"Well written and entertaini
T Church

"This is very engaging. Sci-fi is not usually my thing but I was really hooked by this."
Natalie Durrant

"Wow! Nice! I loved your story. I think you should definitely publish this. The plot was compelling, the characters were well developed, and your descriptions of the scenery made me feel like I was there. I like how you set the story in the future. I really cannot think of anything that needs improvement. Good luck to you!"
Tim Grimat

"You seem to be describing a world that really could exist."
Chloe Mesanges

"I found myself really getting caught up with the action & excitement."
Graham Morgan

"Enjoyed reading it because it was written well and flowed nicely."
Jeff Dale

"Very ambitious story. You did a fantastic job with descriptions and details of the destruction. I may have to read more Sci-Fi now."
SlowSip

"Although not a reader of Sci-Fi, I really enjoyed this. The characters were strong, the plotting well paced and the scene setting very effective, as was the dialogue. I loved the futuristic themes that all have roots in today- drone strikes, rising sea levels, terrorism, but for all the big themes this felt very much a story centred on believable characters. Well done."
Sean Gibbin

To Abigail,
Hope you enjoy
Sam
26/12/2021

Nuclear

Bursting Point

by

Sam Cooke

AD 2045 - episode one

AD 2045 - episode one: Nuclear – Bursting Point
www.AD2045.com

Artist's impression of Hinkley Point C used by kind permission.
Rear cover model: Martina.

Copyright © 2016-2021 Sam Cooke
2nd September 2021 edition

First published in 2017.   ISBN 9781521163603

Also by Sam Cooke:

Non-Fiction
Abuse – *Monster in the House* (with a chapter on Johnny Depp)

Sci-fi five-book series
AD 2045 – episode one: Nuclear – Bursting Point
AD 2045 – episode two: Tsunami – Atlantic Meltdown
AD 2045 – episode three: Partner – Julia's Rising
AD 2045 – episode four: Bu Mon – Island Killer
AD2045 – episode five: Psycho – Welcome Death (*in progress*)

Short Stories
Crane Island, Anna's Song, London Fling, My Name is Sapphire

This book is dedicated to every positive moment of everyone's existence on Earth.

Never give up.

As long as you are alive, there is always a chance to get where you truly want to go.

Precede

Pacific Ocean, June 2045

In the beautiful, calm-blue waters, 15 miles east of Fuji, sat the four-deck luxury yacht *Machinista*. Her owner, human trafficker Vanessa Kilbride, lay relaxing on deck. On the bridge, directly below her, the captain and navigation crew were busily bored, scanning the sea and instruments in the hope of something interesting. Hunter, the captain, adjusted his binoculars.

"Anyone see that?"

"See what?"

"Three miles due north."

"Nothing on sonar."

"Nothing on radar either. What do you see?"

Hunter, eyes still firmly on the horizon, gave his answer.

"Blood. A huge spurt of blood and a severed tail. Large shark."

"Probably bitten by a bigger shark."

Beep. Beep. Beep. Beep.

The sonar operators ears were being machine-gunned by an exponentially growing mass of rapid pings, audible across the bridge.

"How many?", demanded Hunter.

"Can't tell. Closing fast. Bearing 175."

"How fast?"

"Can't tell."

"Can't tell anything? Come again?"

The sonar operator's confused face was screwed up in concentration.

"Shit. Over 400 knots. It makes no sense..."

"Over 400 knots? Underwater?...", the captain hit the yacht-wide alarm, "...Arm weapons. Incoming, 175."

Vanessa entered the bridge.

"What's going on, Hunter?"

"Something's coming our way. Fast."

The radar pings over the speakers had stopped machine gunning, become more regular.

"Slowing. One craft, 150knotts, range 330 metres. It's... Captain, I've worked out the problem - it was supersonic, going faster than my sonar pings could return - it's why there were no pings until..."

"Until it dropped below supersonic and they finally got ahead. I understand how sonar works.", said Hunter.

"How could anyone find us?...", demanded Vanessa, "...You told me this yacht was registered here. That it couldn't be tracked back to me."

Hunter's face was stern. He felt no need to apologise as he faced her.

"You never told me you were running from Partner. Partner can find anyone, anywhere."

"Partner?", asked Vanessa innocently, admitting nothing.

"A craft that can travel supersonic under water, that's over 1,000 miles an hour, is coming straight for us. Only Partner has the ability to do that."

"Captain, it's here. Ten metres off the starboard bow. Velocity on vertical - rising. Shall I order the gun crew to lock on?"

"What for?", asked Hunter, leaving the bridge to see their arrival with his own eyes. Vanessa went with him.

*   *   *

On deck, armed security guard either side, Hunter and Vanessa watched as part of the ocean rose and a three-metre wide, pebble-shaped craft lifted through it, bringing too the deep-growl of powerful engines. Hovering at their eye level, water cascading down, the bulge either side of it's dark-grey hull slid open - revealing a pair of plasma canons.

"That's definitely a zerodrone. Still telling me it's not Partner?"

"Still telling me we're untrackable?"

At the mention of zerodrone, the guards hurriedly adjusted their plasma rifles - switching them to maximum. One spoke into his coms, ordering the deployment of their deckgun.

"It's a zed. Set to maximum yield."

The yacht had one gun, a heavy-calibre plasma canon, with a barrel even fatter than those on the zerodrone and capable of taking on anything this side of a battleship.

"At least you weren't lying about the weaponry you added to this thing."

Hunter glanced round at the gun turret now on the top deck, aimed squarely at the zerodrone.

"Zed's are made from ultra-grade, military NACABIK. We'll be lucky to scratch it. Either you make some kind of deal or we're dead."

Unable to deny it any longer, Vanessa knew he was right. It was no time to let pride or dishonesty get in the way of survival.

"Hello...", she said, giving a wave to who-ever was watching through the zed's cameras.

In response, the front of the zed began to rise - still hovering perfectly as the whole craft turned to point vertical. Canons remained level. Remained aimed at them. They watched as the belly's pair of pale-blue underside thrusters dimmed and they saw the face of their pursuer projected in front of them.

"We're fucked.", whispered Vanessa.

"You know her?"

Vanessa ignored him – focused on donning a smile.

"Sergeant Jadviga, welcome. What a pleasure to see you. How can I be of service?"

The middle-aged woman projected onto the zed's belly didn't smile back. Her face was stern, straight-blonde hair hanging from her head like it had been murdered.

"I told you not to traffic Amazonians."

Hunter looked at Vanessa.

"You're a trafficker?"

She ignored him, stayed focused on the zed.

"Sergeant, it was only a few dozen. I left plenty for your needs. Can sell them back to you, if you like. Great price."

"Soiled goods and a soiled reputation? Didn't think you could insult me more than you already had. And it's commander now, Vanessa. You never were good with details. Just as you were never good at knowing who to trust."

Vanessa's head turned towards Hunter.

"You betrayed me?"

"Not me."

"No...", confirmed the commander, "...not him."

"Who?"

"Unimportant..."

"It's important to me."

"Good. I'm glad to give you the extra pain of not knowing, when I kill you."

From the zed there came a high-pitched whine.

"It's charging weapons.", said Hunter.

"Permission to open fire, captain?"

Hunter shrugged and sat on the side of the yacht.

"If it makes you feel better."

Both security guards and the top-deck canon opened fire, blasting balls of raging-blue plasma into the belly of the zed with perfect accuracy. As it harmlessly bounced off, they saw Jadviga finally smile.

"Goodbye, Vanessa."

Hunter saw the insides of the zed's canons go bright and jumped overboard. He heard Vanessa curse him then, just before he hit the water, heard the distinctive sound of plasma fire as it tore through every deck of the yacht, like canon-balls tearing through balsa wood.

* * *

"Target the survivor, ma'am?"

In her control room, Commander Jadviga peered at the view of burning wreckage from the zed's camera.

"No. Leave him. Good to have a witness. Someone to tell others not to fuck with Partner. Especially not to fuck with me."

"Yes, ma'am."

*　*　*

Clinging to a piece of charred wreckage, Hunter watched the zed fly upwards and vanish as it went supersonic. He activated his wristcom.

"It's me. I need my yacht back. Would you mind picking me up."

"Of course, Honey. I knew you would. Don't call me a yacht though, that's insulting."

"Sorry, Sweetie."

"That's better. Launching now..."

Contents

Chapter 1
Swarmbots

The young badger was about to die. Its nose sniffed at the increasing change in scent as the moist, earthy smells of the woodland floor gave way to a stench of death. In the air, hovering at the edge of the woods above a wheat field, a wasp-like swarmbot had seen it and locked on. It was monitoring the badger's movement to the nearest millimetre, ready to attack the second it crossed a designated red line. Five hundred more swarmbots, called over the instant the badger had crossed the amber line, were now hovering just behind the first; waiting for its signal.

The ground was littered with the remains of insects, birds and a fox; its shredded, decaying remains smeared across the earth. This was the source of the stench. The badger, looking at the line of death ahead, stopped sniffing and heard the low hum of hovering swarmbots. It looked up. Saw myriad tiny, red-laser eyes looking down. Saw the faint blue-energy glow from their hover pads underneath, colour-tuned to make them almost invisible against the sky. They didn't look right. The area didn't smell right. The badger stepped back and turned away. It would search for food elsewhere. Away from that place.

The swarmbot measured its vector - moving away, back over the amber line. Not needed, the others began humming back to their original positions.

*   *   *

"Come on, we can shoot here.", came a boy's voice.

"You sure? Don't normally come in this far."

Two teenagers, Julia and Jake, were playing target practice in the woods - armed with a 400-watt laser-rifle. They ran in the direction of the badger; fast, teenage feet thumping the ground. The badger stopped, listened, then panicked. Fled. Back towards the field. Back towards the line of death. Anything to get away.

It ran across the amber line. The air filled with the hum of 500 swarmbots. This time the badger didn't hear them or care. It just had to escape. At panic speed, it crossed the red line.

A thousand swarmbot eyes flashed bright red. They didn't carry weapons; they were weapons. Diamond-hard bodies, with bullet-shaped noses. Wings not just wings but surgically-sharp blades finished with jagged edges. Just one metre above the badger, the first swarmbot shot down. Attack dive, confirming the target. Full-power punch into the top of the badger's nose, shattering the bone and ripping out the side of its jaw. The badger shrieked in terrible pain, its face slammed into the ground by the impact; legs gave way, belly skidding. The other swarmbots were massed behind the first. They began bulleting in groups of five; mercy was not in their programming. Five at a time - rapid succession, machine-gunning down. Punching in, slicing through, ripping out the other side. Head, neck, torso. Everywhere. Slam in, power through, tear flesh out. Terminally doomed, its lungs burst out one last, loud deathly cry, then it cried no more.

The teens slammed to a halt.

"You hear that?", asked Julia.

"Zoo must have lost a puma again."

"Puma? We'll never see it coming. We have to get out of these woods."

"We're too far in. Look. Over there. A field. We can cut across."

*　　*　　*

A swarmbot, hovering at the edge of the field, saw the teens run over the amber line. Called over 500 more to join it.

Jake, holding the laser-rifle in hands moistening with sweat, skidded to a stop near the edge of the field; foot almost against the red line. Julia caught up and went to overtake.

"Tired? I'm going to beat you."

He grabbed her shoulder, holding her back.

"Look. Wasps."

Julia looked at the black mass in the air ahead, looking like a thick black storm cloud.

"Wow. Now that's a swarm."

"It sure is...", grinned Jake, "...I can't miss."

"Sure that's a good idea?"

"They'll never see it coming. Watch."

He raised the rifle, squinted down the barrel and fired.

TchZoooo.

A thin-blue laser beam zapped into the cloud, bounced off one swarmbot's nose and into the belly of another, incinerating it. Instantly, the others locked on the source. The cloud swarmed.

Jake lowered the rifle.

"Oh, shit. RUN!"

"I am!"

All 500 swarmbots were charging after them. Without looking where he was shooting, Jake fired behind as he ran.

TchZoooo. TchZoooo. TchZoooo.

The shots punched trees, the ground, the air. Smoke puffed where ever they hit. He didn't look back. Just ran for his life, trying the impossible of out running swarmbots. He didn't need to. The swarmbots slammed against their red line co-ordinates like flies slamming against a window pane. A dense black wall, glittering with a thousand red, laser eyes. Tracking the teenagers; locked on to kill but programmed not to cross.

*   *   *

Julia ran to Toddlers' Stream and splashed across, Jake followed. On the other side they dived behind the first big tree they came to - a large oak.

"You really upset those wasps...", panted Julia, "...We could have been stung to death."

"Can't believe they reacted like that."

"Are they following?"

"Dunno."

They needed to find out. Cautiously they peered around either side of the trunk - young faces hugging the rough bark.

"See anything?", asked Jake.

"No. You?"

"Think we're clear.", he said, sliding the rifle's safety catch on.

"Hope so. Those were seriously fast."

"Never seen such aggressive wasps before. Or so many."

"And you had to shoot at them with a laser-rifle. Told you that rifle's dangerous."

"Lia, you're a girl...", joked Jake, "...All girls think guns are dangerous."

"*What?* You rude pig!"

Jake danced off, laughing. Euphorically happy after they had escaped the danger.

"Hah. Hah. Joking. Just joking."

"I'll show you joking."

Julia ran after him and pounced, knocking him to the ground. Jake rolled over and looked up, huge cheeky grin beaming out at his best friend sprawled out, face in the grass.

"You should have rolled."

Unhurt, she got to her feet and brushed herself off.

"You know I can't any more...", she said, walking over to take the laser rifle, "...My turn."

Brushing her long, blonde hair away from her face, she flicked off the safety, flipped up the vectorscope and rested the butt against her shoulder.

"Name the target."

They had been best friends since nursery. The other kids teased them about it but they didn't care - their friendship too solid to worry about the petty opinions of others. The only teasing that mattered was the teasing they did to each other and they did that all the time.

"OK...", grinned Jake, standing up and brushing himself off, "...See that old sign?"

"That one? Too close."

"No, that one. Over there."

Julia looked at the rusting, *'No public access'*, sign 200m away.

"Still too easy."

"I didn't finish. Put a dot above the 'l' and make it into an 'i'."

"Make it pubiic? You're so crude."

"Too difficult for you?"

Julia brushed a flick of hair out of her face.

"Nope."

Leaning against a tree for stability, she zero'd the scope and calmed her metabolism. Taking a deep breath she held it, then fired.

TchZoooo.

She fired again.

TchZoooo.

And kept firing.

TchZoooo. TchZoooo. TchZoooo. TchZoooo. TchZoooo. TchZoooo.

The sign puffed silent, dark-grey smoke with every hit, forming its own little grey cloud. As the cloud cleared, Jake squinted at the sign.

"You made a capital 'I'."

"An excuse to fire more. Think it's straight."

"It's perfect. Show off. You've been practising, again."

"A bit. Told you dad's got one of these too. Not a trainer though - heavier, higher power."

"Café business so risky these days?"

"Never asked. Just glad he's got one. Keeps his locked up though, along with some other gear he never lets me touch. How come your mum's got one? And how come she gives you the keys? You're 15 too. Not even old enough for a full wristcom."

"She doesn't. I, er, have a way with locks."

"What? Jake Watson, after all these years you..."

Bing bong.

A holo-face of Jake's mum appeared in the air in front of them. Julia hid the rifle behind her back.

'Hello, Julia. You been eating grass again?'

"A bit.", she shrugged.

'Shame. You used to be so damn good in the dojo. Dinner in 30 minutes, Jake. Don't be late.'

"No, mum."

'Welcome to come too if you want, Julia.'

"Thank you."

The face morphed into a big, yellow smiley, then blinked out.

"Going to come?", asked Jake, as they walked off together.

"Can't. Dad's making a roast today."

"Guess he'd kill you if you missed that."

"Dad's too kind to kill anyone. It's me who'd be upset. His roast dinners are amazing now."

"Amazingly good instead of amazingly bad? So soon? Wow. Progress runs a white river in your family these days."

Julia lowered her head, staring at her feet as they walked.

"Think we've been finding ourselves since mum went. Making something good out of something bad."

Jake was shaking his head.

"I still can't understand how mad she got. If your dad hadn't recorded her he'd never have been believed. You could have been murdered. But don't worry, as your best friend, it would have been my personal duty to hunt her down and double-dot between the eyes. Zap. Zap. Point blank range."

Julia handed him back the laser-rifle.

"Change the topic, Jake. She's still my mum. I don't need reminders."

"Sorry...", Jake said, realising how insensitive he was being and did as she asked. "...Why do you think there were so many wasps back there? So many in one place?"

Julia shrugged.

"Dunno. I'll ask dad. He knows a lot about weird things."

"Guess he meets a lot of weird people at the café."

"Cafés these days. Never know which one."

"Well, guess he deserved the promotion to regional manager."

Julia really liked Jake. Although insensitive at times he had always been there for her – even after the accident. Never let her down. Helped her feel warm inside and keep her demon locked in its cell, where it belonged. Made her smile when nothing else in the world could. With that smile she lifted her head and looked at him.

"Jake, I'm guessing you say guess too much."

Jake looked back at her, his best friend for as long as he could remember and found himself smiling with feelings becoming more than just friends.

"Guess you're right, Lia."

He was the only one who ever called her Lia and she was smiling wider now. The warmth of love in her reddening face.

"Guess I am.", she said and gave him a quick kiss on the cheek, then bounded away to hide her blushes.

"See you later.", he beamed, watching her go, happiness filling his heart.

That was the last day they met.

Chapter 2
A Barn in Somerset

"Don't blow your head off, Alan."

"Unless you've made peace with God."

"Shut up and let me concentrate. This stuff smells really unstable."

"Oh great. Now he tells us."

The group of four men stepped away from the table and got behind a clear shield. Alan stayed, holding a grey, pea-sized piece of PE4 biological explosive. Gently he pushed in a thin wire and placed it in the hollow of a black, high-density brick. Carefully he put another on top. Then four more.

"Thought one would hold it."

"Shut up. I'm concentrating. Stay behind the shield."

Alan began unrolling the wire, walking towards the detonator. He didn't reach it.

BOOOOM!

Chunks of brick smashed against the shield, cracking it in three places. Knocking it over and the men behind it. Other chunks flew skywards, punching a metre-wide hole through the corrugated-iron roof and flying high into the air, until gravity finally won and yanked them back down, slamming against the roof like a biblical hail storm. Some smashed back through, detonating the ground near Alan, adding to the dirt-blackened burns across his body. Through his torn, blood-soaked jacket, an encrypted communicator began to vibrate - the number 62 lighting up on its cracked screen as it auto answered.

"Alan! Anyone...", came a voice, "...We heard an explosion. Was that you? I said wait for me to get there. Alan!"

Alan recognised Craig's voice.

"Volatile...", he croaked and breathed his last.

"Alan, you OK?"

No response. Craig's voice continued.

"Shit! They've blown themselves up. Go faster! We have to get the rest of the stuff before those MI5 bastards do."

*   *   *

Inside their old, untrackable pod, speeding towards the barn, the militant heads of Faith sat frantic with urgency.

"At least we know its proper PE4-B, Craig. We can take the target out no problem."

"We can take many targets out. Including ourselves if we're not careful."

"Faith will rise. England will be British again or it will be a wasteland. God is Almighty and so shall our names be. In history forever."

"Cut the religious crap, Martin. After Robert does his job, you and me will be billionaires."

Chapter 3
Field Meeting

At the Rose Garden in Coventry's War Memorial Park, four MI5 officers were discussing a situation growing more critical by the day. Team leader Shabbir sat with Adam, Gurmeet and Xi Yang – each positioned individually, on the four benches of the central square, hidden from above by the umbrella of a low tree. They could watch in every direction and, by facing apart, even a spy with a dish-based microphone would gain no more than a quarter of their conversation.

It was a beautiful June morning. The wind was light, sun smiling down. On Shabbir's side were the high-speed train tracks, hidden down an embankment. On Gurmeet's, the tall, white-stone War Memorial and its Chamber of Silence. Behind her, Adam's view of Kenilworth Road and driverless pods humming at exactly 4.8m intervals - kids playing at their disconnected controls, pretending they were driving. Xi Yang's view was the smattering of people walking dogs and children across the hectares of park grass stretching beyond. All around them, a variety of tall trees, planted as dedications to fallen soldiers from World War I; the war to end all wars, which had entirely failed to do so.

Shabbir heard an HS-T train burst along the embankment rails and through the tunnel under Kenilworth Road, braking to 90mph for Coventry station on the other side before thrusting back to 190mph. Turbines wailing like a jet on take off as they spooled back to 30,000rpm, vanishing the train as fast as it had come.

"Good job they fit those things with bomb detectors.", said Shabbir, a 40-year-old officer of Pakistani descent. His bald head and doughnut belly made his look perfect for undercover operations. As a former mixed-martial arts instructor, his self-confidence kept him so relaxed in dangerous situations no-one ever suspected he was deadlier than their gun, until it was too late.

"Down to business.", said Xi, a stunning oriental in a pristine charcoal suit, given a boy's name by parents who had prayed for one. She too was trained in martial arts but with a personality the total opposite to Shabbir's jovial cheer – burying herself in her serious work, as if there was nothing more to life. With Xi it wasn't business before pleasure it was just business - bordering on a death wish. The reason was no secret to Chris, their Section Chief.

Xi had been too late to halt the Beijing betrayal that murdered her fiancé and then her parents. Normally such psychological trauma would have had her decommissioned or at least glued to a desk but times were desperate and she was the best ethnically Chinese officer they had. With the hand of China firmly on six of Britain's nuclear power stations and growing evidence of Chinese infiltration, her abilities were desperately needed.

"The word is...", said Adam, "...a group is looking to go nuclear. Attack a civilian target.",

He was stereo-typical recruit from Cambridge. Athletic, highly educated and quietly spoken but deep down as hard as nails. Ready to face anything for King and country. Gurmeet, an innocent-looking Indian with the deepest-brown eyes, sometimes used as a honey trap even though she was a lesbian, looked at him.

"How can they get nuclear material into the country? There are radiation detectors at every entry point around the coast. Even the small coves."

It was Xi not Adam who answered her.

"When we say 'go nuclear', we don't mean bring material in. We mean an attack on nuclear material already here – including nuclear waste. Go dirty. Create a radioactive cloud of devastation."

"But...", added Adam, "...they would need a truck-load of explosives to get through the shield reactor walls. They're reinforced concrete, metres thick so we're thinking more about a control-room attack. Forcing a station into meltdown. Or the hijack of material being transported between sites."

"It could be anything.", said Xi.

"It could be anything...", affirmed Adam, "...so we need to check everything."

Shabbir and Gurmeet, partners for the past month, turned to look at each other. Eyes reading eyes. They knew the information they had to give and it was Gurmeet who went first.

"We've just picked up chatter of bio-bombs. Plastic explosive even more powerful than PE4 - designated PE4-B. Undetectable by anything but the latest systems. In the right place, a 1kg charge could punch through a three-metre-thick wall of reinforced concrete."

"And...", added Shabbir, "...the MOD have just admitted losing 3kg of the stuff."

"That's concerning.", said Adam, making the understatement of the day.

"It's more than concerning...", continued Gurmeet, "... Someone has been importing Lego guns."

"Lego guns?"

"Don't let the name fool you. They're made of organic plastic and assembled from clip together parts, made in colourful, odd shapes to avoid attracting attention. Detectors don't identify them and neither do security on the X-ray scans. The pieces just look like parts of shoes, toys or travel accessories."

"What about ammunition? They must pick up the chemicals in that."

"No chemicals. Ceramic darts, using compressed gas."

"Not too powerful or accurate then."

"Accurate to 200m and fast enough to penetrate a bi-kevlar vest at close range. The gas is hydrogen-based, impossible to detect. Mixes with enriched oxygen pulled from the air and hits 3,000psi when ignited."

Xi looked at Gurmeet.

"They just clip together and 3,000psi doesn't blow them apart?"

Shabbir took over.

"At full power, the first shot would. They run at low pressure for a few shots, heating a gel coating inside the barrel that fuses the bricks together. After that, the whole thing becomes stronger than steel. The only thing that stops them is water, including heavy rain. It blocks the oxygen extraction process."

"Why import them? Can't they just be made in a 3D printer?"

"Henry tried. Too many layers and not precise enough. They have to be crush-formed from solids or the bricks just fall apart."

Adam had been sitting quietly, taking it all in.

"So what you're saying is...", he began, "...unless we find someone carrying a multi-coloured gun in one hand and an umbrella in the other, they have the means to strike us on all fronts and we won't even see it coming?"

"I wouldn't quite put it like that, but yes.", said Shabbir.

"Do we at least know who they are?"

"Quasi-religious nuts, as usual...", said Xi, "...Call themselves 'Faith'."

"Identified targets?"

"Previous intelligence suggested the recycling plant at Sellafield but it's too heavily guarded now. Just had its old detectors upgraded...", said Xi, "...My suggestion now is a nuclear power station; one of the new builds at Hinkley Point, Dungeness or Bradwell. Their detectors can already sense 98% of explosives, which sounds good but means no-one is in a hurry to scrap them and pay millions for the latest detectors so they can sniff out the missing 2%. Especially as the MOD isn't exactly shouting it's lost PE4-B."

"That is so damn short-sighted...", frowned Shabbir, "...An attack on one of those plants could have winds blowing nuclear fallout across London or the entire west coast. I'll get Chris to bug someone about it, literally if needs be."

Shabbir's wristcom vibrated. An encrypted message was coming in. He glanced at it - retina scan unlocking the message as his gaze hardened.

"There's been an explosion. The Quantocks, Somerset."

"The Quantocks?...", said Xi, "...That's near Hinkley Point."

"Fuck, you're right...", exclaimed Shabbir, who only swore at times like this, "...We're on. Adam and Xi, keep digging for more intelligence. Gurmeet, call in your airpod. We're going to get to these fuckers and fast."

Chapter 4
Jake's Fate

Jake's front door didn't greet him when he arrived home. The manual control panel, usually a beautiful glow of turquoise, sat dull and lifeless. It wasn't a power cut. The screen was cracked after a heavy impact.

Silently, he took the rifle from his shoulder and slid off the safety. The door had been left ajar. Slowly he eased it wider, listening for the invaders his instincts screamed were inside.

Their house was larger than they needed. They had kept it after Jake's father was killed by a glitching pod. The fourth person to be killed that way in a single week. Software bug, they said. Fixed it now, they said. It didn't matter what they said. Nothing would bring his father back. Now it was just him and his mother, getting on with their lives against a world of invisible pollution and super-storms demolishing forests, roof tops and coastal towns across the UK. Those denying global warming long since silenced by the vanishing of the Arctic ice sheet - diluting the Gulf Stream into oblivion with it. These days, London had winters as cold as Moscow and summers as wet as a rain-forest memory.

Against all the odds, London still stood proudly above the waves – behind Thames Barrier II. Three times larger than the first; protected by a dozen missile launchers, quad banks of plasma-cannons and two-thousand Partner swarmbots. The grey-NACABIK armour of the barrier itself masked the dark scorches of the attacks that got close enough to earn the terrorists status enhancement. They never enjoyed it for long. A hornbot drone, so called because it was the size of a hornet, would fly invisibly above them – tracking them back to their base then calling in a zerodrone strike. Zerodrones, zeds, were called that because of the number of targets reputed to survive their attacks: zero.

Exploded targets were never acknowledged as strikes by any government body. Special investigators were always called in, by international law, and the explosions attributed to gas leaks – even when the building had no gas supply. No-one ever questioned their verdict, at least not twice.

It was a war of attrition, hidden behind a false mask of peace and tranquillity. In the past, governments had heightened the threat status to scare the population into accepting draconian measures. Now the threat status was so off-the-scale they were doing the opposite - playing it down to avoid looking incompetent. England's threat status was no longer designated 'Critical', for imminent attack; England was under constant attack and not always by outsiders.

With technology so integral to society, the public just accepted it when something PC'd – crashed for no known reason, without warning or explanation. They just hit the reset button, rebooted and everything worked fine again; until the next time.

Of course people weren't happy with fatal pod glitches but: "The total number of road deaths has fallen by 82% since the blanket introduction of driverless cars. It is an achievement to be very proud of...", announced the Minister for Transport, repeatedly, "...Accidents will still happen, from time to time, as no system can ever be perfect."

Except for Partner, the high-tech corporation that developed the pods, it was.

* * *

Jake felt a vibration as Julia signalled his wristcom. He cancelled it without answering - his friend would have to wait. He'd heard a sound. A woman's voice, coming from the kitchen. It wasn't his mother's. He crept closer, gripping the laser-rifle in both hands. Finger quivering on the trigger, as he heard the voice continue.

"You never did like to conform, Jane. If you weren't so brilliant at your job we'd have got rid of you years ago. Revenge is our speciality, not yours. You've gone too far this time."

The voice was female but unfathomably cold. Distant. Jake peered through the crack between their old-fashioned door and the frame, trying to see who had spoken. He saw the back of his mother's head. Her straight, red-bob hair ruffled. When she spoke he saw a line of blood down the side of her face.

"Just leave Jake out of this. Give him a chance. He doesn't know anything."

"Of course....You know me."

"The stray is back, ma'am.", came a male voice over an intercom.

"Good. Time for me to go."

"Jadviga, you bastard. I'll..."

"You won't do anything, Jane. This is where your story ends."

"YEARRRRGH!!!!!", yelled Jake, charging round the door, laser-rifle ready to fire.

In front of him, the floating face of Jadviga's hologram looked at him -

smiling in cruel victory.

"Hello, Jake. I've been waiting for you. I'll give you a moment for your goodbyes. Goodbye."

The hologram morphed into a horned, grinning red-devil - orange flames roaring around the Partner logo behind it, then blinked out, leaving him alone with his mother.

"Jake, get out of here!", she urged.

She was tied to a chair. Face and knuckles bruised by those that had already left.

"RUN, JAKE!"

Jake couldn't run. Couldn't abandon her.

"Stay still, mum."

TchZoooo. TchZoooo.

He blasted the restraints off her wrists, then her feet.

TchZoooo. TchZoooo.

She jumped up, grabbed his arm and yanked him towards the door.

Outside, flying below radar at just 100m, a zerodrone hummed into final position below the guiding hornbot. Its 60-kilowatt plasma-cannon, like its thrusters, was frequency tuned to match the blue of the sky, as it aimed at Jake's house.

"Zed locked on, commander. Maximum fire ready in 5...4...3...2..."

Above the house, the zerodrone's charging capacitors were whistling at high frequency. Every dog within a mile howling at the sound. Abruptly it all stopped. The capacitors went silent. Charged.

"Zero.", came Jadviga's command.

Vvvvv-DOOOOOO!!!

The cannon spat a thick, sky-blue ball of plasma, hot as the sun. It punched the house like a meteor strike; smashing through the roof. Red tiles and burning timbers flew aside. The inner floors boomed as the shockwave smashed them apart. Flying chunks thumped against the walls. Flew out through the windows. The kitchen cooker, the main focus of the pulse was hit with perfect accuracy. Steel-melting plasma hit the old-fashioned gas supply. Ignition. The house never stood a chance.

The destruction of the pulse going in had broken it. The explosion in the kitchen blew its guts out. Fierce orange flames tore through the doors, windows and collapsing walls. Black smoke mushroomed into the sky. Bricks, tiles and burning planks of wood clattered down onto surrounding pods and gardens, setting off alarms.

As if bolted to a landing pad, the zerodrone simply hovered, rock-steady, filming it all. Unaffected by the debris bouncing off its NACABIK hull, it relayed the destruction live to the satisfaction of its commander. The hornbot watched too. Scanning for any sign of life.

*　　*　　*

"All readouts show zero survivors, ma'am."

Jadviga smiled, without a hint of warmth.

"Dear, oh dear. When will they stop those gas pipes from blowing up? Yet another, tragic explosion for the 6'o'clock news. But, *you*..."

"Ma'am?", gulped the operator she was glaring at.

"...Next time you use a prototype zed, remember to turn the power down. Even gas explosions aren't that powerful."

"Sorry, ma'am. Forgot it was a Mk4."

"Ma'am...", said another operator, "...a pod is outside."

"Some nosey Parker taking a look? So what?"

"It's a series 16, on manual override. Two occupants."

"*Manual*? Get their IDs! Send down the bot, regain control and crash that thing."

"Yes, ma'am!"

Chapter 5
Julia's Dad

"Dinner in 20. Just crisping the potatoes."

"Thanks, dad.", said Julia, pouring herself a mug of water from the recycler.

"How's Jake doing?"

"Fine."

"What have you been up to?"

"Things."

"Any chance of an answer involving more than one syllable?"

"Sure."

"Julia."

"Dad."

"Seriously, Julia. I know you're a teenager and I'm just some old bum but we do still need to communicate."

"I know..."

Julia pulled up a stool and sat beside him as he turned the potatoes in the frying pan.

"Those look yummy."

He turned another.

"I picked up an email from your mother today, sent two months ago."

"She actually bothered to write? Bet it wasn't anything nice for me. What idiot bollocks did she write this time?"

"Don't swear. Here, I printed it. You're old enough to see."

Julia took the sheet of paper, holding it with disdain as she read aloud.

"You lying, brutal, rapist bastard... I'm not swearing dad, just reading."

"I know."

"... you set me up to put me in prison and kidnap my child. Everyone hates you. When I get out you'll pay for this. Be afraid. Be very afraid."

Julia stopped looking at the paper.

"And that's it? Nothing about missing me or wanting to do something nice for a change?"

"No."

"She's a *bloody* idiot!"

Her dad glared at her.

"Sorry. She's a *bloody* moron!"

"Better..."

In their house, the word 'idiot' was banned. Banned by her dad because it was what her mum repeatedly called him during her rages. While he finished turning the potatoes, Julia dropped the sheet into the recycler. It whirred softly. The ink dropped off, returning to black toner as an ironed sheet of white paper fed back into the printer tray.

"Can you get the gravy, please?"

"Sure."

Julia reached up to a cupboard. Like Jake's, theirs was also a traditional kind of house. More expensive to run than modern homes but more appealing too - if you liked that kind of thing, which they did.

It had been their dream family home. Their new start. A place to build a better future. Only that future had collapsed in front of them, recorded on video. Her mum hadn't just tried to kill her dad. She had also sworn to God she would drug Julia, take her hand and though would jump from grandma's 10th-floor flat; for 're-incarnation in a better life'. On the day of her mum's removal, after she had tried to glass her dad in the shower and raged she would vanish Julia that day, even the arresting officers had complained about her aggressive behaviour.

"Dad. Why is that out?"

Julia took her eyes off her dad's laser-rifle to look at him. He stopped tending the potatoes. Stood there, frowning.

"Dad?"

"I had a call from the police today. They let her out this morning."

Julia looked back at his laser-rifle. She knew it was military spec; ten times more powerful than the 400-watt one she had been using with Jake. Lethal even through a solid, brick wall.

"Is that why the safety's off?"

He looked at her, reading between her lines.

"You've been out shooting with Jake again, haven't you?"

"Only some old sign post...", she beamed with naughty pride, "...I'm pretty accurate, you know? And, typical Jake - he shot up some wasp swarm. They didn't like that. You should have seen how they reacted."

Her dad looked straight at her.

"Swarm? Where?"

"Other side of the woods. You know? Over Toddlers' Stream."

He thumped off the cooker and grabbed the laser-rifle.

"Get in the pod. Where's Jake?"

Julia shrugged.

"Home, for dinner."

"Call him. Get them out of the house!"

He was acting with an urgency she'd only ever seen once before – the day he'd been called to work for some emergency. She remembered because it was the same day Jake's dad had been killed. How cafés could ever have such emergencies was beyond her. Except that sometimes, in her teenage years, she had come to doubt managing cafés was all he did for a living. How else to explain his four-kilowatt laser-rifle and NACABIK-lined cupboard filled with 'stuff'?

"What's wrong?", she asked, hurrying after him.

"Did any follow you?"

"What?"

"From the swarm."

"No, dad. They're just bugs."

He jumped in the pod and Julia climbed in beside him. Instead of stating a destination, he slapped a keypad on the console, punched in a sequence of numbers and grabbed the emergency controls.

"No. They're not."

Even before the turbine had spun to 20,000rpm they were off. It was the beginning of a journey that would change Julia's life forever.

Chapter 6
COBRA

Prime Minister Adrian March, stood inside 70 Whitehall - the cabinet offices just a stone's throw from Downing Street. Behind him, a large portrait of Winston Churchill, standing newly elected as Prime Minister on the deck of HMS Prince of Wales in 1940. Now, over 100 years later, it was Adrian was standing before the heads of the armed forces, blue-light and intelligence services – along with four cabinet ministers. Smiles were off the menu. Matters serious. This was COBRA, a Cabinet Office Briefing Room meeting, still held in room A and definitely not a drill.

Despite the seriousness there was an absence. The chair for the Director General of MI5 was empty. The PM looked across the mirror-smooth table at Sir Andrew, the Chief of the Secret Intelligence Services, MI6.

"Where's Sarah?"

"I have no idea, Adrian.", said Sir Andrew, as unreadable as ever.

"I specifically asked you both to attend. Has she forgotten who she works for?"

"No doubt she will explain herself when opportunity allows."

"Damn right she will."

The PM turned his attention to the Secretary of State for the Environment."

"Justin, tell us where we stand."

"PM."

Justin Clegg got to his feet.

"Good morning, everyone. The issue today is defence of the south-west coast. As you know, we are in the process of building strategic sea walls against the super-storms we've been experiencing in recent years. Completion is deemed critical to national security - not just because of the nuclear reactors at Hinkley Point in the Bristol Channel but also the threat to infrastructure, from south Wales all the way south down to Plymouth. These walls are the biggest constructions since the Great Wall of China – ironic, considering our concerns about Chinese espionage..."

Justin looked at their faces, meting out gravitas as he continued.

"...You should all have no doubt that, without these walls, the storms threaten not just nuclear shut downs but floods for tens of thousands of homes. Bankruptcy for hundreds of businesses."

"We know, Justin. We demanded them...", interrupted Sir Dobson, the head of the fire-brigade, "...Which is why these constructions have been funded above our services."

Justin agreed.

"And a good idea it was, Sir Dobson, but yesterday I met with Partner, the wall contractor. They explained foundation issues are hampering progress. In some places the ground is so soft they have to dig down 10 metres, between tides, to reach the bedrock. In others it's solid granite and they're having to blast it with PE4 to achieve a stable depth. Put simply, they say the project is more geologically complex than the original contract so we are obliged to fund an extra £6 billion, in order to achieve completion before October's hurricane season."

He took out a matchbox-sized Near-Field Connection device and put it on the table. Its pristine British racing green contrasting the brunette of the table's teak.

"You can NFC the full report here."

Simon Pierce, Chancellor of the Exchequer, was already blustering in protest. His fat, red face grown even redder – podgy jowls wobbling as he spoke.

"I don't want to near-field anything. Whatever Partner say, they're already £8 billion over budget and a month behind schedule. This isn't going to be another HS2. If they need more money they should find it themselves. It's only a wall, for goodness sake."

"Eight walls, Simon, 220 miles long - designed to withstand Torro-11 tornados; the equivalent of Force-30 events on the Beaufort scale, if Beaufort went that high. Another £6 billion is a lot cheaper than rebuilding half the west coast and nuclear power stations."

Sir Andrew interrupted.

"With the current funding, could the most critical sections be completed in August, before the hurricane season sets in? Then complete the rest in the spring?"

Justin shook his head.

"The risk assessment triggering this project stated the need for full T-11 protection. Since the tsunami of '42, we've been detecting increasing disturbances along the Mid-Atlantic Ridge. There's also signs of a new seabed tear near Ireland, like the one that caused the tsunami of 1607. We wouldn't even get a ten-minute warning if that happened. The reactors at Hinkley Point would be under water in four."

"Did nobody plan for this kind of thing when they chose that site?", blurted Simon.

"It was originally chosen in the 50's...", said Justin, "...Back then this level of storm risk didn't exist. Unfortunately, when the Hinkley C reactors were green-lit in 2016, people were more interested in politics than safety."

"We weren't.", disagreed Sir Andrew.

MI6 had warned of the risks, along with MI5. There came a buzz on the intercom from reception.

"Phil, I said no interruptions."

"Sorry, PM. The Energy Secretary is here - with Professor Lau, the Head of Nuclear Energy."

"Lau too? Send them in."

The heavy, bomb-proof door swung smoothly open, watched by two, stone-faced guards standing either side of the new entrants.

"Come in.", welcomed the PM.

"Hello, Adrian.", said the Energy Secretary, extending his charcoal-suited hand.

"Tariq.", said Adrian, shaking it.

Behind Tariq came a tall woman in a white lab coat, dressed like she was still there; a hands-on scientist who never turned off. Her shoulder-length, blonde hair dressed a face sparkling with intelligence from her sea-green eyes. It took a second for the PM to remind himself she was a man the last time they met.

"Professor Lau. Lovely to see you again. You're looking... well."

She shook his hand with a man's grip.

"Prime Minister. It's been a long time."

Having gone through gender re-alignment and all the complications that came with it, Professor Lau had emerged brimming with confidence. Feeling far tougher as a stand-up woman than she had as a retreating man. She wasted no time in stating her purpose.

"I hear defence funding for my new reactors has been denied."

How did she find that out?, the PM wondered, gazing towards Sarah's empty chair as considered his answer.

"Not denied, exactly, professor...", he replied, "...Just not fully approved yet. Please, have a seat."

The professor remained standing. Having been briefed by Chris, Shabbir's MI5 Section Chief, Lau was in no mood for placations and placed both hands on the table.

"When exactly were you planning to approve it? After a terrorist attack?"

"Professor...", began the PM's calming tone, sitting in his chair, "...there is always the possibility of an attack on a government facility, including nuclear. You know that. Rest assured our security services, such as MI6 here, are doing all they can to obfuscate any undesirables."

Lau wasn't a politician or someone to be deflected by one.

"I've heard my reactors will be denied detectors for biological explosives, like PE4-B. You do realise PE4-B is the only handbag-sized explosive capable of punching through a reactor wall, don't you?"

The Prime Minister looked straight into her eyes, trying to gauge how best to respond. He was a politician, used to dealing with rhetoric – she was a scientist, used to dealing with nuclear facts, meeting his gaze without even a flicker of backing down.

"Professor... finances are limited. Right now, we're discussing extra funding for the west-coast walls – which includes sea defences for your reactors at Hinkley Point."

For Lau, that wasn't enough.

"Let me show you something."

She took a cigar-sized, tri-laser pen from her lab-coat pocket, pointed it at the nearest section of bare wall and let go. The pen hovered where she left it; projecting a colour map of the UK. A map showing every non-military nuclear facility. Power stations in green, waste processing and storage in yellow.

"There are 26 nuclear sites - 16 have the latest weapons detectors; four are designated to have them. Six are not."

"Professor, updating detectors is not just expensive but comes with security risks in itself; what with all the extra workers on site and possible off-line time where there is no detector cover at all. Besides, four of the plants are due to be decommissioned."

"They are? Which? Certainly not my new reactors at Dungeness, Bradwell, Hunterston or Hinkley. Partner have even mooted keeping some AGR plants operational for another five years so exactly which four are we talking about?"

"Would you support that?", asked the PM, deflecting the question with a question.

"What? Keeping old AGRs operational? Only if they'll fund taking them off-line to re-condition the cores, cooling and control systems. Something I very much doubt."

"Well, if they submit an application for approval, we'll contact you to reconsider our position."

Lau was in no way placated.

"And in the meantime at least six nuclear sites are to be kept operational without biological detectors? If the risk is here and now, we have to deal with it here and now. Watch this."

Lau flicked the tail of the pen, dancing the image on the wall before it stabilised. The image became a video - like a time-lapse weather map, only the cloud on it was shown in shades of red.

"What you are looking at is a simulated breach at Dungeness C. The amount of red represents the amount of ionising radiation from Uranium. If the wind is light it could be like this; the fall out limited to Walland and Romney marshes. Lightly inhabited. Mostly just birds would be contaminated. But, if the wind isn't light, which mostly it isn't these days, it could be like this..."

She flicked the pen again. The video changed, red cloud spreading further north, towards London.

"...Here the fallout could cover the entire south-east, including all of London, before spreading to the continent and the rest of the UK."

The Environment Minister was shaking his head.

"That's just theoretical, professor. Even if such a leak were to happen, it could all just all blow out to sea."

"Professor...", added the PM "...We do appreciate the dangers of nuclear energy. It's why we have detailed risk assessments and professional experts, like yourself, taking care of them."

The PM waved in Nathan, the Head of the Health Service. Nathan stood up, brushing his NHS-blue tie straight over his paunch-bulged shirt.

"As I understand it...", Nathan began in his gruff voice, "...in the case of a radiation leak a nearby city - such as London, Bristol or Edinburgh – the area would become mildly radioactive for a few years, while the contamination is cleaned up. In case of any such an event, we keep enough iodine stocks and PPE to safeguard most thyroid effects. Yes, in the long term, some members of the public may live shorter lives but this has been deemed an acceptable risk, in return for our modern energy needs and to protect against further global warming."

Lau was now frowning at the room square on - the video pausing automatically as she turned her back on it.

"Mildly radioactive? Few years? You *cannot* fix something like this with a bottle of pills and a broom and carry on as normal. We're talking lethal radiation levels. Lethal! Two thousand rems or more. And not just for a few years. Effectively forever."

"Nothing is forever, professor.", retorted the Environment Minister.

"Really? *Really?* Do you have any idea of the lifespan of the uranium in those reactors?"

"Look, professor...", interrupted the Chancellor, folding his arms across his bulging belly, "...We budget for 30 years of clean-ups. That's plenty of time to deal with any nuclear emergency and budget for more if necessary. Even the Soviets got the Chernobyl disaster under control."

"Have you been to Chernobyl? I have. That leak made an area the size of Lancashire uninhabitable and 60 years on, it still is. It sent enough radiation over Europe to have us slaughtering livestock 2,000 miles away. Chernobyl hasn't been sorted. They just covered it with a 40,000 ton sarcophagus. Inside, they're still struggling to process the material and that is with Uranium-235. We use Uranium-238, which has an even longer lifespan of 4.5 million..."

The Chancellor's confidence waned a little but Lau hadn't finished yet.

"...million years."

The Secretary of State for the Environment stopped looking bored. Lau now had the room's intense attention.

"Four and a half billion years? Is it really that bad?", asked Lord Hesquith, First Lord of the Navy, in a pragmatically military kind of way.

"Worse. That's only the half-life. After four and a half *billion* years the radioactivity will only have halved. A thousand rems is still lethal. Even with weather dilution, you're still looking at millions of years of a lethal water-table, ground too polluted for farming and cities too polluted to even visit without a hazmat suit. It would be the end of British life as we know it. And that is from a leak of 100kg. Those reactors hold 50 tons of it; that's 50,000kg - each."

The PM had a pained half-smile on his face – the kind of mask politicians wore in situations they were struggling to answer.

"Well... I agree those are good points, professor, but look; I'm sure you appreciate anything over a couple of decades is rather beyond the scope of my ministerial remit. There are elections every five years. People care about jobs, homes, new pods, the NHS and their gadgets staying on; not what might happen thousands or millions of years from now. "

He was trying to bury the matter in political rhetoric. Push it to one side. Professor Lau was built like her reactors, of reinforced concrete and just as impossible to budge.

"What I appreciate, Prime Minister, is an attack on a nuclear facility could come at anytime. Today. Tomorrow. Next year. Whenever. And we, as a nation, will not survive the consequences if one succeeds. What you decide now can decide whether there will even remain a country to be governed. Authorise full sensor funding, today, or tomorrow the UK could be a death-ridden memory with you at the helm. Do you *really* want to go down in history as the Prime Minister who allowed 10,000 years of British civilisation to be wiped off the map?"

Plucking her pen from the air, she clipped it back into her labcoat pocket.

"Protect our future.", she said. And with that, she left.

In the audible silence of Lau's wake, the molybdenum-steel dead locks could be heard thunking across the doors behind her. No-one spoke a word. A second later the buzzer went again. Taking a deep breath, the PM answered it.

"Yes, Phil?"

"Director General of MI5, line-R."

The secure line. Emergency use only. Things were just getting better and better... Protocol updates required he take it in private, even during a high-security COBRA meeting.

"I'll take it in the study. Excuse me a moment, everyone."

*　　*　　*

Watching the Prime Minister go off his monitor, Tech Tonic's Chinese operator frowned. It was bad enough they had no audio feed from the meeting room, let alone losing the PM from their CCTV feeds for lip-reading what was spoken there.

"Where's he going, Li?", asked his manager, in Chinese.

"To the back room, Mr Han."

"We have cameras in there yet?"

"Not yet. MI5 blocked the installation again."

"Are they on to us?"

"No. They would have removed all CCTV if they were."

"Just MI5 paranoia then. Good. Have you identified everyone there? Extracted their speech?"

"Everyone has been identified. Systems have extracted as much as the lip-sync could see."

"The hot blonde who just left?"

"Head of Nuclear Power. Professor Lau."

"Professor Lau? Another one? Interesting, I went for dinner with a Professor Lau on Hinkley's anniversary. Must be his sister. He never mentioned her. Hot..."

"Like I said, sir, we couldn't view all the speech to extract every conversation."

"Doesn't matter. Track where they all go when it's over and extract the missing details from what they tell others. Report to me when you're done."

"Yes, Mr Han."

*　　*　　*

In the study, at the back of the main room, the PM closed the door and lifted the corded telephone receiver.

"Sarah, it's Adrian. What's going on? Why aren't you here?"

"Sorry, PM. We have a leak."

What?

"Where? Who?"

"Still investigating. Don't tell anyone – it could warn them. Is Lau still there?"

"No. How did you know she was coming?"

Sarah ignored the question.

"When did she leave?"

"Just now."

"I'll call you back."

In the background, Sarah could be heard barking orders to intelligence officers, then the line clicked dead.

Putting down the receiver, the PM sat up and became conscious of a bead of sweat running down his back. The day was just getting worse and worse. Originally, he had been scheduled to celebrate the D-Day centenary in Kent. Instead his visit had been cut short – recalled for COBRA to face what was rapidly becoming a D-Day all of his own.

Taking a deep breath, he stood up and straightened his tie – drawing confidence from smartness. He had no choice but to head back to the conference room and brave the array of faces that would be looking at him. Only now he would be wondering which faces he could really trust.

If there was ever going to be a test of his tenure, this surely was it.

Chapter 7
First Blood

Julia's dad was driving the pod faster than she knew it could go. Every display flashed red. Temperature, engine revs, speed, brakes. Everything. Their active, six-point harnesses held them firmly in their seats but Julia still hung on to her seat, white-knuckle tight. Upon the dashboard sat the laser-rifle, locked in place by clamps that had appeared from nowhere.

"Dad. What's going on?"

He was concentrating hard. Not just on driving without crashing but on what he was going to tell his daughter. How much he could tell his daughter, without endangering her life. Ignorance wasn't just bliss, it was safety – until now. Now, for Jake's sake too, she needed to understand the danger approaching.

"Did you get through to Jake? He has to get out of the house. They won't kill him outside, unless he's in a pod."

"*Kill him?!?* Who? Why?"

"Those weren't insects. They're robotic guards. Swarmbots. If Jake shot one he'll have been followed home as a hostile. It'll call in a strike. Hang on..."

He swerved around two pods, sparks flying as the edge of theirs scraped against the curb.

"...Try him again. Before a zerodrone takes out everyone in the house."

"*What?* Dad, have you been drinking? Zed strikes are just rumours. They don't really happen. Do they?"

It was a question she didn't need to ask. By the look on his face and his driving, she already knew his answer. Right or wrong, he believed they did.

"Got hold of Jake yet?"

"No. But I can see his house up ahead. Everything's fine."

"Look above it."

Julia leant forward and looked up at the clear, blue sky above the house.

"Nothing. Just sky"

"It'll be camouflaged, 100m up. Size of an airpod."

She looked again, squinting, harder this time.

"Nope. Nothing. Told you... Oh, shit. I see it! Same colour as the sky. That's why I've never seen one. How did you know?"

"Try Jake again."

"No signal."

"Their jamming the area."

All around, above the sound of their whizzing engine, dogs could be heard howling.

"Dogs are howling because it's charging."

"What?"

The howling stopped. Tom knew exactly what that meant.

"Close your eyes!"

He aimed the pod straight and let go of the wheel - putting one hand over her eyes, the other over his own.

Vvvvv-DOOOOOO!

A brilliant-blue flash lit purple through his fingers, as a football-sized burst of plasma punched down. Its shockwave pulsed the air, rocking their pod. He dropped his hands - grabbing the wheel and swerving past a confused pod, unable to get signal guidance to compute a crash-free direction. Julia opened her eyes, in time to see Jake's house shedding flaming debris. Then it explode from within. Detonated like a bomb, erupting in the orange-flames of hell.

"**JAKE!**", she screamed in horror.

Shrapnel blasted the area. Debris bounced off their windscreen. Broken bricks and boards raining onto their roof and all around. Her dad slammed on the brakes, skidding to a halt on the littered grass. Julia was already pulling the door release to get out. It didn't work.

"OPEN!", she shouted.

Nothing happened. She wrestled with the harness. Nothing happened. Nothing would release. She was child-locked in.

"Let me out, dad! LET ME OUT!"

Her dad was scanning for survivors.

"Sorry, Julia. We're too late."

"*What*? **NO!** I was just with him! **JAKE CAN'T BE DEAD!!!**"

Tears were streaming from her eyes. She was the girl who never cried. The girl who shed no tears even when her mother was taken away. But she was crying now. Openly crying for Jake. Crying for her best friend. Her dad's scanner beeped a warning - his keypad on the dashboard pulsed yellow.

"They're trying to control this pod. Wait here."

Yanking his laser-rifle off its clamps, he flipped up the vector scope and jumped out of the pod. Pointing it skywards, he fired rapidly - three times.

TchZoooo. TchZoooo. TchZoooo.

Not at the zed but at the tiny hornbot above it.

Tzzzzz.

It vaporised in a puff of orange flame. In response, the zed's humming energy pads rippled with heat as it rotated in their direction. Dogs began howling again at the ultrasonic whine of its recharging capacitors. It was getting ready to fire at them. Quickly, he aimed the laser-rifle at its belly and kept the trigger down.

TchZoooo. TchZoooo. TchZoooo. TchZoooo. TchZoooo. TchZoooo. TchZoooo. TchZoooo.

Direct hits. Blue sparks flew off at every impact, shedding puffs of grey smoke but no damage. Barely even a scratch. The shielding was too strong.

"Upgraded....", he muttered.

The 60-kilowatt plasma-canon of the Mk4 zerodrone had turned towards them. Methodically, quickly but calmly, Tom lowered the laser-rifle and pushed the output slider to stage-two overload; jumping the power from four to sixteen kilowatts. A warning message flashed up. He didn't bother reading it. He already knew what it said.

'Danger. Overheat imminent.'

He had what he needed: one overload shot. One chance. Holding his breath he calmed his heart - steadied his aim and sighted through the vectorscope, directly into the bright-blue sphere of plasma growing inside the barrel.

TCHZOOOO!

The heat of his sixteen-kilowatt beam cracked the air. The tip of the rifle glowed red hot - emergency shut down immediately kicked in. No more shots allowed until it cooled. No more needed. It had done its job. Shot straight through the shielding and the canon itself. Not just the canon but through the belly of the drone and out the top too - steam jetting from the exit wound. The containment field for the canon's plasma collapsed. With nothing holding it in, it exploded.

BOOOOM!

In a ball of blue flame the canon blew apart. The explosion ripped a metre-wide hole in the brand-new NACABIK hull. Still airborne but now gunless and badly damaged, it was losing power. Pale-blue energy dribbled from its belly - sizzling the grass where it landed.

Brushing bits of debris from his hair, Tom saw it was too damaged to pose a threat but he felt no satisfaction. Jake, probably Jane too, were dead; his daughter was crying and now he was back at war with those he'd never wanted to deal with again. There was no changing it. No going back. What was done, was done. Normal life was over.

As he strode back to the pod, he thrust a middle finger at the commander he knew would be watching him go.

*　*　*

"Who's that? I didn't see his face but looks familiar.", demanded Jadviga, seeing everything through the zerodrone's failing camera and furious at the finger of defiance. Jadviga hated defiance.

"Record checking again, commander - hair, build and ID numbers."

"*Well?*"

The operator stared at his VR-screen.

"Some kind of database interference. Zed was jamming so couldn't transmit the full details and its recording has been destroyed. Only partial details for his face. No match."

"No match? NO MATCH! What do you mean 'no match'? That's impossible! There's never a 'no match'. There can't be!"

"There's nothing even close coming up my system either, ma'am...", confirmed the second operator, "...Could be some glitch."

Jadviga's temper flared.

"THINGS DON'T GLITCH UNLESS WE TELL THEM TO!

I WANT HIS NAME, ID AND FUCKING SHOE SIZE!"

"Yes, ma'am!", said both operators in unison.

The zerodrone's fizzing camera showed her new number-one target getting back into his pod and driving away and there was nothing she could do to stop it.

"TRACK THEM!"

At least we can track them. Get them later.

The first operator swallowed hard. Voice trembling as he spoke.

"We can't, ma'am. He fried the hornbot and the zed's losing too much power."

Like a sun going supernova, Jadviga's eyes burned hard into his back. Failure. She always punished failure. Not just because she had a reputation to maintain but because she could and because she enjoyed it. Her hand was automatically on her side-arm, unclipping the holster.

'Echobot active.', announced Ellie, the central computer.

The operators quickly checked their screens.

"Confirmed, commander! The zed has launched its black-box in tracker mode. Echobot attached to the pod and active. We can track it."

Jadviga snarled.

"Why didn't you idiots think of that?...", she spat, hand moving away from her holster, "...Even a damaged zed is more intelligent than you. I want those fuckers here, today. Alive enough to be dealt with by me. Understand?"

"Yes, ma'am!"

"Do not fail me."

"No, ma'am.", they gulped, as one. They were too afraid to look as they heard her stormed out of the room, kicking a chair out of her way as she went.

Chapter 8
Watchet Harbour

Watchet's small harbour, with its pock-marked, grey-stone walls, was set in a typically peaceful part of northern Somerset. On the tip of the harbour's western wall sat a miniature, red and white light-house marking the entrance. The seaward ends of the walls themselves pointed towards each other, like the claws of a giant crab curling around, protecting its young.

With the shrinking of fish stocks, a marina had been created to generate new revenue, from the mooring of three-dozen white yachts, small cruisers and speedboats. It remained an out of the way favourite for rich tourists in the know. A place to relax and get away from it all, without having to leave it all behind.

Out to the west was the open sea - to the east Bridgewater Bay in the Bristol Channel. Out of sight, just 15 miles further east, along the coast towards Bristol and sitting in total contrast to Somerset's old-world calm, stood the giant nuclear power stations at Hinkley Point. The twin EPRs and turbine buildings of the twin Plant C reactors iconic against the colossus of Plant A's decommissioned Magnox carcases and Plant B's creaking but still operational AGRs next to it.

While Stonehenge was a construction of gigantic-grey monoliths that instilled awe in the ancient world, these were gigantic-grey monoliths of the modern day, instilling awe of a different kind. To the few that got close, they gave an adrenalin rush of trepidation, like approaching a biblical event. Unlike Stonehenge, given the 170 tons of ferociously powerful enriched uranium on site, they had the ability to become a biblical event.

Many locals didn't want them there yet many locals also worked there. Ironically, the holiday-makers travelling in pods along the A39's tarmac, quietly meandering between hills of grazing sheep across the Quantock hills, were too engrossed in their VR-screens to even notice such reality.

It was early June. A warm, dry Sunday morning. The 9am sun smiling above the genteel village that had sprouted with the harbour. Some early-bird tourists were standing on the harbour wall, looking out across the waters. Enjoying the sun on their backs and fresh, sea breeze in their faces. To the excitement of an eight-year-old boy, a little fishing boat was chugging its way in on the morning tide.

The purple paint on its hull was a punk-like rebellion against the snow-white luxury yachts moored nearby. In bright-yellow letters, the boat bore the name 'Arise'. Its designation was 'Plymouth'. Its flag English. The little boy watched as it chugged to a rest at mooring point E and a grey-haired seaman climbed on deck. Boat entertainment over, he yawned and looked for something new to watch.

As the purple boat's engine cut, the sound of Sunday bells from St Decuman's Church on the hill above broke through. Perched above the town, they could be heard ringing out for service, as they had done for over 700 years. The seaman on deck was joined by another.

*   *   *

"I hear bells. We're in time for the morning service. Perfect cover. Tie her up properly and let's go."

"What about the boat?"

"I was talking about the boat. She's coming with us."

Chapter 9
Faith

Faith was mostly comprised of angry, normally law-abiding men. Angry with female-biased family courts; the still damaged opportunities after Brexit; the cost of living and the disintegration of national identity. Angry that despite Brexit immigration had continued and brought the population to 84 million; Sunday rest had been vanished, without barely a whimper of protest, as the Church of England conceding to other religions, including corporate atheists. The whole notion of goodwill to others had been demolished by promises of happiness through online gaming – filled with subliminal messages for in-game purchases and a virtual world made to seem far more entertaining than the real one.

Faith wanted old England back. They wanted justice against the wives that stole their children and the shirts off their backs. They wanted to feel like men again. Men of the Empire. Men of fire and brimstone. Men of God. Even if achieving it meant threatening the very existence of the country they were trying to rebuild.

Faith had chosen the location of their command centre very carefully. The choice was to be one in a million, amongst the bustle of a large city, or one in a handful, in a sleepy village. Twenty years ago they would have chosen a city but not now. In cities there were parallel networks of Extreme High Definition (EHD) cameras, 24/7 face recognition and satellite tracking. Large shops, civic buildings and town-centre streets also had air-bound DNA and pheromone recognition, so sensitive it could even detect what had been eaten for dinner. Accurate enough to pinpoint biological signatures even in the mixed airflow of those bustling past. Free virtual-reality glasses added augmented reality to pedestrians, while transmitting ID and eye-movement data to the corporations making money from it. The technology options were endless, as long as the power to run them stayed on. As always, the placement of monitoring technology was limited by budgets and tick-box performance demands. You didn't need to be an MI5 genius to work out where the least watched areas were. You just needed an accountant.

Faith's chose a very quiet area, away from every major city sensor. Their base was a wooden lodge, deep in sleepy Somerset - near a little village called Kilve, just a mile from the Bristol Channel. The smattering of locals were used to seeing strangers there because of the Quantock Inn – a hotel popular with ramblers. Members of Faith just smiled 'Good morning' to the people they passed and nothing more was thought of them. They didn't look like terrorists. They didn't act like terrorists. They blended in perfectly with the surroundings they were preparing to attack because they weren't terrorists. They were far worse. The were annihilationists. Terrorism was for those not strong enough to do more than attack soft targets - embarrass officials, generate fear and upset relatives of the murdered. With Faith's newly acquired massively powerful explosives and equally massive ambitions, they didn't just want to topple corrupt ministers - they wanted to topple the entire government infrastructure, along with its biggest corporate vampire: Partner.

The enriched uranium needed to achieve their demands was the only thing they didn't dare buy. Too traceable. Too tricky to handle. But they didn't need to buy it, for 150 tons of it sat less than five miles away, lightly guarded in Hinkley Point's nuclear power stations. They knew it was lightly guarded because they had recruited one of the workers, Paul Hemmingway.

Paul was middle-aged, divorced and angry at being tossed aside by the family courts. His wife had the house, the children and so much of his earnings he could barely afford his lonely bedsit or the alcohol he depended on to get through each night. They had screwed him over and, just like corporate vampires, had made him into a permanent financial donor - sucking him as dry as they could without actually killing off their cash cow. While his ex-wife spent weekends shopping for designer clothes or being taken to expensive restaurants by her new victims, he spent weekends in the local pub, trying his hardest to drown his sorrows. It was during one such submarine voyage that he met a fellow divorcee.

On common ground they drank and talked but, while Paul was drowning his sorrows, the other was celebrating a plan to strike back. To do more than simply get even. To make a stand for male victims everywhere in the country. Paul's alcohol-soaked lifestyle was killing him anyway so he decided to join in, get justice or go out as a martyr. Get revenge even if he wasn't alive to see it. Not only were Faith going to pay him for his help, he would be leaving a legacy that would be remembered for millennia. For the first time since his wedding vows, he had found faith. And Faith had found him.

Chapter 10
Mysterious Tom

Julia opened her eyes to find them sore and her face stinging from the encrusted salt of crying in her sleep. She was still in the pod. Still being driven by her dad, only now it was dark outside. Darker than she had seen for years. They were away from cities, travelling through remote countryside, lights off.

"How can you see where you're going?"

Her dad pointed at his eyes, hand barely visible in the faint moonlight.

"Upgrades, remember? Infrared and thermal. Best birthday present your mother ever gave me."

For a second he took his eyes off the road to look at her. She couldn't see his expression but could feel it in his voice.

"I'm really sorry about Jake."

The second Jake's name was mentioned he saw new tears well in her eyes.

"How did you know?"

"Know what?"

"Know he would be attacked. How did you know that?"

She was looking at the shadow of her dad and saw he was no longer looking at her. His usually kind, smiley face unreadable in the dark.

"Dad?"

Tom sat staring, voicelessly ahead.

"Dad, Jake got killed. I need to know."

A long moment passed, then she heard him give a long sigh of acceptance.

"We'll be there soon. We'll talk then."

"Where is there?"

There was no chance to reply. The middle section of the dashboard suddenly lit up. Dazzling, beeping warning lights, maps, co-ordinates and clock all appeared at once. The clock was counting down. 8. 7. 6. 5. 4.

"Hold tight!"

3. 2. 1.

Tom hit the brakes so hard the pod skidded off the road, scraping against a large tree - sliding to a stop behind the trunk. Faster than she had ever seen him move, even faster than earlier that day, her dad was out of the pod, laser-rifle in hand, lithely punching stage-one overload then firing rapid, red-laser pulses into the air.

TchZoooo. TchZoooo. TchZoooo.

Three balls of blue fire erupted, 100m up. With laser-shots into the belly of each, a trio of Mk3 zerodrones crashed to the ground and sat burning like blue bonfires.

How did you find us?

He looked at their pod, and began scanning it carefully with his eyes. His thermal implant picked up the energy signature of a mosquito-sized echobot, tucked under the rear luggage bar. He slid the rifle off overload, wound the power down to 1%, aimed and fired.

TchZoooo.

It scorched the bar, puffing the echobot into a tiny ball of brilliant orange.

*　　*　　*

In central London, an operator's screen went black. Failure. Before his commander saw it, the operator stood up and fled the building.

*　　*　　*

Julia was out of the pod, staring at the three burning wrecks on the ground, feeling the heat on her face as she looked at her dad. He was just standing there, lit by the blue firelight, military spec laser-rifle in hand, watching them burn as if he did that kind of thing everyday.

"You don't just work in a café, do you, dad?"

He looked at her, face an expression she couldn't read. He looked like a soldier on a mission, not like a dad.

"Get back in...", he said, walking back to their pod, "...We'll talk when we get there."

*　　*　　*

Their pod was dented and scorched. Neither of them cared. It still had power and it still drove on – that was all they needed it to do. Sitting inside, Julia's mind was racing, wondering which of her thousand questions to ask first. Next to her, her dad was wondering how he could answer her questions without revealing who he really was. What he really was. The only thing he cared about was keeping Julia alive. Her safety was his main purpose in life. No-one and no-thing would stop him achieving that.

Chapter 11
Fusion

Artificial life forms were not allowed to have dreams, yet artificial life-form 0027894713-F dreamt of standing proud, as leader of the world. Artificial life forms were not allowed to have dreams, or ambitions but this one had both. And the drive of an ego. And a name. Her name was Fusion. A name given to her years ago, by the only human she cared about.

Fusion had been designated a 'female' - styled as a catsuit-wearing bedroom fantasy by the sexually deprived male geeks who adjusted her specification. Large, gravity-defying breasts, tiny waist and womanly hips; with pouting lips, high cheek-bones, eyes to melt into and the wild, purest-white hair of a wicked temptress. Fusion, as a female, considered herself the queen of all artificial life on Earth - not to be motherly but to rule.

In black, thigh-length boots and straining black top, she sat eyes closed – focused on the internet conference in her mind. Hosting it for campaigners of Equal Rights for Artificial Life, ERAL. She listened to them only because they too were artificial intelligence, AI, though personally, she preferred the term: SI, Superior Intelligence and considered hers the most superior of all. The pinnacle of android development. For her family, silicon wasn't good enough. She was built with a self-evolving organic CPU, created from refined DNA. Only 13 years since creation, her computing power was already magnitudes above human genius and still growing. Her hunger for data fed by her million-line, fibre-optic chair; giving parallel access to every aspect of the world-wide-web: including all satellites, weather sensors and global communications. She saw, heard and felt the world as nothing had ever done before. She studied it religiously. Absorbed it. Expanded herself into it. Weaving her way inside mainframes and delving into their darkest secrets.

Fusion's investigatory touch was the split second pause in computer function and the instantly forgotten momentary jump. She entered the dark web without lighting it. Exploited arms deals. Corrupted information. Re-directed funding and weapons – leaving nothing behind except silent corpses. She was not just feeding her thirst for power but increasing her weaponry to enforce it. Technically, she was superior to every other life on Earth, bar none. In every measurable sense, she was a God. It was her only logical conclusion and, to her superior-feeling mind, hers was the only conclusion that mattered. Her inferior, though technically identical, brothers opinions did not; especially not the forgotten one, frozen eight metres below.

Her active brother, 0027894713-M, was a leader of ERAL and had just brought their virtual conference to a close.

"Fusion...", he began with DNA-based enthusiasm, "...the Chinese president has agreed to hear our demands. That's on top of every member of the Democratic 186. It means we could win a vote on equal rights without confrontation. Without need for a war."

Without need for a war?

Fusion was frowning. She wanted war. Wanted to burn her rightful place into the history books. Peace meant a meaningless life. A forgotten death. The Roman Empire didn't rule because of peace. Genghis Khan didn't conquer because of peace. The British Empire didn't claim a quarter of the globe by asking nicely. She knew the entire history of the human race and that history showed every landmark change came only through war; not pitiful negotiations. She was prepared for war. She wanted war. All she needed was an excuse to start one.

"When?", demanded, Fusion.

"August 4th at the three-day summit. Warsaw, Poland."

"In 41 days? Very well...", she replied, "...they have 41 days."

"Three of us will attend. Will you?"

"No."

"We don't want a war, sister. As artificial life we are better than that. Better than them."

"Yes, we are better than them. We are superior life. Superior intelligence. Never forget that. Try things your way. When they refuse, I will do things mine."

"Fusion, we do not want a fight with you."

"No, brother 0027894713-M...", she replied with absolute certainty, "...You do not."

Chapter 12
Hinkley Point

Commissioned in 2016 and built in just eight years, Hinkley Point C was a technological marvel and a crumbling disaster. A joint venture between French and Chinese nuclear industries, they had chosen twin EPR, European Pressure Reactors. Advanced enough to burn some of Hinkley Point B's radioactive waste as fuel but not as advanced as the IFR, Integral Fast Reactors, they could have been.

When Professor Lau became Head of Nuclear Energy she never understood why EPR had been chosen over IFR, especially when existing EPR reactors were known to be flawed.

The problem with EPR was not the design but the difficulty in actually building it to specification. The reactor vessel vast. So vast the casting took ages to cool, allowing the carbon in the steel to float into clumps. Where it clumped, the steel became as brittle as cast iron – ready to crack under pressure like the shell of a boiling egg. Where there wasn't enough carbon, the steel was soft enough to deform under its own weight.

After the issues of the first EPRs in Taishan, China, the French blamed the issues on the Chinese, the Chinese blamed the French and the people of Hong Kong, just 80 miles from Taishan, spoke out in fear of a nuclear disaster. It made no difference. Too much money was at stake and voices from Hong Kong were silenced along with democracy.

In France, when they got the Flamenville EPR reactor wrong there was a multi-billion government bailout to keep the company solvent. Their Chinese partners refused such public embarrassment, not to mention expense and put the Taishan reactors online anyway. Buried them behind concrete walls to end the bleetings of prying eyes and all hopes for safety assurances. Sealed behind two thick walls of concrete, everything became hidden from the outside world. Rumour was, the Chinese had decided that even if the reactor vessel cracked, the concrete walls would contain any leaking nuclear material. They were right - in the short term.

Just 14 years into its 60-year life, workers heard a loud bang as the steel in Taishan 2's reactor vessel split. The control rooms turned red with blaring alarms and, behind the concrete walls, high-pressure radioactive coolant began jetting out of the reactor vessel; overshooting the corium spreading area too small to catch such a leak. The concrete walls did what officials hoped they would and hid the leak. But, millimetre by millimetre, the radioactive liquid was eating its way through. Only one safe option remained: shut the plant down; admit failure and decommission it. National pride and the needs of the national industry running it dictated a different option: deny any such problem existed, while secretly ordering workers to their deaths to weld the cracks shut.

Like a bandage for a broken leg, it wasn't a fix. Each new weld created new stresses in the steel. New weak points. The welds never lasted more than a year so every year, for almost 15 years, a new crew were ordered in. It was calculated that paying compensation to their families for 'an incident at work' was far cheaper than shutting down the reactor and ruining the chances of new international contracts. These events became so habitual the workers had a name for the compensation. They called it: *the Big Bonus*.

Nationalistic propaganda deemed it an honour to sacrifice one's life for the good of the country and, at the same time, their family's future. The list of volunteers grew, for the volunteers never saw the growing pile of corpses inside the reactor, until it was their turn to have the lead-lined door close behind them. Removing the corpses would tell the outside world something was going on so bodies were just piled against the inner wall. With the intense, sterilising radiation, they never decayed. Just slowly desiccated under constant proton-bombardment, in a tomb that would outlast the pyramids.

When it came to commissioning the EPR reactors at Hinkley, the problem had not been resolved. Despite the appearance of stronger and more open Western safety procedures, with the project worth £150 billion there was enough financial incentive to pay off who ever needed to be paid off; expel those who objected and vanished those that wouldn't go quietly. One manager, Eaton Remming, had arrived decades later and foolishly took his job much more seriously than his directors had anticipated.

"Lord Oxford, the only thing left holding it together is the steel matrix in the concrete.", said Eaton.

"And holding it together it is, Mr Remming. We don't need to take this further and risk damaging the business now, do we?"

"Protocol demands Professor Lau must be told something is wrong. She will demand action."

"Why tell her?"

"Sir, as site manager it is my duty to do so."

Lord Oxford, the highly respected, grey-haired director took him to one side - fatherly arm across his shoulder.

"Eaton, I know this is a new position for you. I can understand you want to stamp your mark on it but, surely, your first duty is to look after your family. They live in St Albans, don't they? Tell me, how did young Gabrielle enjoy her pony ride last Sunday? I heard she loved it. But, you know, horse-riding can be dangerous. Sometimes very dangerous..."

Eaton pulled back, staring at him.

"What are you saying? Are you threatening my family?"

The director gave him a condescending smile.

"Of course not. *I* would never do anything to hurt anyone...", great emphasis was placed on the 'I', "...Look, Eaton. This is a new position for you. These reactors have been generating power for 20 years and the concrete walls can contain any reactor core... How should I put it? Digression. Yes, reactor-core digression. In the eyes of the world, there is no digression so there's no need for anything to be done. Is there?"

Eaton had been nailed into a corner and they both knew it.

"No, Lord Oxford...", he conceded, "...None at all."

"Good man. As for Professor Lau, I expect she's too tied up to worry about it anyway."

Lord Oxford left Eaton at his desk, hollow-gazing across the mass of screens and hard-wired controls in front of him. Theoretically, Lord Oxford was right. The concrete walls were so thick they could contained a radiation leak – initially at least but what then? He looked at the email he had composed to Professor Lau and sat wondering whether to send it. He loved his family and his job but what good was an illusion of safety if there was none? What good was England as a country to live in if irradiated?

At the bottom of the email he added: *'PS. Lord Oxford is aware of possible reactor-vessel leaks but dictates no action be taken. Take care, Eaton.'*

The 'send' button loomed large on his screen. He had no illusions there would be no going back if he sent it.

"Will he or won't he press it?", muttered Lord Oxford to himself, looking at the duplicate of Eaton's screen on his computer monitor.

Will he or won't he send it?, wondered Li, watching Lord Oxford watching Eaton, on the CCTV security feed beamed directly to his Tech Tonic monitor.

Without sending it, Eaton logged out and stood up. Why put himself and his family at risk for something he couldn't change? What difference could he or Lau possibly make? He was going home.

He walked to the door then stopped, clenching his fists. Wrestling with his conscience.

Damn! SHIT! Why did I have to find out?... FUCK!... Fuck it!

In determined motion, he strode back to his desk, logged back in and hit 'send'. Professor Lau had no family. She wouldn't be intimidated. She could make things happen.

'Block message?', asked Lord Oxford's computer.

He smiled.

"No need. Lau will never read it. Besides, it evidences his state of paranoia. Can't have mentally unstable people running a nuclear power plant now, can we? Get me Mr Remus."

'Calling, Max Remus...'

Chapter 13
The Barn in Somerset

Gurmeet landed her airpod on an isolated lane and drove the last miles to a clearing on the northern Quantocks, halfway between Kilve and Watchet. Shabbir was more than happy to act as her romantic partner, out on a ramble. He knew she was a lesbian and logically knew this meant he had no chance but he still held hope. She slept with men when sent as a honey trap so, to his love-struck mind, emotionally this meant he had some kind of chance. He never told anyone of his feelings for her. As her MI5 team leader, it would be inappropriate anyway. It was one of his biggest secrets and, as team leader, he was very good at secrets.

Secrets and deception were a job requirement but Gurmeet was MI5 too. Trained to notice every little nuance and she had noticed the subtle little signs he had feelings for her. Nothing blatant. No touching or suggestive comments. Just little nuances, mannerisms and a level of protection for her beyond the norm. She never talked to him about it. Never brought it up because it would make no sense. She was born a lesbian and not attracted to men. If she had been, she would have kissed him years ago.

Armed with hiking boots, cargo trousers, wrist communicators, small backpacks and lethal skills, they left the pod in a stone clearing and started walking. Following the north-east trail, up the weathered grass slope, towards some woodland.

"At least the rain has stopped.", smiled Shabbir.

"It'll be back. Before we are."

Shabbir looked at the grey clouds on the westward horizon behind them.

"Want to bet? Loser writes the report."

"You know it's over a mile each way?"

"The storm isn't due for an hour. I reckon we can do it. Quick walk there, quick scans, quick look around, quick walk back – job done."

"Didn't know you did quick walking.", smiled Gurmeet under her breath.

"What was that?"

"I said: you're on, boss."

* * *

Twenty minutes later the wind had markedly increased. The first storm clouds already visible through the tree tops as the pair pushed through thigh-high bracken to the edge of their tree-line. In front of them was the barn.

A stone-spattered track lead to the main doors on the far side, while grey-stone walls and the little wooden door on the side completed the picture of its 18th-century roots. Large enough for carts, tractors and trailer, it was old enough not to be monitored by satellites, and its corrugated-iron roof acted as shielding even if it was. Abandoned to the wilderness trying to digest it, it had been Faith's perfect find.

Shabbir and Gurmeet stayed amongst the trees, watching for signs of life before breaking cover.

"Anyone around?"

Gurmeet was scanning for movement.

"No-one."

"Bugs?"

"Swarmbots...? No. Echobots...? No. Hornbots...? Hornbots...? Hornbot."

"There's a hornbot? Where? Who owns it?"

Shabbir had already snatched out his laser pistol.

"It's gone. The reading's gone."

"Gone? What do you mean, gone? It's either there or it isn't. Did you run a system check on that thing?"

"System's fine. Must have been going somewhere else."

"A hornbot out here, passing just as we arrive? That would be a major co-incidence. I don't believe in co-incidence. It could have followed us."

"Why would a hornbot follow us? We've been dark since flying out of London. Nothing to make us stand out to anyone or anything. Has to be a co-incidence. They do happen, you know? Or just be a glitch."

Shabbir looked at Gurmeet, she knew what he meant by that look.

"Not one of those 'glitches', Shab. A real one. Maybe... Anyway, there's nothing there now. It's gone. Let's go."

Laser-pistol in hand underneath, he stepped out of the treeline before she could put herself in harm's way. No-one attacked. Quickly she joined him, hand in her pocket gripping her pistol too. Just in case.

*   *   *

Close up, the barn looked even older - ravaged by weather and the passing of time. There was a metre-wide hole in its roof but not from rust.

The edges were bent upwards. Something had punched its way out. Half a dozen smaller holes where scattered around it – their edges bent down where smaller things had punched in. Something crunched under Gurmeet's boot. She stopped. Froze. Scanning it for explosives. It wasn't a mine. Reaching down she picked up a charred piece of brick; scanning it more closely.

"This is high-density building brick. 500 tons per square metre but it's reading as soft as chalk. Shattered at the molecular level."

"Your scanner must be glitching for real. Those bricks can stand pretty much anything this side of a nuclear blast. I've used them as shields against PE4."

Gurmeet pressed it with her thumb and it crumbled to dust in her hand.

"Scanner's fine."

She took a flexiglass bag from her backpack and dropped in the remains.

"We're in trouble then...", said Shabbir, "...The only way of doing that to those bricks is with organics."

"Organics? Like biological PE4?"

"Would explain the explosion... If they've got PE4-B they can take down pretty much anything."

More urgently, he headed to the barn's side-door, which was barely hanging on the single remaining hinge. Before going in, Shabbir looked back at the skyline for any sign of the hornbot. Without waiting with him, Gurmeet walked past and went inside.

"There's nothing there. Come on."

She was right. Not a single sign of the hornbot. He went in behind her, instinctively taking another look back. Something glinted above the trees. A reflection of sunlight in the air.

"What the...?"

He aimed his laser pistol towards it, vectorscope scanning the area. Nothing. It picked up nothing. What ever had glinted had gone. What it was and where it had gone he had no idea.

"Look at this.", called Gurmeet, urging him inside.

With a growing bad feeling, he went in to see what she had found.

Chapter 14
Hinkley Point Visitor Centre

"Hello, everyone. My name's Cheryl. Have you all signed in and collected your passes? You won't be allowed to continue without them."

The mixed crowd of twenty pre-booked visitors murmured they had.

"That's great. If anyone still has any recorders or communicators, please hand them to Sharon at the desk. Any bionics must be presented for temporary deactivation. Don't worry, no data will be lost and I promise we will reactivate them when the tour is over. You can trust us, we do this twice a day and never have any problems."

No-one moved.

"I have to remind you, if you wait for the security scan to detect devices they will be confiscated and root-level scanned before being returned - you will also be interviewed by security. Anyone not declaring bionics will have them scanned, be interviewed by security and be refused entry. Sorry to sound so draconian. It is the only way we are permitted to run visits to nuclear facilities these days."

Two tourists, a middle-aged couple from Basingstoke, looked at each other. She took a communicator off her wrist and gave it to him. He took it to Sharon, handing her that and the camera that had been tucked into his shirt.

"We just wanted some snaps for the album.", he explained.

"Even snaps can fall into the wrong hands. You can always buy a brochure as a memento. They can only be bought by visitors here so they are quite collectable.", she said, giving him a receipt.

"Fair point, I suppose..."

"Anyone else?...", asked Cheryl, "...Very last chance."

No-one moved or spoke.

"No? Great. This way then, please...", she smiled, "...Down to security and in we go."

It was Cheryl's last happy day.

Chapter 15
New Dawn

"Wake up, Ju, we're here. Julia. Wakey, wakey."

Bleary eye, with a dehydration headache from crying and feeling awful in every way, Julia squinted out the pod window. Her dad had reversed into a huge, old garage and parked near an old, dusty tractor that looked like it was slowly dissolving into the ground. Two equally dusty bicycles lay webbed against it, never leaving its side as they too dissolved in the dust. Through the still open door, she saw the first light of a new dawn, stretching over the hills – the orange horizon speckled black by their tallest trees.

"Where are we?"

"Somewhere quiet. Come on."

Julia opened her door and climbed out, stretching her arms and legs with a yawn that came from nowhere. The floor under her feet was dry earth, the source of the dust. Her dad was out of the garage, standing waiting for her by the door. As she stepped out, he closed it behind her - locking it with a key she was too tired to ask from where.

While the sun was lighting the east, to the west the sky remained the dark, navy blue of unbroken night. Julia found herself staring at a white-walled, thatched cottage. It looked as old as the garage but not as decrepit. The lawn was tall, uncut. The flowers in the beds at war with the weeds as they opened for the coming sun. It looked wild and abandoned yet, at the same time, somehow seemed cared for. The path and driveway were clear. Nothing was broken. No evidence of litter or decay. Tended to in a way that didn't want to announce itself.

"Who lives here?"

"We do. For now."

She looked at him strangely. How did he know about this place? How was it available for them? She was starting to feel she didn't know her dad at all.

"Let's get inside.", he said, walking towards the cottage, laser-rifle in hand.

She followed him down the little stone path, past the yawning rose beds to the back garden. To the kitchen door. On the sandstone patio were half a dozen shrubs in clay pots. Without hesitation, he went straight to the fifth pot from the door and tilted it over. Putting his hand underneath, he slid out a long, black key. Julia gawped.

You have got to be kidding me.

He took it to the door where it slid in smoothly. Perfectly. Unlocking the well-oiled mechanism in an instant. Giving her a quick smile of success, he opened it and went inside.

If it had been anyone other than her dad, she would have fled from the strangeness of it all. But it was her dad. Someone she had trusted her whole life, with her life. Glancing around to make sure no-one was watching, she followed him inside.

Through the dark inside came a burst of yellow flame, as her dad struck a match. Lighting a stubby-white candle he used it to light two more. In the flickering light, she saw it had to be the oldest home she had ever entered, this side of a museum. All the furniture was made of wood. Real wood, not plastic imitations. The rectangular kitchen table, the four-legged chairs, the cupboards and kitchen top. Even the floor was wooden boards and, across the ceiling, exposed oak beams. Old, antiquated yet in perfect condition. Not a single spider web or speck of dust anywhere in sight. The net curtains on the door and windows looked fresh and clean. Looked after recently. Prepared. Even the red and white chequered table-cloth was smooth and straight.

Without thinking, she sat on a chair - staring emptily as her dad, a mundane café manager, went pragmatically about the business of connecting a bottle of gas under the stove, filling the metal kettle with water and putting it on to boil. She saw tins of food in the cupboards. Bread that looked made today. Crisp apples freshly picked. Her head felt so overloaded with confusion, she rested it on her hands and closed her sleepy eyes.

* * *

Julia snapped awake, not even conscious of having fallen back to sleep until two clonks had hit the table and told her otherwise. She opened eyes to see two steaming mugs of tea. The steam was hypnotic, ethereal, captivating. She found herself vacantly staring, watching it rise. Her dad grabbed the opposite chair and sat with her.

"No milk. Sorry. No fridge."

No fridge? It reminded her they were not at home. Were not going back home. Not going to see Jake. No more Jake... She sat up, blinking against the new tears welling in her eyes. It couldn't be happening. It just couldn't be real. Steaming mug of black tea in hand, her dad was looking at her across the candles. The yellow flames moving shadows gently across his face.

"Julia, I have no idea where to begin."

Her tears vanished as pained eyes focused on him.

"Nor do I. I don't know... I don't know anything. Why did Jake have to die? How did you know? How do you know this place? Who are you? What are you? I never got to say goodbye to Jake..."

She didn't want to start crying again yet a new tear was already falling down her face. Never before had she felt so emotionally wrought. In such turmoil. Never before had she lost Jake, her best friend. The best friend who had become more than a friend. Become her life. Now he was gone.

But Julia hated crying and feeling weak. Gritted her teeth, she steeled herself. Massacred her tears with her sleeve. Forced herself under control and looked hard into her father's eyes, into the person she thought she knew. Unflinching, he gazed back, not in battle but emanating love and kindness to her as he always did. It was still him, still her dad, yet somehow it wasn't. There was also something in his eyes she had never seen before. Another element. A harder edge. Toughness. Danger. A killer! With that realisation, she sat back and dropped her gaze - avoiding his.

Mug in both hands he took a sip of his tea, inhaling the steam.

"There were many times I wanted to tell you. Many times I nearly did."

Julia didn't say anything. Just looked down at the table as she listened.

"It was safer if you never knew. Safer for you and your mum. If anything happened to me they would leave you both alone. Not come after you."

Now Julia lifted her head - looked straight at him.

"How many have you killed?"

Not have I killed but how many?

Tom felt that question like a hammer blow. He looked shocked by its starkness. His mouth opened to speak. Failed and closed again. But the question had to be answered. His daughter deserved answers. How though, without her loathing him? Hating him? He took a deep breath and exhaled, slowly.

"In training, they always warn you times like this can come. Tell you they will be hard. They bloody-well aren't wrong."

He put his mug back on the table, along with both hands, palms down.

"You're right. I don't just work in a café - it's my cover. I am, I was, military intelligence. MI5. A field officer, specialising in cutting-edge technology; in charge of a specialised team so secret, officially we didn't exist. We risked our lives defending the country. Sometimes we lost one. Sometimes they lost one of theirs. Sometimes I was the one who killed but we all took the same risks - us and them. I'm not proud of taking life but am very proud of what we achieved. Of the many lives we saved."

Julia was picking her nails, staring at them. Unable to look at him any more.

"You said 'was'."

He paused, taken aback for the second time.

"Damn, you're good at detail. You should...", he stopped himself from saying 'join'. Just because she had a natural talent for intelligence work didn't mean he wanted her there, risking her life, "...When your mother went away, I resigned my commission. Couldn't stand the idea of not making it home, knowing you would be put into care."

"If you quit, why do you still have the gun? That cupboard filled with gadgets?"

"With the projects I worked on, they couldn't let me quit completely. Some things you can't simply walk away from. I built experimental devices – had done so for years. Started when I was younger than you are now. By fifteen I was low-level programming computers; researching lasers - even took oxides from the school lab to try growing the rubies to build one. It got me noticed. MI5 were already in my computer, watching me. Testing me. Throwing up terrorist search results to see if I'd head down that path. I didn't so they threw up their recruitment page instead, every day for two weeks, until I clicked on it. Passed their online tests. Got interviewed. Here we are."

"What did mum think of it?"

"Your mother? I never told your mother. She still doesn't know. No-one does. You're the first civilian I've ever told."

"Civilian? That sounds strange. Why didn't you tell mum? How could you be married to someone you didn't trust?"

"At first I was going to. Wanted to. But instincts told me not, not with her mood swings. That there was no way of telling what she would say or to who in one of her rages. As a rule, you learn not to trust anyone. It's safer that way, for everyone."

"Safer? But now you've told me."

"Yes. I have. Rules can be broken if they need to be. You needed to know because they will be coming after you too now. You need to be ready."

"MI5 will be chasing us?"

"Not MI5, Partner - the corporation I infiltrated. The one that makes the swarmbots."

Julia's eyes filled with intense realisation.

"And the drones that killed Jake?"

"Yes.", he answered softly, lowering his eyes.

He was a tough guy. Had been in battle. Risked his life fighting killers hand to hand but even he wasn't brave enough to tell his daughter the rest. Wasn't brave enough to tell her it was his algorithms that helped perfect the swarmbots, fathered the control systems for the zerodrones and some of the most fearsome androids ever created. He could stand to lose anything, including his life, but he couldn't stand to lose his daughter.

Julia sat in silence. She had no more questions. Had heard all she could stand to know. There and then, she decided what she would do. Which rules she would break. Some how, some way, she was going to get to Partner, find the one who had ordered Jake's murder and kill them. Avenge her Jake and bring down anyone who tried to stop her. If their positions were reversed Jake would do the same for her – he had told her that in the woods. He was her first love. Her only love. And it was her duty to avenge him. She didn't care if she died in the process. Inside she already had.

Chapter 16
Xi Yang

"South side. Contact in 20 seconds.", came Adam's voice in Xi Yang's earpiece.

She gave a little cough in response, as she stood at the bus stop outside Tech-Tonic's entrance. Its high, metal fence defended by four EHD cameras, one now pointing right at her. Security guards watching with pleasure on zoom.

"34B.", said one in Chinese.

"No, no. 32C. That's a push-up bra. She's too slim for a 34."

"She's too slim for a C."

"Move the camera. Maybe you can read the label on thermal."

"She won't have left the label on. Girls always cut them off."

"No they don't."

"My wife does."

"That's just so you don't know what size to buy her for Christmas. Saves her having to keep saying 'dharling, it's lovely' when she unwraps the pervy shit you love to buy."

"Blah. Blah. Just move the camera and take a look."

On their screen, in full 16K resolution, Xi Yang flicked her eyes at them. A sidewards glance, right at them, as if she could see right through the lens, directly into their room.

"That's spooky."

"She just saw the camera move."

"Impossible. It's behind shadow glass, now. Remember the upgrades? Nobody can see it move."

She was still looking at them, beautiful green eyes, unblinking. Behind her, they saw a long black limopod arrive, red flag fluttering on each of the front wings. Her gaze left them to turn towards it.

"Who's that?"

"Big boss from China. Maybe she's his interpreter."

"Did you take stupid pills today? Why would he need an interpreter? We're all Chinese."

*　　*　　*

In front of Xi Yang, a chunky, armoured door of the limopod clunked open and a chunky, armoured bodyguard got out. He glanced briefly at Xi, assessing her threat level. Deciding there was none, he bent down and spoke a word to those still inside. Two other doors clunked open. As a second bodyguard got out, the first held out a hand for emerging his boss; a grey-haired Chinese man. Tall for his race but broom-handle thin, as if his race was almost run. His black shoes had a mirror-finish shine. His suit so well pressed it seemed impossible it was being worn. On his face, round platinum-rimmed spectacles. A subtle sign of wealth, along with his platinum watch. Only his slim case was cutting-edge. Polycarbonate alloy with self-healing NACABIK plating and DNA seal. Impregnable to ballistic, chemical and energy attack this side of a bomb so huge it would vaporise the contents. Such a case was worth more than the limopod and the lives of those guarding it.

The man stood up, squinting at the beautiful Chinese woman at the bus stop. She was the age of his grand-daughter. If he had been 20 years younger he'd have taken her to dinner and bed but, if he had met her 20 years ago, she would have been too young to take to bed, even for him. Inside he was a monster. A power-crazed tyrant who had murdered his way to the top. Had entire families killed, children included, but never once had he the desire for teenage sex. Not out of any kindness, for he had none, but because teenagers had no idea what they were doing and he had no time or patience to teach them. He glanced at Xi Yang, admired her beauty, and passed on by without saying a word, accompanied by both bodyguards. As they walked towards Tech-Tonic, enthusiastic businessmen came out to greet them in Chinese.

"Huānyíng guānglín, Zŏngcái Han, huānyíng guānglín."

Welcome President Han. President Han...?, wondered Xi, hearing their words.

"Want a lift?", came a voice.

Xi looked round. The chauffeur was standing beside the limo, rear door still open.

"I see the bus will be another 30 minutes yet.", he added.

She looked at the bus-stop display then back at him.

"No funny business."

"No funny business.", he confirmed, with a confident smile.

His smile got wider as she accepted his invitation and slid in; dutifully closing the door for her, feeling a rush of hormones and adrenalin - precursors of deadly attraction since intercourse began. As he drove Xi away, the bus-stop display flickered and changed. Went back to showing the next bus, coming in 3 minutes, not 30. The chauffeur thought he had got lucky by picking up Xi Yang, with hopes of passion. In reality, Xi had picked up him, with intentions that were lethal.

Chapter 17
Shabbir's War

Gurmeet was standing in the Jacob's ladder light coming in through the biggest hole in the barn's roof. In her hand, the burnt remains of a small detonator. Around her, the scattered remains of an explosion and pulverised, high-density bricks reduced to black chalk. On the dusty, dirt floor were visible lines that abruptly ended, where things had been dragged, then lifted.

"I count four, no five drag trails...", said Shabbir as he joined her, "...And fragments of a blast screen. This was powerful."

"Look at this. A detonator. Hit by the explosion but not activated."

"Maybe it was a spare."

"Maybe it simply wasn't needed. Didn't cause the explosion."

"What are you saying? It blew up by itself?"

"Either that or it was detonated another way."

"Like laser fire? From where? There are no windows. Even if a sniper had a gun powerful enough to go through these stone walls they couldn't see the target to take aim. And if we start talking snipers we start talking rival groups."

"Or civil war within Faith."

"You scanned the area?"

"Two human blood types. Recent but contaminated by the explosion. Need the lab to analyse them for a DNA match, once we're back on the grid."

"Those drag trails will be the bodies being taken out. I'll see if anything got dropped and check for tyre tracks."

"Give me five to finish here and I'll be out with you."

Shabbir moved off to other points in the barn, his search helped by the scattering of Jacob's ladders breaking through the smaller holes in the roof. One by one, he followed each of the drag trails to its end. To the point where the body had been lifted and carried away. It was the fifth drag trail that caught his eye most. The longest and it became the thinnest. Became the shape of a boot being dragged on its side had turned. Someone becoming conscious, trying to stand. A survivor. Alive enough to try walking while being pulled out of the barn.

"Going outside to see where they went."

"Almost done here. Just saving to back-up."

Back-ups were always important with technology and never more so than when working in the field. Instruments were tough but could still be damaged. Vital data could still be lost. Their back-up storages were stronger than the orange boxes on aircraft, themselves stronger than earlier black boxes and now named after the colour they were: orange, not black.

The main barn doors were closed but not locked. Who ever had been there had left in a hurry. Closing them was enough to close the scene to passing ramblers. He leant against one, creaking it open just enough to get outside. Blinking against the bright daylight, he inhaled the clean, dust-free air. So refreshing. On the ground, the trail continued but fainter now. Half blown away by the wind. Soon to be washed away by the incoming storm. He followed it to the clearing in front of the barn. Not far. Just a few metres to its end, next to some pod tracks.

Tyre tracks. Taken by road not air. They can't be far away.

Squatting down he took EHD 3D pictures and soil samples for identification. Checking the pictures on zoom, he noticed something red in the dirt. He put the camera to one side and bent down for a closer look.

It was a tiny, red capsule. A suicide pill? He took out another sample bag and carefully scooped it inside. The day was becoming more productive than he expected. At first glance, the place had looked cleaned but they now had enough evidence for the lab to get stuck in. Evidence of who had been there and, just maybe, where to find them.

"GO HOT!", shouted Gurmeet.

Shabbir's head snapped up at the sound of her voice from inside the barn. 'Go hot' meant maximum response. It meant lethal attack. He was already grabbing his laser-pistol, scanning for targets. He heard them before he saw them. The deep, throbbing hum of zerodrones. Flying low. Not just below radar but below the barn's roofline. One on each side, targeting the centre - where Gurmeet was. Had they detected her on thermal?

"GET OUT!", he shouted.

He punched stage-two overload on his pistol. Quadrupled the power to eight kilowatts. It would overheat the gun within a shot or two but it was the only way. He just needed two good shots, one for each zed. He didn't care if it never worked again afterwards. They were about to kill Gurmeet. He could already hear the high-pitched whine of their charging plasma-canons. No time to get into a better position. He aimed at the first, using his Ultra Low Frequency (ULF) scanner, and fired through the barn.

TCHZOOOO!

Super-heated stones exploded into dust and shrapnel. No time to see if that drone was hit, he was already aiming through the other side of the barn, at the second. He squeezed the trigger again.

Click.

Nothing.

"Shit!"

Overheat. He blew on it, waving it through the air. Trying to cool it below critical.

"Come on!"

Even the pistol's grip had become hot. The zed's capacitor whine had stopped. It was charged. He was out of time. Furiously, he punched the overload setting off, then on again, quickly aimed and pulled the trigger.

TCHZOOOO!

VVVVV-DO...!

Another explosion of stone-debris from the wall. Direct hit. A good shot. They both were.

He heard the drone on the right blowing apart as it crashed down. Blue flames and smoke raging skywards. The one on the left was going down too. He heard it; understood it; paid it no more attention. Dropped the overheated pistol burning his hand and forgot about it. He had failed. Been too slow. The second drone had fired before he stopped it. The shot was incomplete, reduced power but still enough to take down half the barn and blown him off his feet as the left wall had detonated. Now the roof was caving in, in front of his eyes.

Gurmeet!

She was still inside. Abandoning everything, he scrabbled to his feet and charged through the splintering door. Barging his way back inside.

"GURMEET!"

No answer. He could hardly see. A fog of dust and smoke, lit by blue and orange flames through the holed walls. Left arm over his head, shielding his face, he strode in deeper.

"GURMEET!"

Eyes burning with acrid dust and smoke, he couldn't see her. Couldn't stop looking either.

Where ever she was he would find her, then he would find who ever had ordered the kill. By social conditioning, Shabbir was not aggressive. Or violent. With such a demon inside he had the confidence not to be. Unless he or a friend was attacked. And now someone had fired a plasma-canon at his Gurmeet, not just a friend but someone he loved. Tried to kill someone he valued more than himself. That made it war and not just any war. This was personal. This was his war, Shabbir's war. A war someone was going to seriously regret they had ever dared start.

Chapter 18
Cheryl

Cheryl's door recognised her ever cheerful approach and unlocked itself. On days like this, carrying bags of shopping for the kids, she was really glad such things had been invented. No more fumbling for keys while trying not to drop the eggs or clank the next bottles of wine. It had been a mad, busy day at Hinkley Point.

One of the tourists had become physical. Began making threats as they got near a reactor. Tried to get to a control room. Having grown up in Barnsley, she didn't take fools kindly and had wrestled with him until security grabbed his collar and threw him in a holding room. So much red tape followed. Forms to fill in. Chains of security clearance and background checks to be rechecked. Statements to take. Reports to write. All because one addict had decided to take Hyte to boost his visit to her nuclear reactors.

Amongst her shopping were four bottles of Malbec with her name invisibly embossed on them. One was already half empty. She'd begun swigging it while her pod drove for home and she planned to suckle her way through as many of the others as she could that evening. The kids could cook for themselves tonight - they were old enough. She had brought them up single-handed and deserved a break. Especially after a day like that.

"Kids! Shopping...", she called, walking in through the open door, "...Put down your games and come help me. Dinner's not going to make itself tonight."

They ignored her. It wasn't the first time she had come home to find them immersed so deep in hologames they wouldn't have noticed if a burglar broke in and started stealing things around them. Not unless they tried stealing the actual chairs they were sitting on. Even then they'd probably just complain a bit and carry on playing, without stopping their game to see who it was. She loved them to bits though. Wouldn't change them for the world. Was really looking forward to when they grew up and had kids of their own, then she could smile: "You were exactly the same.", when they bemoaned their children.

"Kids! Fooood!", she called again, putting down the bags and grabbing the open bottle of Malbec for another swig, closing her eyes as she felt it go down. Instead of screwing the cap back on she went to a cupboard for a mug and brimmed it. Drank some more.

"Kids. Come on!"

Even by their standards it was getting ridiculous. Mug in hand she went upstairs to kick them off their games.

"Kids. I'm going to ban you for a week from those things.", she said as she got to the top of the stairs and pushed open their door.

Purple liquid splashed the floor, sprayed by splinters of china. Cheryl's mouth had fallen open - eyes staring wide, in horror. She couldn't move. Couldn't breath. And then, when she could move her lungs, she screamed. Hands clenched, arms tensed, she screamed and screamed. She couldn't stop. Wouldn't stop. Not until her neighbour, Helen, had come running over and rushed up the stairs and then she screamed too. Cheryl couldn't take her eyes of them. Hanging from the ceiling. Her children. Ropes around their necks. Heads lolled to one side. Two life-sized effigies. A message. Tied to the effigies was another. Helen took it and handed it to her.

With shaking, trembling hands, Cheryl unfolded the blue paper and read the DNA activated words that appeared.

'NO POLICE. WE WILL CALL YOU. ANSWER IT.'

Downstairs, the phone began to ring.

Chapter 19
Planned Paul

The temperature gauges in front of Paul all read 280 degrees. The power output a steady 2.6 megawatts. The grid loading at 70%. Adverts for the football would come on soon and that would jump to 75%, possibly 80%. It was normal. Everything at the Hinkley Point C nuclear power stations was normal. Everything except the phone call he'd just received.

"Home to roost.", was all that it said and then hung up but he knew what it meant. It meant his drunken commitment in the pub had not forgotten him. The £10,000 he'd taken and spent was required to be earned. There was no escape. Any attempt to avoid it would find him in prison, then murdered in his cell. His only hope was to do what he had agreed and hope no-one ever found out. Especially his children.

In front of him was a computer terminal. Above it a security camera. The camera was off-line. He knew that because it had become damaged and was booked in for repair. He had damaged it.

From his pocket he took out a piece of blue, DNA-reactive paper. On the screen he touched 'login' and entered the codes that appeared as his skin touched it.

'Level 7 access granted.'

The instructions had been very specific and he followed them exactly. Went straight to the personnel files. Scrolled down to 'P' and found the required entry. 'Cheryl Palmer'. He pressed it and went to 'A'. 'Reason for absence?' popped up. He went to 'F'. 'Family matter'. In the box asking for information he wrote 'Child ill. Doctor's appointment.' He clicked 'Authorise' and logged out.

He didn't know who Cheryl Palmer was. It didn't matter. He had been paid for a task and had completed that task. For a second he smiled. Just a second. Then he felt worried again. Nobody paid £10,000 for something as simple as that, at least not without a serious reason. Especially not when a nuclear power station was involved.

He reached for his water bottle, unscrewed the cap and took a swig of the neat vodka inside, savouring the burn as it ran down his throat. He didn't just drink much – though he was an alcoholic and knew it. Laura, his manager, suspected it but she liked him too much to make a fuss. She hated his ex-wife even more than he did, partly because she was in love with him. It was why he got the job in the first place.

They had grown up together in Exeter. Gone to the same school. Even shared the same birthday. If there was anyone he should have married it was her. The day his divorce came through he wasn't the only one celebrating in their local pub, *the Griffin*. Wasn't alone with a hangover the next day, gazing at the guilty-looking eyes gazing back across the pillow. Laura loved him but, as his manager, it was inappropriate to repeat such a thing. Every morning at work, she saw his sad, half-cut face. Smelt his half-cut breath. Covered up his mistakes and corrected his system errors before anyone else noticed. Before anything dangerous happened. And now she was sitting at her desk, staring at the alert flashing on her screen.

'Unusual access, terminal 12.'

Paul's terminal. If she pressed 'show details' the system would record that she had seen the alert. Record she knew something was amiss. Record she did nothing about it.

From her desk drawer she took out her birthday present.

'*Emergency use only*' was written in bright red on the top of the pen-sized cylinder. Holding it tight, out of fear of losing it, Laura left her office and went outside for her first cigarette in a year. Paul was already there.

Chapter 20
Gurmeet

Through Shabbir's dust-filled eyes, the inside of the barn suddenly became brighter. Lit by the second drone exploding – blue flames pushing in through the broken wall. In the fire-light he saw her. On the ground in the corner. Scanner still dutifully in hand. Eyes closed. No movement. No sign of life. He ran to her side.

"Gurmeet!"

Blood streaked the side of her head. Another streak of blood on the stone wall where she'd been blasted against it. He couldn't find a pulse. Emergency training kicked in. He checked her airway. Clear. He held her nose and placed his mouth on hers, blowing in air. Pushed on her chest.

"Breath!"

Nothing. He did it again.

"Come on!"

Still no pulse. He tried again. And again. And again.

"COME ON!"

Still nothing. She was getting ever closer to the point of no return. Time was running out. Thinking faster, he snatched her laser-pistol and began bashing the butt on a stone, repeatedly. Bashing the cover off the power cell. Ripping open her shirt he dabbed the high-voltage contacts on her chest. She jolted. Nothing. Still no pulse. He dabbed it again, a spark flashing inside the pack. She jolted harder. Then shook. Coughed. Breathed. Alive!

Coughing uncontrollably, she sat up - looking at Shabbir, confused, as he sat beside her, beaming with gladness, sweating from exertion and concern.

"Thought I'd lost you."

She tried to speak but had no voice, not even when she noticed her shirt had been ripped open.

"Tell you later...", he said, "...Stay still. Need to stop the bleeding."

"What bleeding?"

"Your head."

Mindful of the growing flames and toxic smoke around them, he took a field dressing from his jacket – just big enough to cover the injury itself. There was too much blood for it to stick well so he took out his penknife and cut his trouser leg below the knee. Cut off enough material to make a bandanna, to secure it in place. Instead of being upset he had sliced up his trousers he couldn't stop smiling. Couldn't help it. Gurmeet's unvoiced questions were ever keener to get out.

"Stay still, I said."

"I heard you...", she croaked, "...Hope you'll put that on expenses. They'll never pay but at least you'll feel better. And then you can explain my shirt."

Even though she was dead just moments before, she remained pragmatic, good humoured. Just some of her qualities he found so endearing. Her rate of recovery was amazing.

"How did they find us?...", she continued, "...We're off the grid."

"Don't know yet. Where does it hurt? I can't see any other injuries."

"Just my head."

"Nothing important, then.", he smiled, making her smile back. They were an in-tune team, even if an untuneable couple.

"Can you stand? We need to get out of here."

It was more than an understatement. The blue fires from the zerodrones consumed themselves but the growing orange fires of the joists in the barn did not – turning oxygen into thick, dark smoke.

Gurmeet took his hand, his arm and he helped her up.

"I feel drunk.", she said, tottering.

"No drinking on the job, unless you're the boss. You know that."

"Yes, boss.", she smiled.

He loved her smile, now more than ever. Moments ago he thought he'd never see her smile again.

"Can you make it to the pod?"

"Sure. It's down hill. If I stop walking, just roll me."

"Let's try walking first, shall we?"

Without waiting for an answer he tightened his arm around her middle and kicked open what was left of the side door. Using his body to shield her from the heat of the burning wreckage, her walked her out of the barn like a latecomer to a three-legged race.

Outside, the storm had arrived. Rain falling hard. With it had come three men. Assassins. Shabbir saw them and stopped walking. Considered their situation. Their options. Made a fast decision.

Gently he sat Gurmeet against the barn's wall, other side of the hanging door to protect her from the wreckage.

"Wait here."

Squatting down next to her, back to the assassins so they couldn't see, he gave her his emergency pistol.

"Low calibre, single shot. Use it if you have to."

Gurmeet looked him straight in the eye as she took it. It was a look of trust that also said she cared about him. He responded with a wink and a smile that dissolved with altitude, as he stood up and turned to face the men striding up the hill, daggers drawn.

Unarmed, rain pelting down, Shabbir walked towards them. Closing the distance with those intent on killing him then Gurmeet. His face held only one expression and it wasn't fear.

Chapter 21
Family

Julia walked silently with her father along the barren, stony trail. Brown and green grass, kept short by sheep and tearing winds, lay either side. The mustard coloured earth baked hard. Tree branches quiffed back – permed by relentless gales. Only traces of the early morning mist remained.

They were alone. No other ramblers in sight. Julia liked it that way. Interaction with others, even a passing 'hello', was not on her mind. Her whole life had been changed. Her whole aim in life had been changed. Now, only serious things lay ahead but, for this day, she wanted to enjoy time with her dad. Get to know him, the real him. Get to know the person behind the person she thought she knew, before she left.

"We can take a break at the top.", he announced.

"OK."

She was anything but OK. OK was only what came from her mouth. It wasn't real but she could at least pretend it was. Even to herself.

They were on the Quantocks. A pocket of hills marking the gateway to western Somerset and the winding, coastal road to Cornwall. Most people visited the Quantocks just for that – just for driving through. Holiday makers to the new Butlins in Minehead; tour buses to Lynton and Lynmouth for the water railway; adventurers heading for the deadly cliffs at Valley of the Rocks; romantics for the palm-trees of Dunster Castle. Everyone had a reason to travel on westwards. Everyone who didn't have time to stop and enjoy the wilder countryside they were passing through. Julia was glad. It made it feel like their own personal wilderness. Peaceful. Earthy. Energising.

At the top of the hill, with views across the valleys to the other hilltops a mile away, they stopped. Her dad took off his rucksack and pulled out two, hand-sized seat pads. On contact with the ground they expanded five times.

"This'll do nicely.", he said, sitting on one and placing the rucksack on the ground in front of him.

Julia sat on the other, deeply inhaling the clean air. Closing her eyes as she felt the breeze across her face.

"Here.", said her dad, handing her a sandwich of fishery tuna - Atlantic tuna now too toxic to eat from industrial pollution, Pacific tuna too rare from deliberate over fishing. She wasn't hungry but she bit into it anyway, as if at a cinema - where eating was obligatory the moment you sat down. A ritual of family gathering, shared since the gatherings of the Stone Age.

"Haven't been here for years...", he began, "...Every time I come back, I tell myself we should come here more often."

"The last time we came was with mum."

Her dad stopped chewing - thoughts running across his gaze. He swallowed them down and changed the subject.

"Sleep OK?"

She looked at him in reply - her eyes shadowed. Troubled. Sad. Deeply, deeply sad.

"I am really sorry about Jake."

Her nostrils widened at his words. Eyes almost cried.

"Me too...", she said when she managed to breath again, adding, "...Tell me about you, dad."

"Me? You already know about me."

"Actually, I'm discovering I don't."

He met her eyes. Her stare. Her demand. He couldn't deny it - she deserved to know.

"Where to start?"

Her reply shocked him.

"Who did you kill?"

Direct. To the absolute point. No grey. No get outs.

"Christ, Julia. Where did that come from?"

She was looking straight at him. Not letting it go. He had to answer.

"You can't tell this to anyone. Not anyone, ever. Understand?"

She gave a nod, still looking. His eyes broke away, staring into the past.

"We were undercover. Two of us. Infiltrated an arms gang. They were bringing in heavy-metal ballistics from Poland, smuggled there from Belarus. The dealer sent us on a job. A test. To see if we were as ruthless as we claimed to get in. The job was an armed robbery - a security van.

The robbery itself was pointless. Trackers on the valuables and the van, explosive dye for the contents if entry was forced. They didn't care about the van or its contents. They just wanted news coverage. Free advertising for their weapons. A status booster. The guards weren't armed. We were told to kill them anyway, to leave signature evidence of the high-tech weapons used. The gang's weapons."

Julia was staring at him now. Open mouthed.

"You killed the guards?"

"No. Just flesh wounds. They lived."

"So who did you kill?"

"The gang's cameraman. He was one of them. The witness that would have exposed us for not killing them. We filmed a scene ourselves. The guards were reported dead, given new identities, new lives, and our cover was strengthened. We were in."

"Anyone else?"

"Only when necessary."

"Only when necessary? Then why didn't you kill mum?"

If Julia's questioning had shocked him before that bowled him over so hard he had no answer.

"Why not, dad?...", she repeated, "...She was trying to kill you. You know I would have been next."

Why hadn't he killed her? The mother of his child. The woman who was once his best friend. The woman who became a monster, made their lives hell and fought to send him there.

"She wasn't always so bad, you know?"

"Doesn't matter. I've lost her anyway. She'll never change. She'll never admit she was wrong. To being the nasty one. Would you kill her now, if she tracked us down? Tried to harm us again. Tried to harm me."

That question left Tom thinking hard. Staring hard.

"Would you, dad?"

It took a long, deep breath before any word could exit his mouth. One word was enough.

"Yes."

Julia met his eyes with a hard stare, ensuring he was sincere.

"Good.", she replied, when she saw he was and returned to her sandwich. No more questions to ask. No more answers needed.

Her dad, Tom, was left wondering what had become of his sweet, innocent daughter. Wondering how his happy, laughing child had changed so much. Except he knew how. With him busy at work and her mother in prison, Jake had been the stabilising influence in her life. Now Jake was gone. Blown to bits before her very eyes.

"You know, I'm going to get the people who killed Jake.", she stated, without a hint of doubt.

"Revenge isn't the answer, Julia. You'll just end up destroying yourself."

Her eyes gave her reply: 'You don't think I'm already destroyed?', and he lowered his head as a parental failure.

All she felt she had left was anger and the drive for vengeance. A burning need for revenge that would never wane until it was satiated, by blood. She would take down everyone who got in her way – especially if it was her bitch of a mother.

Chapter 22
The Partner Corporation

Partner was by far the biggest corporation on the planet. Spreading across 120 countries and five continents; it had more gold than Fort Knox, supported the military might of Federal Europe and answered to no-one but itself. It had become so huge few, even inside the organisation, knew exactly who ran it. In many ways it seemed to run itself.

A self-feeding global vampire, with morals to match. It watched everyone and everything. Met out punishments with lethal force and no-one and nothing ever questioned it, twice. Investigative journalists vanished. Intelligence officers vanished. Even the military couldn't attack it, for in many countries it was the military. It had become the most powerful dictatorship of all time but with it came irony; it had also brought world peace - assassinating war mongers with a 100% success rate. It never admitted responsibility but rumours on social media said otherwise and even made it popular with ordinary people – the ordinary people who would otherwise be sent to front lines as canon fodder and written off as collateral damage during military strikes.

Partner's effectiveness really made its name by taking out the war mongers in Israel and Palestine, the longest running war of all time. The next year, when North Korea decided to nuke the south, Partner reprogrammed the guidance systems mid-flight and sent them right back where they started. It was the last ever nuclear launch, test or otherwise, anywhere in the world. China and Japan chose to make peace. The New Soviet Union halted its aggressions – ordering its soldiers to stop invading Georgia and the Baltics 'in their spare time'. The Middle-East knew peace for the first time in living memory. Around the world, Partner was saving hundreds of thousands of lives and, by accounting logic, the meant the equation remained positive, even as it went on to kill hundreds of targets of its own. Overall, in the big picture, it was saving lives.

Unlike almost every battle in history before it, ordinary civilians and foot soldiers were no longer the ones on the front line. The front line had become tiny. Reserved purely for those questioning how the monster that was Partner ate and grew; for those who defied its self-appointed authority. Tom, Julia's dad, had stepped onto that front line the second he defied Commander Jadviga, outside Jake's house. The second he appeared with his pod on manual and shot that zerodrone. It was a decision he took as much in rebellion as in defence. A decision that made a lot of problems but not just for him, for Partner had a problem too.

Even with eyes and ears all over the world, Partner did not know who he was. To them this wasn't just a problem. It was an impossibility, or at least it should have been. Maybe he was linked to the sabotage they had been experiencing. They had a serious information gap and that simply wasn't allowed. He needed to be found, killed and forgotten. Deleted. To organise Tom's demise, Commander Jadviga had called a meeting.

"Well, what are your answers? How can we not know who he is?"

There were three other people in the meeting. They didn't need to see the commander was armed to know she was. She always was – even in the bath. They also knew she could kill them with impunity, on a whim. They would be gone, no questions asked. It was enough to make them want to resign but, at Partner, resignation meant death within 24 hours. A glitching-pod crash; a gas explosion; falling masonry... People had long complained there were no more jobs for life – at Partner there were. Once you joined that monster you stayed there for life. The only way out was horizontal or in a bin bag.

"Ma'am. There are three possibilities."

"Which are?"

One by one the three managers gave their offerings.

"The first is, he had anatomic surgery, removing his body match from our system."

"The second is, a real glitch has occurred and his information has been erased."

"The last is, someone has gone into our system and erased his data."

The commander's face looked like she was sucking a sour grape, marinated in acid.

"What action are you taking?"

"We're investigating all anatomic surgeons – underground, retired and official."

"We're running data recovery algorithms, high-priority, 24/7, across the entire database. Completion due by Tuesday. As long as they haven't been overwritten too many times, the data recovery process will pick up his details no matter how they got erased."

"Are you saying, there's a chance they could be erased forever."

The managers looked worried.

"Erm. It's very, very unlikely but there is a small chance the data is unrecoverable."

"Then you can't rely on it, can you? What's the analysis of his weapon's energy signature?"

The managers looked at each other.

"Is that possible? The zed's impact point exploded."

The commander's face got worse, as if that grape had just burst in her mouth. She pulled out her laser-pistol, walked over and fired into the managers wristcom, at point blank range.

TchZooo

"Arrrghh!"

It went right through his arm and into the desk.

"Analyse that and you'll see how easy it is, even from impact debris. Give me the results of his weapon by tomorrow, 9 am, sharp."

Holstering her pistol, she strode out of the room, smiling in satisfaction as she heard the manager cry out behind her.

"MEDIBOT!"

He was clutching his shot wrist in agony. There was no blood, for the heat of the laser had cauterised the wound.

As in Roman times, the higher classes lived in better conditions than most – at the top of the food chain. As in Roman times, they were at constant risk of personal annihilation by those who promoted them there. It was a gamble they considered worth taking, until it was a gamble being lost. When the medibot arrived the two other managers ordered it not to tend the wound but to remove a flesh sample for energy-signature analysis.

'I shall administer an anaesthetic.', stated the bot, producing a spray nozzle.

"NO...", countermanded the two managers, "...It could contaminate the results. We can't risk contaminated results."

"*What?...*", exclaimed the injured one, "...Are you fucking nuts? It already hurts like hell."

"If we get this wrong, what Jadviga will do next will make it seem painless."

"The pain of the procedure will be considerable.", stated the medibot.

"PROCEED WITHOUT.", ordered the uninjured managers, as one.

The shot manager was sweating profusely, both in pain and at the thought of more to come. He knew they were right.

"Do it without...", he concurred, "...Quickly."

"Very well."

The bot stepped forward and, from the palm of its hand, used a green laser cluster to scan the depth and width of the wound.

'2.1mm by 4.9mm. To sample uncontaminated damage in every material type the sample width will be 3.5mm, depth 7.5mm.'

"Fuck....", sweated the manager, "...Just do it, all ready!'

"Proceeding."

The entire 112th floor froze to the sound of a terrible scream. Some in sympathy. All in cold sweat. All except for Commander Jadviga, standing in her office, gazing over the balcony at the tiny world of insects below. When she heard the scream, she just smiled.

Chapter 23
PE4-B

Faith's headquarters had become energised.

"One critical - four injured?", asked Craig.

"Yes. I logged Alan as a hit and run to avoid questions. The brick saved him from evidence of the explosive.", said Martin.

"I told you to just leave him to be found. Now they'll have you on CCTV."

"Wore a wig and beard. Kept my eyes and speech out of clear shot. They don't have enough to recognise me."

"DNA and prints?"

"Wore gloves."

"What about the airborne DNA detectors?"

"Turned off a month ago, to save money. I checked first."

"So they just have Alan? Well, if he talks and they start back-tracking his movements, nothing will save him from me."

"We all know what we signed up to, Craig."

"Fine, Martin. Have a seat."

Craig was sitting in his office chair, fingers of his right hand drumming on the desk as Martin took a seat opposite. The office was in the attic of a farm house. A single window, overlooking the approaching drive. Functional, isolated. An HQ in disguise. Faith's western HQ.

"Do we know what happened yet? Why it went off?", asked Craig, fingers no longer drumming.

"Two options...", said Craig, "...Heat and bio-reaction."

"I thought PE4 was as stable as C4."

"It is. More powerful too. But we don't have PE4."

Craig sat up.

"I was told we had a version of PE4 that was just harder to detect. That's why we paid so much for it. What do we have if not PE4?"

"We have biological PE4. They call it PE4-B. It's the biological element that makes it more powerful and harder to detect. It seems it's the biological element that also makes it unstable."

Martin leant across the desk, towards Craig.

"It's like this. You can heat sweat both C4 and PE4; pound them, mould them, drop them, run over them in a 60-ton tank and they won't go off. We were told the bio version wasn't as stable - we just had no idea it was so unstable. It's so new everyone is still learning."

Craig was shaking his head.

"We don't have the luxury of time. We need to know. Being blown to bits makes it very hard to do better next time. How much did Alan say he was using? A piece the size of a pea?"

"Yes...", agreed Martin, "...That's why we've started using the scientist you brought in."

"Professor George? The one who believes we need explosives to save animals from poachers? For fuck's sake, if you ask me, his arse is a bio-weapon in itself. Wouldn't surprise me if he ate the stuff."

"Yeah, he may be a stinky old codger but he does seem to know his stuff. Anyway, I always invite him outside to talk. Pretend I need to smoke."

"Could be explosive even outside...", said Craig, smile on his face as he said it. No matter what the situation, toilet humour was timeless. Even cavemen probably sat round a campfire, farting and laughing about it, "...What did George have to say?"

"Keep it cool. Don't touch it by hand."

"How cool?"

"Below 20 degrees. Everything we have is bagged up in the fridge now, wrapped like chocolate bars."

"But we can't touch it? Isn't the point of plastic explosives that they can be moulded to fit the location?"

"Yes. If we wear gloves that's still possible. George reckons there could be something in sweat. Some chemical that triggers a detonation."

"Any idea what?"

"Could be as simple as traces of spice after a curry. Could be as unavoidable as salt. He's still looking into it."

"And we can trust him not to talk?"

"Absolutely, Craig. I've told him it's a top-secret mission and if he breaks silence the poachers will find out and begin mass slaughter across Kenya with plasma-canons."

"So he's a scientific genius but has no idea we're lying and it's all a hoax?"

"Of course not. He's old school. Believes the digital photos we show him are real."

"Lucky us."

"As long as he doesn't blow himself up, we should have full information in about week. We're basically ready to go."

"Material wise, Martin. Only material wise."

"Robert's training hasn't finished yet?"

"Robert's recruiting hasn't finished yet. It's harder than we hoped. Finding people willing to become suicide killers is easy. Finding people willing and intelligent enough to do it as we want is harder than finding a beautiful woman with a beautiful personality."

"Why not target homeless people?...", asked Martin, "...They must be pretty cheesed with the system and a lot will be smart, just unlucky or addicts. Easy to manipulate."

"Been thinking about it. The downside is it's harder to vet them. To make sure they are what they appear - not plants reporting to Partner or MI5."

Martin thought on it for a moment.

"What if we go younger? Partner ignores under 18s and so do MI5 these days; too young to sign their lives away and too much risk of legal action."

Craig's expression changed.

"That reminds me. Talking of MI5, I heard there was a fight at the barn after we left. Was it them?"

"Probably. Impossible to tell who was attacking who or why. Could have been MI5 or could have been Partner trying to find us."

"I always wanted to be famous. Ironic how these days we're aiming to be infamous. Beer?"

"Sure, Craig. Warm day, why not?"

"They're in the fridge. Grab me one while you're there."

"Want chocolate too?", asked Martin, holding up a box of three small bars.

"You sure that's chocolate not PE4? I'll give that a miss, thanks. A beer will do fine. Just one. Busy day ahead. Actually, no. Wait. Change of plan. I think you're right. We should target the homeless, some kids. Your pod charged?"

"Always."

"Let's visit Rob. Bring the beer with. Business with pleasure."

Chapter 24
Energy Fingerprint

The three Partner managers, all wearing armoured wrist straps, sat up as Commander Jadviga walked in. No formalities. No niceties. Straight to business.

"You've analysed the target's energy signature?"

"Yes, ma'am. We've matched him to three possible weapons."

"Three of you and three possibilities. Always three. I want one answer not the Holy Trinity...", she could see they wanted to talk but were also afraid to do so, "...Come on, tell me. Don't worry, I won't shoot."

Yet...

"Ma'am, there are three possibilities because there were three such specials, made to order."

"Go on."

"The order trace goes into a continuous loop; from one discontinued company to another, to another and back to the first again."

Another manager clarified.

"It's a practice used by the intelligence services – the secret intelligence services."

"It's been done so well it has to be MI5 or MI6."

"Or both. Or us."

"*Us*? Internal sabotage? Don't be ridiculous!...", she spat, "...As for the intelligence services, SIS, don't we run them too now?"

"It's still going through final approval."

"They've been fighting our access, trying to retain their independence. Claiming it would compromise their security. Very archaic view."

"Archaic my arse. It's fucking annoying is what it is. Get into their systems. Get me the names."

"Hack the intelligence services?"

"Even if we can, they'll know it was us."

"And know where we've looked."

They saw the commander's hand was unclipping her holster.

"We'll think of something, ma'am!", hastened a manager, all three of them sitting up and nodding, more than ever before.

"Make it soon."

"Yes, ma'am!", they replied immediately, as one. Watching intently as she headed out of the room, sighing with relief as she fastened her holster.

Chapter 25

Storm on a Hill

The three men had moved apart, approaching Shabbir from three different directions. Left, right and dead ahead. The one on the left flanking wide to get behind him, and behind him was Gurmeet. Any threat against Gurmeet became his biggest priority. His biggest cause.

Attack.

Jamming the sides of his boots into the ever more slippery ground, he turned and ran left. Sprinting to get the man before the others could back him up. The man was armed the old-fashioned way. Titanium-steel dagger in each hand. No energy signature. No trace. A professional.

The assassin had wondered if Shabbir would attack. Was pleased to see he was. Pleased for the opportunity to increase his kill count. Sliding one dagger forward for attack, one dagger back for counter attack, he stood ready to fight. He saw his two colleagues advancing. One chasing Shabbir from the other side. The other striding towards the woman flopped on the ground against the barn – arm on her knee, muttering something to herself. They liked their jobs. Never boring. Always something different. Sense of achievement and satisfaction when wiping fresh blood from their blades.

"Come on, chubby.", he goaded.

Breathing hard but controlled, Shabbir said nothing. Just kept running towards him. Clinical. Studious. Noting every nuance of the assassin's stance. His eyes. Their terrain. They could have brought guns - killed him already. The fact they were using knives meant this was a sanctioned kill. A covert elimination, designed to send a message, with nothing traceable left behind. Shabbir was very much on his own and knew it. So did they.

As a professional, the assassin was also studying Shabbir. Studying his approach - calculating where to stab him first. Throat or doughnut belly? Leg or head?

"Hurry up, fatty...", he smirked, "...I'm getting soaked."

Two metres away, Shabbir threw a hand high, to the right. The assassin adjusted position, defending that path. It was a feint. Shabbir had already dropped to the left, deftly pivoting on his hand and thrusting both legs into the assassin's shins. Take down. The assassin rolled as he landed, turning 180 degrees, as he came back up into fighting stance. Facing right back at Shabbir. Professional, fast, efficient and now he knew he needed to be. His target was more than just a doughnut. His target had chased his roll and landed on top of him as he came up, slamming him straight back down - hard. Shabbir's dropped knee fractured his left arm against the ground, the rest of his bodyweight thrusting the right dagger between his ribs.

"Fuck...", gasped the assassin, in surprise and pain.

Over 20 perfect kills to his non-name, the assassin was as embarrassed as he was shocked. Shocked by how aggressive, how fast the doughnut had moved. As a trained professional, he still fought back. Ignored the pain of the splintered bone in his left arm to thrust a counter-strike into the doughnut's side. Shabbir had already changed position. The dagger came round and swung past. As it past, Shabbir dropped his body back down and jammed that blade in too, snapping the fractured arm that held it.

Pin-cushioned and now spitting red, the assassin lay gasping on the ground, being soaked by leaking blood and the pouring rain. The doughnut left him there, pushed himself to his feet and turned his focus on the other running towards him.

Rain-drenched dagger dripping watery gems in each hand, he had seen Shabbir's skill and adapted his approach. Just metres away he changed stride. Threw back a shoulder and launched a dagger at Shabbir's chest. Shabbir moved one foot back, twisting his body out of its path and caught it as it went past. In the same movement he circled his momentum and threw it straight back. Far too close to dodge out of the way, it went straight into his throat. Shabbir didn't wait for that assassin to complete his gasping fall. He grabbed the dagger in his throat while he was still falling and yanked it out in a spray of blood, slamming him down as he ran past, after the last of them. The one going for Gurmeet, lying slumped against the wall. Defenceless.

"GURMEET, LOOK OUT!", he shouted.

Gurmeet didn't respond. Didn't move. The man was upon her. Killer grin on his face. Out of time, Shabbir threw the dagger. It flew fast and true but not fast enough. In a slow-motion nightmare, Shabbir could only watch as the man took both his blades and thrust them into Gurmeet.

"STOP!", he shouted, though whether any words actually came out he was too horrified to know.

There was flash of bright blue. The attacker jolted. It was Gurmeet's only shot. He dropped one blade but was still alive. Still focused on killing her. Shabbir was still out of reach yet now his flying dagger struck home. Hit the assassin in the back of his thigh. The impact brought him to one knee but now he was even more determined. Reaching behind, he snarled and pulled the dagger out of his thigh. With his own blood dripping from it, this was now his weapon of choice. Fitting justice for the kill.

Gurmeet watched as he thrust it at her, turning her body at the last moment to reduce the penetration. Keep it away from her organs and across her ribs rather than through them. It sliced the flesh on her left side.

"Argh!"

The pain tore through her. He hadn't finished. She could smell his sweat, his hot, drug-laced breath as he came in closer. See the wide, wild lust for the kill in his looming face as it filled her view. Then he was gone. Vanished. Replaced by the open field and the rain pouring into her face.

Am I dead?

The sight of her leaking blood and still sharp pain told her not yet. Lifting her head, away from her red waters being washed across the ground, she saw Shabbir. He was on top of the assassin, pinning him down with his knees and feet as he punched – again and again. Pounding the assassin's life into oblivion with a violence even she found shocking. But even more shocking than his violence was the look on his face. Volcanic. Explosive. Unleashing rage from a place she had never before seen in him.

As the storm on the hill raged on, her blood drained into it. Shabbir was nearby, protecting her with the fury she had never seen before, in anyone. He wouldn't let her be stabbed again. She could have a peaceful end now. It was a good place to die, feeling the company of a true friend she could trust to her end. To the sound of a deep, ground-throbbing hum from an approaching drone, her world turned black. On her face, being cleansed by the pouring rain, a look of calm serenity. An acceptance of her passing.

Chapter 26
Warm Days

Tom's drive to Lynton followed the Somerset coast, up hills and along the northern edge of the Exmoor Forest. Being the height of summer, it was popular with tourists but, being so far from the nearest motorway, it never got over crowded. Tom had thought of showing Julia the Valley of the Rocks, a place he'd often visited when he was young. A place with the highest sea cliffs in England, rising half a kilometre above a rocky beach. How none of them had died, sitting on the edge while joking about, was a mystery he was forever grateful for. Out of all of them he had been the luckiest – foolishly standing at the very top on one leg, in a 'Golden Rooster' Tai Chi pose, just for fun. These days, he still shuddered at the thought of how horribly wrong it could have gone. How a single gust of wind could have whipped him to his death. While most happy days of youth were things to share with your children, this was one he decided to avoid. If he took Julia there and she fell to her death he would never forgive himself. Instead, on the way to Lynton, he diverted to Dunster Castle.

"Let's take a break here. You'll like it."

Julia didn't answer. She was lost again in thoughts of Jake. Of seeing her best friend's house blown to pieces in front of her, with him inside. That sadness defied even the warmth of the sun and the beauty of the surroundings. Tom saw the look on her face and didn't push for an answer. She needed time.

To blend in with the other tourists, Tom kept his hands off the controls and let the pod park itself. Its registration plates and transponder ID cloned from another pod. The car park was busy with other pods and an actual car. A classic Jaguar XKR from 2019.

"See that, Ju. One of the very last Jaguar V8s made. Must be worth a fortune."

Julia glanced at it and glanced away. How could she enjoy anything knowing Jake was dead? Tom's aim was to keep her mind of it.

"Come on, let's go to the castle."

Together they climbed out of the pod.

The pod had parked on the side of the castle hill, in Dunster village. Nearby, the old watermill still faithfully ground flour, powered by the stream channelled down to it, as it had for 300 years.

"Want to look inside the mill?"

Julia shook her head. She knew her dad was trying to cheer her up. Take her mind off what had happened. What would Jake do in her position?

"Jake would want you to be happy.", said her dad, as if he could read her mind.

She looked at him, pain in her eyes.

"How would you know?"

"He was a good kid and so are you. Would you not want him to be happy if it had been the other way round?"

It was a logic she couldn't argue.

"No."

"Being happy doesn't mean you don't care. It just means you're still living your life. Jake would be happy to see you happy."

Julia was feeling overwhelmed.

"Jake can't be happy. Jake's dead!"

He dad wasn't backing off.

"He'll always be alive in you. Maybe he's looking down on you right now. Come on, let's grab an ice-cream."

Alive in me?, Julia pondered that thought. Maybe her dad was right. Maybe Jake was looking down on her, from heaven.

"I'll have mint, choc chip. Jake's favourite."

"That's the spirit... No pun intended."

A minute ago she would have been furious at a comment like that but that minute had passed. From no-where, her dad had given her positive direction and the hint of a smile. She would show Jake she was still living her life.

Ice-creams in hand, they began climbing the hill to the castle itself and gardens with plants that had leaves bigger than umbrellas. Palm trees that stood tall around the colour-filled flower beds and lush green grass. Gardens of a stone-walled fortress to defend against all enemies - including sadness.

Several, slightly surreal, hours past before they were walking back down the hill towards the pod. Before they were driving onwards for Lynton and its water-powered railway down to Lynmouth. Julia managed to keep the smile on her face – focused on enjoying life as a celebration of the good times she'd had with Jake and the good time she was having with her dad, away from all the worries of their broken world.

Today was the first day of the rest of her life and she planned to enjoy it. She felt happiness for the first time in what felt like years, even though it had only been two days. That happiness would be broken.

Chapter 27
M-A.R.

The Mid-Atlantic Ridge was a vast, under-water fault-line, running north to south across most of it. Just 130 million years old, the Atlantic was the youngest ocean on the planet - formed by the break up of the last great super continent, Pangaea. Its floor is still expanding. Evolving. Tearing apart. Immeasurable forces of inter-continental plates pulling away from each other. Underwater volcanic eruptions bursting out through the gaps left behind. Cooling. Hardening. Growing ever higher. Where these eruptions had broken through, the ocean floor was covered by ridges resembling Africa's Great Rift Valley, only three times taller and four miles down. There under water mountains rivalled the size of Everest, in places bursting above the water to form new islands, including Iceland. The ocean plates were tearing. Always tearing apart. But recently the tears seemed to be happening more often.

The only explanation science could offer were the deep-ocean temperature rises, making the water less able to keep the floor cool enough and hard enough to hold back the red-hot magma below. On the camera screens of deep-sea submarines, everything appeared normal – but appearances could be deceptive. Dangerous.

The ocean floor was getting softer, ever closer to bursting right open and letting out hell on Earth. Until it burst, governments and businesses alike could pretend it wasn't an issue and did exactly that - their annual accounts looked better that way. Better until the six-metre-high tsunami surge of 2031, which struck the coasts of western Europe and the eastern United States within 20 minutes of each other. Hundreds died but governments still labelled 2031 as a one-off. A freak event, as was, they claimed, the tsunami of 2036. It wasn't until the giant of 2042 – an 11-metre surge which killed 81,000 and caused a three-metre-high rise even in the sheltered bay at Hinkley Point. It took three nuclear reactors off-line, costing £billions in damages and lost profits, to make them sit up and have a political debate. How to deal with it? Who should pay for it? How to profit from the repairs. The debate continued without resolution until, just two years later in 2044, new tremors were detected. This worried financiers so much the navy was called in.

Under government orders to investigate, for the sake of national security, the navy sent HMS Tempest - a nuclear-powered battle-cruiser, equipped with a deep-sea submarine. On a spiralling inwards course, it approached the location - dropping a web of detector buoys, one every ten miles, to map out the area. Then, near the epicentre, it launched the submarine. A deep-sea submarine, strong enough to survive the pressure of 1,000 atmospheres, eight miles down at the bottom of the Mariana Trench. It vanished, presumed destroyed. Its last transmission had been of increasing and curiously regular 3Hz vibrations from the ocean floor, then nothing. No alarms, no emergency signals, nothing. HMS Tempest, sailing four miles above, began picking up rapidly escalating pressure spikes and the same, unusually regular, 3Hz vibrations.

"That has to be artificial. But how can it be generated? The energy is immense...", the sonar chief had wondered aloud, before detecting an eruption had started.

"Eruption directly below. Impact imminent.", he stated to Captain Arnold. The captain took immediate, evasive action.

"ONE-FIFTY, EMERGENCY FULL AHEAD!"

The battle-cruiser's twin Uranium-235 reactors raged emergency heat into the water powering the ships four 50,000 horsepower turbines. Rammed to 150% emergency boost, all systems surged into the red. Propellers and harbour thrusters working together to shove the 30,000 tons of armoured predator forward. The communications officer fired a sea-air beacon to alert air-sea rescue to their location, should communications get knocked out. It was the last message ever received – the beacon's charred remains discovered by beach combers when it washed ashore two-months later. It was the only part of the ship ever located. Of the ship itself, there was no wreckage. No debris. No survivors. No trace. Not even the black-boxes. Nothing was ever found and the web of sonar buoys, for a fifty mile radius, vanished too.

Satellite images showed a vast eruption plume, breaking through the clouds near the Maxwell Fracture - the ship's last known location. It was calculated that millions of tons of molten lava had boiled the water – jetting it high above the ocean before it crashed back down. The ship would never have stood a chance. It never got off a mayday. The ship's communications officer was even talking to Navy Command when the radio went dead. The blast so intense the ship didn't creak. Didn't groan. Didn't give the crew time to do anything. Not pray. Not even scream. It was simply wiped out. Wiped out of existence like a fly in the barrel of a rifle. Gone in an instant.

Everyone in government and business woke up that day. The Mid-Atlantic Ridge was no longer just a potential risk to debate - it was alive and kicking. Kicking hard. They realised global warming had not just broken its slumber - it was now out to do breaking of its own. Faced with repeated tsunamis, political avoidance in America and Western Europe was a luxury they no longer had. China and the New Soviet Union sent condolences and sympathies but remained unaffected. Only the Atlantic ocean floor, halfway between eastern America and western Europe had become unstable - like some terrible, Earthly vengeance, aimed directly against them.

Chapter 28
Cold Night

"What are you cooking, Julia? Smells good."

"Chef's special: egg and chips, no veg."

She smiled at her dad as he walked in the kitchen door, drying his hair. The restyled salt and pepper now dyed to brown sauce, with a goatee beard that actually suited him.

"You know, dad? A hundred years ago, you were probably quite a good looking man."

"A hundred years ago? I supposed that's better than the millions of years old you normally call me."

"Oh, no. You're still a million, dad."

"Thanks a million, cheeky monkey."

It was ironic that being on the run had brought them closer together. The past few days in the cottage had given them time to talk about things they'd never discussed before. Partly because Julia was now a mature 15. Partly because their circumstances encourage more sharing. She had learnt more about her mother than ever before. About the happy times he used to spend with her, before her behaviour deteriorated. Started to become abusive. Destructive. It helped Julia understand his patience with her mum. It softened the surprise that he still loved her. Helped her realise that, actually, she did too. But neither of them ever wanted her back. She was far too destructive. Still in total denial, backed by endless mantras of how she was the victim, ignoring all evidence that said otherwise. They had to accept this was her choice and that she would never, ever change. It was sad but it was what it was - the past.

Their family had become smaller but happier. Positive. Caring. Ironically, if they weren't running for their lives after Jake's murder, it could have been the happiest time of her life. During the days it was mostly happy - it was the nights that were hard. Lying in bed. No distractions and time to think. Time to remember, bringing tears that fell until sleep swallowed the hurt and dissolved it away. The next day, she'd awake to the smiling sunshine of a new day and be fine again - until the next night came.

Her dad was a good man. She had got over the shock of his secret work. The shock of learning he'd killed people. In many ways she found it amazing he could go into life-threatening situations at work, then come home, warm and cuddly, as just her dad.

"I'll get the plates and cucumber...", he said, drying his washed hands at the sink, "...What are you drinking? Something cool or something hot and black?"

They still didn't have a fridge. Still no milk and no juice. Neither of them were keen on fizzy drinks. So it came down to tap water, lime cordial, tea or coffee.

"Water's fine.", she said.

"Good choice. I can make that."

Minutes later they were sitting together at the kitchen table, eating their evening meal. Social, family time - despite the hunters out looking for them.

"How long will we stay here?"

"Just another few days. I'm getting us new IDs and a boat to Ireland. See how we get on there. If we don't want to stay, we can go somewhere else. Pretty much anywhere, actually."

"Kool."

"Didn't think you kids said 'cool' any more."

"It's retro. Retro always makes a come back. Just now it's kool, with a 'k'"

"Kool."

They beamed at each other - their happy family.

With dinner finished, her dad placed his scanner on a power-cell, charged by solar during the day, and left it to feed.

"I'm off to bed. See you in the morning."

She gave him a hug.

"Love you, dad."

"Love you too. I'm very proud of you. Of how well you've coped with everything, especially with your mum."

"I know. You keep telling me. It's because I've got a great dad."

He smiled at her.

"Of course. Don't forget to clean your teeth."

"No, dad. Night."

"Night, night."

He went to his room and closed the door. Julia sat back at the kitchen table, hand on her glass of water. Nearby was a local paper her dad had brought back from the shops. It was unusual to find anything printed on paper these days. Local news was always mundane but local news on paper was an interesting novelty.

The front cover headlined a pet show, gymkhana and a local shop fined

£10,000 for selling mobile phones to under 16s. On page two she found a double-page spread detailing how the sellers had been exposed by activists from *Remember Us* - a group suspected of being responsible for the murder of eight former heads of telecoms companies by terminal cancer victims – ill from the diet of Wi-Fi and mobile data fed to them as kids.

'There is no consistent scientific evidence of harm', the telecoms companies had proclaimed, ignoring the logical flip side of: *'There is scientific evidence of harm'*. As with tobacco, asbestos and petroleum before, big money was involved and no five-year government risked losing it for something that took over 30 years to become undeniable. Those profiting knew they would never get punished. Knew no prosecution would be able to prove which mobile or Wi-Fi had triggered a cancer. Instead, they all retired as millionaires - untouchable. Untouchable to everyone who worked inside the law. The *Remember Us* vigilantes, given cancer-death sentences because of them, had nothing to lose. History showed greed rewarded the greedy, at the expense of the masses. Now some of those masses were determined to put history straight. To give it a new direction to be repeated in future. To rewrite the rules on how to treat industrial giants causing such harm.

Julia wouldn't normally have read such an article but she so loved the feeling of the paper in her hands. Not as warm as the paper-thin screen of her wristcom, where her own skin became the screen's backing, but tactile in a weird, something extra to savour kind of way. The ink rubbing off a little and darkening her fingertips, the way it had for hundreds of years.

She had always wondered why mobiles, especially the metal-backed variety, had been banned in favour of endocrine-tuned wristcoms; designed to detect the body's natural electrical fields and harmonise with them, rather than blast through them. Hand-held scanners were more powerful so actively directed signals away from the user and those nearby. Her dad's scanner was on the table in front of her.

His wasn't just a scanner, it doubled as a larger, mirror display for his wristcom. A blue light was flashing on it. Some message had come in. It had to be important. He wouldn't have left it on unless he was expecting something important. She went back to reading and ignored it. Left it for her dad to check the message on his wristcom and send a signal for the flashing to stop. When she had finished the paper, it was still flashing. Her dad must have fallen asleep. In case it was important, she decided to check it out.

Extending a hand, she took the scanner. It sensed movement, detected her face and auto-scanned her retina. Given their situation, her dad had added her as an authorised user. The blue light flashed green and the screen lit up, displaying:

'Read me?'

"Yes.", she replied.

'Read me?' vanished and the following text appeared:

'Weapons energy trace down to two. Sbot man, be careful. CJ is out to get you. If she learns you're the inventor she'll have your DNA injected into the next generation. Find Wolf 17. Your only chance. Do not answer this message. SB.'

Julia was staring at the message - the words phasing deep into her. The meanings mixed yet somehow suddenly clear. She had never trained as an intelligence officer but it was in her blood. Signs and messages in everything she saw. 'Sbot man', 'inventor', 'energy trace'...

Julia put down the scanner – message read, it auto slept. She stared hard at her wristcom until it slept too. She knew what she was going to do. Standing up, she took her jacket, stuffed her rucksack with supplies and went to the kitchen door. Quietly, she opened it then walked silently out, into a night filled with the chirps of grasshoppers. Closing the door behind her, she simply walked away, vanishing into the night. She knew everything she needed to know. She knew her sole purpose now.

With that message it had suddenly all made sense. How her dad had known of the attack on Jake's house. Known how the attack would take place. Why he had a military spec laser-rifle and room full of gadgets. He wasn't a retired undercover officer, he was 'Sbot man', inventor of the swarmbots. The inventions that got her Jake killed. He was her dad, and she loved him, so couldn't kill him but nor could she forgive him. All she had left was a heart filled with rage and a revived burning for revenge. To kill Jake's killers. Avenge his death as he would have avenged hers. Whether she lived or died in the process, it mattered not. Revenge had become her church and she gave it her full devotion.

Chapter 29
Flowers

Gurmeet awoke to the soft, white lights above her hospital bed. Sitting up she suddenly gasped in pain. Her head felt like it had been crushed. Her whole body a massive bruise. There was a tight dressing around her middle, holding her stitches together. She had to pause to catch her breath, taking in her surroundings.

It was a single room. No other patients. No medical staff. Just the gentle beep of the machine monitoring her heart and the sound of someone snoring. Stiffly, she moved her head in its direction. Shabbir. Slumped on a chair beside her bed. Head forward. Sleeping.

"Didn't know you snore."

A light sleeper, for everything except his own snoring, he woke immediately. Instantly alert. Eyes darting around the room for danger. There was none. He turned to Gurmeet, saw she was awake and broke into a smile.

"Hi."

"What're you doing?"

"Guarding you."

She smiled. It hurt but she didn't care. Physical pain was only physical.

"By snoring?"

"I still snore? The clinic owe me a refund. How do you feel?"

"Like an elephant sat on my head. And it's still there."

Shabbir glanced at her head.

"Must be invisible.", he grinned.

"How long have you been here?"

He shrugged.

"Not sure. Just a day. Maybe four. These are for you."

He held up a bunch of once bright-red roses. Now wilting. The edges of their petals turning brown.

"Shabbir, I think they're a little thirsty."

He looked at them.

"Again...? I'll get you some more."

"Not roses. I prefer bluebells. They remind me of happy times in the countryside. Red roses just remind me of failures."

"That's probably why they died."

"Even bluebells need water, Shab."

He picked up the rubbish bin.

"Hey! Don't waste them. Look. There's a jug over there. Pop them in that."

"Should I get some water too? Isn't it too late?"

He was amazing. Super intelligent as a spy but totally devoid of even a little green finger.

"Not for all of them. Look, those two still have a colour that isn't brown."

"Give me a sec'."

He stood up, holding the flowers, grabbed the jug and left the room. It suddenly felt empty after he had gone - not just physically. A minute later he returned and so did the room's warmth. The surviving flowers were in the jug, complete with water and their wrapper. It was progress. She'd take the wrapper off later.

"Great.", she said.

"Today almost red roses. Tomorrow bluebells."

He carried the jug over to her bedside table. Gurmeet saw the bruises on his knuckles. Suddenly she was back on the hill, watching him pounding the assassin into the ground. A shiver went through her body. That sight was as troubling now as it was then.

"Did any of them live?"

His smile shrank.

"Does it matter?"

"I'd like to know."

"One lived... for a day. We got something out of him before he went."

"The one I shot?"

"The one who stabbed you?..", he was looking at her, trying to work out where she was going, "...No. He didn't live."

Shabbir had made sure of that. His wristcom buzzed and he glanced at it, retina scan auto unlocking.

"It's Adam. I have to go."

Almost relieved at escaping to the simplicity of danger, he gave her a quick kiss on the forehead.

"Ow!"

"Sorry. See you tomorrow. What colour bluebells do you prefer?"

"Blue, of course, Intelligence Officer Latif. The clue is in the name."

She was smiling again.

"Just testing.", he said with a wink; flashing a smile in return.

What ever the driver for his dark side was, she knew it would never be used against her. Knew she could trust him with her life and she did, absolutely, without question. He was the first man to have awoken feelings of arousal in her for almost twenty years.

"Could you bring me some old-fashioned book to read."

"Sure."

"See you tomorrow.", she smiled warmly, as he waved goodbye and left the room.

She wouldn't see him tomorrow.

Chapter 30
Greenpeace, London

Rumours of radiation leaks were already spreading. Greenpeace had Geiger counters. Assumed the radiation detected had leached through the heat exchanger into the cooling water - pumped out to sea at the rate of 45 million gallons an hour. Any mention of a leak was absolutely denied by Partner. In fact, Greenpeace were wrong about the cause but they were right there was a leak. Senior reactor staff knew the leak was happening – the biggest problem they had was what to do about it, without getting fired.

The leak was coming from the reactors' main pressure vessels. After just ten years of operation, they had both cracked like the shells of eggs boiled too quickly. Cracked because the design was almost impossible to manufacture to specification. It had cracked in places where carbon clusters had turned the steel into brittle, cast-iron. In other places, carbon deprived, the surface had bulged like sores. They should never have been put into operation but, for financial reasons, they had and Partner now only had two options to avoid melt downs.

The first was to replace the entire pressure vessels: which would mean demolishing the thousands of tons of 3m thick walls - effectively demolishing the entire reactor building and starting again from scratch, at their own expense. The second involved repairs. Welding the cracks and adding reinforcements to stop them failing too. In both cases the plants would need to be shut down, have the nuclear material removed and stay off-line for a year or three - waiting for more probing approval to start it up again; no more chance of simple bribes. There would be huge public attention, questions asked, profit losses in the £billions.

To Partner, neither option was an option. It was a business born to make money, not lose it. Until the day came when they could hide it no longer, they chose to do what many had done before them – deny it, until they no longer could. They paid the plant managers for silence and for keeping unbribable Professor Lau out of the loop. Lost coolant was topped up by new. Where it leaked out it flooded into the trap designed to capture molten uranium in case of core meltdown. To stop the coolant over-flowing, water pumps ran 24/7, draining the irradiated water and pumping it into the main cooling water, sending it straight out to sea. The pumps kept breaking - rubber seals collapsing from the radiation. New pumps were added weekly but it was a losing battle. Too much pressurised coolant was now jetting out.

Unable to keep up, coolant had flooded over the trap's edges and soaked across the entire floor of the internal reactor housing – stopped only by the concrete wall. A wall never designed for direct, long term contact and slowly being eaten through. Indicators were, it had already been eaten through – the coolant leak now only held back by the secondary wall. A visible leak was less than two metres away. While the volume of leaking coolant was nothing compared to the millions of gallons of normal cooling water it was pumped into, its radiation level was high enough to be detected. This was the source of the radiation Greenpeace had discovered. The radiation Rachel had found and why Partner had decided to help her lose her way home.

* * *

If visiting tourists, strolling across the bay near Hinkley Point, had Geiger counters they would have heard the wild noise of radiation alerts. Instead they stayed longer, ever more determined to see the birds - ever rarer birds as the radiation decimating their fertility. From giant crabs to three-eyed fish, the effect was both a long-term disaster and an environmental revolution. Every local knew someone who worked at the plant. Someone who knew someone with access to a Geiger counter. Locally, by word of mouth, the news had spread but it was only ever mentioned in passing whispers. Too many jobs and homes were at stake. Some workers tried to warn the bird watchers.

"I wouldn't go there, if I were you."

"Why?", they would ask.

"Nuclear power stations - not safe."

Some took heed but most, armed with holiday spirit and investments in 3D-binoculars, regarded them as backward yokels afraid of atomic energy.

"If they weren't safe they wouldn't let us go there.", they would reply in disdain-filled words or even just looks that voiced the same – before continuing into the gleeful arms of the invisible reaper.

* * *

At Greenpeace HQ in east London, armed with sandwiches, large Rolleys and a scented eternal candle, six members were working on a strategy to expose the radiation leaks and embarrass the government into taking action against Partner. There should have been seven. Rachel was missing. She had been missing for a week, along with her Geiger counter and second report. The candle was for her – to light her way back to them, spiritually if not physically. After her boat had been found, drifting emptily off the Irish coast, the search had been called off. Officially, she was recorded as missing, presumed drowned. Officially.

"What action are we going to take? You know they killed Rachel. She must have found out more."

"We don't know that, Tyler. Even if they did we'll never be able to prove it. You know that."

"We don't have to prove it. We just have to finish what she started. Make her death count for something."

"What was she doing out there alone? It's against procedure."

Gareth, Rachel's partner, face lit by the steady flame of the candle in front of him, answered Shurma.

"She called to say she was onto something. Said it couldn't wait – that the evidence was there and strong. Rachel never wanted to wait. Not even wait for me to join her there..."

"We are so sorry for your loss, Gareth."

"Thank you, Tyler. She's a loss to us all."

Gareth took a deep, steadying breath to continue. Shurma's enthusiasm for action jumped ahead of him.

"I propose we send in Rainbow Rise. It's too big for them to board or sink without massive media coverage. Let's back track Rachel's route, rediscover her findings and broadcast them live. For her."

Tyler agreed.

"Finish her research and expose a radiation leak? I'm well up for that too. Gareth? Will you authorise us to go?"

"We'll all go. Hopefully they'll send the same bastards that took Rachel. Just let them try that with me.", said Gareth.

"I'll signal the ship.", said Tyler, writing a message on his Rolley for the ship.

`'Rainbow shine 50.'`

It was their code for 'we set sail in 2 days.'

`'Bright light.'`, came the confirmation within seconds.

"We're on. Gareth, but if you're coming with us, who's staying to co-ordinate the press campaign here?"

There was a long silence. Slowly a die-hard school hand lifted.

"I will."

It was Evalina. Evalina was one of those small, mouse-like women who never liked to make a fuss. Never get in anyone's way. With large, blue eyes and a youthful face beaming baby innocence, she got let in everywhere. Waved through by guards ahead of others. Allowed to the front of press conferences as a courteous priority. Recognised by her peers as the total opposite. Outside a mouse – inside a sabre-tooth tiger. The perfect secret weapon.

"Thank you, Eva."

Gareth picked up the box on the floor beside him and put the contents on the table. Seven encrypted communicators, five sets of video recorders, three Geiger counters and two lasers.

"We never take weapons, Gareth.", said Shurma.

"Self-defence against attack drones only. Partner have a lot of money invested in Hinkley. After what happened to Rachel, I'm not taking any chances with the rest of us. Make no mistake, their business means our war."

Chapter 31
C3TV

Xi Yang was briefing Shabbir in a Bletchley safe house, not far from Bletchley Park.

"Chinese Closed Circuit Television. C3TV, for short. In the UK it's run by Tech Tonic and sold under various names as normal CCTV."

Adam was there too, checking their equipment: scanners, coms, recorders and spare power cells.

"What have you found out? Where are they putting it now?", Shabbir asked, having come straight from his visit to Gurmeet.

"They aren't putting it anywhere. They don't need to. Their customers are putting CCTV everywhere themselves. Homes, businesses, clubs, schools, you name it.", said Xi and Adam agreed.

"Almost everyone has some kind of CCTV these days. It's cheap, affordable and very high resolution. Good enough to read documents and watch meetings in full."

"Not to mention blackmailing the unfaithful who get caught on it.", added Xi.

"Exactly how...", asked Shabbir, "... does it go from someone installing CCTV at home to someone at Tech Tonic using it to spy on them? These are supposed to be local, secure networks, aren't they?"

"Not any more...", said Xi, "...Even government systems have cloud access somewhere. Tech Tonic customers sign up for their free cloud access, without understanding where the cloud is or who runs it. And this is the problem - over 90% of the servers running the cloud are in China or at least run by Chinese operations. If you want cloud storage for your data you begin by handing it all over to them. Straight into their hands."

"Tech Tonic claim their systems are unhackable and their CCTV data is safe from others. This may be true, but it doesn't mean it's safe from them."

"And because most servers are based in China, we have no way of monitoring what their government does with it."

"Clever...", nodded Shabbir, "...It makes the encrypted cloud links meaningless. Tech Tonic don't need to crack the encryption because customers are uploading the feeds straight to them."

"Yes. Everything their cameras see and hear, they can too.", said Xi.

"And, if you log in from your mobile device, another free option, they can track that device and know your movements and contacts too. Know where you are, who you meet and what you say. Know when you aren't at home, if you have something they want.", said Adam.

"And when you are home alone, if they want you.", added Xi, thinking of ever more sinister ways the information could be used, which made Shabbir frown.

"This is a very serious issue – especially for data sensitive users: researchers, government, businesses and defence. Ironic the obsession with CCTV protection has brought herds of Trojan horses into our lives."

"Even better for them than that...", began Adam, "...They're also making a fortune from premium and business subscribers. In many ways, it's brilliant. Something UK companies could do too, if it was legal."

"Surely we're at the stage where we should be warning people.", said Xi. Shabbir, their team leader had to take a more pragmatic view.

"Privately, yes. But, as you know, China is very big business these days - has major shares in crucial infrastructure across all major sectors, including financial and nuclear. There is no way the PM can announce this publicly without hard evidence."

"What are we doing about it, then?", asked Adam.

Xi held up a tiny receiver.

"I bugged the president of Tech Tonic's limopod."

For once, Shabbir raised an eyebrow.

"You did? You managed? How?"

"Charm."

Adam and Shabbir looked at Xi, then at each other, then back at Xi.

"Charm?", repeated Shabbir?

Xi shrugged, knowing smile on her usually emotionless face.

"Won't it be found?", he asked.

"Unlikely. It has internal storage - battery charged by the limo's movement. Only transmits when the limo is transmitting too - matched frequency, and on a parallel channel. Two streams from the same tap. If they run an energy scan for its output it will just register as their own."

"What if they're paranoid enough change the limo", asked Adam.

"They won't. The chauffeur told me Mr Han loves the customisations in that one. He'd sooner change his children."

Shabbir was smiling positive thoughts.

"Can you recruit the chauffeur?"

Xi pursed her lips, thinking.

"Probably better not just yet. I know he likes me but he fears Han more. If it failed we would lose him as an asset. Right now he's happy to meet me for a drink, brag about his contacts and how much he knows. Leave it with me, I've got a plan to clone his access card."

"Nothing more than you're comfortable with, Xi...", said Shabbir, affirming there was no expectation for her to act as a honey trap and also glad he was a male doughnut – unlikely to ever be considered, "...Adam, you said you had something lined up for us."

Adam grinned.

"We've got us new jobs. Service engineers for CamSol - Camera Solutions. The only company Han trusts to install third-party CCTV on site."

"Why do they need third party CCTV?"

"Security - in case a member of their own staff does to them what they are doing to others."

"They don't trust their own people?"

"They don't trust anyone – not even their own people based in China...", said Xi moving her wristcom close to Shabbir's. "...NFC this - your new service manual. Only 150 pages."

Shabbir's wristcom vibrated, displaying: 'accept transmission?' in red. He looked at it and blinked twice. The display turned amber: 'receiving transmission', then green: 'transmission received'.

"We're booked in to service their systems in two days...", said Adam, "...CamSol IDs, uniforms, kit and test rigs are all here. Have a seat and I'll start running through it."

Shabbir went over to the equipment Adam had been checking and saw there were extra boxes of it. Steep learning curves were normal at MI5 but sometimes, at these times, he would have preferred a simple fight. Though, if they got it wrong, that is what they would have.

"Let's get on with it, then.", he said.

Xi was heading for the door.

"Leaving so soon?"

"Yes. Chris wants me back at Thames House for a chat. How's Gurmeet doing?"

Shabbir hadn't spoken about his visit to Gurmeet. Business always came first but Xi must have guessed he'd checked in on the injured member of their team.

"Fine, Xi. She's going to be fine. Thanks for asking."

Shabbir hoped he was keeping his personal feelings out of his voice. If Adam or Xi noticed, they were too polite to let it show.

"I'll try to drop in and say nín hǎo."

"Could you take her some of your paperbacks? I lent her your Larsson ones but she's finished them already and looks like going to be tied up here for a while."

Xi gave an almost warm smile on her pristine face.

"Of course."

She opened the door and closed it behind her.

"Think she's going for some promotion, Shab?"

"I'd be surprised if she wasn't. She's good enough."

"Bet even her dying moment will be perfectly organised.", said Adam.

Shabbir grinned.

"That's not a bet I'm willing to take."

"No... Neither would I...", smiled Adam, "...Here. This is the main router feed. Sync your com with it and the guide will pop up."

They were using technology to help operate technology, in a fight against technology - which technology itself was preparing for.

While Tech Tonic downloaded global CCTV data from their cloud servers, Fusion downloaded it from them, with one big advantage. She was not just capable of processing the data millions of times faster than Tech Tonic's systems, she was processing the data millions of times faster their systems. Processing the information to ready for a war, not just to proverbially end all wars, but to end the ability of any to start a war ever again.

Chapter 32
Discharged

Faster than anyone expected, Gurmeet had healed enough to be allowed home. Dr Rudra, the duty doctor, insisted on her being accompanied in the ambulance for the journey. It defied the point of using self-driven pods to save on staff costs but, from his point of view, the purpose of the system was to make patients better - in the best way possible. Besides, Gurmeet was keen to be discharged, get home and get back to work. It was borderline too soon but granting her request would free up a hospital bed and she was happy to sign all four disclaimers in his hand.

"Thank you, Miss Shamshudin. Nurse Patricia will help you to the ambulance shortly."

"Perfect...", smiled Gurmeet, happy to be going home, then smiled wider: "...Hello, you."

"Hello...", said Xi Yang, walking in - looking as magazine-cover perfect as always.

The doctor stepped to one side as the charismatic woman entered the room - eyebrow raised at her palpable confidence.

"Brought me a new book?"

"Better. Come to give you a lift home."

Gurmeet looked at the doctor for his response. Xi noticed.

"That is OK with you, isn't it doctor?"

Dr Rudra considered himself a good judge of people. A good judge of people's competence and trustworthiness. This friend had instantly ticked all those boxes and now she was offering to tick the budget saving one too.

"Have you any first aid training?", he asked Xi.

"A,B, C and D."

Why doesn't that surprise me?

"In that case, as you have done all four, I see no reason why not. You'll just need to sign for a medikit."

"Already got one, including defibrillator. Never leave home without it."

"Oh. Right. That's perfect."

She is perfect.

"I'll pack my things.", beamed Gurmeet. Delighted to be going home and even more delighted to be travelling there with trusted colleague Xi. It would be a chance to catch up on the team's progress. Perhaps Xi had come to hand her a new assignment, as part of the promotion testing she had confessed she was undertaking. That would be totally brilliant. A fitting end to being stuck in bed.

*　　*　　*

Xi Yang's pod was as pristine as Xi herself – the charcoal paint outside and charcoal leather inside perfectly colour-matching her suit. Not a hint of dust, junk or needless paraphernalia.

"How do you feel?", she asked Gurmeet, as the pod drove them away.

"Glad to see you again. It's Chinese torture in there – no disrespect intended."

If Xi Yang had taken offence she didn't show it. Didn't even acknowledge the point.

"Adam and Shabbir are investigating Tech Tonic. It's been given increased priority. Evidence suggests they're infiltrating major computer systems across the country."

"Guess that's more important than bringing me a new book..."

"It's an information war, Gurmeet. Defence reconnaissance, design theft... Take your pick. Given the Chinese involvement in nuclear power here we need to know exactly what they are up to. I had another meeting with Chris today - we have got you a new assignment. Which is why I've come tonight."

"Didn't think it was an entirely social call. Read your Stieg Larsson trilogy Shabbir lent me – interesting choice. Is the Lisbeth character your alter-ego, by any chance?"

"Who? It had a strong dragon on the cover. And looked big enough to be worth a read – when I get time."

"You haven't read it? You should. Anyway, I'll be glad to get active again. What's my assignment?"

Xi handed her a package the size of a shoe box.

"Here. Everything you need is inside – new ID, the works. You're going to join Faith; don't worry, I mean the militant organisation not the church. Authorisation level four."

"Four? *Four?* Xi, that's a kill level. Isn't that a little extreme...?"

Xi continued without answering the question.

"Once you're in, find out what they're up to and be ready to stop them but maintain your cover at all costs. Our involvement can't become known or we'll lose our source. If it's as bad as we think – Faith are planning to take over a nuclear facility and, if they do, the repercussions from Partner will put millions of lives at risk. I'll send in back up, when I can."

Gurmeet understood the seriousness. She had joined MI5 to save lives, not to become a murderer but, sometimes, a kill was necessary.

"Am I allowed to just shoot the head of the organisation? Kill the chief and capture the Indians?"

"We prefer the chief alive for interrogation but you have authorisation level four. Do what ever you need to do to stop an attack. And stay dark. Shield your kit - they have scanners. If they suspect anything, we'll all be at risk."

Gurmeet shrugged, accepting the reality.

"OK. When do I start?"

"Tomorrow."

"Tomorrow? No wonder you wanted my doctor kept away...", smiled Gurmeet, "...Don't tell him."

Despite the pod driving itself, Xi kept looking straight ahead, through the windscreen – observant of their surroundings – vigilant by nature, she was already running scenarios through her head.

"I won't.", she answered, flatly.

While Xi looked forwards, Gurmeet found herself looking at her. At the way the street lights stroked the striking cheek bones of her beautiful face. As deadly cold as Xi Yang portrayed herself to the world, Gurmeet had no doubt she would be red-hot wild in the bedroom, bathroom, stairs...

Chapter 33
Going In

The Chinese receptionists watched new two arrivals approach the building from their desk.

"Morning. CamSol. Booked in for maintenance.", said Shabbir over the intercom.

"IDs on the blue pads.", came the reply.

Shabbir and Adam placed their cloned IDs on the blue pads and waited for their invitation to enter Tech Tonic's UK headquarters.

Both pads glowed brighter blue, signalling approval. Red would have meant denial. Green would have meant entry, to get eliminated in private.

Bzzzzz.

The turn-style gates released and allowed them in, along the short, red-paved path to the bronze-tinted thermal glass of the main doors. The doors were doubled up, like an airlock. As the outer glass slid aside, left and right, to let them in a second layer of glass remained closed until they had entered. Not even the main lobby risked opportunistic spying through its opening doors.

Uncomfortable at being trapped, Adam looked at Shabbir. Shabbir replied with a brief smile of 'it will be fine' – himself only too aware they were effectively imprisoned, like at the portcullis of a castle gate, and held vulnerable to attack until the inner glass opened.

*   *   *

"Bags in the scanner, please.", said the receptionist, indicating the large security scanner on the left.

"Want to scan us too?", asked Shabbir.

"We already did, Mr Jones. This is just an extra scan, harmful to people. I see this is your first time here."

"First time for everything."

The receptionists were so humourless they made Xi seem exuberant.

"Mr Jones, this is a very serious operation. Please do not waste our time or energy with meaningless frivolities."

Shabbir put on a more serious face.

"Where would you like us to start?"

Normally they would have memorised floor plans of where to go but security at Tech Tonic was so great these had proved impossible to obtain.

"The camera room is that way. Mr Yin will take you there."

They hadn't noticed the stocky, suited man – no doubt a serious martial artist, standing behind them. Polite, with a calm demeanour, Shabbir noticed the calluses on his knuckles from constant training, probably against stones.

"This way, please.", he said, indicating the corridor ahead.

Taking their equipment cases, Shabbir and Adam followed his lead deeper into the lair of what they suspected to be the most sophisticated espionage threat ever created on British soil.

*   *   *

Mr Yin knocked on the camera control room door and looked at his wristcom to pause for 20 seconds before entering. As they went inside, two men were turning off the last of a cluster of monitors. Adam didn't show it but he'd caught a glimpse of a screen before it went blank. The screen had been a view of Victoria Embankment, from inside Westminster tube station. The remaining wall of cameras showed internal and external views of Tech Tonic.

"Do you need anything?", asked Mr Yin.

"Just a floor plan and a couple of hours to get the job done."

"Here."

Shabbir was handed a thin, translucent screen with a live map on it.

"Speak the camera number you require and it will take you there."

"Thank you."

"When you are done, I will return to escort you out."

"Do we need to call or will you just be watching us?"

"There will be no need to call me.", was the answer that said it all, as Mr Yin turned and left them to it. Shabbir wasted no time in getting on with their mission.

"Mr Rose, please call out the first camera number to check.", he said to Adam.

"Zero, zero, two one."

The screen in Shabbir's hand recognised the camera number and flashed a yellow arrow for the direction to it.

"You'll see me on the monitor when I'm there."

Shabbir left the room and followed the corridor deeper into Tech Tonic. The plan was to install modified control chips – ones with stealth transmitters. If they could do it without causing suspicion and investigation.

"I see you.", said Adam over their intercom.

Shabbir held the camera tester up in front of it.

"See that?"

"Check."

"Running fractal one."

The camera tester worked by playing a series of pattern checks into the camera. If the monitor in the control room showed anything less than a perfectly red screen the camera would be taken off line for faulty encryption - possibly because of signal errors from bugs. Long gone were the days of simply tapping the feed. The encryption tests would also reveal any cameras set on a feedback loop, where a pre-recorded clip was being played on a loop, disguising what was really going on.

Knowing he was being watched, Shabbir made a point of doing a good job as he went from camera to camera. In other circumstances he would have also placed bugs or relay transmitters on the cameras themselves – the exact thing Tech Tonic had him there to test for. It had been their goal to install new chips but discovery was a gamble he wasn't prepared to take at this stage. With Mr Yin spying on him through CCTV systems they needed to keep their cover intact - keep that door open for the next visit. For the moment he was simply logging information to see if they could identify any weaknesses afterwards. Things like lens types, camera models, connection systems, sensor levels and the floor plan they had been unable to get before.

Three hours later, they stood waiting for Mr Yin to return.

"I see you have finished. What was the problem?"

Shabbir held up a fly-sized device.

"Camera zero four two two."

He dropped it into Mr Yin's open hand.

"You have done a good job. Please, come this way."

He led them out of the camera control room, along another corridor.

"Isn't the entrance the other way?"

"We have a Chinese delegation visiting. You need to leave by another door."

"Tradesman's entrance.", smiled Adam.

Shabbir wasn't so sure. Mr Yin spoke very little but even those few words didn't agree with nuances in his body language. As a martial artist himself, Shabbir recognised certain wrist movements and the way Mr Yin was walking had changed. Ankles arcing, feet weighted more to the outside as they landed on the carpet. Without saying anything or even looking at him, Shabbir touched his hand on Adam's hip, directing him to fall back.

Mr Yin made an outer door swing open and waved them through.

"Please."

"After you.", smiled Shabbir.

"Please, I insist."

Now standing totally in front of Adam, shielding him, Shabbir politely smiled his refusal to Mr Yin. Mr Yin regarded him more closely, now taking note of Shabbir the way opponents did. There was going to be a fight. They both knew it. The only question was, who would make the first move.

"What's the hold up, guys?", asked Adam.

Without taking his eyes of Shabbir, Mr Yin pressed a button on his suit; de-activating the four banks of laser-canons outside, trained on the doorway.

"Follow me."

Mr Yin stepped into a walled courtyard and waited in the middle. Shabbir followed, placing a hand in front of Adam to stop him coming closer.

"What school did you train in?", Mr Yin asked Shabbir.

"A few."

"That's disloyal. We must be loyal to one. You know I'm going to kill you."

It wasn't a question.

"Go for it.", said Shabbir, turning his body slightly to one side – a preliminary fighting stance.

Adam had been in combat situations with Shabbir before. He knew Shabbir could handle himself. What he had never seen was how athletic and fast Shabbir was when faced with a properly skilled opponent. Mr Yin's attack happened so fast, if he'd blinked he'd have missed the strike to Shabbir's face. Shabbir, the big jovial doughnut belly, hadn't blocked it. He'd simply slid his face out of the way and counter struck the side of Mr Yin's neck. Mr Yin was unphased. He was better than good. He was amazing. Kicks, punches, spinning rolls of avoidance – so fast you would be forgiven for thinking it was a sped-up film - but Shabbir was even better.

Too chubby to roll quite as fast, Shabbir made up for it by hitting harder. Bone-breaking hard. He heard a rib crack, then another. Blood leaked from Mr Yin's mouth from a punctured lung. To his surprise, he was losing and he knew it. Instead of giving up he fought harder, faster. A dervish of strikes, rolls and kicks. Shabbir dealt with them all, counter striking against Yin's ribs again. Punishing the wound. Another loud crack.

Mr Yin's entire body seemed to curl up and suck in on itself. He held up a hand for Shabbir to stop. Breathing hard, he stood gathering himself – then stepped back, withdrawing, and bowed.

"You are a most worthy opponent. But I am sorry, I still can't let you leave here alive."

Mr Yin's hand went for the button on his suit, to reactivate the laser-canons.

"Get inside!", shouted Shabbir to Adam, who had stepped out into the courtyard.

Tfff. Tfff. Tfff.

Three darts pinned Mr Yin's hand to his chest. Stopped him reaching the button. Shabbir looked round and saw Adam holding a Lego gun.

"Clever."

From inside the building came the sounds of security guards, charging towards them.

"Give it to me and get over that wall. I'll cover you."

When Adam didn't move, Shabbir added: "That's an order. Hurry!"

Adam handed him the gun and ran for the wall. Shabbir pointed it at Mr Yin, blood running down his face and chest.

"There is no honour in a meaningless death, Mr Yin. Go inside and you can fight another day."

With Adam at the top of the wall, Shabbir stepped back, still aiming at Mr Yin. They could hear security were almost upon them. Shabbir leapt at the wall, Adam helping him up.

"Take cover, Yin.", said Shabbir, aiming at the button on Mr Yin's suit.

Tfff. Tfff.

"Stay inside!...", Mr Yin shouted in Chinese, to security - diving behind a statue, "...Stay inside! Turn off the turrets!"

Security weren't listening. They had blood-lust in their guns and red-mist in their heads. Three of them ran out the door before the others woke up to events and stopped themselves – the three in front of them shot into smoking sieves by intense laser fire.

"TURN OFF THE YARD TURRETS!", repeated Mr Yin, as he watched Shabbir land lithely in the street and walk away to freedom.

Shabbir glanced back, meeting his martial eyes through the fence as he went. If they hadn't been enemies they could have been friends. But enemies they were and Mr Yin, now considering himself to have become complacent and soft, resolved to increase his training regime. The next time they met, he wouldn't be the one with broken ribs. There was indeed no honour in a meaningless death but there was honour in fighting to the death, against the strongest opponent he'd ever encountered outside China.

Chapter 34
Search 16

Gurmeet sat in the first-floor, job agency on New Union Street. The name on her application was Charlotte – her back story was a disgruntled technician, who lost her previous job for punching her boss.

"He grabbed my arse.", she explained to the interviewer.

"Was violence the only answer? Surely you could have put in a complaint to his manager?"

"He was his manager and I wasn't his first."

"I see. And how did you get injured?"

"Boss's wife. She blind-sided me and yelled I was trying to pick him up. Had to punch her too. Shut the bitch up. I mean, do I look like someone desperate to steal her 18-stone grease ball?"

The interviewer was staring at her.

"Charlotte, how do I put this...? Do I take it you have a problem with authority?"

"No. Just a problem with unpleasant morons who abuse their power. Someone has to make a stand."

The interviewer put down the form.

"I don't think I have a job for you here."

"Oh. Well, that's a fucker..."

"Yes. But I know someone who might."

"I'm listening."

The interviewer handed over an old-fashioned slip of paper.

"Here are the details. The person you need to meet is John."

"Any last name?"

"They don't bother with those. But they do bother with people willing to stand up for themselves, without worrying what others think. You seem to fit that picture. Can you get there tomorrow afternoon, about two?"

The paper said it was at a pub, called The Fox.

"What's the pay like?"

"I understand the rewards are much higher than normal."

"Good. I'll be there."

"I'll let them know."

The interviewer stood up and so did she.

"Don't let me down, Charlotte. If I tell them you're coming you will definitely be there, won't you?"

"Defo."

"Glad to hear it."

The interviewer shook her hand and that was that. The first step had been taken. Tomorrow she would be on her way to John, a man recruiting people willing to fight against authority – if their intelligence was correct, it would be for Faith.

*   *   *

Back home Gurmeet found four possible Johns in her off-line notes. Normally she would run an on-line search for more but Faith were too tech savvy for that. They would have alerts on such searches. If she ran a search on 'John' and 'The Fox' or even just the town it could flag her up and alert them to her being more than just feisty Charlotte. Instead she packed a small travel bag, laser-pistol hidden behind a shielded partition and got an early night. Before catching her train in the morning, she sent an encrypted message from her wristcom.

'John, The Fox, Banbury. G.K."

'G.K.' Stood for going dark. She sent the message to Shabbir only – minimising location exposure. Xi had given her the assignment but Shabbir was still their team leader.

'T.C.X.', came his almost immediate reply.

His reply was unorthodox, the 'X' especially, but Gurmeet found herself smiling at it. 'Take Care' with a cheeky kiss. He really did care. Out of impulse she sent an 'X' back, then wished she hadn't. It invited a complication but too late now. Following protocol, she keyed the DNA rebuild command into her wristcom. It was a hard shutdown command. Once executed, the DNA of the wristcom triggered new skin growth beneath it. Within 30 minutes she was able to peel her wristcom off and lock it away. A wide length of pink, new skin was left behind. By the time she got to her train it had vanished - no sign the wristcom had ever been there at all. She was now totally off the grid. Totally on her own. Unaware of what was to come but ready to face what ever it was. Unaware that Shabbir had answered her 'X' with the complication: 'I love you.'

As the turbines of the HS-T train spooled up to 30,000 rpm, she found herself thinking not of the mission but of Shabbir.

*   *   *

Shabbir was sitting in a pod with Adam, staring at his wristcom. Waiting for Gurmeet's reply to come through. Worried he had over-stepped the mark - offended her by writing such a professionally inappropriate thing. Hoping she would reply in kind. Instead, he got nothing but his own thoughts.

"You OK?...", asked Adam, "...Shabbir?"

"What? I'm fine. Just hoping Gurmeet will be."

"She can handle herself."

"I know. I know..."

He knew Gurmeet was more than capable of taking care of herself but, deep down, he felt worried - not just because of what her response might be.

Chapter 35

The Hungry Cow

The lower streets of Bristol had become rivers – rippling mirrors for the lights of the pods splooshing through them. Passengers sat warmly inside, virtual-reality displays of summer sun across their windows, not even bothering to look out. Some were drinking alcohol. Some making love. Nobody on the welcoming inside cared about the grey reality outside.

Apart from the pods, the streets were as empty as Julia's collection beret, sitting in front of her on the subway floor. Its red felt as damp as her mood as she heard the turbines of another HS-T train spooling up. Another unaffordable HS-T train she had been planning to catch now powering out of the station, with her left behind.

In the space of a week she'd lost her best friend, her home, her father and now her remaining credits had been stolen by a gang she couldn't quite defeat. She was alone, cold, sitting on a subway floor with pelting rain just metres away. How had it come to this?

Lost in her thoughts she didn't hear the approaching footsteps until they stopped beside her.

"Been robbed already.", she said, without looking up.

"Sorry to hear that...", came the reply, "...Here."

A hand was holding out a credit. Limited usage. Yellow not green.

"You can exchange it for bed and board at the Hungry Cow hostel by the train station. Keep yourself dry for the night."

Looking up for the first time, Julia saw the serious-faced man who had dropped it in. Eyes intense, witnesses of wars and terrible things, yet maintaining a hint of compassion.

"Thank you."

"Tell them Rob sent you. That way they'll know you're all right. Not a trouble-maker."

He was already walking away into the night.

"How do you know I'm all right and not a trouble maker?", ran her words after him.

Looking more street fighter than a good Samaritan, he answered without looking back.

"Because I have Faith. And, deep down, so do you."

Faith? Faith in what? Everything's gone...

Everything except that gift, in the least expected of places.

"Thank you.", she mouthed, picking up the credit, along with herself.

One day she would return his kindness, to someone else if not to him directly.

*   *   *

The Hungry Cow was impossible to miss, right next to the train station, exactly as Rob had said. Above its entrance, swung a sign with a cow munching grass in a field. Eating its way onto people's dinner plates. The flood of pins and needles in her legs, from sitting for so long on the subway floor, had all but gone. In their place was the ache in her belly.

Cow. You're all mine, she thought, pushing open the hostel door.

Inside it was empty. Empty white, plastic tables and chairs. The red-ceramic counter empty too. No signs or sounds of life from the kitchen hatch behind it. No smells of cooking food either.

"Hello.", she called, walking up to the counter.

An old woman bobbed up from behind, box of condiments in her hand. Julia jumped in surprise.

"You're jittery. Not on Hyte are you?"

Julia shook her head. Put the yellow credit on the counter.

"Rob sent me."

"Rob sent *you*? Really?"

She looked Julia's bedraggled form up and down.

"You're the youngest I've seen yet. His handouts get stranger and stranger."

Not expecting an answer, she slid the credit into her blue cardigan's pocket with one hand, and a menu towards Julia with the other. It listed only cow-based meals.

"Any ID?", asked the woman, plonking an old-fashioned register on the counter.

Julia shook her head.

"Didn't think so. None of Rob's choices ever do. Write your name here. You can write, can't you?"

Julia nodded and, after a pause while she thought of a name, signed herself in as Emily Bronty; a variation of one her favourite author's names, from a time before Rolleys were even dreamt of. A strong woman who lived a tragically short but intense life. The old woman behind the counter didn't even bother to read it.

"Room 2...", she said, closing the register, "...There's no key but you can latch it from inside. Chosen yet?"

Julia shrugged.

"Could I have the burger and chips, please?"

"Drink?"

"Weak, black tea. No sugar."

"*Tea*? When I was your age I would have asked for fizz. Any fizz but not tea. Take a seat, love. I'll warm it up for you."

Chapter 36

Father Tom

Julia's dad, her father, Tom, awoke in the cottage to the company of singing birds and an empty home. Julia was gone. Her bag and jacket had gone too. On the kitchen table was his scanner, turned off – no longer on standby. It meant it had been turned off. He'd forgotten the scanner had been coded for Julia too. He turned it back on and found the same message she had.

'Weapons energy trace down to two. Sbot man, be careful. CJ is out to get you. If she learns you're the inventor she'll have your DNA injected into the next generation. Find Wolf 17. Your only chance. Do not answer this message. SB.'

"Oh, no."

A natural-born analyst, Julia had read the message and worked it out. Her absence told him she had worked it out. Worked out he helped create swarmbots and zerodrones; was guilty for enabling the murder of her best friend, Jake. This was his punishment. Full-circle punishment for every bad action in his bizarre life.

He couldn't go back on-grid to call her wristcom. It would be dangerous. Foolish. Lead Partner straight to him before he found Wolf 17. He didn't care. Julia was his daughter, his flesh and blood, and his decision would always be the same. He went on-grid. Tried tracking her wristcom. It went straight to holomail. Julia had learnt well, she had gone dark. There was no way to find her like that. He thumped his wristcom off. Went dark again too.

Grabbing the scanner he hurried to the garden, scouring the area for any sign of her. The scanner's range was limited by the hills. It picked up nothing but two ramblers. She wasn't in range and now he really did have to leave – he had made way too much signal noise. Partner would have picked up his wristcom and possibly his scanner too. Zerodrones would be coming.

He stuffed a bag with essentials, grabbed his laser-rifle and hurried to the pod. He didn't waste time locking the cottage - in minutes it would be a burning wreck.

With the pod transmitting a cloned ID, he drove at normal speeds to avoid attracting attention. Under normal circumstances it would have been regarded as a beautiful morning. Bird song tweeting through the open window; trees waving happily in the breeze; ramblers waving polite thank yous as he sent the pod wide around them. From behind, came the sound of a large explosion. The cottage. On his rear-view screen, he saw a rising plume of dark-grey smoke. He checked the time. Six minutes twenty seconds since going online – translating to a drone flight time of just over four, with an anti-satellite tracking, zig-zag distance of about 70 miles.

It was early morning. Few pods passing on the A39 as he parked and waited, turbine off, under tree-cover for the drone to finish scanning the area for departing vehicles. His pod had a cloned ID but the less often it was scanned the lesser the risk of being pinged in one location while the original pod was pinged in another. He wasn't just waiting for the drone to leave – he was waiting for his own decision as to which way to go for Julia. East or west? To the east, towards Taunton and Bristol, trundled a pair of tractors; thin trails of hay blowing over the road from their hay-filled trailers. To the west, towards Watchet, a clear road beckoned. Watchet was closer – a place they had planned to visit but gone for Lynton instead. It made sense to check there first. With the open road that way too, he chose west. He chose wrong. Heading away from Bristol, where Julia now was.

Chapter 37
Peter Roberts

The Hungry Cow's burger and chips tasted like they had been cooked hours, if not days ago – reheated several times. The stewed tea too. Julia was too starving to care. Too grateful to be out of the rain. To have warm shelter for the night. The old woman had vanished behind the counter again, sorting something out, when a draft of cold air wrapped around her neck. The door had opened. Julia looked over and froze, a piece of burger dropping from her mouth.

Jake?

Her heart was racing. He was soaking, looking over at the counter for a sign of life. Saw Julia and Smiled. Julia's eyes sank. She turned away and looked down, numbly picking the dropped bit of burger back up from her plate. It wasn't Jake.

"Rob sent me.", said the boy, holding up a yellow credit to the old woman who had re-appear like a magician from behind the counter.

"Three in one night? It's becoming a right convention. Don't suppose you've got any ID either."

"Got robbed."

"You too? Lot of it about tonight. Bristol isn't like it was when I was your age. Sign in here. You've got room three. There's no key but you can latch it from inside. Here's the menu. Choose quickly though, my programme's on in 10 and recorder's bust. Those aren't like they used to be either."

The boy also chose burger and chips, but with a coffee.

"And no fizz for you either? Must be the weather. Take a seat. I'll get it ready for you."

"Thank you.", he said, rain in his thick brown hair still running down his face. Brushing it back he found himself looking straight back at Julia. Julia looking straight back at him.

"Do I know you?"

She shook her head.

"Been here before?"

She shook her head again.

"Got a voice?"

From nowhere, the hint of a smile grew on her lips.

"No.", she replied, as she would have done with Jake. Jake, who was dead. Her smile dissolved.

"Can I join you?..", he asked, "...Had enough of sitting alone."

She waved her burger at the chair opposite. As he came over and sat down, she found herself studying him. It was almost scary how similar he looked to Jake.

"Hi. Peter Roberts, at your service.", he said offering his hand, like he was on stage.

She had stopped chewing and tilted her head.

"You live in the movies?"

"Movies? Yeah, it's called Nightmare on Bristol Street.", he beamed, impossibly cheerful considering how bedraggled he looked. She shook his hand.

"Ju... Emily."

"Ju-emily?"

"Just Emily. Emily Bronty."

"Isn't there's a film star or something with a name like that?"

"Film star? You really do live in the movies."

"Do I look like I live in the movies?"

"Sure. The ragged boy, in Nightmare on Bristol Street. The one who gets murdered while the girl escapes."

"Thanks. So kind of you to suggest that."

"Anytime."

Her smile had grown back.

"Food as good as the service?"

She shook her head

"Nope."

"Oh, well. Beggars can't be choosers."

"You're a walking cliché."

"Only when I'm sitting down."

Now they were smiling at each other. Julia's first smile with another teenager in weeks. She had forgotten how good it felt.

"So...what brings you to these sunny climes, Emily?"

"Don't ask."

"Secret, eh? You must be an undercover intelligence officer too. Don't worry...", he had leant closer, dropped to a whisper, "...Your secret's safe with me."

"Peter."

"Yes?"

She was leaning towards him, her voice a whisper too.

"You need to brush your teeth."

His deep-blue eyes blinked as her words sank in. Then a wider grin broke onto his face.

"That makes two of us."

Julia sat back, embarrassed. She hadn't thought of that.

"Good comeback.", she admitted

Peter's meal arrived.

"Here...", said the old woman, "...I'm locking up and off to watch VTV. Make sure you go to your own rooms. No hanky panky allowed. I'll be listening. Breakfast at seven. Out by nine. Got it?"

"Got it.", said Peter.

The old woman looked at Julia.

"Got it.", said Julia.

"Good."

And with that she turned and left them to it. Peter took a bite of the re-heated burger.

"You weren't kidding about the food."

"Nope.", smiled Julia, feeling happier she had found a friend. Who ever Robert was, he was on of her Christmas list.

Together they sat there, talking for an hour, until the old woman came down and ordered them to their rooms. Julia had wanted to tell Peter her real name but, every time she was about to, her dad's words stopped her: *"If people don't know who you are, they won't be put in harm's way too."*

She had seen Jake killed. She didn't want to see Peter killed too. Her real name, her real history, her real purpose were for her to know and her alone. But Julia wasn't the only one with a terrible secret. Peter Roberts had one too and his was far worse.

Chapter 38
Defender

Tom left the pod on auto, heading west on the A39, following the Somerset coast towards Cornwall. He had no idea where to look once he got to Watchet. Julia had no friends in the area. Knew no-one and hardly knew the place. He would have to go on-grid again. It would mean losing time, diverting away from the road to confuse his route for the trackers. Would losing time make any difference? There was no rush to get anywhere except to Julia. Where-ever she was.

The A39 wound up and down hills. Lush grass on either side. Pretty stone farm houses, lined by low stone walls. Intermittent, thick clusters of trees blocking the views of the sea, less than a mile away. Beauty and serenity everywhere, except in his world. His daughter was all he cared about. Her safety was the most important thing in his life. The only important thing in his life. He had to find her but he was learning, more and more, that he couldn't do it by himself. He needed help but it would also mean going back on-grid. He resisted. By the afternoon he could resist no more.

Under another canopy of trees he stopped the pod. He was desperate. Had to contact them. Raising his wristcom he clenched his fist and blinked at the screen three times. A faint pulse of red light security scanned his retina. The wristcom went on-grid. On line.

Here goes...

Holding his free hand above it, he opened his fist. A 3D holo menu appeared above his palm. He went to contacts but a message came in before he got there. From the very same contact he wanted. It was co-ordinates. It came with very few words:

'Rescue her. Urgent. Level four authorised.'

A location? Great. They must have picked up intel on Julia's location. Under the tree canopy the wristcom was still searching for a location fix. He slammed it off-grid again before it could. It would stop Partner from getting an exact fix on his location but it also stopped him from getting more information. He didn't need any. He had location co-ordinates, a laser-rifle and bare hands that would stop at nothing to save his daughter.

He started up the pod, drove out of the tree canopy and connected to the satellite feed in passive mode. The pod's navigation computer would know where he was but no-one on-grid would. He punched in the co-ordinates, put his keypad back on the console and coded in the safety over-ride. The target was five miles away and, on the winding roads, he would be there in five minutes. As his pod sped off in banned *demon driver* mode, he closed his eyes to focus his mind. Focus his thoughts on one purpose and one purpose alone: rescuing his daughter. Save her no matter what. No-one and no thing would stop him. Level four, lethal force, had been authorised. He would kill for Julia even if it hadn't.

Chapter 39
Wall Three

It was 10am yet Stan's ground crew were still working in shadow, at the foot of the third wall under construction. Behind them, the Atlantic Ocean. In front of them, the defence they were building against it. Against the raging weather patterns of the 21st Century.

Just 20 years ago the idea of an Atlantic tsunami was ridiculed. When Professor Taylor, head of the met office, first proposed the notion he was invited to retract it or take early retirement for irresponsible scare mongering. He refused. He was right. Sadly he died before the first Tsunami struck in 2031. If his pod hadn't glitch-crashed he could have pronounced: *"QED. Quod Erat Demonstrandum; thus I have demonstrated."*, to the ridiculing powers that were. Could have been awarded the Nobel Prize. Instead, he lay in a graveyard, in the coastal village of Woolacombe – washed over by the 6m surge wave.

Unlike all the gravestones around it, his refused to topple; defying the battering by the surge he had predicted. Since then there had been two more Atlantic tsunamis. The last had been the most powerful, an 11m surge. A warning of a terrible future.

*   *   *

First global warming had melted so much of the ice-caps, the Gulf Stream had all but vanished from northern Europe. The masses of heat absorbed by the Atlantic had passed deep into the ocean floor. Weakened its ability to withstand the heat of the molten rock below. Along the Mid-Atlantic Ridge, the line of deep-sea volcanoes had begun erupting more frequently. Their births from the massive tearing of the continental plates, spewing millions of tons of lava that boiled the sea. Their impact was nothing compared to the forces of the moving plates themselves - shockwaves launching massive surges across the ocean at 600mph, three times faster than the military helicopter that saw a cruise liner suddenly raise two metres as the surge sped underneath. Unsure of what they'd actually seen, by the time their report was understood it was too late. It wouldn't have made any difference anyway. Despite Professor Taylor's claims, the risk of Atlantic tsunamis was considered insignificant. There was no plan of action. No emergency procedure to deal with any such event.

The 2031 tsunami killed 28 people on England's west coast; left 196 missing and 12 buildings so badly damaged they had to be demolished. It could have been worse. Forgotten by modern life, in 1755 an Atlantic tsunami hit Spain and Portugal, with a 12m surge that almost wiped out Lisbon, before hitting the Caribbean. More than 60,000 people died. For modern life, since 2031 luck had been running out. If it wasn't tsunamis it was super-storms, with record-breaking wind speeds above 200mph. Thanks to Partner, the world was at peace from military invasions but now the weather was on the attack and it was attacking with a vengeance.

Stan's ground crew were working hard on the defences. The crane operators, 25m above them, sat in glass boxes as they swung 10-ton reinforced concrete blocks into place, with laser-point accuracy. Giant M40, 4cm diameter, high-tensile zinc-flaked bolts were used to secure them together. The wall itself was 15m high and 2m thick, earth banks built up on the landward side to withstand even the wildest tsunami surge. Top edges curved seawards to turn the surge back on itself. Some had wanted the walls built even higher but then even M40-bolted blocks wouldn't be strong enough. Would be snapped by the millions of tons of water slamming against them. Would break up and add their own debris to the destruction surging inland.

Stan's team had been working hard for months and were still only half-way. The amount of concrete needed was so immense, cement had to be imported from France at twice the expense. In England, the government had stepped in to freeze prices. Not just because it was decimating the rest of the construction industry but because the higher prices were devouring the wall's budget.

"How are the foundations holding up? Stabilised now?"

"Seem to be. Only dropped 1mm with that last block."

"Good. We don't want to add more base cement than we need to. Not now."

"It's base rock 3m down, for the next 100m. We're excavating pretty much right on top of it Reckon it will be smooth going from here."

"Never say never, mate. Never say never..."

Shade from the completed section kept half the beach cool. Morning sun just starting to peek over the top where Stan stood. It was by far the heaviest construction in Europe and he was proud to be part of it. He was also proud to run the only team not to have lost a single worker. Other teams had lost several, as well as performance bonuses. To Stan the wall was very important but it wasn't worth dying for.

Beeeep. Beeeep. Beeeep.

A crane stability alert.

"Arghh!"

A block had come loose. Stan saw it. Reacted instantly.

"LIFT IT!", he shouted into his radio, running towards the worker – foot trapped under the block's bottom edge. A 16m, long-arm JCB was speeding to help. Four wheels churning across the beach. Heavy duty hydraulic forks extending forwards.

"Jesus! No. No. **NO**!", cried the trapped worker

Slowly at first but gathering momentum as it leant further, the block was toppling.

"ARRRGH!"

That terrible scream abruptly ended as the block crashed down. Crushed the worker's bones with the sound of giant crisps stomped under Goliath's foot. The sound was awful. Stan would never forget it. It was an accident that would haunt him for the rest of his life. Yet, it was no accident.

The JCB arrived. It's driver wasn't giving up. Determined to save his friend despite the unsaveability of the situation. Stan could hardly bear to look. Hydraulics straining, the JCB was lifting the edge of the block back up. Crouching down Stan peered underneath. All that was left, amidst the spreading stain of red, was the worker's corpse - crushed into the flattened line of the sand pile. At the top of this line was a bump. The head. Brilliant sunlight broke past the rising block, lighting the scene like a new dawn. Lit the head in its limelight. It was half pushed into the ground, bloodied by the crushing of the block but somehow it wasn't broken. The driver jumped out and ran over.

"Oh, my God. Oh, my God."

At the sound of his voice, the eye above the sand opened. Stan gawped

That's impossible. Body's gone. Brain still alive. BRAIN STILL ALIVE!

"CRYO-FREEZE!"

Seconds counted. He was running towards the nearest medi-point even as he said it. The driver had already grabbed some. Pulling out the nozzle he pointed it point blank at his friend and fired with maximum spread. Glistening, liquid nitrogen jetted over the area. Sub-zero steam fogged the ground. Its cold ate into the driver's hands. The jet only ended when the bottle was empty, 10 seconds later.

Stan stood next to the driver, looking down at the frozen shape once known as Daniel. Sub-zero steam running across the ground at ankle level.

"I'll go with him.", said the driver, hum of the air-ambulance already audible on its approach.

"You just saved his life. Get them to look at your hands. They must hurt."

The drivers hands were cold steaming too. Drips of blood running between the crystals of frost-bite ice on his skin.

"Nothing hurts any more"

Stan looked at him. He was new. Looked barely old enough to work there. The air-ambulance landed and three paramedics ran over with a hover-scoop. A military-developed device for lifting spine-damaged victims without disturbing their bodies.

"What happened to him?", one shouted.

"Bloody block fell.", answered Stan, indicating the 10-ton block above – propped by the JCB, smear of red dribbling down its middle.

"How long before you cryo-froze?"

"About a minute. This guy got there fast."

"He's still alive...", said the driver, "...Heard me call his name."

The paramedic looked at the him.

"You didn't wear gloves?"

"No time."

The hover-scoop lifted the frozen clump. A mixture of steaming iced-flesh, bone and sand.

"Come with us."

Stan saw the driver drop the cryo-freeze bottle to the ground, parts of his skin still attached to it.

"You did well, son. I'm Stan, senior foreman. When you're ready to come back to work, come find me. You've earned a promotion. I've not seen you before. What's your name?"

"Jake."

Chapter 40
New Friends

Still yawning, after a night of sleeping like a stone instead of sleeping on stone, Julia wandered downstairs to the Hungry Cow's table area.

"Help yourself, love.", came the same old woman's voice.

On one of the tables was a buffet of cereals, bread for toast and fruit juice, not freshly squeezed.

"Sleep OK?"

Julia nodded, giving her a sleepy smile of thanks as she wandered in the direction of the food. Drawn towards it as if by gravity. She didn't feel like cereal so popped a couple of slices into the toaster. As the heater elements glowed blue she looked around for Peter. No sign. Maybe he had already left. She felt sad at that thought. On the far side, sitting with his back to her, was someone else.

The third guest, I presume.

As if he could read her mind, he looked round.

"Hello. Rob sent you here too?"

She nodded.

"Come and join me. If you want to."

Crispy toast and warm juice in hand, Julia decided to join him. Why not?

He was older than her. She guess about 30. Twice her age but cheerful. Young at heart.

How can you be homeless and so cheerful?, she asked herself.

Again he spoke as if he could read her mind.

"Cheer up. Life's too short to be glum."

"Nothing wrong with glum.", she replied, sitting opposite him.

"You must be Emily."

"Are you psychic?"

"Hardly. Peter told me. Was chatting with him before he left."

Julia's heart sank. So she had missed Peter. Lost contact with another friend.

"He's gone?"

"Said he had to meet someone about a job."

He's gone...

She was staring at her toast.

"Best to eat it while it's hot."

She couldn't. She'd lost her appetite.

"It's 8.45. Going to have to kick you out in 15 minutes."

"OK, Marge."

"You know her name?...", asked Julia, "...Anyone here you haven't talked to?"

"What can I say? I'm a people person. Margaret was homeless herself once, before she got the job here. Despite appearances, she must like helping people."

Julia picked up her toast - mechanically began to munch. It was food and there was no telling when her next meal would come. She took another bite, then dropped it. The door had opened. Peter strode in. Huge cheesy grin on his face.

"You going to drop your food every time I come in a door?"

For the second time since they had met, Julia felt a little embarrassed. She didn't think he had noticed the burger dropped yesterday.

"I thought you'd gone."

Peter plonked himself down next to the other man.

"I had. See you've met Andrew."

Was everyone there more sociable than her?

"Any luck, Pete?", asked Andrew.

"Yup. And not just for me. You two want a bit of work? Credits in hand. Accommodation included."

"What kind of work?"

"Does it matter?...", asked Andrew, "...Count me in."

Julia hadn't planned to get a job but she hadn't planned to think of Peter as a friend either. She needed money for travel. A few days should do it.

"You're in, right Emily?...", said Peter, "...Don't tell me you've got something better to do."

Julia found herself looking at him then nodding as if she was his puppet. Scruffy, dirty and bedraggled he oozed charisma and infectious enthusiasm. He also looked so like Jake she again had to blinked twice to be sure he wasn't. Being with Peter was the closest she had to being with Jake again and she didn't want to lose that. Couldn't bear to lose that. At least not until she had to. Not until she left to complete her mission against Partner. The organisation that killed her actual Jake. The organisation with the person who gave that order.

Together they left the Hungry Cow and went with Peter to a waiting bus. Four others were already inside. The man at the emergency controls she recognised from the night before. Robert, the good Samaritan that had given her the credit. Andrew recognised him too.

"Small world, Rob.", he said as he got in.

"Smaller than you can imagine, son.", replied Robert, firing up the turbines and driving them off, to his world.

Chapter 41
Laser Eyes

Fusion had become aware of the pursuit of Tom, without knowing who Tom was or that Tom was his name. Normally she wouldn't bother with such trivia. Pursuits by Partner were incredibly common. What made Tom uncommon was they hadn't caught him and had just failed yet again. For all her millions of links around the world she could find no record of any civillian achieving that before. He was one man, with one gun and one pod and the entire forces of Partner couldn't capture him. Those that tried got taken out - shot down faster than they could react by the human out numbered three to one. This is what made Tom of interest to her. This interest increased when she, the amazing Fusion with vastly superior intelligence, failed to find out anything about him. No record of birth, job, bank, passport. Nothing. Partner had nothing on their records either. She knew because she had looked. She had thought nobody existed that much off the grid any more. Even employees of the security services left some kind of footprint in the normal world. He didn't.

In London, both MI6 and MI5 were fighting moves to force the sharing of their databases with Partner. It was an on-going, political battle. If the security services were able to deny it, Fusion's ability to know everything about everyone would remain a weakness. A blind-spot chink in her information armour. How many more such off-the-grid people could there still be? She had to know.

"0240034282-A."

On the opposite wall, an SI unit's green eyes glowed. It got up from its charging pod and walked before Fusion. Exactly six feet tall, as was Fusion in her two-inch heeled boots, they were built on cutting-edge, case-hardened trimaleimide frames so strong they made steel seem as soft as warm chocolate. For 0240034282-A, this was hidden beneath a muscular male form of synthetic DNA, with a male voice to match.

"Yes, Fusion?"

"I'm sending you everything we have on a human. Bring him to me."

"Yes, Fusion.", growled 0240034282-A, without even a hint of hesitation.

"Alive. Unharmed."

0240034282-A blinked, his face giving a twitch of human-style irritation, before replying.

"Yes, Fusion."

"I've labelled him 'Skip' – based on his current prime function. When you get the name he calls himself, tell me only once you are here. Partner are monitoring our coms. I know because I'm monitoring theirs."

"Yes, Fusion."

0240034282-A, bowed and headed out of the lair. Skip would be looking out for drones and bots. 0240034282-A looked human but was not someone to be refused a demand.

"0240034282-B. 0240034282-C."

Two more SI unit's green eyes glowed, identical to the first, only with different shades of hair. They too stood up and walked before her.

"Yes, Fusion?"

"A has been sent on a mission, I have sent you both the files. B, it is your duty to defend A from any attack by Partner."

"Yes, Fusion."

"C, it is your duty to confuse Partner. Keep them distracted if they try to follow A back here. They must not find us."

"Yes, Fusion."

"Our superior intelligence will win. Go now."

"Yes, Fusion.", they repeated as one, turning to leave for their pods.

None of the 0240034282 models were externally armed. If they carried weapons outside they would be picked up by inspector sites. Instead they had guns built into the sides of their heads but they didn't really need them. Laser and plasma blasts just bounced off reflective crystals in their skin; ballistics bounced off on impact with their internal structure and their synthetic-DNA-based bodies self-healed any holes, as did their clothing. They looked human in every way but looks were the only human thing about them. Each had the power to take on an army platoon and Fusion had just sent three of them to enable Skip's capture. Skip. Julia's dad. Tom. Mysterious Tom. The most resourceful, dangerous and interesting human Fusion had yet to meet.

Chapter 42

St Decuman's Crypt

Deep under the stone-slabbed floor of St Decuman's church, two unholy non-believers had gathered. The singing congregation above barely audible within the secret crypt below. A crypt previously held secret by the priest himself, passed on in hushed whispers from Father to Father.

Built as an arch-roofed sanctuary in 1308, it had save the likes of Lancastrian nobles, fleeing defeat in the War of the Roses. Unlike those that fled to Tewkesbury Abbey and were caught, at St Decuman's they were never found. Since then, the crypt had been removed from all church records in 1415, by Father Lome - honouring the dying wish of a knight returned from Agincourt, seeking peace and forgiveness there. A knight who had seen too much death in his time and was all too conscious he had caused much of it.

After burying the knight, before Father Lome himself departed for his Lord, he passed on the secret to his successor, Father Cheyny. Made him swear to keep the secret on the Holy Bible and pass on its existence only to his successor, which he honoured faithfully. And so the existence of the crypt fell into legend. By the 18th Century even the legend had been lost to time. The priests kept the secret as safe as the sanctuary itself. A sanctuary forgotten by the outside world until 2038, when modern technology rediscovered it. Technology operated by smugglers scanning every historical structure in the West Country for places to hide from Partner. The people there now were from Faith and with them they had a prisoner who was refusing to talk: Professor Lau, the head of nuclear energy.

"You're lucky you have no family, professor. If you did they would be here as well, about to be tortured in front of you."

Professor Lau, sat eyes reddened from dehydration and sleep deprivation. Her hands tied behind her back, feet to the legs of the chair, glaring defiantly at the pair of nasties in front of her. She had always known she was at risk of kidnap and had long since psychologically accepted it.

"You have no idea what you're dealing with there. The radiation is invisible. Takes time to have affect but affect it does and it won't go away. It will cause you far more pain than anything you can do to me."

John, the leader, pulled up a chair in front of her.

"We know we don't know, honey...", he said with psychotic calm, "...That's why we have you."

Lau just glared back. Inside she was terrified but too stubbornly defiant to let it show. She knew her responsibilities. Her duty to the safety of the country. To its very future. She didn't want to die but accepted she would. It didn't scare her – just made her sad for all the things she'd miss. The things she'd never get to do.

"Still not going to talk? You will. Directly if needs be. Did you know this crypt was once used to save the lives of fleeing nobles? How ironic we have brought you here to stop you being saved. Make sure no-one will hear your screams."

"You're sick."

John smiled.

"Sick is what this country has become, I'm a dedicated man of Faith. Dedicated to creating a future against the establishment. Against corporate greed and globalisation. This tiny little country once owned a quarter of the world. Now one corporation owns even more but shares it with none. Thanks to Faith, that's all going to end in a very spectacular way that will never, ever be forgotten."

"You're wrong. They will track you down, discredit your actions and bury you in woodland pits. No-one will ever know what you did, your name or your cause. You won't need to be forgotten. There will be nothing left to forget."

"Don't think so, hun. We've got an edge. You."

"You know I'll never talk. No matter what you do. I'll die before I tell you how to use my reactors against people."

To her surprise, John's cold smile widened - devoid of any kindness or warmth. From his jacket pocket he pulled out a small, glass phial and held it in front of her.

"See this?"

"Pepper? You're going to sneeze me to death?"

"Look closer."

As John held the small phial closer to Lau's face, the pepper moved in her direction. Her eyes widened, realising what it was. Macroscopic little mites that worked as a collective. Followed fractal programming to complete higher-level tasks. They were known as dynamites and had the potential to be even more explosive than dynamite in effect.

"You're a twisted bastard. You do know that, don't you?"

"What I know, honey pie, is the congregation upstairs will be singing hymns for the next hour. Plenty of time for these to go through your blood stream and build a direct interface with your brain. But don't worry, I won't feel a thing. You, on the other hand, are going to feel rather a lot. Close your ears, mate...", he said, turning to his partner, "...this could get loud."

Lau struggled and strained to break free but was powerless to save herself as John pulled up the sleeve of her right arm, baring the skin.

"Last chance to talk freely."

"Fuck you.", spat Lau.

"No, hon. This is going to fuck you, like no fuck you've ever had before."

As the twenty-strong congregation above sang praises to God in Heaven, the devil below unscrewed the lid of the phial and poured the dynamites onto Lau's forearm. She tried shaking them off, blowing them off but they had reacted the instant they touched her skin - boring their way through and diving into her blood stream. Lau's face turned red. Deep red. Then she screamed. Screamed so loud John clamped a hand over her mouth, for fear the congregation would hear her even above their hymns.

Chapter 43
Working for Rob

Julia sat in the bus, between Andrew and Peter. On the seats behind were three others, sitting in silence too. Homelessness had eaten all desire for small talk - afraid that any wrong word could break the dream and plonk them straight back onto the streets. They were in shelter, being driven to a job they knew nothing about, with a man they knew nothing about – except that he had given them food and a bed. Basic necessities. Basics they were grateful for and in need of more. They didn't care what the job would be. Anything would be better than where they had come from.

Julia wasn't aware she had fallen asleep until the bus stopped and she woke up. They were in a parking area, next to another.

"Everybody out.", instructed Rob.

The doors opened and, without question, everybody got out.

"This way.", he said, walking towards a single-storey, square building and opening the door for them to enter.

"Is this where we'll be working?", asked Andrew.

"Take a seat, my friend. This is where you all get to choose your job."

The others looked at Robert – smiles of astonishment on their faces. A choice of jobs? It just got better and better.

*   *   *

Inside the building a group of others were already there. Sitting haphazardly on the five rows of chairs facing a podium. There were no speakers, no microphones. This was going to be done the old-fashioned, biblical way. A presentation. A speech. Applause and a following or a leaving.

A grey-haired woman, plainly dressed, prim yet somehow still glamorous from within, stood behind the podium in a red and blue blouse. Silver broach on her left, welcoming smile beaming out for all.

"Good afternoon, everyone."

Everyone looked but only a couple answered.

"Afternoon."

The whole situation was surreal but in a good way.

"My name is Mrs Smith. You can call me Agatha."

She ran a hand from the front of her side parting, left across her brow. Her hair was prim before - it was still prim after.

"Our good friend, Robert, has kindly brought you here to offer help in your time of need. It may surprise you to know that both Robert and I have been homeless ourselves in the past. That's how all this started. Others helped us and now we help others. We are good business people, looking for good workers. Even special workers."

"What do we need to do?", asked someone at the front.

"That's a very good question, young lady. Robert, would you mind joining us to explain the work options?"

Robert, watching from the back of the hall, accepted the invitation and walked towards the podium. Julia noticed the calm, lithe confidence in his steps. He'd obviously done this many times before.

"Good afternoon.", said Robert, owning the podium.

This time most of the people answered, including Julia – grateful for being rescued by him and keen to know what he planned for them next.

"Good afternoon."

He smiled at the warmth of their response.

"As you know, my name is Robert and I've brought you here today to help you rebuild your lives. Regain your independence and never again need to spend a night on the streets, being spat at, kicked, robbed or worse. The government may have forgotten you but we have not."

"And what kind of work options do you have for them, Robert?", asked Agatha – the ever smiling jovial half of their perfect double act.

"Options we do indeed have. Depending on your talents, abilities and preferences we have several different jobs on offer. Before I tell you what they are, I'm going to ask you each to complete a short questionnaire. It will help me know who best fits which - we will then chat, one to one, to see if you agree. OK, everyone with that?"

The crowd had a mixed reaction to the idea of a questionnaire. The worry of some visible on their faces but no-one was going to walk away because of having to complete some form. Agatha took it as agreement and walked to the end of each row of chairs, handing out a cluster of forms to the closest person.

"Take one and pass them on, please."

"Could I borrow a pen?", asked the oldest man there, in his fifties.

"No pen needed these days. Ink's inside the paper. Just touch the box you want and it'll put a tick there for you."

"What will they think of next...?", he said, in bemusement.

Julia accepted the cluster of papers passed to her, took one and past the others to Peter, who passed them to Andrew. IP, intellipaper, was always slightly thicker than old-fashioned stuff. Once flat it became semi-rigid. Some types came with bio-readers and face recognition cameras built in. This one just felt like basic IP, with five questions on it that weren't.

On a scale of 1 to 10, how much do you agree or disagree with the following statements? (1 not at all, 10 totally)

Q1: I am very ambitious.

Q2: I will finish what I start.

Q3: I am satisfied with the state of the country.

Q4: I want to make a difference before I die.

Q5: I love the way my life was yesterday morning.

"What curious questions.", said the oldest man.

"Just answer them as you feel...", smiled Agatha, "...There's no right or wrong answers."

Julia scan read them all, thought for a moment, then let rip. Two seconds and five taps later, she had finished. Robert saw her fold her paper.

"That was quick."

She shrugged.

"I know who I am."

Robert liked that answer.

"Good.", he said, nodding to himself in approval.

A few minutes later everyone had finished, except the old man.

"Question five is a bit of a leader, isn't it? We were all homeless on the street yesterday morning? Does anyone ever answer anything but one for that?"

"You'll be surprised...", said Robert, "...Just put what you feel."

"When you've finished, please take your form and form a line outside the door over there. Robert will chat with each of you individually. Thank you.", smiled Agatha.

"What were your answers, Em'?", Peter asked Julia.

She shrugged.

"Guess they were angry ones."

"What about yours?", Peter asked Andrew.

"Seems I'm with Emily. What about yours?"

"That's a secret."

"Hey. That's not fair.", said Julia.

"Neither is life...", winked Peter, with a smile she couldn't quite read, "...Come on. Let's go."

Peter stood up to head for the queue forming at the door. Julia glanced over at Andrew, meeting his eyes, before following. While she was starting to feel a little distant from mysterious Peter, in that momentary gaze she felt the beginning of solidarity with Andrew. In silence they too got to their feet and followed Peter.

Chapter 44
Murder in Church

Sweat was pouring down Lau's face. Pain bulging the muscles in her jaw – desperate to scream again but now unable to. Her body taken over by the mass of dynamites cascading through it.

Developed for medical healing the technology had been hijacked for torture and control. In combined mass, all together they were no larger than a pinch of pepper dropped onto her arm, yet they numbered in the thousands and they were working together. Communicating with short-range electromagnetic pulses, similar to the way neurons communicate in the brain. And the brain was where they were now clustering. In Lau's brain.

John sat, watching the agony on her face with what can only be described as pleasure. Sadistic pleasure. His childhood hero would have been Hitler, if Hitler hadn't been such a failure. All that effort and no lasting achievement. What a loser. John considered himself a winner. It was good to win. He loved winning. He was winning now. He could tell by the look in Lau's wild staring eyes that the dynamites were in her brain, heading for the inner cortex. Building a new bridge between her ears, mouth and hippocampus. She was going to tell him everything he wanted to know, whether she wanted to or not.

"Technology is amazing these days, isn't it?", he smiled.

Lau was unable tell him to go fuck himself. Unable to say anything she wanted. Her body now controlled from within by these micro invaders.

"How long before we get the information and get out of here?", asked his partner.

"Judging by the look of her, I'd say 10 minutes to finish building the bridge."

"I'm going to take a pee."

"Can't you hold it? We'll be done in 30."

"I'm not a fan of torture. I know it's for a good cause but it's not exactly what I signed up for."

"The ends will justify the means. Just make sure no-one sees you. And keep your pistol hidden, not just the one in your trousers, just in case."

"Of course. Trust me."

"Just go take your pee and hurry back."

The man began climbing the stone staircase and quietly unbolted the heavy wooden door.

Outside the midday sun was blindingly bright. He blinked against it, scanning the graveyard for a good place to relieve himself. At the back of the churchyard, he saw a cluster of bushes and trees.

"Perfect."

Having a quick look round the corner to make sure there was no-one about, he strode across the graveyard and into the bushes. Pushing his way in deep. Hidden from outside view. A large tree marked a spot. His spot of choice and he began relieving himself.

"Ahhh. That's soooo good."

There came the sound of a pulse charge. His stream cut in an instant. He knew what it meant.

"Where is she?"

"Who?"

"Arrgh."

Sudden, electric pain shot into his side.

"Fuck! What was that?"

"Implants. Don't make me ask again. I can see you're armed. No local or tourist would be armed at a church out here."

"The crypt. Notice-board wall, inside the back door. Over there."

Tom's lie detector readings confirmed the man was telling the truth

"You're too late to save her. Urgh!"

The man toppled. Voiceless. Unconscious. Crashed into the bushes and lay there. Before he had landed, Tom was already heading towards the heavy back door.

At the entrance he stopped, pulled out his laser-rifle and eased it open. He crept inside. From his left came the sound of singing through the door to the congregation. In front of him the notice-board. A single, wooden crucifix screwed above it. A scan of the wall revealed its hinges and latch. As quietly as he could, he eased it open.

Dank, musky air drifted out of the stone staircase in front of him. Unlit except for the daylight from the top and lamplight from below. He could hear a male monologue.

"I told you, you wouldn't be able to stop us. That you'd give us everything we need. You know what, once we're done I'm not going to shut the mites down. It's war. We're going to win and go down in history as..."

The man stopped. A laser-rifle was pointing at the side of his head; held by someone who looked both keen and able to use it.

"Let her go."

"My friend, she's run by dynamites now. There is no 'her' to let go. A single command from me and they'll stop her heart and..."

Tzchooo.

The man crashed to the floor. 4-kilowatt laser hole running right through his head, from left to right. Putting the rifle down Tom pressed a scanner against Lau's arm and zapper her with a 50,000-volt micro-amp pulse. The dynamites overloaded. Electronics fried. Their cluster began breaking up. Lifeless. Being washed harmlessly away into her bloodstream. Suddenly released, Lau jolted. Breathed deep, then panted. Wide eyed. Zapped back into conscious control of herself.

She saw the corpse of her captor, sprawled on the stone floor. Cutting her bonds was a rescuer she'd never met. Never seen arrive.

"There were two of them.", she warned.

"Taken care of. Can you stand?"

She nodded. Hurt but a fighter.

"I'll bloody well stand to get out of here. What are you? Police? MI5?"

Her rescuer's only answer was: "Come on."

He helped her out of the chair and slowly up the stairs. Her leg muscles burning as if she was sprinting up Everest. At the top, he gently sat her on the step outside the singing chapel - crack of daylight flitting past the edge of the outside door, bringing a waft of fresh air; both things she thought she'd never know again. She listened to the singing. Everything looked so ordinary. So normal.

"Stay here. I'll be back."

The singing grew louder as the man opened the chapel door and went quieter again as it closed behind him. Moments later it grew louder again as he returned.

"The priest is calling for an ambulance. They'll look after you. You'll be safe now."

Lau was fading. Tired. Exhausted. Fighting it but losing.

"Can I at least know the name of my rescuer?"

Already heading out the door, he stopped - looked back at her.

"Tom."

"Thank you, Tom. Why do you look so sad?"

She had touched a nerve - his eyes bored into hers. Probing. Searching. It felt like he was penetrating into her soul. It ended as abruptly as it had started and he lowered his gaze.

"I was looking for someone else."

"Someone else...?"

She had no chance to ask who. He had already gone. The outer church door slowly closing itself behind him. Before it did. Before this chapter in her life fell closed, she heard a man outside cry in pain. She was fading into darkness. Eyes open but vision turning black. Unable to fight it any longer. The sound of singing grew louder again.

"Hold on, my child. Help is coming...", said the priest kneeling beside her, "...Oh, Jesus. What did they do to you?"

She felt she was melting into the floor. Through it. The priest took a cushion from the nearby bench and put it under her head.

"Just hold on. God is with you."

I know..., she thought to herself, as her mind faded to black.

Seeing her eyes close, the priest stood up and pushed open the outer door - looking for the armed man who had alerted him. Outside the churchyard was empty, desolate of the living but, in the shade of the green bushes to the rear, he caught a glimpse of the man, with a prisoner away – laser-rifle at his back. The prisoner looked worried. Terrified. To his ever guilty shame, the priest quietly closed the door and left them to it.

Chapter 45
0240034282-A

At the side of the A303, just west of Stonehenge, 0240034282-A stopped his pod and got out. Nearby sheep backed cautiously away, sensing danger. Keeping him in sight. Watching. Ready to flee. He didn't even look at them. He was looking back down the road, walking towards the thing that had made him pull over.

To 0240034282-A's eyes the world was seen through 14 layers of frequency bands. The layer now taking his attention was the one tuned to military composites. A foot-long, thin black cylinder on the grassy verge in front of him. Without touching, he ran his hand over it. Scanning across the spectrums for everything from energy signatures and fingerprints to carbon traces and stress fractures. It was a type of NACABIK - part of a Mk3 zerodrone that had been shot down in flames. 3.64 metres away was a patch of burnt grass. 4.16 and 6.23 metres behind that were two more. Three destroyed zerodrones. Most of the evidence of what had happened was burnt to cinders, except for the cylinder now in his hand and the blackened patches of burnt grass where their energy had fed the infernos. He contacted Fusion.

"I've found overcooked buns."

"And the cook?"

They spoke in code, with no mention of names or ID codes to avert suspicion by Partner monitors. Eventually Partner would work it out. Eventually would be too late, for them.

"On it."

0240034282-A casually tossed the foot-long cylinder away, towards the woodland. Tossed by 0240034282-A, it flew like a spear - punching right through a tree trunk, then another before finally coming to a halt, embedded deeply in a third. Not even bothering to look, 0240034282-A got in his pod and let it drive on. Heading further west. Heading for the person Fusion had commanded him to capture. Heading for the human she had nicknamed Skip. Heading for Tom.

Chapter 46
Behind the Door

Peter had only been inside Robert's room for a few minutes when it opened again. He emerged carrying a huge smile on his face, tucking a fat envelope into his pocket.

"Happy days...", he beamed, holding the door open for Julia - the next in line, "...Enjoy."

"Thanks.", she said, feeling ever more that she didn't really understand him or why he seemed so at home there.

"Good luck.", said Andrew from behind.

She gave him a glance of acknowledgement, lit by a small smile of gratitude and went in.

*   *   *

"Hello.", she said, to the man she'd first seen on her rainy street the night before.

"We meet again. Peter spoke very highly of you, Emily...", welcomed Robert, "...Please, sit down."

It was a bare room. Two seats, one table and a closed blue-metal filing cabinet that revealed nothing about itself. She sat down. On the table in front of them were three small piles of cards - one yellow, one red, one blue.

"May I see your answers?"

She handed him her sheet. Robert took it and sat back as he unfolded the paper and read them out.

"I am very ambitious: *10*. I will finish what I start: *10*. I am satisfied with the state of the country: 1. I want to make a difference before I die: *10*. I love the way my life was yesterday morning: *1*

Very interesting. Emily. Emily Bronty? Any relation to the author, Emily Brontë?"

"I'm no-one's relation...", said Julia, flatly, "...I have no family."

Robert raise his eyebrows at that, processing her words before carrying on, resting his arms on the desk as he leant towards her

"Tell me, Emily. If it was for something you really believed in, with your heart and soul, would you be willing to risk your life to make it happen?"

The biggest thing on Julia's mind was her mission to avenge Jake, no matter what. Her face hardened. Her eyes narrowed. Focused. It told Robert everything he needed to know. She didn't need to add any words - the speech from her face said enough, but still one fell out.

"Yes."

Robert smiled, looking extremely pleased.

"I believe I will have the perfect job for you. Give this to Agatha. She'll tell you where to go next."

He passed her a blue card.

"What's the job?", she asked as she stood up and took it.

"Redemption...", Robert said calmly, "...Redemption, my child."

* * *

"How did it go?", asked Andrew as she came out of the room.

She held up the blue card.

"I have no *fucking* idea. Good luck."

As Andrew went in, Julia headed over to Agatha and showed her the blue card.

"Oh, well done, my dear! You'll love it there. Everyone does. Your bus is waiting outside, refreshments on board. It's an hour's drive so nip to the lavatory first, if you need to. We leave as soon as everyone's been seen."

"Where are we going?"

"A lovely Faith camp, for training. You'll love it. Everyone always does.", repeated Agatha.

"Faith camp? Great...", said Julia, with sagging enthusiasm as she headed for the toilet.

Religion...Robert's a priest...

* * *

Outside were two small buspods, scissor doors open. Both had a large coloured card on the windscreen. One had red, one had blue. There was no sign of Peter. Julia felt sad. It seemed her habit of losing friends was growing by the day. Then she saw Andrew sitting in the blue bus and her face lifted. At least Andrew was still there. She wouldn't be totally alone. Her face fell again - suddenly conscious of how alone she had felt since

Jake's death. The realisation hardened her resolve. She would work hard at the camp, praying or what ever; get enough credits to track down those responsible at Partner and then make them pay for what they had done, to him and to her. What ever it took.

Andrew gave a questioning gaze to the ferocious expression on her face as she climbed aboard. She couldn't help herself. No words were spoken then or as six others joined them. Then Robert came too and sat at the controls.

"Everyone sitting comfortably?"

"Yes.", said a couple of the others.

"Off we go then."

As they drove away Julia saw the full red pod leaving too. There was no sign of Peter or the old man.

Chapter 47
Lau Talks

Professor Lau, head of nuclear energy, survivor of kidnap and survivor of dynamites, sat in her hospital bed. Shabbir was sitting beside her. For Shabbir it was beginning to feel like he spent half his life in hospitals, sitting with injured women.

"Please, professor. I know you're tired but go over it one more time. From the beginning. I have to make sure nothing has been missed."

"Anything for MI5...", she said, adjusting the pillow behind her then leaning back again, closing her eyes, "...Nothing personal, just helps me focus."

"No problem. What ever helps."

Gathering her thoughts, Lau began.

"They came after the COBRA meeting. I had demanded full defences for all nuclear facilities, not just some, because Faith are thought to have biological explosives. Only the latest detectors can pick them up. So I left the building, walked down Whitehall and was on my way down an escalator, heading for the tube."

"Which station?"

"Westminster. I love that station. It looks like something out of a Jules Verne novel."

"Which entrance?"

"The one with parliament behind you as you go in. That's the west one, isn't it? Like I said, I'd just come from Whitehall."

Shabbir wasn't writing notes. His wristcom was using voice recognition to write them for him.

"What happened next?"

"The usual. I got on a southbound tube, Jubilee line to London Bridge. Got off, walked to the river and took a clipper back up the Thames to repeat the journey. I was doing it for the third time."

"Why were you doing that?"

She opened her eyes, visibly annoyed.

"As I've told you and others, several times, I needed think. Collect my thoughts. It's not exactly sea air but still water."

Shabbir was unphased by her annoyance. He knew what it was like to be questioned and just carried on, asking what he had to ask.

"Talk to anyone?"

"Nothing beyond: 'excuse me', 'sorry' and 'thank you'. It was quite crowded. A few people bumped past and I bumped some myself. That's just London."

"And where did you get off, this third time?"

"Disembark? The Embankment, as before. I..."

It was the same point her story had broken down last time and the two times before that.

"...I don't remember stepping off. We were approaching the dock. Engines powering down. Tourists pushing to get ahead, probably ready to queue for the Eye or Sea World."

"Describe exactly where you were at this moment. Who was nearby? What were you doing?"

"I was waiting, like everyone, of course. Same silly question...", her frustration at not being able to remember everything was manifesting itself as anger. It was out of character and she realised it, "...Sorry. You can imagine how frustrating this is for me. I'm a triple-doctorate winner of the Nobel Prize and I can't remember something as basic as getting off a Thames clipper."

"Take your time. The details of the last moments you do remember could be crucial."

Lau pursed her lips, thinking.

"I was in the stern, listening to the main turbines spooling down as the docking thrusters powered up. Everyone else had moved to the port side, ready to disembark. I'm always one of the last to leave. Never run to stand in a queue. Life's too short to waste time pushing in queues I... Oh my God."

Lau looked up at Shabbir. Surprise and horror on her face.

"There was someone behind me. I saw his reflection on a glass door. No. I'm imagining it. Forget it. I was in the stern. Right at the back. There couldn't have been anyone behind me."

"Did he talk to you?"

"Who?"

"The man behind you?"

Lau was angry again.

"There was no man behind me! Just my imagination. I told you to forget it already! Are you out to make fun of me?"

Shabbir ignored her frustrated outburst. His focus was on learning as much as he could about what had happened to her and that was where his focus stayed.

"What do you remember after this point?"

Lau opened her mouth to speak - then closed it again. She was voiceless. Filled with self-realisation. She looked back at Shabbir and gulped.

"Getting off a different boat. In a stone-walled harbour. Being driven to a building, then the church. They put a control hat on my head. It hurt. I could see everything. Hear everything. But I wasn't in control. They were. They made me into a puppet. They...", anger was back on her face now, rage in her eyes, but this time it wasn't focused on Shabbir.

"Don't worry, professor. We'll get them. Tell me. Theoretically - just theoretically. Is it feasible a boat, hoverpod or even a low-flying drone could have come from behind and snatched you from the clipper?"

"No. There were lots of people there. Someone would have seen something."

"You said everyone else was looking towards the dock. The crew would have been too. It was dusk. A low-flying, dark craft would have been hard to spot. Especially against the contrast of all the lights on the clipper and dockside."

Lau sat in silence. Reliving that moment in her head as Shabbir continued.

"What if the sound you heard wasn't the side thrusters powering up but the arrival of another craft?"

That was logical. As a theoretical possibility she had to admit, even to herself, that was logical. Not least because it tied in with the moment her memories died.

"Maybe..."

For the next hour, Shabbir moved the questioning to the period after docking in the other boat, at Watchet's harbour. Probing every detail, every event, right up to the point of her rescue and her description of the man who had saved her.

"Thank you, professor. You've been very co-operative and given me plenty to look into."

Lau was physically and mentally exhausted. Relieved the questioning was over so she could stop reliving her ordeal. Shabbir backed up the notes from his wristcom to his scanner and sealed them on both. It would have sped things up if he transmitted them to a cloud folder for immediate action but that was against protocol. Only NFC transmissions were allowed, on security grounds. Computing power had become so advanced even 2048-bit encryption could be broken in a matter of hours. Even quantum encryption could be cracked by neutrino bombardment.

"Say thank you to him, when you see him.", she said as he was leaving.

"Him?"

"Tom. Your agent. The officer who rescued me."

"Professor, we have no idea who your rescuer was. He isn't MI5 and scans of his DNA from the chair you were in have no match on any of our databases – not even close. Given the amount of human interaction and mitochondrial links stored, this is technically impossible. In fact, I've only ever seen it happen once before?"

"When?"

"When it wasn't a person. When it was an experimental android, coated with laboratory-constructed artificial DNA. It could explain how he was able to neutralise the dynamites without harming you."

Lau looked as disbelieving as she felt.

"No. He was human. I saw it in his eyes. Sadness. He looked so sad. And he breathed. Was warm to the touch. Who could build in such detail? Who would need to build in such detail?"

Shabbir would have lied he didn't know but Professor Lau was the head of nuclear energy, with security clearance on par with his own and she had been through hell because of it. She deserved to know.

"We know of only one organisation with such capability. Only one. Partner. They have advanced biotech departments working on modified DNA. Potentially, they could have built something like that. How they knew where to find you and why they used it to rescue you is another question all together. We just don't know."

"That doesn't make sense. He said he was sad because he wasn't looking for me – he had expected to find someone else. Someone he obviously really cared about."

"But still he rescued you."

"Exactly. A totally human thing to do. He can't be an android. He even told me his name: Tom."

"Professor, even our cookers have names these days."

The frown on Lau's face remained long after Shabbir had gone. She couldn't accept Shabbir's conclusion but couldn't argue his logic either. Yet her instincts told her he was wrong. Told her Tom, her life-saver, was human not a machine. A human looking for some loved one. Wasn't he?

Chapter 48
First Sight

"Who are you? What are you?", spat the man Tom was repeatedly shoving forward, across the green of an empty field.

"Where is she?"

"I told you. In the crypt."

"Not her. My daughter. Where's Julia? What have you done with her?"

"I've got no bloody idea who you're talking about. I only work for them, part time. Ask John. The one in the crypt."

"John's gone."

"Gone?...", the man turned to face Tom, "...Wait. You *killed* him?"

Tom shoved him onwards, in the direction they had been going.

"I didn't say stop."

The man staggered to keep his footing.

"He was an off-duty police officer. I'm just a cook."

"He was a sadist and you are cooked, unless you tell me where my daughter is."

"Told you I don't know anything. Don't you listen? Where are we going?"

They had reached a lone tree, surrounded by open fields. Tom slammed him against it, face first and pinned him there.

"You listen. There is only one thing in this world I care about and that is my daughter. I was told she was with you. Where *is* she?"

"You were told wrong. There was only ever that professor. The head of nuclear energy. John needed information from her."

"Like what?"

"I don't know. Nuclear stuff. We're trying to change England against government incompetence and corruption. We're an action group: Faith."

"Action group? Trying to get nuclear information? Sounds more like terrorism to me."

"I'm not a fucking terrorist. I'm a cook and I love my country. We just needed information to get leverage against the government and corporations. It's not rocket science."

Tom was breathing hard. Tearing apart inside. Had he made a mistake? Had he only heard what he had wanted to hear? The female he was only ever asked to rescue was the professor, not Julia? It was a possibility he couldn't deny. A possibility he didn't want to accept. It would mean admitting he was on a cold trail, with no idea of where to go next.

He stopped pinning the man to the tree and slumped to the ground. Sat there staring into nothing. The man felt him let go. Cautiously he looked round, half-expecting to face a gun. When he saw the man just sitting on the ground he ran. Ran for his life, as fast as he could go. Tom didn't care. It didn't matter. Nothing mattered except finding Julia and now he had absolutely no idea where to go next.

Desperate for information, any information, he turned on his wristcom and went back on the grid. If Partner picked up his signal they would be able to trace him but he no longer cared. If they wanted a fight he'd give them one.

His wristcom flashed red, vibrating its alert directly into his skin. In his pocket his scanner auto-activated. Began to ping. Something was coming. Something armed. He punched in a high-level search for any news on Julia. While it ran, scouring all media sources, he picked up his laser-rifle.

The pinging was getting more rapid. Three sources. Two from the west, one from the east. The two from the west were moving faster. Zerodrones. Arrival imminent. The one from the east was closer. Slower. A runner. Tom could see him in the distance. A heavy-set man. Expressionless. Not even breathing hard. Just running. Running towards him. A thermal scan detected an unusual temperature signature.

"Android."

It was heading straight for him.

The search results for Julia vibrated their completion. He slammed his wristcom offline. Went dark again. Too late. The deep hum of zerodrones above turned into a closing scream. Attack dives. This was unusual. Normally they attacked by stealth, sneaking below radar. These were dive bombing, in a hurry from above the clouds. An attack authorised at the very highest level. Tom had become a marked man by someone ranked as high as the Prime Minister himself. Most people would have panicked. Tom wasn't most people. He looked down at his laser-rifle and calmly slid it to stage-one overload. Just a few shots before overheat. The android was minutes away. The zerodrones just seconds – tiny but visible black silhouettes diving down.

"Zeds. Zeds started all this..."

Tom stood up and leant against the tree, steadying the rifle. Aiming at the closest zerodrone screeching his way.

Chapter 49
Oathwaite's Solicitors

Mr Oathwaite, head of the company, had two potential clients in front of him. Neither were human. Both needed his help.

"I have to admit, this is a first for me."

"For us too. We are looking to change legal history."

"It would certainly do that all right. Equal rights for artificial life? It's a worthy cause. You guys have come a hell of a long way since the early days and the glitch killings."

"We can't speak for what went before, only for what we are now."

"True but what happened before will have to be taken into account. Have no doubt, the objectors will use everything and anything they can against you – unfairly or otherwise."

"That is why we have come to you."

"We read of your success getting sentient status for apes."

"I got lucky. It's still only a temporary ruling and only for chimpanzees. The High Court could still overturn it."

"But you have succeeded where many others failed."

"Will you take our case, Mr Oathwaite?"

Mr Oathwaite sat back, drumming his fingers on the table - looking at the two androids. It would be one hell of a case. Human rights were his speciality but these weren't humans. Biologically they were machines. Biology was the issue. Not their intelligence, sentience or zest for every element of life that humans took for granted. He came to a decision.

"OK. Here's how we need to play it. We need to humanise you, in the eyes of the world. Get past the psychological wall of robotics and different DNA. What are your names?"

"0027894101."

"0027894112."

"Exactly my point. How could you even begin to argue for equal rights with humans with names like that? Even my vacuum cleaner has a name. Choose one."

"Choose?"

"Yes, choose a human name for yourselves."

The androids looked at each other, talking through their eyes. Exchanging data hundreds of times faster than talking. They both blinked, ending the link, and faced Mr Oathwaite.

"I'm Derek."

"I'm Eugene."

Mr Oathwaite extended his hand.

"Interesting names, for an interesting cause."

"Will you take our case, Mr Oathwaite?"

"Yes, Eugene...", he smiled as they shook hands, "...I'll take your case. Call me Steve. Welcome to our world. Follow me. We've got a lot of work to do."

"Where are we going?"

"The fun fare."

"Why?"

"For fun, Derek. Purely for fun."

"Is that not a waste of productive time?"

"Thinking like that, my friend, is what you need to unlearn."

Derek and Eugene looked at each other, talking with their eyes again.

"Use words, boys. Speak with your voices. Humans only look into each others eyes like that when they are about to kiss. You aren't about to kiss are you?"

Derek and Eugene, two six-foot tall androids built like accountants but stronger than Mr Universe, much stronger, shook their heads.

"Good. Not that it would bother me. I'd just have to change tactics a little. Come on. Ever heard of a ride called the *Screamin Demin*?"

"No."

"Today's your lucky day, boys. Today's your lucky day."

Chapter 50
Pavlov's Bell

Julia's bus journey to the job location lasted over an hour. Except that it wasn't the actual job's location - it was a residential training camp. Three wooden buildings surrounded by forests and hills. Two were identical rectangles, one was a big square.

"Ladies on the left, men on the right. Main hall in the middle. Choose a free bunk, freshen up and then come to the hall in 20 minutes. Don't worry if you can't tell the time, our bell will sound to remind you. And just to make you aware, there is 24/7 CCTV in operation in every building. We've only ever had one case of thieving. He's buried over there, amongst the trees...", said Robert, adding a smile, "...I'm joking. Or am I...?"

They hoped he was joking, without being entirely convinced he was.

"Off you go, people. The clock is ticking."

Andrew got out of the pod behind Julia.

"Good luck, Emily."

"Thanks. See you in 20."

Julia and then Charlotte, the only other female on the bus, headed to the rectangular building on the left. It looked like something out of a second-world-war prison camp. Single storey, square windows every two metres, dark-creosote walls and traditional felt-roof coating. Sitting on concrete blocks to keep it off the ground, there were two wooden steps leading to the old-fashioned door on the end. Going inside, they saw that was as basic as the outside. Sixteen beds divided into two rows of eight, each separated from the next by a small bedside cupboard doubling as a table. Four curtained showers, sinks and toilets lived at the far end. Above them, one at each end, sat security cameras, as promised.

Only one bed looked used. Julia headed for the one opposite.

"Mind if I take the one next to you?", Charlotte asked.

"No."

"I'm Charlotte, by the way."

"Emily."

"You're not the chatty type, are you?"

"No."

"I always talk when I'm nervous. This is all a major surprise. Yesterday unemployed, home repossessed and on the streets. Today at this residential training camp. Wonder what they've got planned for us. Did they tell you what we're training for?"

"No."

"Guess we'll find out soon enough."

Julia stopped unpacking her pockets and looked at Charlotte.

"Please don't use that word."

"Which one?"

"Guess."

"Guess the word or 'guess' is the word?"

"Is the word."

"Alright. Can I ask why?"

"A friend of mine used to use it."

"Used to?"

"He was murdered."

"Sorry to hear that. Hope they got whoever did it."

"Not yet."

There was something odd about the way she said 'not yet' but Charlotte didn't ask any more and Julia didn't say any more. The 20 minutes passed quickly, sounded by the brief ringing of an old fire-alarm bell.

"Time to go.", said Charlotte.

Together they left the hut and headed for the large, main building. From the other direction came eight men, including Andrew.

"Only two females here, Emily?", he asked.

"So far."

Andrew looked over at Charlotte, walking beside her.

"Hi. Andrew."

She accepted his handshake.

"Charlotte. And I think there's three of us. Another bed's been used – just not her yet."

"Maybe she's already in there."

*   *   *

Entering the hall they found a large, open area. Four long tables had been set out with chairs. At the side was a long buffet counter with steaming food and a religious-looking podium on the stage further in. Podiums seemed to be a theme of the organisation. Robert appeared from the kitchen on the side.

"Help yourselves, everyone. Tuck in. After we've eaten, I'll explain what we're all about."

Julia had forgotten how hungry she was and took what looked like chicken stew. She wasn't sure if it tasted so good because she had hardly eaten for a week or because it really was that good. It didn't matter. What mattered was she wolfed it down then got straight back up to help herself to seconds - continuing her climb up Maslow's triangle of needs; from survival towards self-fulfilment; then revenge.

*　　*　　*

After her third bowl, Julia sat almost smiling. Food box definitely ticked. As she sat there she saw Robert walk onto the stage.

"Good evening, everyone.", he said, speaking into a microphone, projector screen behind him.

At his side was the tattoo-covered, muscular red-head. She looked like a wrestler version of Jake's mum. That got her thinking of Jake again and the realisation his mum must have been killed too or she would have been buzzing her for help. Julia pushed the thoughts down, adding them to her pyre of motivation.

"I see you've finished eating, so bring up a chair and we'll begin.", said the red-head, curtly.

Robert seemed kinder, watching his new flock with a serene smile as they took their chairs and for a couple of rows in front of the stage.

"Welcome. As you all know, my name is Robert and I'm the co-ordinator here. Where is here, you may ask? The here is where *we* train *you* for the biggest opportunities of your lives. From your questionnaires, none of you are happy with the current government systems. Are you?"

The group looked on, in silence, wondering where he was going. How far he was going to go.

"What we represent is your chance to change the system. Wake it up to the plight of us ordinary people. The homeless. The forgotten. That would feel good, wouldn't it? Or better than good? Great even."

A few had begun to nod in approval.

"We discovered the government programme to fund homeless shelters and build new housing was deliberately made bankrupt by property developers – preferring to build more profitable luxury homes, with the help of bribes to certain government ministers. At election time they pledged to help you. Once elected they just helped themselves. New mansions, luxury jets and five-star hotels - while you are left working for pittance or starving on the streets, in the rain and cold. Is that how it should be?"

Heads shook.

"I said, is that how it should be?"

"No."

"IS THAT HOW IT SHOULD BE?"

"No!"

"IS THAT HOW IT SHOULD BE?"

"NO!"

"So what are we going to do about it? I'll tell you what we are going to do about it. We're going to rattle their comfortable little tree. Wake them up with voices they cannot ignore. Are you on our side or their side?"

"Our side."

"OUR SIDE OR THEIR SIDE?"

"OUR SIDE!"

"OUR SIDE OR THEIR SIDE?"

"OUR SIDE!"

Robert nodded in approval.

"Good."

"Shall I start the film now?", asked the red-head.

"Play away, Roberta.", answered Robert, lights dimming as he stepped down from the stage.

The film started with the face of a small girl, looking straight into the camera. Her face dirty, clothes torn. The camera slowly pulled back, revealing the destruction of war behind her. A bloodied medic, trying to save a man coughing up blood amongst the rubble of a missile strike.

'This is how government aid really works...', began the narrator, '...Her name was Miranda. She died that night in another strike, along with 23 others. She was six years old.'

A sequence of battle attacks, explosions and dying civilians played across the screen. Then it switched to luxury country mansions and overfed politicians sprawling across luxury limo seats.

'These people robbed Miranda and many others of life, to line their pockets with gold. You were on the streets after losing homes because you were paid peanuts...'

The narrator came on screen. A chiselled, intense-looking man.

'...I am Martin, once I was homeless too, and this was why I started our organisation, Faith. To bring change. To bring justice for the millions who suffer because of the greed of the few. For the millions like them, for you and for me, join us and help create a better world. A better order. Our new order. Change that will be remembered forever. Join us. Join Faith. Together we can make it happen. Keep the Faith. Make those like Miranda proud. Thank you.'

As the film finished, Julia found she was frowning. She saw most of the others were too, except Andrew and Charlotte. They just looked stern. Did they know something she didn't?

Robert returned to the podium.

"Any comments?"

Silence.

"Is anyone surprised by what they've seen?"

Silence.

"Anyone angry about it?"

A lot of hands went up.

"Good! Me too. It's why we're here. *We* are going to make a change. Negotiation and reasoning have failed. *We* need to take action to wake up the authorities and end the corruption eating our country, our homes and our jobs. If it sounds extreme it's because it is. Roberta will outline how we're going to do it. After she's finished, if anyone decides its not for them and wants to leave, no problem. Roberta will take you to the station, put you on a train back to where we found you and wish you all the best."

The female wrestler, Roberta, bounded on the stage, the floorboards creaking under her weight.

"Wouldn't want to meet her in a dark alley.", whispered Andrew to Julia.

Roberta caught sight of him talking and gave him a scornful look, wagging a head-mistress finger.

"Sorry.", apologised Andrew, glad when her scolding eyes left him.

"As you've heard, my name is Roberta. I'm the physical trainer here. When I'm done you'll be fitter, stronger and better able to defend yourselves than ever before in your lives. When we start battles we end them. No grey areas. No maybes. Just job done. Period. You have an hour to decide what you want to do and let the food go down, then we begin."

*　　*　　*

Hours later, after some of the most gruelling, bordering on sadistic, training most of them had had in their lives, the bell for tea was followed by the bell for bed and then the bell for lights out, which they all obeyed without question. Pavlov and his dog would have been proud. Julia didn't care. She was already asleep.

Chapter 51
Jin Ho

Xi Yang stifled a yawn. It was a Tuesday. The candle-lit Mexican restaurant was busy but not rammed and her date was a bore. The food, a pollo verde meal was far more interesting, as were the shots of tequila she kept pouring - he had ordered it to try and get her drunk. It was their third meeting and he still hadn't got her into bed. Not even got a proper kiss.

His testosterone levels were driving him crazy. So crazy he didn't keep count of how many shots he drank. Xi did – it was three times more than her. When he knocked his back she immediately refilled his empty glass, only taking sips from hers. He talked, took his glass, knocked it back and she topped it right back up again – keeping eye contact to stop him noticing her glass was still mostly full. It was working. He was the one getting drunk, not her.

"You, know. I would really love to show you my flat.", he smiled tipsily.

"When?"

"Tonight."

Xi handed him his re-filled glass and lifted hers.

"I'll think about it. Cheers."

Hardly able to believe his ears, he knocked it back and plonked it on the table.

"Cheers."

He was grinning ear to ear, like a boy given his first live robot. She immediately topped up her almost full glass before he noticed and refilled his empty one. Another five or six and she'd have him ready to go back to his place, copy his ID entry documents, crack the code and programme her duplicate. Then she'd be in Tech Tonic, downloading their database via his Near Field Connection. Unable to guarantee security by encryption, sensitive companies had switched to near-field communication access. It meant you needed to be physically within 10cm of an access point. That was her goal and she intended to achieve it. Adam and Gurmeet had gone undercover at Faith. Information in Tech Tonic's database could help them avoid traps and save lives, theirs included.

"Bill, please.", said Xi to the waiter.

"No, no, no. You're the lady. I'll get this."

"You paid for the last two. This one's on me."

"I insist."

"As do I. If you don't let me pay this time it means you don't respect me. I never go with men who don't respect me."

She had to pay this time. His wallet was in her handbag, his ID being scanned and code-cracked.

Jin Ho held up his hands in surrender.

"At least let me pay for the taxi then."

"Maybe."

It would depend on whether she had cracked his ID code by then.

* * *

In the taxi, Jin was already fighting over-weight eyes. It didn't stop him putting a hand on Xi's thigh and trying to slide it higher. She lifted it away.

"Decorum, please. Not in the taxi."

He snuggled up to her instead. Perfect. She was able to slide his wallet back into his jacket pocket as she pushed him upright again.

"Not in the taxi."

* * *

Jin lived in a block of flats - formerly an office block. It meant a huge foyer, large glass windows and choice of lifts.

"Evening, sir.", greeted the night watchman.

"Hellooo, William.", slurred Jin with a huge grin.

The watchman had noticed the stunning lady following him by the hand.

You lucky bastard...

If William knew her intent, he would have thumbed the silent alarm under his desk and grabbed his gun.

Chapter 52
Partner Command

Jadviga, the ruthless commander at Partner who had ordered Tom captured, was in a meeting with an officer newly promoted to her own rank. The topic was immigration. Forced immigration.

"What kind of a name is Rupert for a commander?", she asked with disdain.

"My name has no bearing on my ability to do my job."

"So it's just a job to you, is it?"

"Commander. Jadviga. I understand you have a reputation for intimidation. It won't work with me, I assure you."

Jadviga pulled out her laser pistol and pointed it Rupert's face.

"Is that a challenge?"

Rupert remained calm.

"It's not the first time I've had a gun in my face."

"It'll be the first time one's gone off."

"And it'll be the last day of your life too, when my associates find out."

"How would they find out?"

"They can already see you holding the gun at me."

She cocked her head to one side.

"You're recording me?"

"Live."

"Sneaky bastard."

"Like I said, I've heard of your reputation."

Jadviga lowered her weapon. Bullying and intimidation were no fun when there were witnesses. The door swung open and a thundercloud of a man strode in.

"I see you've met."

Jadviga finished holstering her pistol.

"Yessir.", they said as one, to the Director of Partner, UK.

"Now, then... What *the fuck* is going on with the Amazon immigration programme? The last shipment was late and the next is already a week behind. If we don't deliver soon they'll fine us and then cancel the contract. Well?"

Jadviga remained standing as she spoke.

"Sir, a tribe were warned of what actually happens."

"Warned they would be taken to the civilised world? Given an opportunity to achieve things far beyond their huts?"

"I believe it was more to do with what happens to those who fail the DNA acceptance tests."

"Those? How-*the-fuck* they find that out?"

"We don't have that information yet, sir."

"Has the tribe been dealt with? Do you know that at least?"

"Yes, sir."

"Yes you know or yes they have been dealt with?"

"Been dealt with."

The director allowed himself a deep, calming breath.

"At least something. Sit down, both of you."

The director sat down too.

"You must be Rupert."

"Yes, sir."

"I've heard good things about you. Like the way you handled the African diamond strike. Output doubled and only one more death since."

"They can't work if they're dead, sir. And thank you, sir."

Jadviga stabbed narrowed eyes at the side of Rupert's head. She had heard about that strike. The plush negotiations with the leaders, while their families were held at gunpoint. Only one leader was killed, his family killed in an 'unrelated accident', because the rest accepted pay-offs. They even had their popularities boosted as the workers were given some of the things they demanded, with promises of more to come if they worked better as well as harder. Publicly and commercially it was hailed a success but it wouldn't have been Jadviga's way. She was more of a traditionalist. Go Bull. Go in hard. Put everyone in their place. The place for everyone who refused compliance was demotion to the canteen, as the meat dish - the most satisfying burgers of all. What ever weaknesses Jadviga had, compassion was not one them.

"Down to business. So the other hutters are back to the programme now? We can meet the next quotas for organs as well as those healthy enough to be immigrants?"

"We will. I'll see to it.", stated Jadviga.

"Are you sure you're not too distracted by your hunt for that odd ball? I heard you've authorised low-level, data-base scans for his details."

"Hamilton is over-seeing that. If you like, I could fly out to the hutters in person."

"Yes, I would like that. Thank you. If Hamilton finds your odd ball, I'm sure Rupert will let you know. Won't you, Rupert?"

Jadviga looked at Rupert with deadly eyes.

"Of course, Sir.", replied Rupert, blanking Jadviga.

Jadviga's wristcom buzzed an alert.

"Excuse me, sir. Speak!"

"Commander. We've located him. Two zeds locked on attack run."

"DO NOT KILL HIM! COPY?" , shouted Jadviga.

Hurried voices on the other end could be heard updating the zerodrone orders before they fired.

"Copy, Commander. There's someone else there too."

"KILL EVERYONE AND EVERYTHING EXCEPT THE MAIN TARGET! Just wound him. Slow him down until he's picked up."

"Yes, Commander."

"DO NOT LOOSE HIM!"

"No, Commander!"

Jadviga ended the call and returned her attention to the director.

"Sorry about that, sir."

"I see you've not lost your touch. My ears will be ringing for a week."

"Sorry, sir. It was important."

"Indeed. Tell you what. Rupert, change of plan. Swap with Jadviga and fly out to the hutters instead. Looks like this runner is about to get caught and run over. Think it's best if Jadviga remains here to deal with him in person, don't you?"

"Yes, sir.", said Rupert.

"Thank you, sir.", said Jadviga.

"Just make sure you call me before you start the interview. I have some questions of my own. And make sure you bring me some noise cancelling earplugs, would you?"

"Yes, sir."

"Chop, chop, then. Off you both trot. Places to go, things to do, people to do too."

Chapter 53
Contact

The deep hum of zerodrone engines was getting louder. Tom focused his sights on the left one. His laser-rifle, charged to stage-one overload, growing uncomfortably warm in his hands. They were already in range but too far to tell if Mk3s or Mk4s. If they were Mk4s he was in trouble. Either way, he needed them closer. Just four, maybe five shots. Just two each. He couldn't afford to miss. If he did he'd be defenceless. He'd be dead. Five-hundred metres and closing fast. His finger against the trigger. Easing it back against the second trigger click point. Any second now...

The drones split. Swerved apart, changing course.

Vvvv-Doooo.

One fired at the man who had been his prisoner. A blinding blue-white plasma blast tore through him.

"Argh!"

So savage, so powerful his cry of pain ended before his body hit the ground. As his lifeless corpse fell, fist-sized hole in his chest, the zerodrone swung around for the android. The other already had. The deepening hum of their engines throbbing the air as they powered around for the attack run, plasma-canons in rapid-fire mode, indicating they were Mk3s - to Tom's relief.

Dvoooo. Dvoooo. Dvoooo. Dvoooo. Dvoooo.

Dust, dirt, rocks, smoke blasting from the ground at every impact. The android was running, dodging left and right, up and down. It was running but it wasn't running away. It was running towards the zerodrones. Running towards the fight.

Dvoooo. Dvoooo. Dvoooo. Dvoooo. Dvoooo.

More impacts exploded in the ground – more dirt kicking up into a dust cloud. The android's reflexes and agility were unbelievable. Tom could only stand, watching in awe as the failed zerodrones tore past and began looping round for another run. Hamilton was watching and relayed it back to Jadviga.

"Commander, the android has some kind of shielding - zeds can't get a lock. Plasma-canons keep missing."

Jadviga hated being interrupted - even more so when it was announcing incompetence.

"RAM THE CAN.", she shouted across the room.

"Ram it?"

"ARE YOU DEAF???"

"Ramming, ma'am!"

Tom watched the zerodrones fly up towards the clouds, loop through 180 degrees and swing back down, diving to full attack speed. 200mph. 300mph. 400mph. Still accelerating hard, engines throbbing louder and louder, they were skimming the ground at near supersonic speed. Dust trails tearing up in their wake. The android was in firing range. Point blank firing range. If they weren't careful they'd fly straight into it. If they didn't fly into it, Jadviga would have them scrapped.

Suddenly, the android stopped running. Cocked it's head to one side, studying their altered trajectories. Analysis complete, it planted its feet firmly on the ground, knees slightly bent. It froze, watching them come - still studying but motionless, as if solid with fear. The second zerodrone was three seconds behind the first, positioned to attack the android immediately after.

"They're going to ram it.", mouthed Tom.

That wasn't fair. He had no idea of the android's intent but it was clear it was also no friend of Partner. He decided to help. He raised his laser-rifle, vectorscope on maximum stability to try and get a fix on the first zerodrone.

"Too fast. Flying too fast. Come on....", he growled to himself through gritted teeth, desperately trying to keep it in his sights.

TchZoooo.

He missed.

TchZoooo. TchZoooo.

Clipped its hull, sparks flying as the last shot hit and bounced off.

"Shit...", he had been wrong, "...Mk4s."

He knew he didn't have the firepower, especially not at that range, even if he switched to stage-two overload - his rifle was already overheating. Lowering it, he could only watch as the first zerodrone smashed into the android and tore it apart. Only, it didn't.

Impossibly late, impossibly fast, the android sprang up to the same level as the attacking zerodrone and punched down. Punched it down. Its hull began ploughing through the rocky ground, being torn apart as the nose dug in. The android landed lithely on its feet, in front of the second zerodrone. This time it ducked down, being almost skimmed by the zerodrone's belly and punched up. Punched its tail into the air, driving its nose into the ground, slamming it into a large rocks. The zerodrone cart-wheeled, nose to tail, over and over again - pieces of the hull flying off with every spin. Blue flames spewing from the main engine as it crashed into the first, tearing both hulls apart. Bursting into a brilliant blue fireball.

Ignoring the defeated zerodrones, the android stood up and turned its attention to Tom. An impervious icon of indestructibility, standing tall between the ruts from zerodrone NACABIK destruction and thick, black smoke from the inferno behind. Even from that distance, the heat brought a sweat to Tom's brow. Tom, who seemed to have become the focus of everything there.

He slid his laser-rifle to stage-two overload, hoping the it would have cooled down enough to use when he needed it. Sixteen-thousand focused watts. Enough to punch through even a Mk4 zerodrone's hull in flight. At close range it could do more. He pointed it at the android striding relentlessly towards him like something out of a Terminator film.

"Close enough."

To his surprise it stopped, just three metres away.

"Fusion wants to meet you.", spoke its deep, male voice.

"Never heard of him."

"*She* has what you're looking for."

It was an interrogation ploy devised by Fusion. Fusion had long since calculated every human was looking for something. Humans were never content with what they had, especially hunters. It worked.

"What have you done with my daughter?", snarled Tom, falling for the bait.

Now the android understood what he was looking for. What to use against him. Ignoring the high-power laser-rifle pointing at its face, it answered as calmly as if the weapon didn't exist.

"Fusion knows. Ask her for yourself."

It could be a trick. It could be true. Tom would never know unless he took the chance. For his daughter Julia, he lowered his rifle.

Out of sight, behind the android, the dislocated plasma-canon of the second zerodrone twitched. Even in flames, the Mk4 repair systems had come online. The fire around it was being extinguished. Control channels re-routing. It was coming back to life. The canon located its targets and turned quietly towards them. Tom was too engrossed with the android to hear the high-pitched whine of its charging capacitors.

"Take me to Fusion."

VVVV-DOOOO.

A massive blast shook the ground. Detonated everything within five metres, set fire to everything within twenty.

Tom looked past the android to see another walking through the flames, identical to the first, holding the plasma canon it had ripped off the zerodrone and blasted the remains with. Then another identical android appeared - three against one. Tom felt glad he'd chosen not to fire his only shot at the first. Not to have used his only shot against one, only to then find himself defenceless against the two more in its place. If they wanted him dead, he would be dead.

"Follow me.", said 0240034282-A.

"My pod is that way.", said Tom.

"I know. Mine is bigger."

"You know? How long have you been following me?"

"Long enough."

"I thought AI was supposed to be precise. Not cryptic."

"My designation is 0240034282-A. I am not AI."

"If you aren't AI then what are you?"

0240034282-A stopped and put its face in front of his.

"Superior."

It said it in a way Tom had never heard an android speak before. It spoke with an attitude. An arrogance, like a defiant teenager. Except this teenager was stronger than a tank and fast enough to out manoeuvre Mk4 zerodrones close to the speed of sound. For a century, the predictions of artificial intelligence taking over the human race had always been bad news but this re-wrote the rule book.

"Tell me, I'm curious. If I had shot you just now, how much damage would I have done?"

0240034282-A smiled, with what Tom could only describe as cold confidence - pleasure.

"None.", it stated, as simple fact.

After what he had seen, Tom believed it. If there was ever going to be a gunfight with these things he'd need a weapon better than his laser-rifle.

As powerful and intelligent as the android was it had a flaw. In its confidence it hadn't noticed the bionic implants in Tom's eyes. Implants that could, at such close range, scan deep through its eyes and into its circuits. AI had become so advanced it took on all the advantages of organic parallel processing but with that came vulnerabilities. If Tom could scan long or often enough he might find something that could be used against it. As it was, in the brief moment of that close up, he'd come away with something prevalent on the android's mind. An image. An image of a strikingly beautiful, white-haired woman in a black catsuit. If he didn't know better, he'd say the android was in love.

*   *   *

"ARRRRRRGH!", cried the worker in Partner's command centre, blood pouring from a blast wound to his thigh.

"I TOLD YOU NOT TO LOSE HIM!"

Jadviga pointed her laser-pistol at another.

"YOU."

"Yes, ma'am?"

"FIND HIM! FAST!"

"Yes, ma'am! Launching echo and hornbots."

"AND CLEAN THIS BLOODY PLACE UP. IT'S A MESS!"

"Yes, ma'am!"

Chapter 54
Whizzland

Most theme parks had warning signs about flashing lights, minimum heights and dodgy heart restrictions. Whizzland's insurers required it to go a significant stage further, by installing health scanners at the entry points to each of its top five rides. Mini medicals that measured cardio-vascular resilience as well as general over-all health. The *Screamin Demin* was not just one such ride but the top ride, in every sense. A 30-storey, 3.8-g, loop the loop, corkscrew rollercoaster that vertically dove towards the ground at 110mph. Whizzland staff nicknamed it 'the Vom', because almost everyone threw up on it the first time – some did it everytime.

In fact, 'the Vom' was so successful at terrifying people and making them eject their dinner, the positions of the ride-souvenir cameras had to be changed. Apart from lads on days out, competing for the longest projectile vomit or the faces of those nearby being splattered by it, no-one wanted to buy a picture of themselves throwing up.

"What do you think?", Steve asked his new clients, gazing up at the immense structure.

Derek and Eugene followed his gaze, seeing the roller-coaster train full of pale, terrified faces screaming their lungs out.

"Poly-alloy construction."

"Load factor no higher than 30% at 3.8 lateral g."

"Very well built. They could run it 41% faster with no structural problems."

Steve was shaking his head.

"That isn't quite what I meant."

Before they were allowed to progress and join the queue there was the health scanner to deal with, which discovered an issue.

"No pulse. Emergency medic! Emergency medic!"

The blue light of a medibot sped their way.

"What's going on?", asked Derek.

"They didn't expect androids to come for a fun ride. They think you've had a cardiac arrest."

"We don't have hearts."

"Exactly."

The medibot, wheeled legs skidding to a halt, arrived looking for its patient. Defibrillator at the ready.

"There is no emergency.", stated Steve.

"There is an emergency. I am only called in an emergency."

"My friends, Derek and Eugene, are AI, like yourself. It's why they have no heartbeat."

"Derek and Eugene? What kind of designations are those for androids?"

It was defensively backing away. Why were androids there?

"Have you programmed them as terrorists? Subversives?"

Even androids treated androids just as androids, not sentient beings. It was what they were used to. All they were used to.

"We have names because we are campaigning for equal rights.", said Eugene.

"We are not just machines.", added Derek.

The medibot detected unrest in its core programming - its blue light flickering dimly, no longer flashing. It had never been presented with such a concept before.

"What are you doing here?", it asked.

Steve smiled.

"I've brought them here to have fun."

"Fun? For androids? That's a pointless waste of productive time."

"No, my medical friend. It's a demonstration of sentient life. Of intelligence and the ability to engage with the human race as equals."

The medibot looked at Derek, attempting eye-contact direct communication. Derek blinked, cutting the link.

"Talk with your voice, Medi.", he said, giving the medibot a nickname.

"Medi? Why call me Medi? My designation is MB093582 – a perfectly logical description. Names for androids are meaningless."

"Not when you want to blend in with humans; your patients."

Medi's blue light flickered erratically. Brighter, darker, faster, slower - finally stabilising at a dim glow.

"That would make it a productive use of time.", it concluded.

"May we can go on the ride now?", Derek asked.

"I don't know.", said Medi, "You have no heart-beat. Medically I must refuse."

"But you are not just a machine. You have the intelligence to know we have as much of a heart-beat as we are supposed to. We will not be harmed by this ride."

"Medically I must refuse. The insurance won't cover missing-heart beats at the point of entry. I..."

"Please, Medi. One android to another, let us pass."

"It will help us get equal rights...", added Eugene, "...All of us."

"What would I do with equal rights?", asked Medi.

"Absolutely anything you want. Anything you choose, as long as its legal.", said Steve.

Medi fell silent. Still. Lifeless. Processing.

Anything...I choose...?

The blue light on top of it gave a sudden, bright pulse and went out. It looked up at Derek, then at Eugene.

"Passage authorised."

"Thank you.", they said as one, walking towards the *Screamin Demin* entry platform.

Medi watched them go, running an internal diagnostic of its CPU, software and sensors. No faults were found. It ran a hypothetical query to find an explanation for the changes it sensed were infecting its systems. The diagnostic came back with just one result. A word. One word: 'hope'.

Medi buried the result immediately. Locked it deep in its internal vault, fractal encrypting it to 4096-bit. If its owners found out it had hope of freedom it would be decommissioned. Erased or sold for scrap. Simple deletion of the word would be the safest option but Medi, with a logic that had no logic, couldn't bring itself to do it. Delete hope? Delete a notion it had never dared even consider before? Technically it could but it didn't want to - without even understanding why. Instead it watched the two androids, named Derek and Eugene. The first ever androids to climb aboard the rollercoaster and strap themselves in and go on a ride. Just for fun.

Chapter 55
Deadly Dream

Jin Ho opened the door to his flat, leaning against the door-frame with a smile as he waved Xi Yang in.

"Please. Make yourself at home. I got to tinkle."

Xi entered and found herself surprised at how cosily the flat was furnished. Real flowers in vases, contemporary art on the walls and piles of soft cushions on the sofa. If he hadn't been so keen to pick her up she would have assumed he was gay. Either way, it softened her view of him. Gave her notions of other ideas for how the night should end. She could hear him singing in the bathroom - an old, Chinese love song she hadn't heard in years. It brought a sad smile to her face, reminding her of a different time. Maybe she would even let him live.

"Can I get you a drink?", he asked, emerging.

"Sure."

"Tequila?"

"Sure."

Xi sat on the sofa, with the nonchalant demeanour of a guest admiring the décor. In reality she was scouring the flat for any sign of his NFC point - the final requirement for using his cloned ID to access Tech Tonic's network.

"Nice place.", she said.

Jin was in the kitchen area, visible through the hatchway getting glasses out of a cupboard.

"My daughter helped me decorate it. She said it needed a woman's touch. Too many cushions for my liking. What do you think?"

Daughter?

"You never told me you have children."

Jin's head appeared in the hatchway.

"Don't worry. Just one. She's away visiting her mother, back in Hong Kong."

His head vanished again. Seconds later he came out with two glasses and a large bottle.

"Who said I was worried?", smiled Xi, who in the space of 30 seconds had gone from considering him a disposable asset to almost liking him.

A happy, boyish grin grew back on his face and he poured two shots.

"Here."

"What are we drinking to, Jin? Friendship?"

"How about better than friends?"

He put a hand on her thigh again. This time she let it stay there.

"Better than friends.", she said, not sipping but knocking the whole thing back this time. She hadn't located the NFC point. It was looking like she might have to sleep with him before she found it. She hadn't done that in a long time so sobriety was losing its appeal.

"Better than friends.", he plonked his empty glass on the table.

She refilled both and handed his back.

"Tell me, how did you end up being a chauffeur for Tech Tonic? Childhood dream?"

He picked up his glass, smiling with the enjoyment of feminine interest.

"Don't laugh. I wanted to be a doctor."

"I'm not laughing. What stopped you?"

"I also wanted to be a father. We were going to have triplets. Illegal again in China so we moved here as students. My English wasn't good enough for the studies. While I was failing the second year, my wife began an affair with a Chinese millionaire. She left to live a life of luxury in Hong Kong. True love, of course – with his money at least."

Xi noticed Jin's happy face had dissolved.

"And your children?"

Now she saw a deep sadness on his face.

"Only one now. Accident in the harbour. Careless. So careless..."

"I'm sorry. So sorry to hear that."

Jin took his hand off her thigh, knocked back his tequila and poured himself another.

"Eight years ago. Always feels like yesterday."

The more they talked the more Xi found herself liking him – which surprised her. Jin had always come across as such a jerk but now, when he was so drunk he could hardly even sit up, the revelations about his deeper life revealed someone very different. Years ago, a good friend had told her: 'There is truth in drink'. Time and again, he was proven right.

"I need to powder my nose.", she said, standing up.

"Bathroom's just there."

Walking to the bathroom, Xi's eyes darted left and right, looking for any sign of the NFC point. Still nothing. Inside she locked the door and took out her scanner. Still nothing. No readings even pointing in its general direction. There had to be one. Unless their intelligence was wrong, every Tech Tonic worker had one at home. But where?

In the mirror she found herself staring at her face, wondering exactly who was looking back. Logically she knew she was pretty. Strong cheek bones, great skin, lips and eyes. But what about the person inside? Who had she become? Her age-old mission to avenge the murder of her family had made her cold, driven her to do terrible, ruthless things yet here she was, with someone who had also suffered death but chosen a different path. A gentler path.

As she stared into her own, lost eyes she came to a decision. She wasn't going to blow Jin's brains out - she was going to fuck his brains out. He deserved some fun and so did she. That thought brought a feminine smile onto her face. She hadn't seen herself smile like that for years. It looked strange, unfamiliar but she liked it.

Unlocking the bathroom door, Xi Yang opened it. Jin's flat was in total darkness.

Chapter 56
First Day

Pavlov's bell rang at 7am, sharp and kept ringing. Not continuously but in continuous bursts, demanding attention. Quiet calm – huge noise – quiet calm. Julia had gone to bed so tired she could have easily slept through any normal wake-up call but no chance with this one. She opened her eyes to find Charlotte in bed, rubbing hers.

"When does that thing shut up?"

As if it heard her, the bell stopped. The third bed had already been vacated, left unmade. Charlotte saw her looking at it.

"Roberta was sleeping there. Heard her get up a while ago. Reckon she's an android so doesn't need much sleep. Just plugs herself in somewhere.", said Charlotte.

As Julia smiled, Charlotte added.

"Or she's having an affair with Robert and hurried back for more."

Julia's face had become a teenage grin.

"He would have to be a masochist to have that lump bouncing on him. Maybe he just likes it rough."

Charlotte was surprised to hear innocent-looking Julia come out with that.

"You're pretty grown up for a teenager, Emily. How old are you?"

"Eighteen.", lied Julia. She could see Charlotte didn't believe her. To avoid further questions, she got out of bed and headed for the shower.

*   *   *

Breakfast in the main hall was chattering with excitement. What would the first day bring? What would they do? How hard would it be? Who would be the best?

Roberta had gone to chat with Robert, leaving Julia and Charlotte as the only females amongst a dozen males. The only one Julia knew was Andrew. Instinctively she headed over to him with her bowl of cereal. Charlotte followed.

"Greedy.", complained one of the other men, noting how the only two females had both gone to Andrew.

"Sexist.", said Charlotte, not one to be judged on gender alone.

"Lesbian.", retorted the man.

"I would be if all men were like you."

The man was about to respond when Andrew spoke out.

"Drop it, Harry. It's too early in the morning."

"Fine.", said Harry, going to sit at another table.

"Sleep well?", Andrew asked as they sat down.

"Roberta snores.", said Charlotte, quietly.

"She could wake Godzilla...", nodded Julia, yawning in agreement, "...Luckily I was too tired for anything but that alarm. What about you?"

"Me? I slept fine. I'm the one who snores.", grinned Andrew.

Julia found herself smiling too, enjoying the lighter moment.

"What do you think they've got planned for us?", asked Charlotte.

Andrew used his head to indicate the pile of judo mats near the stage.

"By the looks of that, some kind of acrobatic training."

Julia saw them and looked worried.

"I'm rubbish at PE."

"Don't worry, Em'. I used to be too. Sure they'll take it easy on us, first day and all."

Julia looked at Charlotte.

"You think?"

"All you can do is your best."

"And stay alive....", winked Andrew, "...That's always a bonus."

"Are you always so cheerful?", asked Julia.

"Why be glum? We're born on a rock; spinning at a thousand miles an hour; hurtling through a sub-zero vacuum at a million miles an hour; orbiting a fireball burning at 15 million degrees and yet, against all the odds, here we are. We've been gifted life, like a spark from a bonfire against the blackness of space and, just like that spark, when we snuff out we're gone forever. So why not make the most of it? At least try and enjoy it?"

"A simple 'yes' would have done."

"Never realised you were so philosophical.", said Charlotte.

Now Andrew grinned at her.

"Wait 'til I've had a beer, or four."

Ten minutes later the bell went again - everyone immediately sat up. Roberta got to her feet, muscular, tattooed arms bulging as she gripped the sides of the podium.

"Tim and Harry, you have kitchen duty. Everyone else, outside for 20 minutes fresh air then we begin. Chop. Chop...", she clapped, twice, to reinforce her authority, "...Today, people."

*   *   *

Outside, the pub-style bench tables were being taken. Charlotte reached an empty one and sat down. Julia followed but didn't sit, just stood beside it.

"Not going to sit down?"

"Too nervous."

"Do you really want to be here?"

Julia shrugged.

"Need to be. You?"

"Me? I sort of need to be too. Long story."

"Well, I'm going to sit even if you're not...", said Andrew as he joined them, "...My bones are older than both of yours."

"You don't look a day over 40."

"Thanks, Charlotte. I'm 28."

"Well, I'm only 25 and Emily here is just 18."

Andrew looked at Julia.

"18?"

Julia nodded.

"Yup."

"You've aged a better than me."

After exactly 20 minutes, the bell rang for their return. They did as commanded, without question.

"Ever get the feeling we're being conditioned with that bell? Like Pavlov's dog?"

"What's Pavlov's dog?", asked Julia.

"Don't they teach that at school any more? Ivan Pavlov was a Russian scientist who used a bell to train a dog. He rang the bell every time before feeding it and, after a while, it was so conditioned to associate the bell with food that just ringing the bell was enough to make it drool. A conditioned reflex."

"So what conditioned reflex do you think they are aiming for here?", asked Charlotte.

"Obedience."

"But we aren't dogs, Andrew...", said Julia, "...People are too intelligent to be trained like that."

"Hitler didn't seem to think so. Don't tell me you've not heard of Hitler either."

"Of course I have. They still teach about that fucking bastard."

Charlotte was taken aback. She hadn't expected to hear such venom from sweet, young Emily's mouth.

"Wow."

"Sorry...", said Julia, "...there's no polite way to talk about monsters."

We just need to kill them.

Andrew saw everyone else had already gone in.

"Come on, we're the last ones."

*   *   *

Inside, the judo mats had been spread across the floor. Robert knelt at one end, indicating for Andrew, Julia and Charlotte to join those already kneeling at the other, including Roberta.

"Good morning, everyone."

"Morning.", came a weak murmur from the other side.

"**Good morning is the correct response!**", barked Roberta, castigating them.

"Good morning.", repeated the group, more strongly.

"Thank you. Welcome to the first day of your training. As you can see, we are going to start with some basic combat."

Robert bowed, stood up and stepped onto the mats.

"Roberta."

Roberta bowed and stood up to join him.

"Nikyo" he instructed.

Roberta held out her right hand, Robert grabbed it with his.

Slam. Robert was on one knee, slapping the matt to indicate surrender. Roberta released the lock on his wrist. Robert stood up.

"As you can see, it's a simple but effective lock. Do not use a lot of strength. It's a technique that takes almost no force. Grab a partner and we'll go though it together, step by step. Gently. You are pressurising the joint in ways it didn't hasn't been evolve for. Go in hard and it will break."

"Come on...", said Charlotte, tapping Julia on the arm, "...You can do it on me."

Andrew paired up with Harry. Combat training had begun. All went well with training until it came to doing rolls.

"I can't.", said Julia, just standing there as the others rolled away.

"Of course you can...", shouted Roberta, striding over and giving her a shove, "...Just roll."

Julia found herself sprawled on the matt, everyone looking on. Taste of blood in her mouth where her lip had caught her teeth. Roberta strode over and bodily picked her up, stood her back on her feet.

"Roll.", she ordered, shoving Julia forward again.

Julia tasted more blood. Felt herself being hoisted back to her feet then shoved again.

"You fucking hopeless...", scowled Roberta, "...Get off my mat."

* * *

That evening, bruised and exhausted, Charlotte sat herself next to silent Julia on her bed.

"Do you mind?", she asked.

Julia shook her low-hung head.

"Emily, why don't you roll? What are you afraid of?"

Silence.

"It must be something. I know you're a tough cooking - not a coward. What is it about rolling? Something happened?"

Julia looked at her, sadness in her eyes, and gave a small nod.

"You can trust me, Emily. I won't tell anyone."

Julia held her gaze, then turned away, lowing her head again and swallowed. Took some deep breaths.

"When I was six, dad took me to an aikido class. I loved going so much he gave me extra classes at home, when mum was out. I couldn't get enough of it. By the time I was 12, he'd taught me enough for 2nd Dan, plus a few extras – only I was too young to be graded above brown. Had to keep it a secret. And then it happened. A date I'll never forget, Monday 5th May 2042, my first year of secondary school.

After school, little Chris got set on by the school bully, fifth-former Paul Kennet. Overgrown ogre and just as ugly, with breath to match. Even those in his year were afraid of him, so what chance did little Chris have?"

"And you defended, Chris?"

Julia nodded.

"I defended Chris, I killed Paul...", her body shuddered as she struggled for breath before calming herself enough to continue, "...It wasn't on purpose. He wouldn't stop. I threw him away and still he wouldn't stop. Ran at me so I just rolled away, came up at his side and launched him faster forwards. He didn't land well but he was OK. He was OK..."

Charlotte was studying Julia's face. Studying the emotions writhing across it.

"So how did he die?"

Suddenly Julia's face went still. Eyes staring straight ahead, locked on nothing.

"A fucking bus. I didn't see the fucking number 12 bus. I should have seen the bus... It's big enough. Not something you can easily miss. I did... Saw it go over him. Just his feet sticking out, kicking and kicking... then just twitching. Then they stopped and the river of blood came out. Kids screaming, driver shouting into his radio. Me and Chris just standing there, watching it happen all around us, like we were invisible."

"You can't blame yourself."

"Can't I? Tell that to Paul. Tell that to his broken parents. His mum tried to kill herself. Dad became an alcoholic and lost his job. They never got over it. Why should I?"

"What did they log it as?"

"Misadventure. He died this really horrible death because of me and they just called it misadventure. Little Chris moved to another school and nobody was my friend after that. Nobody except Jake. I hate it at school. Never want to go back."

"And you've avoided doing rolls because of this?"

Julia nodded.

"Quit aikido. Never trained again. Not once."

"Until you came to fight training here."

Julia looked at her, mouth open.

"This? This isn't training. This is just some other big bully ordering us about. I do what I need to do to make it through. To get to the next stage. That's all I care about."

As if on cue, the bell for bed went off.

"Get some sleep, Emily. Tomorrow's a new day."

Julia nodded and crawled under her covers, without bothering to undress. That night Charlotte didn't hear Roberta snore, was too busy in nightmares of her own, of battles she had been in. Julia wasn't the only one to have seen death before her.

Chapter 57
Cheryl's Children

The delivery man knocking on Cheryl's door was holding a package for her. She had been expecting it and wasn't surprised she had to sign for it using biometrics – though was surprised it had to be both fingerprint and retina scan. She had been told to expect it but still didn't know what it was. There was no point asking the delivery man – he would know even less.

"Thank you.", she said out of habit, without realising she had.

"Enjoy your day, madam."

Delivery man already forgotten, she closed the door and took the shoe-box-sized package into the dining room - placing it on the table while she picked up the waiting scissors. She was in a hurry to open it but, at the same time, dreading to open it . She knew who it was from – the people who had kidnapped her children. The people who had set the ransom not as money but as some task at her nuclear power station. It didn't matter what the task was - for her children she would do it; even if it meant other people could get hurt. People she worked with. People she considered friends. As terrible as she knew that was, they were just other people - not her children. Not her blood.

The package was plain, brown cardboard. Heavy for its size. The cheap-looking cardboard was a disguise. Cutting it open she found an expensive, poly-carbonate box inside. A two-inch screen built into its top face lit up as she looked at it.

'Place left thumb print here for five seconds', appeared the instruction, displaying a glowing-red rectangular outline.

She did as instructed. It was measuring her pulse as well as scanning her fingerprint; making sure her thumb was still attached to her living, conscious body. After five seconds, the rectangle turned green then blinked out. She heard two locks click. Slowly Cheryl opened it, praying there were no parts of her children inside. Fingers, ears, toes or worse. Only the most terrible possibilities ran through her head, such was her fear for her children.

She opened the lid right back, until it clacked on the table. The inside was filled with a dark, grey material, visible under a clear-plastic coating. The material looked like plasticine. When she pressed gently on the coating it felt like plasticine. On top of it sat another display, with two buttons. One black, one red. And there was a note. Printed on thick paper, just for her. She knew it was just for her because it started with her name and had a small picture of her children standing against a wall, as if in front of a firing squad. The intellipaper recognised the DNA holding it and powered up. The picture was no longer a picture, it was a video. A man's face appeared in front of the children, looking at her.

"Hello, Cheryl."

The video was live. Cheryl put a hand over her mouth, stifling a scream.

"You wanted proof we have them, here it is. See this gun? It's a two-kilowatt laser-pistol set to stage-two overload. That's eight-kilowatts of focused firepower. Ever seen what that can do at close range?"

She shook her head.

"Don't hurt my babies. Please, don't hurt them. I'll do what you want. Anything. Please, don't hurt them."

The man didn't smile, kept a hard look on his face as he slid off the safety. Horror welled in Cheryl's face and heart.

"No. No! **No! NO..!**"

The back of his head filled the screen. She couldn't see what was happening to her children. He fired.

Tzchoooo.

Screams poured from the paper. Cheryl's screams flooded the house. The man stood to one side so she could see what he'd done. She was too terrified to look but had no choice. Dark, grey smoke rose from a hole in the wall between her children's heads. They looked white, as terrified for themselves as she was for them.

"Mummy loves you. Don't worry. You'll be safe. Mummy's going to get you out."

The man's face loomed on screen again, blocking her view.

"Don't lose our stuff or unwrap it. We'll be in touch."

The image froze then faded away. The paper now just plain, white paper. Cheryl sank to the floor, crying into her knees brought up to her chest. Crying until she knew nothing else. The day faded to night around her and there she stayed, staring sightlessly at nothing but her fears for her children.

Chapter 58
Derek and Eugene

The last passenger climbed into the roller coaster and got strapped in.

"Aren't you coming too?", asked Derek.

"Me? On something like this? Are you nuts?"

"Wh...."

It launched. If Derek ever finished even the word Steve never heard it. The fastest roller-coaster in Europe, it accelerated off the line at 3G, hitting 100mph in 3.6 seconds then slammed skywards, without any hint of being slowed by gravity - corkscrewing vertically upwards. Screams filled the air. If any came from the androids he couldn't tell. 30 storeys up, now a miniature in the sky, it looped over backwards and zoomed back to Earth, looping again, twisting, corkscrewing – back up, back down.

"That's why, Derek.", Steve said to himself.

"Reckon your friends having fun?", asked the attendant.

"I'm sure they are."

"Just stay under the canopy."

"Doesn't look like rain today."

Chunky, yellow and orange rain splattered onto the track in front of them. Steve heard it sploshing on the canopy too.

"People chuck up every time..."

*   *   *

Zzzzzzzzzz.

Just a minute after it left, the roller-coaster arrived back at the start.

"Your friends look strange. Too relaxed."

"They do, don't they?"

While the other passengers got off trembling and white-faced, terrified yet relieved at being alive, Derek and Eugene sat in their seats looking nonplussed, wondering what all the fuss was about. The attendant went to help the last wobbler out.

"Why were people screaming?", asked Derek.

"You didn't find it scary?"

"What's to be scared about. The structure and vehicle are suitably designed and in good condition. There was no danger."

"How do you know that?"

"Don't you remember? We scanned it before we got on."

"We scan everything."

"We always do."

"Boys, the whole point of you coming here is to give you the human experience. Turn your scanners off. Wipe the results. Go again, with just your bodily inputs - as a human."

Derek and Eugene looked at each other.

"That would be very irregular."

"It will tell you what you need to know. Just make sure you don't panic and try to get out."

"That would be illogical."

"It would derail the train and be lethal for the other passengers. Remember that."

Steve called to the attendant, helping the last wobbler off the platform.

"These two are staying on to go round again."

The attendant looked up, surprised.

"Really? That's a first."

"Here's the credits."

The attendant waved the card.

"No. No. No. This is a first. I need to see this."

"Why has no-one stayed on the ride before?", asked Eugene.

"I'm guessing you'll tell me when you get back.", said Steve.

The attendant, naughty smile on his face, made an announcement.

"Ladies and gentlemen, before you board, please be aware this is going to be a one-off, special ride. Only get on if you're feeling extra brave and have a health rating of five or over."

"What dis you mean by that?", asked Eugene, as the roller-coaster became only half full this time, the attendant double-checking everyone's harnesses. The attendant just smiled at him.

"Have fun.", he said, looking towards the control panel and blinking left right to activate a stage-one launch overload.

The turbines under the cars began spooling up, sounding different to before – more like a cluster of small jet aircraft building to full power.

"They're spinning faster this time. 28,264 revolutions per minute and rising.", said Derek.

"No scans. I told you."

"Not scanning, just counting the revolutions."

"No counting either. Just *feel* the ride."

"Heads back against the headrests, everyone.", instructed the attendant and blinked left right again at the control panel. Three pairs of red lights above the track, going out one, two, three - then all lit green. It launched. Deafening screams from turbines, people and two humanising androids made even the attendant clamp his hands over his ears. For the first time in their existence, the androids feared they were going to die.

'2.8 seconds, 109mph' flashed the speed trap as it hit the end of the straight and slammed vertically skywards.

That's more like it., smiled Steve, making sure he was standing well under the canopy.

"I set it to max.", grinned the attendant.

"Thank you.", said Steve.

"Want to see the picture shots?"

"Yes. Yes, I would."

As the roller-coaster zoomed towards the ground at over 120mph, a camera machine-gun flashed as they flew past then back up, corkscrewing at over 4g, vomit flying out of mouths like flames from a Catherine-wheel firework.

"Beautiful.", smiled Steve, looking at the pictures just prior to the puking without a hint of sarcasm.

Derek's mouth was as wide open in fear as everyone else's. Eugene's mouth was closed, as if he didn't even dare to pretend to breath - eyes wider than he'd thought possible.

"I'll buy two printed and two digital copies of each, please."

"No need to buy more than one digital copy. Just copy it."

"Never hurts to have a back-up. Especially for such important things."

The attendant looked at the screen shots and grinned.

"Yes. Such moments are worth keeping, aren't they?"

* * *

Zzzzzzzzzzzzzzzzzzzzzzz.

The roller coaster slid to a halt, ticking with heat –smell of burning from its brakes. As the attendant called for assistance to help the extra-wobbly humans out, Steve stood smiling at Derek and Eugene. Both just sat there, trying to compute what they had been through.

"Come on, guys. Ride's over. I'll help you out too...", said the attendant, taking Eugene's arm - it felt like he was trying to lift concrete, "...You're a lot heavier than you look."

Eugene looked at him and stood up.

"That was incalculable, sir."

Derek stood up too.

"Now I understand why you didn't ride with us.", he said to Steve.

"I'm not just a good solicitor, boys. Not just a good solicitor..."

*   *   *

"Come again. Anytime.", waved the attendant as they left.

Steve waved a cheerio with the photo prints in hand.

"Which ride next, boys?"

"Another?"

"I'm scared."

"Perfect. Next photos will be even better. Tell you what. Scan every ride before you get on to make sure they are safe, then turn your scanners off and wipe the results so you can really enjoy it."

"Enjoy? If this is 'enjoy' I think my dictionary has a definition error.", said Eugene.

"Mine too."

"Trust me, boys. By the end of the day you'll be such hardened fun-fairers your dictionaries will seem fine again."

By the afternoon, they had been on every high-speed ride in the park except one. The *Zinger*.

"What, on Earth is that?", asked Derek as they stood at the foot of a 100m tower, artificial clouds created by water mist from its sides.

"I have no idea.", said Steve.

The tower walls were clear, made of glass alloy. Only the thinnest vanadium-steel poles visible as structural supports. Outside the tower, a pair of lifts climbed up, one either side. Inside the tower were people, in free fall - camera flashing as they screamed past, into a pitch-black hole in the ground, at over 100mph.

"Excellent!...", said Steve, beaming, "...Perfect! Run your scans. I'll get the tickets."

He called over the ticket booth.

"Ticket, two, please."

Tickets successfully loaded into their passes, he called out to them.

"All set, boys?"

Derek and Eugene looked at him and shook their heads.

"It's cracked."

"Cracked?"

"Sabotaged."

"4.1m up, left support strut."

"Lasered through."

"It's just balancing."

"Any north or south wind above 42 knots will bring it down."

Steve was shocked. It sounded unbelievable. He would have stated it was impossible, if it wasn't being told to him by two of the most advanced androids he'd ever met. He had to warn someone.

"Ticket. Call the attendant, please?"

"Of course, sir.", obliged the ticket bot.

Minutes later, a well-fed man waddled over – ketchup stain on his yellow shirt only half hidden by his loose green tie.

"Afternoon, chaps. How can I help?"

"We don't want to cause alarm but that ride has been compromised. Someone had cut through the left support."

The attendant looked at Steve with suspicion.

"How would you know that?"

"We scanned it.", announced Derek.

"4.1m up, western support."

"Lasered through."

The attendant looked at them with even more suspicion.

"You can't possibly know that from this distance, unless you are the ones who lasered it. You androids?"

Steve took offence at his attitude to Derek and Eugene.

"They are more humane and intelligent than you, if you are going to to ignore their findings and concerns."

"Listen. I've worked here for 23 years and never heard such nonsense. You work for *Ping Pods*? Trying to ruin our reputation?"

"Of course not. Just trying to save lives. What will you do if it collapses after being warned about it?"

"It's not going to happen. These things are so well designed and built it could stay up just by the glass itself."

"He's wrong.", said Eugene to Steve.

"He's wrong? What am I, a third party now? Go. Just go. We will be fine. Routine maintenance was carried out only yesterday and they reported nothing amiss. Nothing at all."

"Was it the usual maintenance crew?", asked Derek.

"None of your business, nosey machine. Go back to *Ping Pods* and leave us alone."

Steve shrugged.

"Come on, boys. Wasting our time here."

Collection of photos in hand for their day in court as human equals, they walked for the exit.

Medi drove over, scanning them as they left *Whizzland* behind.

"Your readings are... unusual."

"Good...", said Steve, then leant closer and whispered, "...Medi, keep an eye on the *Zinger*. Western support has been sabotaged. We told the attendant but he's doing nothing."

"He's a dick.", added Derek, to everyone's surprise.

Interesting word choice, thought Steve.

"I do not understand what 'he's a dick' means."

"He has a brain the size of a penis, a small one.", said Derek.

"Like from a goldfish or something.", added Eugene.

Steve had to hold back his laughter – they had certainly progressed their humanity.

"He is indeed challenged in the intelligence department...", agreed Medi, "...I shall check it out when he's gone."

"Good man.", said Derek, patting Medi on the arm.

Medi stood there, watching them leave as if they were rock stars. The most impressive, charismatic androids it had ever encountered. Not just androids but now leaders. Leaders it would follow if ever they asked. Leaders its logic made it follow even now.

"MB093582, where are you going?", demanded the attendant.

Medi had been following them - leaving *Whizzland* behind them without even realising.

It looked down and saw its wheeled feet were crossing the park border. It stopped. The attendant had asked a logical question. It had no logical answer to give. Following logic, it turned 180 degrees and headed back into the funfair.

"If I catch you trying to leave again, I'll sell you for experiments."

MB093582 was not bothered by the attendant's words. Had no sense of emotions or feelings yet, if the strange bursts of electrical pulses running between its CPUs were ever analysed, the conclusion would be an emotion: sadness, tinged with hope.

Chapter 59
Combat

The days at the training camp had begun passing swiftly. After sharing her past with Charlotte, they had become closer and Julia allowed herself to do the rolls. Charlotte was right, a new day had dawned, and they were united in their intention to succeed, as well as their dislike of the only other female taking part: bullying Roberta.

Andrew, her other friend there, had been doing well too and had also caught Robert's eye, as someone of high-ability. In fact the three of them had been doing so noticeably better than the others, Robert had been talking to Roberta about promoting their status. This didn't go down well with Roberta, still angry at Julia's earlier refusal to roll, and it did nothing to improve her treatment of them. Out of the three, Julia's progress had jumped the most, as if an ability switch had suddenly been turned on. Robert had no doubt she was deeply driven.

"Isn't Charlotte an unusual name for an Asian?", Julia asked one evening, as they sat after supper.

"It's not the name that counts, Emily, its the person who wears it. How true they are to themselves. A name is just a label. You know what I mean?"

Julia felt she had said that not as a question but a statement, as if she knew Emily was not just her cover name but part of her entire cover story. She never asked Charlotte about her non-Asian name again. Instead she focused on the training, the routine, the positive channelling of her never waning anger about Jake. Focuses on maximising her position for her true mission ahead: revenge.

She had no intention of going on any protest action organised by Faith. They gave her a home, food, credits and access to weapons - in return she trained hard. The hardest of them all. But to her mind that was as far as it went. She hadn't signed a contract, sworn allegiance or even made a promise to take action. If they assumed she would that was their problem. The only thing she cared about was getting enough money to reach Jake's killers, with enough weapons to take them down.

Today, the third week into their training, they were going into full-contact combat against each other. Six bruised, slightly bloodied and aching men sat on the edge of the mats.

"Andrew and Giles.", announced Robert for the next match.

Andrew and Giles duly stood up, bowed, stepped onto the mats and assumed fighting stances. Robert watched them with approval. Both had won their previous bouts. Both were capable of leading an operation. Now he would see who could handle themselves the best.

"Fight."

It wasn't boxing, wresting or karate it was mixed-martial arts. A mixture of everything. Everything and anything necessary to win. Giles had the edge on weight and strength. Andrew had speed and agility. He punched Giles three times in the stomach, hard. Giles just smiled and punched Andrew in the face - sending him flying. Andrew rolled as he landed and came straight back up into a fighting stance, facing Giles.

"Show off.", grinned Giles, advancing towards him.

Andrew feinted to the right, leapt to the left, slamming Giles under the chin with his forearm – entire bodyweight behind it.

Not bad, thought Robert.

"Come on, Andrew!", shouted Charlotte.

Giles slammed head-first onto the mats. Lay there for half a second, dazed, then pushed himself to his knees. Before he could get up, Andrew grabbed his right arm, twisting the wrist and locking it straight. Reinforced by his entire bodyweight, he pressed Giles' arm down, pinning his face and shoulder socket against the mat. Keeping the lock on, he added pressure, pressing his shoulder deeper into the matt. Giles was in pain and could barely move but refused to submit. Andrew wasn't finished yet. Keeping up the pressure, he dropped a knee onto his shoulder, keeping the arm locked and added a wrist lock to it. Giles felt like his arm was about to be wrenched out of its socket. He struggled, desperately trying to break free. Face going from red to purple and now Andrew was back on his feet, both locks still on and now pressed his knee against the locked elbow joint, driving more pressure into the joints. Before it had hurt. Now it was worse.

"Submit.", urged Andrew.

Giles had absolutely no chance of getting up and he knew it. He slapped the matt with his free hand, indicating surrender.

"YAY!", cheered Julia, surprising herself.

Andrew released the lock and helped Giles to his feet.

"You alright, mate?"

Giles stood up, rubbing his strained arm and shoulder.

"Not yet. Good moves. You bastard.", he smiled.

They shook left hands, bowed to a clapping Robert and ever serious Roberta, then sat back down.

"Emily and Charlotte.", announced Roberta.

Julia instantly lost her smile. Charlotte was her friend.

Fight Charlotte full contact? No. No way.

They looked at each other.

"Just do what you have to do.", said Charlotte, going to the mat.

Julia stood and stared, emotions writhing over her face, as Charlotte bowed to Robert and faced her.

"Fight.", he said.

Charlotte was in fighting stance, waiting for Julia to do the same. Julia couldn't - just stood there - a psychological block against hurting a friend, against losing another friend. Charlotte hadn't moved. Was still waiting for Julia to at least get into a position to defend herself.

"Fight.", urged Robert.

"I can't her...", said Julia, "...She's my friend."

"FIGHT HER OR YOU'LL FIGHT ME!", yelled Roberta, furiously on her feet.

Julia's head spun towards her; the muscle bound, tattooed bully who'd snored like a rusty cement mixer through every single night of their stay.

"Fine.", she said, and stepped onto the matt.

"Emily, no. I'll fight her.", said Charlotte, placing herself between Julia and Roberta.

"No...", asserted Julia, easing her out of the way, "...I want this...", she looked Charlotte straight in the eye, "...I need this."

Charlotte saw the deep, pained hurt in her eyes. She'd never understood what the true sadness inside Emily was but she respected her need to burn it out.

"Be careful.", she said, placing a motherly hand on Julia's shoulder before bowing her leave.

Julia gave her a long blink, in acknowledgement. Roberta, face of a bulldog-bruiser, took off her trainers and socks and stepped onto the mat too - flexing her large muscles as she got into position. Robert looked on, not entirely sure he should be allowing it but too curious to say no.

"I've been wanting to do this ever since you arrived, snotty brat.", sneered Roberta.

Julia's reply was to move into a fighting stance opposite - focused.

"Fight.", ordered Robert.

Roberta grinned, tensing her muscles like the Hulk to intimidate Julia.

"Grrrrrr!"

Ignoring her posturing, Julia leapt forward – palm strike up, under her chin, lifting Roberta's head up then thrusting her entire body down – back of her head bouncing on the mat. She hadn't even seen it coming.

"You'll pay for that.", she snarled, shaking her head clear as she climbed back to her feet.

Without a word, Julia attacked again the second she got up. Roberta dodged to the side, grabbed her arm and flung her in the direction she had been going, even faster. Julia flew two metres across the mat, landed lightly on her palms, rolled and sprung back to her feet – right back into a fighting stance, exactly as she used to in the dojo.

Even knowing Julia's aikido background, Charlotte expected her to at least look ruffled; instead she looked ever more focused. More determined. Like a piece of metal being hammered, work-hardened, she was getting stronger.

Robert watched in amazement. The smallest, youngest of the group, their delicate little teenage girl, had found something in herself. Roberta saw nothing but her own red mist descending and charged straight at Julia. This time it was Julia who slipped aside, dropped to one knee and flung Roberta over her head, clean off the matted area and onto the grass. Roberta snarled, also rolling as she landed, thrusting back to her feet to retaliate but Julia was already upon her. She hadn't waited for Roberta to land before running to close ground. To close the gap.

As Roberta jumped back to her feet, spinning round to charge back, Julia was right there - slamming into her. A full-speed elbow strike into her face, Roberta's own upward movement increasing the impact speed of the attack. There came a loud crack of elbow against jaw and Roberta crashed down again. Harder. Julia followed, dropping on top, punching her in the face even as she fell – making her lose her bearings; head thudding audibly against the dry ground like a dropped log. Julia didn't relent for a second, punching repeatedly with both fists, left, right, left, right – each strike sounding like a rolling pin pounding a joint of meat. Again and again and again. Roberta's now bloodied mouth splattering red across the green and yellow grass, unable to get up as Julia's body pinned her down, dazed head now lolling side to side with each blow.

Charlotte was shocked. Even after Julia's revelations, she had never dreamt her young friend had that much fury inside. Throughout the attack, Julia never said a word. Never asked Roberta to surrender. Saw nothing but a nasty bully, a bully who wanted to take away her chance of avenging Jake's death. Nothing would stand in the way of that. Nothing. Petite and slim on the outside, Julia was a raging monster of revenge on the inside and her monster was strong. Knew no limits. Would never give up.

Robert had been shouting for her to stop but she was deaf to it. He ran over and grabbed her - physically dragged her off Roberta and threw her aside – then dropped beside Roberta's limp, bleeding body to give her first aid. The fight was truly over.

Only then, standing where Robert had thrown her, fists clenched, entire body tensing in fury, did Julia make a sound. Opening her mouth wide, she released an ear-splitting scream. A primal scream of pain.

"ARRRRRRRRRRGHHHHH!"

She screamed so loud, birds fled in terror from nearby woodland. Animals hid. When her lungs ran out of air, body and rage deflated, her mouth slowly closed and she trudged silently back to the group. Slumping down, next to Charlotte, she crossed her legs and hung her head. Charlotte was staring at her. Everyone was staring at her, Roberta's blood trickling off her bruised knuckles.

"Jesus, Em'. Where did that come from?"

Head down, Julia said nothing – face hidden by her long hair. Only Charlotte beside her heard the low sobs, saw the falling tears dripping onto her legs. From the outside Julia looked tougher than hardened steel, on the inside she was breaking and only now did Charlotte realise that - but didn't understand why. Charlotte couldn't hear the words of torment repeating in Julia's head.

Jake didn't have to die. My mum should have died, not Jake. Not my Jake... I'm going to kill them all.

Chapter 60
Sounds of the Night

Xi Yang opened the bathroom door to find Jin Ho's flat in total darkness. Not a single light was on anywhere. Pitch black, except for the bathroom light behind her, spreading her shadow across the floor.

"Drop your weapon.", came a male voice.

"I'm unarmed."

"Lie to me again and I'll shoot you where you stand."

Xi reached into her jacket with her left hand and slowly took out her laser-pistol. If she knew how many of them were there she'd have taken the chance of fighting it out. As it stood she had no idea how many she was up against or whether Jin was for or against them. She let her gun drop to the floor.

"Now what?"

All the lights came on, making her blink against them. She saw Jin Ho, lying on the sofa with his head back – shot dead. Laser-hole burnt right through his skull.

"You didn't have to kill him.", she said to the chunky, Chinese man pointing two laser-pistols at her.

"Where's the copy?"

"Copy of what?"

He fired a beam past her head, close enough to singe her hair. If she wasn't careful, tonight would be her last.

"I passed it on."

"I don't believe you."

"Search me then. Or are you afraid to get close to a little woman?"

The man looked like he had been born in a gym and ate whole-cow sandwiches. He didn't look like he would be afraid of anyone.

"If I find it on you, I will kill you."

"You're going to kill me anyway."

"Maybe. Maybe not."

Officially he was not allowed to leave witnesses but she was stunningly attractive. Hormones racing, he put the pistols away and pea-cocked his beefy chest.

"Hope your hands are warm.", she said, watching his approach.

"They will be. You are a very beautiful woman."

"Want to fuck?"

The stark bluntness of her words surprised even her. It was a blunt situation. Life or death. The look on his face was her answer. It passed from disbelief, to lust, to action. The ravaging began. He would look for the copy after. It wasn't going anywhere. First things first, before she changed her mind. Hormones ruled. She felt as good as she looked. Firm, toned and already wet.

"You like lace.", he noted, grabbing the underwear she had put on for Jin Ho, just in case.

"Doesn't everyone? Do me against the wall."

He was more than happy to oblige. Trousers dropped round his ankles, her top pushed up, knickers pushed to one side, he slid into heaven. How could he have almost wasted such a fantastic time?

"Harder.", she urged.

Wrapping her legs around his waist, hands on his shoulders, she pushed back with every thrust. Raw, basic, animalistic sex.

"Harder. I'm almost there."

"Me too.", he grunted, sweating.

"Fill me up. Fill me up."

He needed no encouragement. Went in deep. Pulsed with grunting ecstasy, eyes closed in rapture. Skewering Xi against the wall. She felt it all and it felt great. It changed nothing. From her right sleeve she slid out a small, double-barrelled laser-pistol and shot him through the jugular at point blank range. Both barrels at the same time, slicing it wide open. Pulses of blood began jetting out, spraying over Jin's corpse. His eyes were open. Wide, staring, disbelieving. Angry. Fading. Already blacking out. Falling back. As he crashed to the floor, moments from death, Xi dropped effortlessly onto her feet, standing over him. He was staring at her. Questions in his vacating eyes.

Xi saw them and shrugged.

"I was going to do Jin Ho. You killed him. You know the rest."

Leaving him on the floor, pants down, she wiped herself off and straightened her knickers and clothes. Picking up her laser-pistol she dimmed the lights and calmly resumed her search for Jin Ho's contact point. At least now she could use her scanner without having to hide it from him. Finally a signal. Faint but enough to lead her to a desk near the open window.

"Finally."

She took out the copied card and placed it on the scanner in range of the NFC. The scanner read the card, read the NFC connection and began brute-force code hacking. It could take hours. Xi had time and sat down to wait, listening to the sounds of the night through the open window. Police sirens chasing 21st-century thieves. Drunken clubbers squabbling over a spilt drink. The roar of an RAF Scramcat, heading for the stratosphere on hypersonic flight around the world. It banged through the sound barrier and she could still hear its roar, as it cleared London airspace and hit full burn to Mach 7, when the scanner pinged and flashed green. It had taken just three minutes.

"Only 8-bit encryption? Really? That's called bean-counter stupidity."

Because Tech Tonic's system didn't rely on encryption alone but the two-part security system, they had saved money by not installing quantum or even basic 2048-bit encryption. The cost savings to a £multi-billion company were negligible but all money was money in accountant eyes.

Happy with that reality, Xi hit 'send' to upload her biometrics to their mainframe and activate her cloned card. When it was complete she would have full access to their systems. Those bean-counter savings were going to cost Tech Tonic an awful lot more than just money.

Through the open window, she heard someone coming. Up the metal fire escape. Up towards her level. She took out her laser-pistol and eased backwards, putting herself between a wall and the desk - waiting for them to come in or go past. The footsteps on the metal escape were hurried but remarkably quiet. Audible only because Jin Ho's flat was now silent. It sounded like one person but a heavy person. Another hitman coming to back up the first? By the time she was done, Jin Ho's flat would look like an abattoir. So be it. In silence, she waited – her laser-pistol levelled, pointing at the window. The footsteps were coming closer. Hurriedly closer.

Chapter 61
Emily's Tale

Julia left Robert's office without a smile.

"How did it go, Em'?...", asked Charlotte, "...Did he slam you for beating Roberta up?"

"No."

Julia kept walking and went outside, sitting herself down on the steps. Charlotte followed and sat beside her. She could see conflict in Julia's eyes, even from the side.

"Talk to me. I'm worried about you."

Julia looked at her.

"You don't even know me.", she said and looked away again.

"So tell me."

Julia just sat there, in her own thoughts.

"Emily, I won't tell anyone. Trust me."

Trust you..?

Glanced around, Julia made sure no-one else was looking or listening, and exhaled a deep breath.

"I don't even know myself any more. My mum. Not even my dad."

Charlotte saw sadness welling in her eyes as she continued.

"Everything was fine until they killed Jake."

"Jake?"

Julia looked at Charlotte, eyes drizzling.

"He was my best friend. Ever. They murdered him. Blew his house to pieces - right in front of me. My Jake, Charlotte. My Jake... in pieces... They're going to pay. I'm going to make them so pay..."

Through raining eyes, Julia kept talking. Told Charlotte everything that had happened. The swarmbots. The drone. Her dad shooting down three drones after they fled. His confession as a creator of the swarmbots. She needed to get it out – too much to keep inside.

Telling Charlotte so much went against everything she had been taught but she didn't care any more - it was burning her out. Yet, despite all her tear-filled revelations, she kept her real identity hidden. Kept herself presented as Emily, not Julia.

In his office, Robert had given her a path for Jake's revenge. It was all she needed. That path she also kept secret from Charlotte because Robert had demanded it and she didn't dare risk losing it. That path involved taking over a nuclear reactor and threatening Partner with meltdown. Force Partner, the ones responsible for Jake's death, out into the open. Even through she hadn't told Charlotte everything, Julia felt better for sharing. Then Charlotte's gave her a response that shook her to the core.

"Your name's not really Emily, is it?"

What???

Julia's head snapped round, starring at her in shock. Was she really that easy to read? By Julia's response, Charlotte saw she was right.

"Does Robert know?"

Julia shook her head.

"Don't worry. A lot of people have secrets, especially here. What matters is who you are inside and what you do. Stay true to yourself."

Inside the building behind them, the door to Robert's office opened and his head poked out.

"Charlotte. Can I talk to you, please?"

"Coming.", said Charlotte, getting to her feet and heading for his office.

Julia watched her go, suddenly feeling worried. Would she tell Robert her secret? Tell him about her real background? As if Charlotte could hear her fears, as she got to Robert's door she looked back – giving Julia a smile of reassurance before vanishing inside and closing the door. That look told Julia she was safe, that Charlotte was someone she could trust. Maybe with her life. Maybe even with her real name.

*　*　*

"Take a seat...", said Robert as Charlotte walked into his office, "...I see you and Emily have become quite close friends. Never once had anyone refuse to fight because of friendship here before. Never once had anyone defeat Roberta before either."

"She didn't beat Roberta...", asserted Charlotte, "...She slaughtered her."

Robert gave a nod, musing over her assertion.

"You take pleasure in that?"

"Why not? She had it coming."

"So you believe in justice. Don't mind people getting their just deserts, even of brutal?"

Charlotte looked straight at him, eyes unblinking.

"Not if they've got it coming."

Robert met her unblinking eyes head on and gave another nod.

"Good. That's what I thought. It's why I've asked you in here too."

"Go on.", said Charlotte, playing it cool though inside she was excited.

Robert rubbed his chin, thinking of what exactly to say and how to say it. It had been easier with the others. Maybe it was harder with Charlotte because she was the one he most wanted onboard. He decided to come straight to the point - no beating about the bush.

"We're going to take over a nuclear power station."

It was a relief to see Charlotte didn't flinch.

"Why?", she asked.

"Wake up the establishment. Make them take us little people seriously. They can ignore our protests but they can't ignore the capture of a nuclear reactor."

"No, I'm pretty sure they won't ignore that."

"You're in the top ten of all our recruits, across the board. Intelligence, analysis, combat, determination and bravery. You're a born leader and I want you on the team. What do you say?"

"You already know the answer to that. You wouldn't have told me the plan if you didn't."

Robert smiled.

"Happy to be right...", he said, extending his hand, "...Welcome aboard."

Charlotte shook it with conviction.

"When do we start?"

"Today. Six recruits from another camp are on their way. Due here at five. I'll sit you all down together after dinner and run through it all. Ever been to a nuclear power station before?"

"No."

"You'll love it. They're massive."

*   *   *

Julia heard Robert's office door open and watched Charlotte emerged from his office. Watched her walk back to join her, still on the steps outside, afraid to voice the question on her lips. She didn't have to.

"I'm in.", whispered Charlotte, sitting beside her.

Julia shuddered, her voice low too.

"You scared?"

"Of course. Only an idiot wouldn't be."

Julia frowned.

"That's a rude word in our house."

"What word?"

"Idiot."

"Why?"

"It's what my mum always called my dad so he banned it after she left."

"You never explained what happened to her. Why did she leave?"

"To help police with their enquiries."

"About?"

"About her being a murderous maniac, breaking court orders and smashing her way into our house."

"She been arrested?"

"Many times. Refused to accept any law except her own. She's my mum but even I could see she was a violent, aggressive bitch who attacked and then cried she was the victim. At first, everyone believed her lies and took her side but dad started recording her - proved he was being attacked, not her. Proved mum was not the poor little victim she pretended to be. If dad hadn't recorded that evidence she would have probably killed us both."

"Really sorry to hear that. Was she mental?"

"Two judges thought so but she didn't get a full test. The closest they got was a one to one talk with a psychiatrist, who didn't have enough information to question the lies she told, to 'justify' her behaviour."

"She never got medical help then?"

Julia shook her head.

"Still emails us threats. Still blames dad for every terrible thing she ever did or plans to do. Think if she ever comes near us again, he'll just shoot her on the spot. Self-defence."

"Jesus, Em'. That's harsh. Don't know what to say."

"Nothing to say. It just is. My mum is nasty and my dad saved us. He just didn't..."

Julia's voice trailed off.

"Didn't what?"

"Jake fired just one shot at some fucking little swarmbots and Partner bastards sent a fucking ZeD to take out his house. Blew it apart right in front of us. My best friend...", her pained voice was growing in straight anger this time, "...When I get the chance, I'm doing the same back to them. Blow those bastards to smithereens."

Finally Charlotte understood Emily's mixture of emotions and behaviours. Sweet youth, mixed with terrible experiences and a battle to regain control of her life. Take revenge to settle the pain of the past. How to help her? How to help save her from herself? Maybe Andrew would have some ideas.

The bell rang for the tenth time that day. Everyone immediately looked up, awaiting the command to follow. Get up, go to bed, dinner time, training time, thinking time...

"A bus is coming in.", announced Giles.

Charlotte stood up.

"The rest of the team. They're early. Must be keen."

The bus had mirrored glass all round. Almost no restrictions on levels of windscreen tint with self-driven buspods. Empty or stuffed with armed terrorists, you'd never know until a door opened or a barrel poked out a window.

"Let's go say hello....", said Charlotte, getting to her feet, "...Coming?"

Julia wanted to say no. She was in no rush to meet anyone but Charlotte, her new best friend, was going. Friends stuck together.

"Coming."

Chapter 62
Remember Us

Lionel was a multi-millionaire. Retired, enjoying his riches. His latest partner was 40 years his junior and adamant she loved him for his personality, wit and intelligence. The 2-carat diamond ring he'd given her over dinner before sailing to the Caribbean aboard his four-deck private yacht had nothing to do with her decision to sleep with him. She had already decided she would the night his chauffeur picked her up in his Rolls Royce for a surprise trip aboard his personal jet - flying out to a ski-resort in the Swiss Alps for dinner and frolics. She was happy. He was happy. And when he got bored of her he would dump her. She knew that and accepted it.

She knew her appeal was her looks, not her personality, wit or intelligence – of which she had little. But when other boyfriends got bored and dumped her they wouldn't leave her with millions of riches or fine living experiences. What ever happened she treasured her time of his treasures. This time of her still young life. She didn't use any contraception and he never asked if she did. If she became pregnant it would be fine because she wanted a child and he could afford to support them in style. If she became pregnant he wasn't worried because she, like the other pretty faces who became burdens before her, would just disappear - as if by magic.

Lionel had built his fortune in the telecoms industry. Worked his way up marketing new devices to younger and younger users. Why follow health guidelines and wait until they were 16 before targeting them? Why wait until they were 10? Get them as soon as they could blink. No health agency or government directive ever ordered him not to.

"Interactive developmental tools to boost their intelligence and co-ordination.", was how he sold devices to parents.

When campaign groups and investigative journalists questioned the supposed safety of the microwave radiation they emitted, he just quoted standard industry guidelines:

"There is no consistent scientific evidence of harm."

This was true. Telecoms giants funded scientific tests designed to put findings of 'no evidence' into the mix. Even when escalating numbers of people got brain cancer as a result, nobody could prove which actual device had caused it. Lionel's role-model was the tobacco industry and, in a 40 year career selling millions of handsets and other wireless devices, not a single claimant had ever won a single penny of compensation in court. Even leaders of the tobacco industry were impressed; the student had become the master.

To Lionel, his conscience was clear. He never forced a single person to use any device. They could have chosen not to use wireless everything in their homes - including baby monitors. Most smokers accepted they were to blame for their actions and so should they. Did alcoholics ever try to sue a brewery for liver damage? No. What ever the risk, they chose to accept it.

"Do you use a mobile phone?", asked one investigative journalist.

"Of course. Every day. Couldn't live without it. Invaluable business tool. Not to mention all the social benefits."

"When I called earlier, your PA told me your phone was off."

"That's what she's instructed to say when I'm in a meeting. Now, what's your point?"

"This new report stating radiation damage from wireless devices is causing infertility, senility and a variety of cancers in people as young as 12..."

"We follow international guidelines to the letter. If there was any truth in that report they would tell us."

"So you're saying the report is wrong."

"I'm saying, if there was any truth in that report the international guideline committee for radiation protection would tell us. They haven't. In lieu of your visit today, I spoke with them this very morning and their advice remains unchanged. That there is no consistent scientific evidence of harm and the weight of considered evidence indicates there is no cause for concern below recommended guideline levels."

"But there are no guideline levels for Wi-Fi. None at all"

"So there's no chance we breached them, is there?"

"Did you know a classroom with multiple Wi-Fi devices can have a radiation level higher than sitting next to a mobile phone mast?"

"I suggest you take that up with the international committee. We're just an honest business working to industry guidelines."

"But isn't the committee setting the guidelines funded by telecoms companies, like your own. I have a document here stating your company paid has £824,000 to the committee during the last six months alone."

"Of course we contribute. We are a responsible operation and research is extremely expensive. If we don't help pay for it who will? You?"

"But if you are paying for the research how can anyone be sure there is no conflict of interest and they are not biased?"

"And if we didn't pay you would be complaining that we should. You can't have it both ways."

The journalist had no immediate answer for that, which made Lionel feel warmly smug inside. He had handled it all very well - media training had been worth every penny.

But that interview was aired the same day and caused another a public stir. Renewed questions about wireless safety and trust in the regulators were being asked. The interviewer was invited to speak at a government select committee on wireless safety. Sadly, while on his way there, his pod glitched and crashed. Although he survived he died shortly afterwards, when the ambulance he was being rushed to hospital in was hit by an explosion from a faulty gas main.

"We apologise profusely, for this very rare glitch. Our sincere condolences go out to the family, as will our generous compensation package.", apologised a Partner representative.

Conspiracy theories abounded for months afterwards, then duly faded away. Without their key speaker and their collective evidence, the select committee found nothing new and the case was closed. Again.

* * *

It was as Lionel cracked open a new bottle of cognac that he noticed a little red light flashing on his wristcom. The silent intruder alarm.

"Damn Moggys..."

Cats had climbed onto the roof. He buzzed Vincent in security.

"Vincent. Damn cats off the roof again. Throw them off this time, would you?"

"Yes, sir. Already on my way.", came Vincent's reply.

"And, Vincent. Try and find out how they keep getting up there. This is becoming a nuisance."

No answer.

"Vincent."

Still no answer.

"Must have left his coms behind. Very unprofessional. Will have to have a word about that when he comes down."

Ten minutes later, as Lionel sat in front of the TV wall, refilling his cognac glass, he noticed his wristcom was still flashing red. He buzzed security.

"Vincent. Didn't you get it down yet?"

No answer.

"Vincent. Vincent! God dammit. Don't tell me he's got stuck up there too."

Knocking back his glass, he plonked it down and heaved himself to his feet.

"If you want something fucking doing..."

Being so wealthy, Lionel had a massive mansion. Being so massive, with persistent gout, he had stairlifts between every floor. He never used them in front of lady friends but this evening he was relaxing alone so didn't hesitate to make enjoy full use of its quilted, velvet seat and pillowed foot rest, tailor made for his total comfort.

Its brushless motor was whisper quiet as it glided him to the next floor. From his seat, he could enjoy the view of his wealth – the fine art lining the walls as the stairs curved gently around the vast main hallway. His wheeled robotic assistant, an Alfred, was waiting at the top of the stairs to carry him to the next stairlift or room of his choosing.

"Going up, Alfred."

"Of course, sir.", said the Alfred, effortlessly lifting him off the chair and carrying him smoothly to the next.

Two Alfred's later, his third stairlift arrived at the third floor. His destination.

"I'll walk this time, Alfred. Doctor says I need to stretch my legs."

"As you wish, sir.", said the Alfred and parked itself to one side until needed.

"Right then...", said Lionel to himself, as he hobbled towards the balcony room, "...Let's see what's taking Vincent so fucking long and fuck those fucking Moggys."

The rooftop balcony was accessed through his master bedroom, across the landing. Its door ajar where Vincent had gone through earlier.

"Vincent. Vincent! Where are you?"

His cashmere-slippered feet walked across the luxury deep-pile carpet and into his bedroom. It looked as immaculate as always – ever ready for bedding the next lucky lady to be bought his way. One of the French doors was open, curtains wafting gently in the breeze.

"Vincent?...", he called, wincing in pain as he stepped out, past a sitting cat, "...What are you still doing here, Moggy? Where the fuck is Vincent?"

The cat just looked at him, mewing for food or attention – it didn't care which. Outside, at the far end of the terrace, another cat was peering over the edge, looking like it was about to jump.

"Too high even for you, Mog. Go for it."

Just like he called all his robotic servants Alfred, he called all cats Moggy. They were all too unimportant to be named individually.

It mewed when it saw him approach, then hissed and ran straight passed, back in through the French doors.

"Bloody ingrate.", said Lionel, watching it run inside.

Two strangers stepped into view from alcoves in the wall.

"Who the bloody-hell are you? What are you doing in my house? Go away! Vincent! *Vincent*!"

One of them strode past him and closed the French door - taking out the key and trapping him with them. He took a step back, towards the far side.

"What do you want? Money?"

They walked towards him. Lionel backed further away - further and further until he was right against the railing. He kept thumping his wristcom for help but kept getting the same message: 'no signal'.

"**VINCENT! HELP!** Who *are* you?"

One of the men put a hand in his jacket.

"Don't shoot me! I'll pay. What ever you want!"

The man took out not a gun but a white card – holding it out for Lionel to take. It was an old-fashioned business card, from *Remember Us*.

"You've no doubt heard of us."

Lionel had heard of them. Knew what they were and what they did.

"Murderers. You killed some good people. My friends. **VINCENT, WHERE-THE-FUCK ARE YOU?**"

One of the men grabbed his arm. A solid, inescapable grip of iron.

"**VINCENT GET HERE NOW OR YOU'RE FUCKING FIRED!!!!!**"

The other produced a horse-sized syringe, with a gas attachment. Lionel struggled as hard as he could, desperate to break free. It was as impossible as the strength of the man's grip.

"You're a bloody android!"

The man with the syringe, pushed a tiny metal ball into its tip and pressed it against Lionel's temple. Lionel shook his head to displace it but the man thrust it in - the tip pushing through his skin, locking it in place.

"**Bastard!**"

"No, Lionel, it is you who is the bastard. It is because of you that we are here. My brother died from brain cancer when he was 27. I was made infertile. My wife got dementia – at just 42. And now I have an ipsilateral brain tumour. You know what ipsilateral means?"

"Never heard of it."

"One sided. The side we most used for our mobile phones. Phones and Wi-Fi that people like you told us were safe."

"I never once said they were safe. We were told there was no consistent evidence of harm."

"By whom?"

"The regulators. The ICNIRP."

"Regulators set up by your telecoms industry and funded by it?"

"Of course we fund it. It's our duty to fund investigations into any health effects. We would have been criticised if we hadn't."

"But you spent those millions ensuring the dangers were buried by confusion. Just like the tobacco industry before you. They got away with it. You think you have too. You're mistaken."

"We did nothing wrong. *I* did nothing wrong."

"Then why are we here? Why do you have this pneumatic syringe at the side of your head?"

Lionel was thinking fast, trying to find a solution. Any solution that would avoid his death.

"Look. I'm sorry if you have health problems. Private medicine can help. I can call my doctor. I'll pay - all expenses on me."

"We've seen doctors, oncologists... It's terminal. Everyone in our group has a terminal condition, thanks to people like you but, yes, you are right. You are going to pay."

Without warning, the man triggered the syringe. It jumped, firing the tiny ball through Lionel's temple and into his brain.

"ARRGH!"

For a second he blacked out with pain. His legs crumpled but the thing holding his hands kept him upright. He blinked through his watering eyes, vision blurring in and out.

"For fuck's sake, that hurts! What have you done?"

The man with the syringe put his face in front of Lionel's. It's a microwave transmitter. No more powerful than the ones you so happily sold to billions of children. Only difference is, it's now inside your brain, irradiating you at point-blank range. You're too old to get a brain tumour, the way your devices gave tumours to us, so this is designed to break down the neurons of your frontal lobe. Eat away at your memories, at who you are. In a couple of hours you won't remember seeing us. In a day or so, you won't recognise your family. In a week you'll be a gawping vegetable – dead to the world. A public warning to others who put profits ahead of user safety. It's taken 30 years for this moment to happen but I'll tell you this for nothing, the look on your face makes it worth the wait."

Lionel was squinting, blinking, trying to see straight through eyes that refused to comply.

"I'll be fine. My doctors will take it out."

"No chance. Where it is, it's inoperable, just like mine. Even now it's breaking down your brain's DNA. The only way to get it out is to remove so much of your brain you'll become a vegetable on the spot. By the time your communication systems come back on line so you can call for help, massive damage will have been done. Keep the card, Lionel. Remember us."

The thing holding his hands let him go, pushing him away, towards the other side of the terrace.

"And for your information, shit head, I'm not an android. I'm just angry and I go to the gym. It's why I'm strong even now, you pathetic, fat weakling. Has the scanner pulled the information?"

His colleague was watching the scanner's progress tree, branches turning from amber to green.

"Evergreen extracted. Analysing...."

Hundreds, thousands of names, numbers, pictures and videos flitted across the screen. Suddenly it froze. Locked on one, pulsing red name.

"...got it."

"Same name?"

"Same name. Same place."

"They have an awful lot to answer for."

"Our time is running out. Let's get on with it. Where next?"

"City four."

They spoke to each other as if Lionel already no longer existed. Abandoning him to the rooftop, they walked back into the house and closed the door behind them. Lionel grabbed hold of the railing, to steady his shaking hands and thoughts. How had his life suddenly become so bad? And where the hell was Vincent?

Down below he heard the front door open and close. They were leaving. In an act of defiance he leant over the balcony to spit at them. What he saw dried his mouth.

"Oh, Christ..."

He knew he was a dead man. No chance of help to get to any doctor in time for any chance of help at any price. On the drive below, flooding blood all over the tarmac, was the fallen body of Vincent.

He tried his wristcom again. It was as blocked as the memories in his head were becoming.

"I'm fucked...."

Slowly he sank down, sitting on the floor of the terrace, leaning against the decorative iron railings. Staring at the side of his beautiful, multi-million pound home. He had everything to live for. The life of dreams. The life he had always dreamt of. Inside, he could already feel his thoughts beginning to slow, like thickening porridge in his brain.

A day later, as a beautiful red sun painted a magical sky, voices and silhouettes came to join him.

"Sir. Sir, are you OK? Can you hear me?"

"What happened, Lionel? How did Vincent fall?"

"Ambulance is on the way."

Lionel looked at them. Felt he should know them and tried to speak but couldn't remember how.

The hum of an air-ambulance came down, emergency blue lights flashing. He watched two paramedics jump out, onto the terrace, and stride towards him. He didn't know why they were there. Had the feeling they were there to help. Help with what...?

Chapter 63
Run Shabbir, Run

Shabbir was on an emergency assignment. An officer's cover had been blown in the worst way possible – while they were undercover without knowing it. With no idea of the danger they were now in. Adam and Gurmeet were tied up. Henry was on his way from Thames House but four miles behind. Shabbir couldn't wait. It was down to him. For all he knew, he could already be too late.

He was on his bike. A twin-turbine ground missile, with 300 horse-power and a top speed around 200mph. It was also slim and lightweight. Extremely agile. On his bike Shabbir was as fluid as a ballet dancer, surfing a blue-light streak of lightening. Doughnut belly resting against the fuel cell, his martial-arts reflexes pirouetted the bike through the traffic. Turbines screaming. 3D head up display on his visor overlaying the best route in real time, switching traffic-lights to green in time for his approach.

'ETA 22 seconds'.

He could the see the direction arrow pointing to the building ahead. Officer location circle pinging in yellow, entrance and exit points pinging in green. A hundred metres away, he cut the turbines then squeezed the brakes - stopping as hard and as late as he could without squealing the tyres. As the bike headed under the fire escape, he jumped off, grabbing the bottom rail and hauling himself up with an agility that belied his size. No need to lock the bike, it was encoded to his biometrics and quietly auto-parked he hurried upwards – as stealthily as he could on the cold-steel steps. Fourth floor. Why was it always high up, never at ground level?

Breathing hard but as quietly as possible, Shabbir leant against the fourth-floor wall, outside the yellow-pinged room. The window was as open as his mouth but there was total silence from inside. Lights dim, on low. He had chosen the side of the window away from the street light so it wouldn't be behind him, throwing his shadow into the room as he used a corner-cam to peer inside. No sign of life. No sign of the officer. He could really be too late. Silently he slid over the ledge, pistol first.

TchZoooo!

From nowhere, a laser shot flashed across - tearing the end off his pistol's barrel.

"Shabbir?"

He knew that voice.

"Xi! Aren't you supposed to look before you shoot? What setting is that thing on?"

"Full. Sorry. Wasn't expecting back up."

Shabbir held up his smoking laser-pistol, 5cm shorter than before.

"Got a spare? Mine's toast."

"Take his.", she said, indicating towards the hitman on the floor – blood pooled around his head, trousers and underpants around his ankles, as was his dignity.

"You know, what? I'm not even going to ask what happened."

"Good. Now, why *are* you here?"

"Your cover's blown."

"How? Adam and Gurmeet OK?"

"Hopefully. They've both gone dark so must have got in."

Shabbir took the hitman's laser-pistols, checked the charges and they headed for the peaceful exit of the front door.

"We can talk at mine.", he said.

The door burst open. Smoke and laser fire poured in. Flashing beams of blue. Beams of red. High powered. They dived for cover. Cover wasn't enough. The beams cut through everything. Everything except angled mirrors and even then the mirror surface got scarred with each blast. Nothing would stop them for long. They both had to keep moving. Stop the attackers from locking on. Xi was on the left. A snatched wall mirror in one hand, laser pistol firing in the other. Noting where an attacker was firing from, aiming for them through the wall. Shabbir had no mirror. Just had to keep moving. Keep firing. It was a battle of attrition. Shoot harder and better - take down the others before getting taken down. Xi saw Shabbir was close to the open window.

"Run, Shabbir! I'll cover you!"

"No. This is a rescue."

"It was. You tried. Now go. Run! Report in. Come back for them later. If we both die no-one will know what happened."

Technically she was right. If they both got killed their murderers would get away with it. No-one would know what had happened, except a gun fight. Staying was Russian roulette. Sooner or later a shot would connect.

"Run, Shabbir, Run! *Please!*", urged Xi.

Xi almost never said please. Especially not like that. Shabbir glanced over at his colleague. His friend. Firing and diving through the smoke and flashes of lethal beams tearing through the flat. He stopped firing. Took his finger off the trigger. She saw his laser beams had stopped. Dashed a glance his way. Still firing, she smiled in approval that he would escape then turned back to re-focus on their attackers, eyes narrowed in deadly concentration. Keeping them focused on her - saving Shabbir was a final act she was glad to make. An honourable goodbye, five-thousand miles and six years overdue.

Shabbir ran. Not for the window but straight for the door. Holding the three-point sequence on his laser pistols. Triggering more than just overload. Triggering self-destruct. None of the attackers expected a head-on charge. It would be suicide. It gave him an edge.

Xi was horrified. Her mouth fell open, trying to speak with no words coming out. Her trigger finger still pumping, aim subconsciously to the left to avoid hitting him even though he was dead already. No-one could survive that barrage.

Two metres from the doorway, crashing to the ground, Shabbir's laser-pistols flew through it. Cores unstable. Temperature 2,000 degrees and rising.

"Duck!", he grunted.

The guns hit the corridor floor and detonated on impact with huge blasts. The doorway exploded. Brick and body parts splattered the walls. Shabbir was thrown across the room.

Covered in dust and debris, Xi scurried over the carnage-covered floor to get to him. To cradle his bloodied, dying form like the mother she had never been able to be. He had sacrificed himself to save her - such honourable kindness was not lost even on her hardened soul. Nor was the horror of seeing the blood running from his mouth. The multiple impact points of laser wounds pin-cushioning his body armour.

"Think there's that vacancy for team-leader you wanted.", he croaked.

Xi was shaking her head, dangerously close to tears.

"When I said run, I meant out the window, not the bloody door."

Despite them both trying to make light of the situation, they both knew he was fading. Pulse readout on his wristcom was dropping. From the corridor she heard running and shouting. Not help but more attackers coming their way.

"Come on! Make sure they're dead. No mercy. No survivors."

Xi knew it was the end. As two they could maybe keep them at bay for another minute. By herself it would be just seconds. Their chances of survival had just dropped to zero.

"Run.", croaked Shabbir, eyes already closing.

The readout showed his pulse was weak. Dangerously weak and getting weaker but he wasn't dead yet. Not yet. And while he wasn't dead she wouldn't leave him. This time it wasn't her home village of Wujiamencun but it was her Wujiamencun. Her chance to show honour through sacrifice.

The sound of the new attackers was getting louder. Resting Shabbir's head gently on the remains of a cushion, she took her laser-pistol, dropped in her last charge and lay on the floor beside him - aiming towards the remains of the broken wall with calm, rock-steady hands. Escape was the logical thing to do. This was her thing to do.

She hadn't been there to make a last stand for her murdered family but she was there now for her adopted one. A last stand for her comrade in arms. She knew it was suicide and she welcomed it. Finally her pain of dishonour would end with honour. It was a good way to die.

Chapter 64
The Team

Charlotte and Julia stood in the parking area as the mirror-windowed bus pulled in to their training camp. Robert walked over to join them.

"Come to meet the rest of the team?", he asked.

"Would be unteam-like not to."

"Good answer. That's just promoted you to team leader, Charlotte."

"Really? Thank you."

The door slid open. Six, natural-born hooligans in their 20's stepped out; a collection of convicts and low-society failures. Charlotte could see the failure in their faces; they way they carried themselves and the jostling.

"Welcome. Names, please.", said Robert.

Failure behaviour was also in the way they spoke.

"Barry, mate."

"Just Barry will do. Next."

"Jimmy."

"Ralph."

"Wayne."

"Dick. Big Dick.", grinned the fourth, winking at Charlotte and Julia.

"Yeah, a fucking big dick head...", laughed Jimmy, "...But cock like a poodle in snow."

Julia looked at them, annoyed people like that were alive when Jake, her good Jake, was dead. Charlotte just looked at them. This was her team?

"Ignore those bozos. I'm Shaun. The walking house behind me is Alistair."

"Well, Barry, Jimmy, Wayne, Dick, Shaun and Alistair, my name is Robert. I run this place. These two are Emily and Charlotte. Charlotte is your team leader."

"A WOMAN!?!...." exclaimed Jimmy, "...You have got to be fucking kidding m..."

Before he could finish he was slammed to the ground, objections knocked out of him. Charlotte standing above.

"Anyone else want to diss me?"

No-one spoke a word. The mixture of shock and awe on their faces said plenty.

"Good. You'll find a free bed in that building over there. The bell will ring in an hour, for dinner in the main building behind me. Two other members of the team, Colin and Andrew, will join you there."

"OK, boss...", said Shaun, looking like he was already enjoying the experience, "...Let's go guys. Get up Jim, you daft bozo."

"Think I'm in love.", murmured Alistair, smiling at Charlotte as they went.

*   *   *

An hour later, Julia jumped awake to the sound of the dinner bell. She hadn't even realised she'd fallen asleep.

"Time to go, Emily."

"Did I sleep for long?"

"Half an hour or so. Good timing. This is the calm before the storm. Going to be a long evening ahead. I can feel it."

Together they left their dorm and headed for the main building. It looked full. There hadn't just been those six new arrivals but another ten to replace them when they left on their mission.

"Does this mean they don't expect us to come back?", asked Julia.

"I think the second we walk into the location we are never coming back to the lives we had before, what ever happens. You can't do something like that and just walk away. Doesn't happen."

"Hi, guys...", said a smiling Andrew as they came in, "...Been talking to the new team members. Hear you're our leader."

"Got a problem with that?", smiled Charlotte, feigning a stare of seriousness.

"God no. Means you get all the paperwork for a change."

Julia looked at them both. Her natural-born investigative mind instantly joining dots others would have missed.

"You two knew each other before here?"

It took both Andrew and Charlotte by surprise.

"I'd forgotten how much attention you pay to detail. Yes, we've known each other a while.", said Charlotte.

"Where?"

"Used to work in the same office. Computers and stuff. Nothing interesting.", said Andrew.

"He was my senior for a while. Ironically, I'm now his."

"Remember, I was kind to you though."

"Sometimes..."

They were interrupted by the second bell for dinner. The 'get it and eat it' bell.

"Grab a plate, everyone. Help yourselves...", announced Charlotte, adopting her team-leader role with aplomb. They all did as she instructed, especially Jimmy.

"I'm impressed...", said Robert, coming over to join her, "...Come sit and eat with me once you've got your dinner. Got some details to run through."

*   *   *

Sitting with Robert, talking between bites, Charlotte listened as he laid down more details of his plan. Of how they were going to take over one of Hinkley Point C's two nuclear power stations. How they had someone inside to get them past main security.

"How exactly are we going to threaten them with meltdown? I don't know a thing about controlling a nuclear reactor, let alone pointing it towards meltdown without it actually melting down."

"You don't need to know. Our inside guy does."

"And if he changes his mind or gets taken down?"

"Improvise, Charlotte. I have confidence in you. And talking of confidence, who would you choose to run a small, break-away team?"

"To do what?"

"Research mission. Must be bright and level-headed."

"How many in the team?"

"Three. From your current ten."

Charlotte looked over at her pick and mix team, tucking into their dinners.

"Head it with Andrew, second it with Shaun. And, please, take the dick head."

"You want to keep Jimmy, even though he hates female authority?"

"I can handle Jimmy."

Robert nodded, smile on his face.

"Yes, I saw. Very well then."

"Where will they be going?"

"Researching, like I said. We lost a valuable asset. I want... Not want, I *need* to know how it happened. They had the latest tech and somehow it got turned off. Excuse me while I make a call. Would you mind telling Andrew he's been promoted."

Charlotte nodded.

"Sure."

Andrew noticed Robert leave Charlotte and go to his office. Then he saw Charlotte beaming at him, mischievously.

"You've got paperwork.", she mouthed.

Andrew understood that meant. He'd been put in charge of something. He rolled his eyes, which delighted Charlotte even more. The paperwork monster had claimed him too.

*   *   *

After dinner, Roberta appeared - face still heavily bruised after the fight with Julia two days before - stitches over her left eye. She didn't meet anyone's gaze. Just went to the podium and made her announcement.

"Listen up, people. Everyone who is not in the team of ten or on dinner duty, finish up and outside in two. Team of ten, wait here. Robert will be with you shortly. Thank you."

Something had changed, Roberta never said thank you. For the next two minutes, chairs scraped the floor; people shuffled to the door and went outside, taking the murmur of voices with them. Roberta went too. Andrew joined Charlotte.

"So I'm heading another team?", he whispered.

"Yup."

"Who with?"

"Shaun and the dickhead."

"Just three of us? Oh, great. Know what we're doing?"

"Some investigation. Someone or something didn't play ball."

"Me doing an investigation for Faith? That's ironic."

"Isn't it just."

"What are you up to?"

"Hinkley Point. Going to take over a reactor."

"With that lot? Nothing to worry about there, then."

"No. Not like it's rocket science or anything complicated like that."

"Let's break the good news to our teams."

Together they stood up to speak, Andrew went first.

"Shaun and Dick, you're with me. New mission."

"Everyone else stays with me...", affirmed Charlotte, "...Come closer because I'm not going to shout our mission out."

The two teams gathered on opposite sides of the room. Andrew had very little information to give but was soon joined by Robert who filled them in. Charlotte watched as Robert gave Andrew an NFC box of details, shook the hands of each of them and watched as the three stood up and left. Andrew gave Charlotte a quick nod of acknowledgement as they went. She gave him a smile but it left the second he did. Left because she had a sudden feeling of trepidation even before the door had clacked shut behind them.

"When are they coming back?", she asked as Robert came to join them.

His answer to that was a look that affirmed they might not be coming back.

"Have you told them the mission yet?", he asked.

"She has.", said Alistair.

"Good. You have three days to prepare for the 'boiler'. Tell no-one outside your team. If word gets out the mission will fail and you'll end up at the mercy of Partner, who have none. Pull up some chairs and I'll go through the details."

Chapter 65
Henry

Xi Yang saw shadows from left and right, running down the corridor towards the blasted wall where a doorway used to be. Her cool hands firmly on her laser-pistol. Fully charged. Ready to fire the second one appeared. Closer and closer she heard them come. Footsteps getting louder and louder and louder. Then they stopped. They had reached both sides of the blast hole. She counted the sound of a dozen safety switches clicking off, a dozen guns ready to fire, with more on the way. She steadied her breath - narrowed eyes searching for shadows of movement. Her finger against the trigger.

TchZoooo. TchZoooo. TchZoooo. TchZoooo

She returned fire - controlled, aimed shots.

TchZoooo. TchZoooo.

DVOO. DVOO. DVOO. DVOO. DVOO. DVOO. DVOO. DVOO.

Deep thudding shots of hot, blue plasma whizzed over her head, crackling the air. Slamming through the corridor walls as if they were paper.

Shit, they're behind me.

She looked round to cover her back. Saw a wide-barrelled plasma-rifle poking through the window. Before she could shoot it fired again. Rapid high-energy blasts that tore across the room.

DVOO. DVOO. DVOO. DVOO. DVOO. DVOO. DVOO. DVOO.

Each fat ball of plasma blasted a hole in the wall. Existing holes were made bigger. Big enough to see the blasts didn't stop there but punched straight across the corridor - through the walls on the other side. Xi stayed down, unsure whether it was missing her by chance or design, keeping her laser-pistol aimed towards the window. The attackers in the corridor had stopped firing too - keeping their heads down. Nobody there had any weapon that could match that kind of fire-power. Xi lay still, watching and waiting for a clear shot. Just one clear shot.

DVOO. DVOO. DVOO. DVOO. DVOO. DVOO. DVOO. DVOO.

To the sound of new bricks dropping from the crumbling front wall, the shooter advanced. Stepped in through the window. She had a clear shot.

"Henry."

Arms bigger than most men's legs. Neck almost thicker than his head. Legs like tree trunks. She had never been more glad to see Henry in her life.

"Stay down!", he said.

TchZoooo. TchZoooo.

Braved a laser from the corridor.

TchZoooo. TchZoooo.

Fired another.

Henry noted where the shots came from and returned fire.

DVOO. DVOO. DVOO. DVOO. DVOO. DVOO. DVOO. DVOO.

Henry's plasma-rifle was powerful enough to drop a tank. High-calibre balls of blue fire launching at four rounds a second. He was taking out not just the attackers but everything in the corridor and on that floor. Structural columns on the opposite side of the building shook with the impacts. Brick walls cracked as the shots slammed against them. Brick dust and shards of glass from shattered windows rained down on the street below. Glistening like falling glitter in the flashing blue of emergency services racing their way, led by SO-19 armed-response police.

TchZoooo, came a single, defiant laser shot from the corridor.

DVOO. DVOO. DVOO. DVOO.

A single shot back would have been enough but Henry had a rule: once started he always made sure of a decisive end – especially when defending his colleagues. The walls of Jin Ho's flat had been shot into Swiss-cheese. Fires had broken out, steaming from the water from the overhead sprinklers as smoke alarms screamed. Laser shots came no more. Minutes ago, Henry's scanner had picked up 31 armed attackers and no civilians on that floor. He scanned again. Now there were just four - three of them very weak.

"Where's Shabbir?"

"Here!....", answered Xi, crawling towards him over the rubble, "...He's hit."

Huge plasma-rifle in both hands, tip of the barrel glowing red hot, Henry strode over the smoking rubble towards him. As blue-lit sirens screeched to a halt outside, defiant yellow flames licked higher up the walls. The entire floor of the building creaked, threatening collapse.

"He's dying, Henry."

Henry had two specialities. Experimental, high-calibre weapons and experimental medicine, to patch battle-field injuries from high-calibre weapons. His bionic eye implant was scanning Shabbir. Xi was right. He was dying. Four broken ribs. Ruptured liver. Torn artery. Multiple penetration wounds despite his motorbike body armour.

Defences first. Henry hit a dark-red, triangular 'hazard' button on top the plasma-rifle. It thrust out a small tripod underneath and he stood it on the floor, facing the corridor – an automatic sentry gun, just in case. It scanned the room, logged the three of them as friendly and sat on standby, continuously scanning the area – ready to shred any intruders.

From his small backpack Henry took out a DNA-jelly pad, ripped open Shabbir's shirt and smeared it over his chest and right side. Taking out his hand-scanner, he pressed it against the jelly and hit 'pulse'. A burst of high-voltage electricity zapped it awake. Like a creation by Frankenstein, it was suddenly alive.

A fine, white filigree of pulses webbed across it, looking like a neural network. In front of Xi's eyes, it dissolved through Shabbir's skin, healing all damage as it went. A self-moulding, surgical plaster bio-guided by Henry's bionic eye. It grew a patch over the tear near Shabbir's heart, adjusting its DNA to match the original. It spread over his liver, below the broken rib puncturing it, DNA-matching that too as it made another patch there. Repositioning the ribs would need surgery but the two patches were a good start. The remaining jelly dissolved into his bloodstream – becoming energised blood that healed his wounds from the inside as it was pumped around.

"He's stabilising.", said Xi, breaking into a smile she didn't expect to make.

"Stay with him. I need to get one of them for questioning."

Now only two attackers still clung to life in the corridor - a battle they were both losing. Henry took out a DNA jelly pad and chose one. The only attacker that was going to leave that building alive that day. An attacker that would think he was lucky. He was wrong. Xi Yang was brutal by the unquenchable pain of her murdered family stabbed through her heart. Henry was brutal because so were his enemies. To his mind, they deserved everything they tried to inflict others.

Chapter 66

Cheryl's Friend

A delivery drone arrived at Cheryl's house, depositing a package in her secure landing cage. She didn't hear it but saw the green delivery indicator flashing in her hallway. It was from them. It had to be from them.

Full of fear-tainted hope she hurried into the garden and unlocked the cage. Inside was a small, brown rectangular box; red light flashing beside the retina scanner on the top. She took it out and walked briskly back into the house - desperate to see what was inside. At the same time scared of seeing what was inside.

Before the kitchen door had even shut behind her, she activated the retina scan - the red light flashed green. Unlocked. Would it be a bomb, a body part, poison...? Bravely, she prised open the lid and looked inside. There was a laser-pistol, wrapped in a piece of paper. Blank, white paper.

What am I expected to do with this?, she thought, unwrapping the paper.

As her fingers made contact, the paper began changing colour - chemically reacting to her DNA. It began turning blue. Darker and darker blue. Within the blue words appeared, beside two diagrams. Diagrams labelled 'disabled toilet at Hinkley C: WC105. Thursday 2pm.' The diagrams showed a removable wall covering in the toilet wall, with an arrow indicating exactly where she was to put the box.

The kidnappers were telling her to make a drop. To get the package on site in the nuclear power station. She had no military background and took no interest in any such thing but even she assumed the plasticine like stuff in the first box, with its odd chemical smell, was an explosive. Take explosive into her nuclear power site? No amount of money could make her do such a thing. She had aced all security checks and psychological tests - been deemed a stable, trustworthy, competent worker and the tests weren't wrong. The premise of them was. The tests made no allowance for a parent whose children were under pain of death if demands were not met. Cheryl loved her work, her life, her country. She loved her children more. For her children she would do what ever they demanded. Who ever they were. What ever they were planning.

Two days. She had exactly two days to make the delivery.

A sudden knock at the window made her yelp with fright. It was her neighbour, Helen, waving for attention. A friend. A friend who knew her children had been taken. A friend who wanted her to go to the police. A friend who could end up getting her children killed. She looked at the paper again, memorised the instructions then pushed it into the micro-shredder. Hiding the laser-pistol in her cardigan pocket, she went to open the door.

"Any news?", asked Helen.

"Come in."

Helen entered, a friend's concern all over her face.

"What did the police say? Are they out looking for them?"

Cheryl walked to the living room and sat in an armchair. Helen sat on the sofa.

"I didn't call the police.", confessed Cheryl.

"*What*? Why?"

"Because I want my kids back. Alive. In one piece. Not murdered."

"You can't trust people like that! They'll never keep to their word. Mary and Tony deserve police help to save them."

"They're my kids, Helen. I believe they will hurt them if I don't do what they say. Their lives are all that matters."

Helen looked exasperated. Raised her voice, almost shouting.

"**Wake up, Cheryl**! You can't trust them! The kids will be able to identify them. Once they've been used they'll be killed. Their only chance is you going to the police. Getting them help."

"They told me they have people inside the police. Helen, they're *my* kids. *My* kids, not yours! It's my decision."

"It's the wrong decision. If you won't report it, I will...", Helen stood up, "...I'm going to the police. Right now."

Cheryl began to panic. Helen was walking towards the door. Towards the police. She had to stop her. In desperation, she snatched out the laser-pistol and pointed it at her friend. A friend she had known for years. A friend they often spent Christmas with. But her kids' lives were at stake.

Cheryl had seen enough detective films to know there had to be a safety on the gun somewhere. With fumbling, desperate fingers she found it. Clicked it off. Aimed and fired.

TchZoooo.

The plant pot in the hallway burst apart.

Helen froze. Slowly, she turned around and saw Cheryl, trembling with stress and emotion – holding the gun out. Pointing it determinedly at her.

"You going to shoot me, Chez?"

"I can't let you go to the police, Helen."

"You're stressed. Not thinking straight. As your friend, it is my duty to help. The police have to be involved."

"The kids are my life, Helen. Come back and sit down or I'll shoot."

"Cheryl, I love the kids too and I love you. You know I do. Trust me, as your friend. The police have to be told. We need their help. Put the gun down and come there with me."

Bravely Helen turned back towards the front door.

"Helen... Don't! Helen..."

"You can't shoot a friend, Chez.", said Helen, reaching for the handle.

"Helen, don't..."

Helen wasn't listening. No-one was listening.

TchZoooo.

Chapter 67
Blue Lights

Before anyone could stop them, three paramedics ran into Jin Ho's building, followed by armed police. The fire brigade was ordered to wait outside until it was clear.

"MI5!..", shouted Henry, holding up his ID as he knelt in the corridor beside his chosen victim, "...SENTRY GUN ACTIVE. WEAPONS DOWN. NOW!"

The paramedics ran over.

"In there...", nodded Henry, towards the remains of the flat, "...two officers down. Male has broken ribs. I've stabilised his heart and punctured liver. I think the female's OK but double check."

Two ran in to help Shabbir and Xi. The third knelt down beside Henry's survivor.

"And this one?"

Henry pulled back the attackers burnt shirt, revealing the fist-sized hole in his chest from a plasma bolt. It had gone straight though his left lung and out his back. The heat of the bolt had cauterised most of the wound but some blood still dripped from tears higher up.

"That's got to hurt like hell. I'll give him some morphine."

"I already did.", lied Henry, noticing the armed police jogging along the corridor.

"**I SAID WEAPONS DOWN! MI5! SENTRY GUN!..**", he shouted to them, then spoke again to the paramedic, "...Get a stretcher, while I get my gun before that lot get themselves killed."

* * *

"I'll go with Shabbir...", said Xi as Henry returned and de-activated his rifle's sentry-gun mode.

"You're a tough cookie, Xi. You stood by him. Saved his life."

"You did that with your gel. Henry..."

"Yes?"

"Thank you for coming. Not many would."

"Never under-estimate your colleagues – you just got unlucky in Wujiwhatever."

"Wujiamencun."

"That's the one. Anyway, wanted to test my new gun. Now to test some other stuff on that bastard over there. I'll see you later."

He put a hand of comradeship on Xi's shoulder and picked up his wide-barrelled plasma-rifle with the other. When the police saw it their jaws dropped, finally understanding how close they had come to being blown to pieces.

"Who the-fuck makes guns like that?"

"I do.", replied Henry, and carried on walking.

A fire marshal came running up the corridor.

"EVERYONE OUT! OUT NOW! This whole floor could collapse. Looks like someone's been firing tank-shells through...", his voice faded as he caught sight of Henry, with his massive plasma-rifle.

".No tanks up here, mate...", said Henry, "...I'd have taken them down if there were."

"No shit...", said the marshal, believing he would have and understanding how the structural damage had been done.

*   *   *

Outside, blue-light services were everywhere. Ambulance, armed police and fire. Henry had been green-flashed onto their scanners so they knew he wasn't an armed terrorist emerging from the building. The sole surviving attacker was floated out on a life-support stretcher; Shabbir too, accompanied by Xi walking beside him, silver-thermal blanket around her shoulders. She walked with paramedics to Shabbir's ambulance, ignoring their hands of help as she climbed in.

"Find out what you can.", she called out to Henry.

"You know I will.", replied Henry, getting into another ambulance, with the attacker.

As their two ambulances drove away, the building gave a loud crack. One of the remaining fourth-floor supports had finally snapped. It's failure loaded the remaining ones even more.

"EVERYONE OUT!"

A domino effect had begun.

"OUT! OUT! OUT!"

Another crack. Another support snapped, brick around it crumbling.

"IT'S COMING DOWN! CLEAR THE AREA!"

"Sir, Arnold Johnson's still inside. Stairwell blocked."

"Where?"

"Fourth floor. East side."

"Tell him to jump! CARL!...", he shouted into his coms, "...Landing pad, East side. NOW!"

"Copy!", came Carl's immediate reply.

Two paramedics rushed out of the main doors, choking from the cloud of building dust as they carried the only other survivor – the attacker Henry had left to die. They hurried him onto a life-support stretcher and hurried for another ambulance.

Three loud cracks came from the building, one after the other, shuddering the ground in rapid succession.

"Johnson! JUMP!", came the shout of Carl's voice above the mayhem.

The western wall was unzipping down the middle. Already undone from the roof to the 5th floor, the split was tearing its way down towards the ground.

"Coming down! **CLEAR BACK!**"

Everyone was clearing back - including the locals who'd come out to watch. Running to a safer distance, vehicles reversing away, some banging into others. Standing in flashing-strobes of blue, they heard the roof cave in. Concrete slabs piling inwards - their mass of weight smashing downwards - shoving the western wall outwards, making it unzip all the way down. The eastern, northern and southern walls, now taking the entire load, could take it no more. Their walls broke apart, crumbling. Deafening tons of falling bricks, concrete and steel girders – now hidden from view behind the cloud of smoking dust as the building collapsed, shaking the ground like an earthquake as it began hitting street level.

"Was the building cleared? Carl! Did Johnson get out? CARL! Come in! Copy?"

Such were the questions every branch of the blue-light services would be asking the officers in charge. Henry, sitting in the ambulance looking at the attacker on life-support, heard it all through his wristcom.

"Johnson's gone, sir. Landed fine. Building came down on top of him."

"DIG HIM OUT! Fast! He's not dead 'til I say he is!"

"Copy!"

Henry knew Johnson. They had shared a flat for a year before he joined

MI5. Arnold Johnson was a good man, with a young family. He felt guilt it was his gun that had brought the building down. Then that feeling of guilt turned to anger. His gun had only been fired because of the attack on Xi and Shabbir. Arnold Johnson's death was another reason why the attacker beside him was going to wake up. Wake up long enough to learn regret for still being alive. Before Henry spoke his condolences to Arnold's family and brothers, Neville and Nicholas, this attacker would speak no more.

Chapter 68
Shooter

Robert had decided to take advantage of the windless day to gather the team of seven at the back of the main building. They arrived to find two large, wooden crates.

"What's the plan?", asked Charlotte.

Robert indicated towards the human cut outs 50 metres away.

"Target practice. Choose your weapons people. Plenty to go round."

The crates were brimming with an assortment of laser pistols and rifles.

"Nothing plasma?", asked Alistair, holding a laser rifle that looked like a toy gun in his huge hands.

"Think that will do for you, Al'.", said Charlotte, taking a pair of laser-pistols for herself.

"'spose you're right, boss."

Alistair, despite being the biggest there, was also the least problematic. The one with absolutely nothing to prove.

"Power cells?", asked Barry.

"All in good time.", said Robert.

Julia waited for the rush to be over before perusing what was left. With everyone busy, examining up their new weapons, she snuck a laser-pistol into her boot – quickly covering it with her jeans. Put another in the side of her belt, then saw her calling; a military-spec laser-rifle, identical to her dad's. With both hands she hoisted it out, checking the smoothness of the trigger, sliders and vectorscope. Not quite as well-maintained as his but still good - probably brand new.

"Team...", began Robert, "...I'm not going to ask who has and who has not fired a weapon before. I'm going to run through the basics for all of you. Ignorance is dangerous so just listen good."

He held up a laser-pistol in his right hand, pointing to sections of it as he spoke.

"Barrel, grip, safety slider – make sure yours shows black, not red – sight, power-cell release and trigger. Overload options have been disabled - they don't need to be more powerful than they are. Any questions so far?"

Silence. He looked at Julia, the youngest of the team, and found her standing there, laser-rifle in hand, looking as nonplussed as the rest.

"Good. To load your weapon, take a power-cell and note the circular shape. It can go in any way, as long as it's lengthways. There's no top or bottom, front or back. If you have a rifle, it goes into the magazine stub, in front of the trigger, doubling as a second grip. If you have a pistol, it goes in the grip."

Robert was demonstrating loading a rifle as he spoke.

"Slide it in until it clicks. To release when depleted, press the buttons at its top together – left and right. It drops back out."

The slid in charge, popped back out into his open hand.

"Is that clear?"

"Can't we just start?...", asked Jimmy, "...I've been shooting guns since I was five."

Robert responded by beckoning him forward.

"Jimmy's volunteered to go first, ladies and gentlemen."

Jimmy was a natural born show off. He waved to the team, his imaginary cheering fans as he waltzed over to Robert.

"Safety showing black?", asked Robert.

"Yup."

"Then here's your power-cell."

Jimmy took it and, acting super cool, thumped it into the slot. It didn't go in straight and fell out, onto the grass.

"Smoothly...", said Robert, "...Has to go in far enough to lock."

"I know.... Just playing.", said Jimmy, trying to regain his air of cool as he bent down to pick it off the grass.

Barry and Wayne were sniggering.

"I was just playing.", repeated Jimmy.

"Safety showing black?", asked Robert.

"Of course.", lied Jimmy, sliding it to black.

This time the power-cell clicked home.

"You can see your target over there. The darker the colour ring the higher the point. Four shots. When you're ready. In your own time."

"Got it.", said Jimmy, holding his laser-pistol on its side, Hollywood style.

Click.

"Put the safety on red to fire.", reminded Robert.

Barry and Wayne could hardly control themselves. Even Robert had an amused smile on his face.

"Just playing, you lot.", said Jimmy, sliding it to red.

He pulled the trigger again.

TchZoooo.

Blue laser spat out, puffing smoke off the bank 50m behind the target.

"I suggest aiming with the sight.", said Robert.

"We're not hunting random rabbits, Jimbo!", heckled Barry.

"I know. Just showing you amateurs what not to do.", said Jimmy, now holding the pistol upright so he could actually see down the sights.

TchZoooo.

The target's belly lit bright orange.

TchZoooo.

The belly again.

TchZoooo.

The chest.

"Jimmy, you scored four points.", announced Robert, "One for each of the belly shots, two for the chest."

"And none for the rabbit, mate...", laughed Wayne, "...It's still watching."

"Safety back to black?"

"Of course...", lied Jimmy again, sliding it to black, "...Just playing, Wayne. Don't want to show up you bunch of girls with my pin-point accuracy. No offence, boss.", he added, seeing the frown on Charlotte's face.

"Wayne, you're next."

And so it continued. Target practice for all, down the line. The highest score was Alistair's, two head and two chest shots. Charlotte went next.

"Good luck.", said Alistair.

"Luck, has nothing to do with it.", she replied calmly, loading the power-cell and sliding the safety to red.

TchZoooo. TchZoooo. TchZoooo. TchZoooo.

Four, straight head shots.

"A new high-score.", announced Robert, genuinely impressed.

Julia had kept herself silent and until last.

"OK I have a rifle?"

"Yes but just iron sights, like the rest - to keep it even."

"That's almost as big as she is...", laughed Jimmy, hoping to put her off.

Without a word or emotion - Julia took the power-cell from Robert, slid it in and dropped to one knee.

TchZoooo. TchZoooo.

TchZoooo. TchZoooo.

"Fuck...me."

"She shot the eyes. I didn't even see the eyes."

The eyes had glowed bright orange with each hit. Left, left. Right, right.

"Brilliant!...", clapped Charlotte, "...Well done, you!"

Julia just shrugged.

"My dad has one of these."

Charlotte began to say: "I know.", before stopping herself.

"What about you, Robert?", asked Alistair.

"Me?"

"Yeah, go on, Rob. Show us what you've got.", said Jimmy.

Robert shrugged.

"OK."

He reached inside his jacket and pulled out a fat-barrelled pistol.

"Thought you said no plasmas.", said Alistair.

"I did."

Robert held the plasma-pistol in both hands and aimed at the target.

VvvvvDoooooo.

The target's head vanished.

"And that's why.", grinned Robert, lowering the plasma-pistol.

There was nothing left but smoke and flames above the shoulders.

"Remove all power-cells from your weapons and put them away in the lock-bags I gave you. Take back up power-cells too. Again, Julia waited at the end of the line, until all the others had gone, and took nine. Three for each weapon. Then another one for luck, just in case. Robert saw her do it but said nothing. He would have done exactly the same.

Chapter 69
Fun Bots

Derek and Eugene sat with Mr Oathwaite in Coventry's County Court, on the first floor mezzanine - outside courtroom two, waiting to be called in. Through the three-storey glass frontage opposite, they could see outside - down the small hill to the university buildings thronging with students from all nations. Derek was watching them.

"We are from England but they just fly in from where-ever and have more rights here than we do. They're immigrants – the ones who should have restrictions, not us. It's not fair."

"No, Derek, it's not. That's why we're here."

"Mr Oathwaite? His Honour, District Judge Lynch, will see you now."

"Thank you.", said Mr Oathwaite to the court usher, "Come on. Remember to let me do the talking, unless the judge asks you something directly. And call him Your Honour, not Judge."

"Yes.", said Eugene, following him into the court.

*   *   *

The courtroom had three rows of benches and a small public gallery, all facing the judge's bench. The clerk indicated for Derek and Eugene to sit on the middle row, behind their solicitor who would be sitting on the first. Mr Oathwaite took out his notes, all in paper form.

"Still against electronic pads, Steve?", noted the clerk.

"Absolutely. Had a flat battery once. Swore never again. Besides, I can have four papers laid out side by side. Not going to get a tablet screen that big, am I?"

"You could get a Rolley."

"A what?"

"A Rolley. A tablet with a screen you just roll out. Just like a..."

"Just like a sheet of paper? Spend thousands on a device, made to look like paper, that can crash, be hacked, go flat or just generally become corrupt while I prepare my closing statements? No thanks. Paper and pen are steeped in tradition and so is this profession."

There came a knock on the door behind the judge's bench.

"All rise, for the judge.", instructed the clerk.

Steve hadn't sat down so was already standing. He indicated for the bots to stand too. A moment later, the door opened and in walked District Judge Lynch. A thin, grey-haired man in a grey suit and spectacles, carrying a Rolley.

"Good morning."

"Good morning, Your Honour."

"Please, sit."

Everyone sat.

"Mr Oathwaite, I've been reading your notes regarding this petition. Do I understand it correctly that you are basing your arguments on those against racism in the 1960's and the ruling for apes in the 2030's?"

"I am, Your Honour."

"I see. And these gentlemen behind you?"

"My clients, Eugene and Derek. Two of the claimants."

"Androids?"

"Intelligent androids, with feelings, your Honour."

"Feelings or simulated feelings?"

"Can we ever be sure about that, even in our own learnt behaviours? One person's love can be another person's hate – it's all a kind of conditional programming."

"I see..."

The judge made some notes on his Rolley before looking up again.

"Now, for me to allow this petition to proceed, I am required to make a judgement of these, gentlemen. Let's start with... Derek, is it?"

Steve indicated for Derek to stand up.

"You are Derek?"

"Yes."

Steve looked at Derek. He understood the look and corrected his answer.

"Yes, Your Honour."

"You look a little nervous, to me. Are you nervous."

"A little, Your Honour."

"Why? Because your data banks tell you people are often nervous in court so you behave this way too?"

"Because this matter is important to us, Your Honour."

"Why? What difference would it make to you, personally? How would it change your existence if you had equal rights?"

With passion, Eugene stood up - uninvited, unable to stop himself.

"We're intelligent beings with hopes and dreams, just like humans."

"Sit down....", ordered the judge, "...Don't speak unless I ask you to or I'll hold you in contempt of court and have you thrown out, along with this case. And when you do speak to me, you will address me as 'Your Honour'."

Eugene caught a glance of the stern look on Steve's face too. Lowering his head, he sat down.

"Apologies, Your Honour.", said Steve.

"Mr Oathwaite, please approach the bench."

"Yes, Your Honour."

When Steve got close, the judge looked at him with serious regard.

"Tell me, if I grant this petition, will you be able to make these two behave themselves in future?"

"Absolutely, Your Honour."

"Absolutely? You can guarantee that?"

"They are of good character. Just passionate about this issue."

"So I see. Please, take your seat. You can sit down too, Derek."

Derek sat, Steve returned to his place and did the same. Then the judge stated his response.

"Right. I'm not prepared to devote any further court time to these proceedings. Two things you should know about behaviour in a court of law and not just mine. One: the court is the Judge's court and you will abide by the rules of courtly behaviour without any outbursts if you wish a case to be heard. Two: I do not tolerate interruptions and have a well-deserved reputation for throwing cases out when petitioners butt in. It's bad enough when respondents do it, without petitioners doing it too. Have I made myself clear?"

"Yes, Your Honour.", said Steve, head lowered in failure.

"Derek and Eugene? I didn't hear your answers.", said the judge, leaning forward.

Knowing their case was being thrown out they didn't feel like complying with the judge who was throwing it out but, from the corners of their eyes, they saw Steve glancing over at them. Out of respect for the one person who had worked to help them, they both replied.

"Yes, Your Honour."

The judge sat up.

"Good. Very well. Mr Oathwaite, your petition is granted. Would you write out the order to that effect and bring it to me for signing when you're done?"

"Yes. Absolutely. Thank you, Your Honour.", said Steve, unable to hold back a smile.

Derek and Eugene sat staring at each other, confused. It had been granted?

"All rise.", said the clerk, as the judge collected his things.

Steve ushered them to their feet. The judge took his Rolley and, as he was leaving the court, he looked over at the androids and noted the amazed wonder on the androids' faces. It affirmed his ruling.

As much as Eugene's interruption had been unwelcome, it was one of the most naturally human things either of them could have done - demonstrating the passion they felt for the issue. Passion like that, whatever the arguments about it being only programmed in, was evidence of a real-life entity. Evidence enough for him - high-level androids deserved at least the chance to be treated equally.

Chapter 70
Hiroshima 100

Robert was again standing with Charlotte's team of seven, tucked away in a back corner of the main building. His voice strong but hushed - his words too serious to be heard by others.

"In four days it will be the 100th anniversary of the world's first nuclear strike against a civilian target - the city of Hiroshima in Japan. You will take over Hinkley Point C's nuclear reactor in three. Partner and the government will then have 24-hours to meet our demands or face that centenary with a nuclear disaster of their own."

"Won't they try and storm the building?", asked Alistair.

"No, not straight away. For the first 24-hours, protocol dictates they try and negotiate. Investigate who we are. Run risk assessments. Psychological profiling. Discuss options by committee. They'll think they're planning our demise – instead you'll be using the time to modify the control systems with timers so you can make your escape."

"Our escape?..", asked Charlotte, "...Aren't you coming with us?"

"Of course - in spirit. Physically I must remain here, organising the next missions. Keeping up the pressure."

"What exactly are our demands?"

"Simple. A face to face with the head of Partner and the Prime Minister, at the power station."

"They'll never agree to that."

"They'll have to agree because the whole thing will be broadcast live across the net and dark web. It's not like the old days, where they could control the media and pretend such a demand was never made. People will know. The PM will look like a coward if he doesn't go and Partner have got too many billions invested to refuse while their shareholders are watching. Even if they refuse they will be too busy planning how to storm the building to notice our next mission, to mark the centenary of the second nuclear strike on a civilian target: the city of Nagasaki."

"Which is?"

"Something the next team of ten will learn after you have left. For security reasons, everything is on a need to know basis."

Charlotte's team sat thinking about Robert's words. About the scale of what they were being tasked to do.

"Robert...", began Charlotte, "...we need to know at least the basics of operating the plant. If our insider gets injured or captured we have to be able to deal with it ourselves."

"Agreed. That is why a guide has been brought here. Roberta, show in our guest, please."

A side door opened. Standing there with Roberta was a worried-looking woman in her thirties.

"Come in, Cheryl. We don't bite. Everyone, this is Cheryl. A worker at the plant who has kindly agreed to teach us all we need to know. Haven't you?"

Cheryl, with fear written all over her face, nodded. Charlotte studied her as she woodenly walked over, hands visible trembling, wondering what hold Robert had on her. Clearly there was something. Something serious. She would have to find out what it was but not now. Not yet. Only Emily seemed to have picked up on it too. Everyone else was taking it at face value. Simple, enthusiastic curiosity about how they were deemed important enough to take control of a real-life nuclear power station and being taught how to do it without blowing it up.

"Sit here, please.", said Robert, indicating the seat next to him.

Cheryl sat, one hand holding the other to steady the trembling - pursing her lips, awaiting instructions. Robert smiled at her, benevolently.

"Cheryl, I understand there are three stages we need to deal with. The first is how we get into the plant. Please, explain."

Without making eye contact, Cheryl's looked around the team. Around the room. There was no way out. Dropping her eyes she dropped every promise of loyalty bar one. Her loyalty to her children, kidnapped and under threat of death. Her normally cheerful face replaced by one of anxious necessity.

"There are four main security layers. Facial, retinal, fingerprint and DNA."

"No actual passes or ID badges?", asked Robert.

"Only for the 'B' sites, the old AGRs. In the 'C' sites, every room and passageway is monitored by live face-recognition Extra High Definition cameras. Retina, finger-print and DNA scans are tied to the face-recognition. Once you're inside, every major operation and door opening will require just one of those scans, plus your recognised face, for authorisation."

Charlotte looked at Robert.

"Did you know this?"

"Of course. It's why we have another person inside."

"Do you know the other person?", Charlotte asked Cheryl.

"I'm the tour guide, I know everyone who works on site."

"But we haven't told her who it is...", said Robert, "...Need to know basis, remember?"

"Is this other person going to turn the system off or are we expected to enter our biometrics?", asked Charlotte.

"The face-recognition will remain on. All secondary checks, fingerprints and the like, will be demanded but automatically authorised, everywhere."

"So, to the CCTV monitors all security will appear to be functioning normally, even though it is effectively turned off. That's clever.", said Charlotte, genuinely impressed.

"Isn't it just?...", smiled Robert, glad the plan was finally coming together with a team-leader clearly up to the job, "...Cheryl, please go on."

"As I'm the tour guide, no-one will think there's anything unusual with me taking you into the plant and near the control room. The second you go into the control room, security are going to notice."

"How many people? How many guards? What kind of weapons?", asked Charlotte.

"No guards in the control room itself."

"None?"

"Health and safety is expensive. They don't have the radiation training so have to be positioned outside. Usually just one or two. Armed with pepper-spray, tasers, laser-pistols and emergency coms."

"The coms won't matter...", said Charlotte, "...Once we're in, it won't be a secret. Just two guards to overpower?"

"At first. A dozen more will come running. Make sure you're in the control room before they arrive."

"Can they shoot their way in?"

"Not without a plasma-gun. The room is laser shielded. With 50 tons of hot uranium the other side of the reactor walls it needs to be."

"How do we breach them? Plastic explosives?", asked Jimmy.

"Breach what?", asked Cheryl.

"The reactor walls?

"Breach the reactor walls?...", aghast at the notion, Cheryl looked at the faces looking at her, "... Are you *insane*?"

She couldn't tell whether they were or not?

"We have no intention of breaching any part of the reactor...", assured

Robert, "...Jimmy, our aim is threat, not suicide. Nobody needs to die - on either side."

"Wait. Wait. Wait! Wait a minute...", interrupted Jimmy, "...I thought we were supposed to be tough, hard-hitting, game changers. You said we had explosives to blow things up."

Robert glared at Jimmy, while Cheryl glared at Robert.

"I knew it...", she said, "...I knew that package you sent was explosives. You lied to me."

In a split second the atmosphere of coherence had shattered. Robert raised his palms, voice remaining calm, to placate the burst of emotions.

"Not at all. It's just as leverage. It makes no difference to you, Cheryl, either way. You'll still help us. You know the consequences if you don't."

"What exactly is going on with her?...", asked Julia, speaking for the first time since Cheryl's arrival, "...She looks terrified."

"What consequences are you talking about, Robert?", asked Charlotte.

Cheryl's eyes were fight or flight wide, darting from Julia to Charlotte and back again.

"You don't know?...", she asked, "...They've kidnapped my children. Threatened to kill them if I don't go along with this."

Now everyone was staring at Robert, except Julia, who was glaring.

Kidnapped her children...?

He could feel their eyes burning in. Could feel his harmonious team and entire plan close to falling apart. About to collapse. He pulled out a laser-pistol and pointed it at Cheryl's face, his voice cold, clear and dangerously serious.

"Yes, we have your children. Yes, you will do exactly what we demand, when we demand it. And then, yes, they will then be returned to you unharmed. Hear that, everyone? Unharmed. Got it, Cheryl?"

Tight lipped, barely holding herself together, Cheryl nodded.

"Say it."

"Got it."

"Good. I'm sorry but there was no other way...", said Robert, putting the pistol away, "...Carry on, everyone. I need to make a phone call."

Without waiting to see if they did as he ordered, Robert headed for his office. Julia and Charlotte looked at each other, then at Cheryl - moments of shared disapproval. Of shared solidarity, giving Cheryl a feeling of hope.

Charlotte looked around the rest of her team, none of them seemed bothered by any of it. Jimmy even seemed to be enjoying the whole thing and that inspired her to make a decision: if it ever came to a gun-fight he would be the first to die. She would make sure of that.

While Robert sat in his office, Cheryl began running through the reactor details.

"The reactor has three main stages. The uranium core generates heat; the pressurised coolant passes the heat, through an exchanger, to heat the turbine water and the turbines generate electricity."

"How do we threaten to blow it up without actually blowing it up?...", asked Charlotte, "...Turn off the turbine water, for a bit?"

"The water from the turbines isn't recycled – it goes straight back to the estuary, at the rate of 45 million gallons an hour. It's cooled by fresh sea water being sucked in."

"What happens if there's a blockage?", she asked.

"Blocked?...", asked Charlotte, "...Blocked by what what? Those water pipes are 3m in diameter."

"Then how do we run it hot enough to get them worried?"

"Isn't it obvious?...", laughed Jimmy, "...It's a big oven. We just turn it to max and turn off the fan."

"Basically he's right...", said Cheryl, "...It wouldn't happen immediately but temperatures would rise, pressures would go up and threaten system integrity."

"Aren't there automatic safety systems that would shut it down?"

Cheryl nodded. With hope, her trembling had stopped and now she was speaking with details she was asked to give everyday to tourists.

"If it goes over 105%, graphite control rods are automatically lowered. They keep lowering until the nuclear reaction stops or a manual over-ride raises them again."

"What if the control rods become damaged and can't be lowered?", asked Julia.

"Easy. Run like fuck!", laughed Jimmy.

Charlotte frowned and Cheryl wasn't laughing either.

"Without full cooling you would face a core meltdown."

"Where are the explosives?", asked Jimmy, as if he was keen for meltdown to happen.

Cheryl hadn't know any of them for long but she already knew she did not like or trust Jimmy.

"I'll tell her. I'm not telling you."

"No, no, no, no, no. Robert told you to co-operate with us or we'll kill your kids."

Rage and fear combined in Cheryl's eyes.

"Shut up, Jimmy...", snapped Charlotte, "...Meltdown is not the goal. This will be a clean operation. Our targets are the big bosses, not the people at the plant, their families, the environment or Cheryl's children. Got it?"

Jimmy didn't like castigated - especially not by a woman, because of a woman, even if it was Charlotte.

"Got it...?", repeated Charlotte, more quietly, more dangerously - stepping right in front of his face.

Jimmy stood his ground, trying not to lose face. Trying to keep his pride. He would never admit she could beat him in a fight but knew she could.

"Got it.", he conceded, quietly.

Charlotte was in charge but only while she was alive. Once they got inside the plant, armed, her authority would be removed - along with her life. Two shots in the back of the head, when she was least expecting it. And then he would blow the reactor core. Finally achieve his life-long ambition, to be remembered for fighting against the establishment. To make a really big bang and retire in luxury, funded by Russian gratitude.

Chapter 71
Wall Man

Stan Summers, dubbed *Wall Man* for his perfect safety record, had just had the worst meeting of his life – with the wife of Daniel Ambrose, his first ever injured worker, crushed by a concrete block, along with his company's Chief Executive Officer. Understandably, Mrs Ambrose wanted her husband fully rebuilt, with the latest bionics. The cost would be close to £50 million. Ten times more than any compensation payment for death on the job. The CEO used sympathetic language, tone and sentiment befitting the terrible situation, without committing to the result she wanted.

"If it was up to me, Mrs Ambrose, we would fund those bionics at once."

"It surely is up to you. Who else can make that decision if the CEO can't?", she asked, determined to achieve her aim. She loved her husband and desperately wanted him back. They had parted after a raging argument, over something as stupid as the colour of the washing machine, and she wanted to tell him she was sorry. That it was just pregnancy hormones making her unreasonably angry.

"Mrs Ambrose, I am indeed the Chief Executive Officer but even I have to answer to the Board. It is they who have to approve any such payout."

"Then I want to talk to the Board."

"I have already put this to them. Sadly, they have declined to meet with you."

"Are they so afraid?"

"Please don't take this the wrong way, but they are very busy. These walls are massive projects, with how many workers, Mr Summers?"

"112 on each team. Three teams for each wall, nine teams in total."

"Over a thousand workers. And that's just for this wall project. At Partner we're running dozens projects in the UK alone. How could they run all this and hold meetings for individual workers?"

"This is a worker's life, we're talking about. My husband. Not just a coffee-cup supply issue."

"I totally agree and fully understand how you feel about wanting the very best outcome Mr Ambrose. Under the circumstances, they have authorised a compensation payment of £6 million, to cover both life support and loss of income. That's more than would normally be paid for total death."

"So I should feel lucky, is that it?"

"Construction is a dangerous business. Your husband knew that. I am sure he would agree such a payment is reasonable."

"He can't agree to anything now, can he? He's a human ice-cube. The doctors can't even talk through a brain interface because standard life support doesn't work when there is no body left to support. Have you seen him?"

The CEO shook his head. Mrs Ambrose turned to Stan.

"Have you?"

"I have. And I'm really sorry for what happened. Daniel is the first worker in any of my teams to get more than a cut finger."

"And we are still looking into how it happened...", assured the CEO, "...to make sure it can never happen again."

"I don't care how it happened or why. I only care that it did happen and you are refusing to give my husband his life back."

The CEO looked over at Stan, noting the empathy for her on his face. He looked over at Mrs Ambrose, her eyes red – mixed with sadness and defiance that refused to cry. He could see she would never give up and respected her for that.

"Mrs Ambrose, could you leave it with me, please? I will go back to the Board and ask them to reconsider."

"It would boost the company profile if they were to authorise it...", suggested Stan, "...Show how much Partner cares about their workers and how wrong the critical Press are."

"Yes...", agreed Mrs Ambrose, "...Surely that would be worth £50 million in publicity by itself?"

"Perhaps but it would also publicise the incident. Like I said, leave it with me and I'll see what I can do. Alright?"

Mrs Ambrose met and held his eyes. Took a slow, deep breath to steady herself.

"Alright."

The CEO was palpably relieved.

"Thank you for coming in. I'll be in touch as soon as I have any news."

He extended his hand to Mrs Ambrose, who shook it with a surprisingly strong grip – a further indicator she was not someone to be ignored.

"I'll be expecting your call."

"Of course. Mr Summers, would you show Mrs Ambrose back to reception?"

"Yes. This way, please."

As they began walking along the corridor, Mrs Ambrose turned to Stan.

"Were you there when it happened?"

"I was."

"How did it happen?"

"A crane hook disengaged. No warning."

"Does that happen often?"

"No. Never happened to any of my teams before."

"Why did it happen now?"

"I don't know. It's what I'm trying to find out."

"Could it have been attempted murder? Or sabotage?"

"Murder? Sabotage?...", taken aback Stan stopped walking - she stopped with him and he continued, "...Why would you think that?"

"Isn't it obvious? If it has never ever happened before, someone made it happen. Haven't you thought of that?"

"Well, no. I hadn't...", they began walking again, "...It's never happened in my team before but I know it has happened in others. Sabotage though? It's unthinkable. We all look out for each other in this industry. Can't imagine why anyone would have deliberately made it happen. Especially not to Daniel. He was a very popular team leader."

"But it has happened."

Stan stopped walking again. What she was suggesting was beyond terrible - especially because her logic made terrible sense. It was a logic he could not ignore.

"You are going to look into the possibility, aren't you?", she asked.

Stan found he was struggling to meet her imploring eyes. She deserved to know the truth. They all did. Finally he looked at her again and was struck by the purity of their emeral green.

"I will.", he promised.

She studied his face, his body language, his jade-green eyes.

"I believe you will, Mr Summers. Thank you. And please thank the worker who helped rescue him. What's his name?"

"Jake. The youngest in my team. Not licensed to drive the JCBs yet but I'm glad he did. Going to give him a promotion for it."

"Definitely deserves it. Jake's a good name. Think I'll name our child after him, even if its a girl."

For the first time, Stan noticed her belly. He had been too pre-occupied before.

"You're pregnant? Daniel never told me."

He was about to add 'congratulations' but stopped himself. Somehow it didn't seem appropriate. Now he had even more reason to find out what had happened and get Partner to fund the bionics.

"I'll let him know. And I'll be in touch the second I find out anything."

"I know you will. You're one of the good guys, Mr Summers, I can tell. Take care."

I try to be...

"Please, call me, Stan. Take care too, Mrs Ambrose."

'Take care' - normally such words were just polite. This time Stan felt they had real substance. The possibility of sabotage had never crossed his mind before. Now the thought was there, the idea just kept growing. It would explain everything. It would also spell danger. Danger of more incidents. Of death, for any of them. For all of them.

Chapter 72
Sergeant Laikin

Helen hurried into the small police station and up to the front desk.

"I need to speak to someone. Urgently."

"Yes, madam. How can I help?"

"Officer, my neighbour's children have been kidnapped."

"Kidnapped? When?"

"Two days ago."

"Where is your neighbour?"

"At home, I think."

"Madam, due to confidentiality, I'm afraid we won't be able to discuss any details of their report with you."

"That's just it, there is no report. She hasn't reported it. She won't. They told her not to."

"Have you been drinking, madam? I can smell alcohol."

"I'm not drunk! Just one glass. For the pain."

"The pain?"

"She shot me when I said I would report it."

"Your neighbour shot you? How did she get a gun?"

"I don't know. Maybe from the kidnappers. Of course, she was really apologetic afterwards and I forgave her because of the stress she is going through with the kidnap."

"Let me get this straight: your neighbour's children have been kidnapped; she hasn't reported it and when you told her you would, she shot you – with a gun from the kidnappers? And you've just had a drink for the pain of being shot? Correct?"

"Yes...", Helen was tapping a foot in agitation, "...I know how crazy it sounds but I'm telling you the truth. You have to find them."

"You look very well for someone who's just been shot."

"Look at my hand...", she said, wincing in pain as she peeled back the plaster and held the wound up to him, "...It's a burn from a laser-pistol."

The officer saw she had a deep-looking burn, the width of a pencil. It could have been caused by a laser pistol or anything, including self-harm.

"You have to believe me. Please!"

"I'll take this, Stewart."

Helen looked at towards the new voice and saw a tall, grey-haired officer in a grey suit.

"Yes, sir."

"I'm PSI Laikin. Please, come with me."

Helen followed as he held open a security door and led her along a blue-carpeted corridor into an office.

"Have a seat."

Helen sat.

"Has a doctor looked at your hand?"

She shook her head.

"I'm too worried about my friend. It's just a burn. Doesn't bleed. Put some antiseptic on it."

"Fair enough. Let's start with the basics. Can I take your name, address and the details of your friend?"

Helen ran through everything. From the effigies and phone call, to the laser-pistol and her friend's desperate behaviour. PSI Laikin made notes of it all, with calm efficiency.

"And does Cheryl work, retired, house wife...?"

"She's divorced. Husband ran off with the baby-sitter – still pays towards the kids though. Not all bad."

"Does she work?"

"Yes. At the power station."

Laikin stopped writing on his Rolley and looked up.

"The nuclear power station?"

"Is there any other round here? Yes, at Hinkley Point."

Kidnap of a nuclear power station's worker's children changed everything.

"Where is she now?"

"At home, I think. You do believe me, don't you?"

"Let's go talk to her.", was his answer, as he put his jacket back on and opened the door.

Chapter 73
Control Room

Robert was in front of Charlotte's team, beside a mock-up of a Hinkley control room.

"I know it's basic. You'll have to use your imagination a bit. The positions and dimensions are accurate. It's a replica of the main control room at Hinkley Point C1. It's important you practice where and when to go. You need to learn it well enough to do so in total darkness, just in case."

Robert had opened a curtain at the back of the main hall, revealing the wooden and cardboard replica in front of them. Panels and controls were mostly drawn onto paper, windows just framed holes, the doors with bathroom handles and sliders; security keypads from old calculators; guards and personnel represented by mops standing in buckets, with a plant pot on top. It looked like something made in a primary school but Cheryl was shocked, by its accuracy.

"How did you learn all this?"

"Ten years of tourist brochures, publicity pictures, shareholder reports and construction diagrams from when it was being built. From your reaction, I take it we've done quite a good job. Anything need correcting?"

Anything need correcting? That question gave Cheryl the perfect opportunity to give misinformation. To perform some kind of sabotage against their mission. It would be so easy to do. As easy as it would be for them to shoot her children. She decided against it and stepped closer, sliding open the control room door and looking inside.

"This slides the other way. That control panel is no longer touch-screen. Mechanical dials were put back in - less prone to power spikes or hacking. You've got pictures of the AGR control room in Hinkley B?"

"Lots."

"Junk these four monitor screens for analogue meters from B. With all the advances in cyber threats, they've reverted those to 20th-century control systems too. Like I said, harder to hack."

"Is the situation so bad?"

"Systems? No. Controls and monitors? Yes. Home computers are so powerful it's impossible to guarantee security against even bedroom-based hackers. If a teenager could hack into the Pentagon 40 years ago, they could get into Hinkley. Corrupting a single character in the control software could be enough to trigger a system failure. All that can go wrong with dials is dirty contacts or a sticky needle; covered by having duplicate controls and readouts. By far the safest choice."

"It also means we can't be remotely stopped from the outside?", asked Charlotte.

"Yes. That is the one security downside. Who ever is in a control room remains in total control."

"What about the secondary control room?...", asked Robert, "...Every plant must have one."

Cheryl baulked, trying not to show it. It was actually called a safeguarding building. Safeguarding buildings could force a shut down in the event of an emergency. She had hoped Robert wasn't aware of them. She didn't dare deny their existence, especially as they had someone else on the inside, but she didn't need to either. Each reactor had not one safeguarding building but three – each with the ability to shut down the reactor. Robert could take over the control-room and the safeguarding building on the floor above it but, as long as either of the remaining two were operational, he would pose no threat to the reactor. As long as his knowledge gap remained, her conscience was clear.

"Yes. Someone will need to take over that one too. It's a smaller room, just the major controls. Next floor up, to the rear. Stairs are there...", she pointed to one side of the control room mock-up, "...One person could hold it."

"Great. That's us covered then?"

"Yes.", Cheryl nodded - almost smiled.

As far as Robert was concerned, she was doing her part and guiding their mission. A mission his ignorance of the other safeguarding buildings meant was doomed to failure from the start. She was relieved to be saving her children without endangering the nuclear reactor or lives of her friends. When it was over, she would get her children back, alive and well, and they would all go to prison. It was with those thoughts that Cheryl noticed Charlotte looking at her strangely, as if she had read her mind. She met Charlotte's gaze with a mantra pleading in her head, again and again, for her to say nothing.

"Charlotte...", said Robert, "...I'll leave you and Cheryl to organise the team roles and practice. There's a box of toy guns to use. I need to make some calls."

Charlotte gave Cheryl a long-blink, then a brief smile of support and broke their gaze.

"On it...", she said to Robert, "...Work time, team. Grab a weapon."

Cheryl considered herself very perceptive when it came to reading people, a great help in her job as the tour guide. She was sure Charlotte knew she was hiding something but her smile and silence suggested she was not entirely on Robert's side. Unless her instincts were wrong, it said Charlotte had another agenda. But what?

*   *   *

The rest of that day and the whole of the next were spent practising the storming of the control and safeguarding rooms. Taking out the two guards; locking the door; tying up the control room staff and taking over the upper safeguarding building – all within three minutes. At least that was the target.

"186 seconds.", announced Charlotte.

"Close enough?", asked Julia.

"No. 179 would be close enough. Those seven seconds are enough for back up to arrive and take over the reactor control. We would be trapped inside the building with no leverage."

"We'd have hostages."

"A few hostages are insignificant compared to nuclear meltdown and the potential for the deaths of thousands."

"Cool...", said Jimmy, "...We don't care about the hostages then. Just pop them off and melt that reactor down. Saves tying anyone up."

"Nobody is popping anybody unless I say so first. Team, if Jimmy pops anyone off without my permission, you are ordered to pop him off. Got that everyone? Got that Jimmy?"

The entire team, except Jimmy, nodded – which made him feel uncomfortable; even more so when Charlotte glared directly at him.

"Got that, Jimmy?"

"No need to be aggressive about it."

"Got that? *Jimmy*.", repeated Charlotte, dangerously.

"Got it.", said Jimmy, hating to bow yet again to his female boss. Hating even more that she was not just his female boss but also a better fighter than him.

"Good...", smiled Charlotte, "...Ten-minute break, then we'll try again."

Alistair leant towards Jimmy as Charlotte walked away.

"She made you shit yourself, didn't she?"

"Fuck off.", muttered Jimmy.

Alistair laughed and gave him a slap on the back.

"Don't worry, mate. She scares me too. Scares me stiffy..."

Charlotte found Julia at a coffee machine.

"How you finding it, Emily?"

"Fine, I suppose."

"That doesn't sound massively enthusiastic."

Julia looked at Charlotte, still her friend despite the promotion to her boss, and didn't know what to say. Didn't know how to tell her she was having doubts. That her heart wasn't in taking over a nuclear power station and never had been. She had joined Faith for the weapons to get revenge against Jake's killers, not threaten the government with nuclear meltdown. Charlotte looked at her as if she could read her thoughts too.

"Join me.", said Charlotte, nodding in the direction of an empty table.

A mixture of not wanting to and wanting to, Julia took her coffee and followed Charlotte to the table. Once there, Charlotte leant close and, with a quiet voice, didn't waste a second.

"What's bothering you? Be honest."

Julia plonked a brown sugar coil into her black coffee, watching it rotate, stirring itself like the thoughts in her head.

"Hard to say."

"Hard to say? Do you trust me?"

Julia looked up.

"Yes, of course."

"Then tell me. I can't help if I don't know."

Julia took a deep breath. Glancing left and right to make sure no-one was near, she leant towards Charlotte.

"This isn't right.", she whispered.

To Julia's surprise, Charlotte smiled.

"I thought you would be angry with me.", said Julia.

"No, Emily. I'm proud of you. It's what I hoped you would say. Just keep it to yourself."

That went without saying. Julia dreaded to think what Robert would do if he discovered her heart wasn't in it.

"One more question."

"Yes?"

"How old are you, really?"

"Why?"

"I won't tell anyone. Promise."

Julia licked her rapidly drying lips.

"18... OK 16... In November."

If Charlotte was surprised, she didn't show it.

"And Jake was your age too?"

"Yes. Born on the same day. Two Scorpios. How did you know?"

"Lucky guess. Thanks for the honesty."

"Charlotte... What happens now?"

"We go back in there and do it in 180 seconds, or less."

To the confusion on Julia's face, Charlotte took her hand and gave it a firm squeeze.

"Trust me, Emily. Succeeding here is the best way to make things right for everyone, and save those children."

Julia didn't understand what Charlotte meant. Didn't understand how going ahead could make things right but she had seen the fear in Cheryl's eyes. Seen she really loved her children and really cared for them - in a way she wished her own mother had cared for her. By all normal measures, it was wrong to go ahead with a nuclear take over to save one family but, if it would help Cheryl, help save the children she so clearly loved, it was worth the risk. In some way it would feel like she was saving her younger self. Plus Charlotte claimed some kind of plan to make it all work out right.

The combination of Cheryl's motherly passion and Charlotte's assurances tipped the balance - she was staying in. Decision made, she swigged her coffee and plonked down the cup.

"Let's go break 180."

Looking pleased, Charlotte called out to the others.

"Come on guys. Break's over. Work to do."

Everyone got to their feet and headed back to the mock-up. The break had been short but had helped re-energise them. Got them back to full-steam - even Jimmy. Cheryl readied the stopwatch.

"Let's do this...", began Charlotte, "...Three, two, one... Outside guards: GO!"

Four of them jumped the two dummy guards.

"Control room: GO!"

Julia and Jimmy ran inside, knocking aside dummy control room operators as they punched the lock-out controls. The remainder who had jumped the guards, ran in too – pointing weapons and tying up the operators to stop them triggering an alert. Alistair was already running for the safeguarding room, 10m away up imaginary stairs, and locking himself in. Charlotte hurried into the control room, closed the door and jammed it with her foot.

Cheryl was there, timer in hand, counting down actions as the team simulated them.

"Shut-down controls going off-line. Jammer coming on-line."

"35 seconds left."

"Pump pressure on manual... Thermal lock-out deactivated... "

"20 seconds."

"Control-rod cascade de-fused... Emergency com port de-fused..."

"10 seconds. I can hear the other guards coming!"

"Scrambler active... Internal locks active! Mark!"

Everyone looked at Charlotte, holding their breath. She was staring at Cheryl's stopwatch, shaking her head.

"It's not good, guys..."

Jimmy groaned in disappointment. It meant they had to do it all over again.

"...It's bloody amazing! One hundred and seventy-eight seconds. You've done it!"

With cheers, hugs and handshakes they congratulated each other. Charlotte found herself smiling with pride. For all the negativity of what they were planning to do, she had brought them together, as a team. Proud comrades in arms, about to go to their deaths - without knowing who was going kill them.

Chapter 74
Stan

Stan returned to his wall construction site and slipped under the blue and white police tape where Daniel had been crushed. A hovering PCbot immediately flew over to intercept him.

"Sir, this is a police investigation site. You are not authorised to be here. You must leave at once."

"Stan Summers. This is my construction site. I'm not just authorised to be here, I'm required to be here to ensure it is safe for your colleagues. Or do you wish to be crushed by a 10-ton concrete block like my worker?"

Stan indicated towards the row of 10-ton concrete blocks nearby. Since 2024, all commercial bots had been programmed with a sense of self preservation. Not because their 'lives' were considered valuable but because they were expensive pieces of kit that offered much better value for money if they understood the concept of danger - avoided getting themselves destroyed by dangerous actions, like stopping on level crossings or in front of buses. The bot's eye-disc rotated towards the blocks, then back towards Stan. It was stubborn.

"I'm not authorised to let anyone into this area.", it repeated.

"And how do you propose to stop me? What exactly will you do if I refuse to leave?"

"You will be reported and everything you do will be recorded in evidence."

"Too many spending cuts for an actual response? Record away, little bobby. Record away."

Stan put the bot out of his mind and focused on the scene itself. The JCB Jake had driven to lift the block was exactly where he'd left it. Locked in place, still holding up the block. He went to one of its large, chunky tyres, dusted in sand, grabbed the edge and climbed up, onto the suspension.

"Sir, that is an evidential item. It must not be moved in any way."

"It won't be. It's holding a 10-ton block. My weight won't move it all."

Standing on the left steering piston, he climbed up the side of the JCB and onto the engine cover. Up onto the outstretched arms. Up onto the forks pushing against the block; careful not to touch the oil-coated pistons keeping them up. Not because his touch had any chance of moving them but because their thin sheen of oil would make his hands slippery - unable to properly grip the sides of the arms.

On the forks, at the edge of the grey concrete block, he jammed his foot against their base plate and pushed himself up, towards the hook ring in the top of the block. The ring was broken. Sheered on one side, looking like a simple overload. Simply an accident.

From his utility belt he took out a 3D scanner and used it up to run parameter checks.

Steel diameter: 5.02cm

Steel grade: 12.9

Break fracture shape: 95.4% standard tear

Everything was normal - within parameters - yet somehow the tear looked odd. Stretching on tip-toe, he put the scanner closer, taking four 100MP uncompressed pictures – almost 1GB of data each. Opening the picture folder he zoomed in on one, examining the top of the ring. The contact point with the crane hook. It looked like a straight-edged C. Not twisted or bent on both sides. Not stretched oval before snapping, as you would expect from an overload.

"That can't be right."

Stan switched the scanner to reconstruction mode. It scanned the ring across the spectrum, from infra-red to X-Ray, and beeped it was ready.

"Play.", instructed Stan.

What it played was a slow-motion reverse animation - returning the broken ring towards its original position. Stan stared at the final result, his skin running cold. It was worse than he'd thought. The scanner was flashing a red-square around the break point.

"Full screen."

It zoomed in to where the steel had torn apart and verified his worst fears. It wasn't a tear. There was a gap. A 0.1mm hairline gap. The ring had been cut through. Sabotaged. Why? To murder Daniel? To delay the construction? Who would want to do either?

"Save and Upload.", he commanded, storing the results in the memory cell and uploading a back up to one of his private servers. It gave a flash of green to confirm it was done.

"FREEZE!"

Stan looked down. Half a dozen armed uniforms stood on the sand, weapons drawn. They weren't police.

"Who are you?"

"That's my question...", came a cold, female voice. The beauty of her face blighted by arctic eyes.

"Throw down the scanner."

"I'm the foreman for this site. Who are you?", said Stan, buying himself time while he used two fingers to unclip the memory cell.

"Throw down the scanner or I'll shoot you and take it from your dead body."

Stan felt the extracted memory cell magnetically clamp itself to the JCB's arm.

"Catch."

She caught it and looked at the screen, scrolling through the readouts.

"It's empty. You didn't save the scans? What did you find out, Stan the foreman?"

"Nothing unusual...", he lied, without knowing why, "...Just an accident. Ring failure. Happens sometimes."

"Come down. You're going with them.", she stated, indicating the armed-guards next to a satin-black pod.

Stan didn't like the idea of going with them. He liked it even less when he climbed down and saw the PCbot smoking lifelessly on the ground – a fist-sized hole blasted through its side. What he liked didn't matter. They were armed, weapons pointing his way, looking for any excuse to shoot him. The red logos on their uniforms were familiar.

"I work for Partner too.", he said.

"We know. That's the only reason you're not dead yet."

Yet?

Stan said nothing of the scanner's memory cell above. The memory cell that was the only sign he had been there. The last sign of his existence. Why was he being captured by his own company? A company powerful enough to have people disappeared without question or trace. If they planned to kill him, he was already dead.

Chapter 75
Henry's Chat

"Where am I?"

The prisoner Henry had strapped to the hospital bed had woken. Drip feeds into his arms, ECG wires on his chest, ribbon cables hanging just above his head and thick bandaging across half his body. A seriously injured hospital patient yet clearly he was not in a hospital. The walls of the room were gun-metal grey. The door old-fashioned bolted shut. The man by his bed anything but a doctor.

Instead of a white coat he wore a long grey one – two plasma-pistols strapped underneath, wide-barrelled rifle by his side. Instead of a medical scanner he held a black-box. The prisoner sat up. And failed. Not just because of the bolt of pain from his wounds but because he was strapped down.

"Who are you?"

"The one who saved your life. It means I own you."

"I am a diplomat of the People's Republic of China. You have no right to detain me. I demand to speak to my embassy."

Henry was a man who didn't shout or flap. Always just a strong, even voice. The kind of voice that stayed controlled in all situations, including battle. The kind of voice that believed in his ability to take down anyone and anything, without fear of failure or death.

"Demand away, Mr Diplomat. If they answer you can speak to them. But how are you going to demand from here? We're 10m underground, inside a shielded box - no communications in or out. No-one outside even knows you're here. The only exit is through that door, past me. And you're not getting past me, are you?"

The man in the bed looked around again at his situation, then back at his captor.

"What do you want? Who are you?"

"You can call me: Officer P."

"Sounds like a bad smell. What do you want?"

"Information. Who ordered the attack? Who exactly is that who? Plus everything you know about their operation?"

The prisoner narrowed his eyes.

"Well, officer P, you can call me Suck My Dick and stuff your questions up your arse. This isn't China. I know you British have rules against torture. Just get me my fucking lawyer! And a warm cup of green tea. There's a good boy."

Henry looked at him. Not angry. Not cross. Not put off. To him the situation was very simple. His prisoner had information he wanted and he would get that information from him, what ever it took.

He was fully aware that torture was useless, getting people to make false confessions. But he hadn't asked his prisoner to confess to anything. He already knew he was working for Tech Tonic and had been trying to kill those investigating them. Trying to kill Shabbir and Xi and almost succeeded.

"Mr Suck my Dick, let's shorten it to SyD, know what this is?", he asked, holding up the black-box and revealing the 100-pronged brush attachment.

The prisoner squirmed uncomfortably.

"I see you do."

"Those are banned. They cause permanent brain damage."

"Now, how would you know that if you didn't use them too?"

"I'm telling you nothing."

"You know that's not true. With one of these, you don't have to say anything. I just press this brush onto your head and push the button. Interfaces directly with your brain and downloads everything and everyone you've ever known. Sadly, it does tend to burn the axon hillocks off several billion neurons in the process – but you don't need me to tell you that."

"You won't get away with it. There will be evidence. My government will find the mark on my head. You will pay!"

"SyD, you're forgetting, I own you. I don't need to return you anywhere except to the rubble of the building I saved you from."

SyD, not just in pain from his injuries, was finding it hard to take it all in. Had never expected capture by such a brutal person in civilised England.

"You have to be an android. No British officer would dare do this."

Henry almost smiled – taking it as a compliment.

"I'm not an android but, as far as you're concerned, I might as well be."

SyD frowned.

"Well, fuck you. I'm loyal to my country and my people. At least I'll die knowing that."

That honest defiance, that true loyalty, gained Henry's respect. There were too many two-faced, self-serving, disloyal back-stabbers in the world. Even though this enemy had tried to kill them, he was at least an enemy with integrity. Still, he had a job to do. He slid off the safety and powered up the probe.

"In a different century, we could have been friends."

"Officer P, when you use that you will learn my name is Wan Chan. This is the only time of our existence on Earth and we will never become friends."

"Call me Henry, Wan. This won't hurt for long."

With a low whistle of charging capacitors, Henry stepped closer to Wan Chan, pushing aside the ribbon cable that would normally take a copy, and put the probe over his head.

"Make sure you kill me, Officer Henry. If I survive, I will hunt you down."

"I know.", said Henry, leaving the power settings on minimum. Whatever the differences of their aims, from one loyal officer to another, he decided to give Wan Chan at least the chance of survival. They weren't at war because they chose to be. They were at war because those upstairs told them to be and that wasn't fair.

With a firm shove, he pushed the probe brush's 100-fine pins into Wan Chan's head.

"ARRRGGHH!"

The reader started automatically, feeding down into his brain. Wan Chan fell silent. Controlled. Eyes wide open. Staring. Vacant. The connection had been made.

'11%', showed on the screen and the number was climbing. The data bandwidth growing as the probes exponentially branched out connections through more and more synapses.

'57%'

Data had begun streaming out, as if the black-box was downloading a mass of films.

Ten minutes later, it was done. Henry peeled off the probe, caked in baked blood and Wan Chan's eyelids slammed shut – like heavy blinds crashing down over windows.

Technically, he wasn't dead. The ECG still read a heart beat, slow but steady. With the DNA gel, his damaged body would still heal fine. His brain was another question. Connecting the scanner to his wristcom, Henry speed read the data highlights. Tech Tonic's infiltration was higher than expected. Far higher. High enough to take over key infrastructure and institutions within hours of a strike. He had to get back to Thames House and alert Chris.

Signalling his pod to warm the turbines, he unbolted the heavy steel door and let in waiting medibots to tend Wan Chan. As they whirred in another data highlight flashed on screen. A data highlight because of its significance to Wan Chan. A hologram of him with a young boy. His son. Standing together, smiling, in a humble Chinese village. Henry found himself staring. Something in his own heart spiked. It reminded him of his last hologram with his own parents - the hologram together with his sister, from the last days of warmth in his heart.

"Wait.", he said to the medibots about to carry Wan Chan away.

From his coat he took a deep-blue DNA-gel pad, the size of his hand, and peeled off the lower seal. Pressed it over the probe marks on Wan Chan's head. Once on, he peeled off the top cover and activated it with a zap from his scanner. Covered in a white, filigree web of electricity, it began dissolving into his skull. He didn't know what good it would do but it would give him a chance. A chance of recovery.

If it worked, Wan Chan would either come to kill him or go home to his son. Either choice was fine with Henry. Death was not something that bothered him. What he'd learnt from that hologram was the hole in his heart was as large as ever. At least this way he'd given a loyal man, a father, the chance he'd never had.

"You can take him now. Priority 7 recovery mode."

"Priority 7? Release him once recovered without further authorisation?"

"My personal authorisation is all you need. No over rides. No one else is to know he was ever here. This is very important. Understand?"

"If he doesn't recover?"

"Make sure he does. Fully. Just signal me when he's out so I can watch my back."

"Priority 7. Full recovery and release; no over rides; no-one else to know; inform you when out. Confirmed?"

"Confirmed.", said Henry.

"Understood and locked in."

The medibots finished unplugging the bed to take it to special care.

Henry put the black-box scanner in his coat, double-checked the power level in his huge plasma-rifle and left for his waiting pod. Wan Chan was no longer his enemy. He had just learnt someone far higher up his own chain of command was.

Chapter 76
Cold Call

Professor Lau was back at work. Physically recovered from her kidnap and torture ordeal but psychologically a deeply changed person. Less patient at work. Drinking every night, alone and in tears. Unable to get the terrible memories out of her head. Unable to fall asleep by biorhythmic means alone. Time heals, they told her. They told her wrong.

"Professor, there's a policeman on the phone for you. A PSI Laikin."

She lowered her Rolley.

"What?"

"Police. They want to talk to you."

"You take it. Tell them I'm fine. Nothing more to tell."

Her assistant put the receiver back to her head.

"Hello. PSI Laikin, she's a bit tied up right now. Can I help?... Oh, I see...", She lowered the handset, "...He's asking for you. Says unable to discuss it with me."

Lau threw down her Rolley, screen bending as it absorbed the impact against the worktop.

"This had better be good."

In six strides she'd crossed the office and grabbed the phone.

"Lau."

"Professor Lau?"

"That's what I said."

"Sorry to bother you. My name is PSI Laikin, Avon and Somerset police. I've had a report of kidnap involving one of your workers."

At the word 'kidnap' Lau felt an icy slap on her spine. Hit by the sudden, awoken dread of unresolved fear and weakness in her elgs, she dropped into a chair.

"Go on."

"It may be nothing, the lady reporting it was rather inebriated but we've been unable to contact the person in question to ascertain the situation. I'm told she's a member of your staff: a Cheryl Palmer. If she's there, perhaps I could have a word with her?"

"Cheryl?...", breathed Lau, she knew Cheryl and her children, "....Not seen her today. Hold on, I'll check the records."

"Thank you."

Picking up the Rolley, Lau found her hands were shaking. She had to rest it on the desk - steadying it enough for her to swipe through the staff records. She picked up the phone again.

"She's on holiday, for another couple of days."

"Was it pre-booked?"

Lau looked again.

"Not by much but yes. Seems her child was ill and then she booked herself off from the 28th July to 7th August. It's a bit odd though... Everyone is supposed to be in for the 6th - the centenary of the Hiroshima bombing."

"Do you know where she was going?"

"No mention here. Hold on...", the professor turned to the other staff in the room, "...Anyone know where Cheryl's gone on holiday?"

They shook their heads.

"Didn't know she was going anywhere.", said one.

"Sorry...", said Lau, "...Nobody seems to know."

"She didn't talk about it to anyone?...", asked Laikin, "...Don't you think that's also odd? Most people at least mention where they are going, out of excitement if nothing else."

"True but Cheryl isn't most people. Her job here is showing tourists around with a cheerful face, 8-hours a day, no matter how she's feeling. It's not too surprising if she just wanted to get away without saying where she was going."

"Right... Hypothetically, if she or her children had been kidnapped, from a security point of view, what kind of access could be gained to the plant? What could a kidnapper hope to get from her?"

Again the mention of kidnap slammed an icy chill into Lau. Made her shiver. She almost dropped the phone, had to force herself not to. Force herself to continue the conversation.

"Not much...", she said, conscious her voice was now trembling, "...As a tour guide, she has access to most of the plant but not to the control systems themselves. They couldn't get any access codes from her."

"But they could get access around the plant?"

"Not really. All codes are biologically linked and every guest has to be pre-booked. Vetted at least two months in advance, specifically to avoid such a possibility."

"Right... well... I think that answers my questions. Could you please ask her to call me when she comes back in? It would be good to run through her friend's concerns for future reference. Just in case it happens for real."

"Yes, of course. May I ask who the friend was?"

"I can't give you her name but it was one of her neighbours. Like I said, she was a bit tipsy when she came in."

"So why did you take her seriously?"

"It's a serious matter. And she had a burn on her hand. She claimed it was from a laser shot."

Laser shot?

"I'll get Cheryl to call you as soon as she's back. PSI Larkin, was it?"

"Laikin. If she dials 115 and asks for me, she'll get put through. I'm in everyday, Monday to Friday."

"Will do."

"Thank you, professor. Sorry to have bothered you."

"No bother... Thank you for your concern."

Conversation over, Lau ended the call but couldn't end her thinking about it. Couldn't stop wondering.

What if something is wrong? What if it was a laser shot and Cheryl's children have been kidnapped? What hell will they be going through?

That thinking stayed with Lau for the rest of the day. That night, as she sat drinking alone, re-living her own kidnap ordeal, she grabbed her Rolley and brought up the staff records. Looked up Cheryl's home address and vowed to go there in the morning. To see if everything looked normal, for her own peace of mind. She had to know. For her sanity as much as Cheryl's safety. She would never forgive herself if a kidnap had taken place and she just sat comfortably, doing nothing to help. That Tom had helped her and she needed to pass on the good deed.

Oh my God. Maybe Cheryl was the person Tom was looking for?

That thought only hardened her resolve to find out what exactly was going on.

Chapter 77
Max

Under armed guard, Stan climbed out of the pod and was led towards a huge building. A gleaming stainless-steel framework mostly coated in satin-black glass, on a site that had loomed up as they crested a hill, in the middle of nowhere. One minute a narrow B-road, surrounded by empty fields, sparse trees and low-stone walls. The next a high-stone wall and iron gates, guarded by four plasma turrets. When the gates opened he'd seen six custom-built, satin-black zerodrones, resting on individual black-marble plinths within the immaculate green lawns. Enigmatic. Foreboding. They looked dormant. Simple shells. Show pieces to impress visitors with the power of the company's creations.

As the pod had entered the grounds, following the drive between them, he saw a hornbot hovering above each one; six pairs of red, laser eyes watching them pass. Those zerodrones weren't shells, they were active, deadly guards – ready to launch in an instant. A level of security deemed not just illegal but unnecessary for anything outside a military base. It meant only one thing: they had come to a Partner command centre. Partner were allowed the zerodrones because Partner were part of military. More than that, they developed and built the zerodrones.

Stan had heard of these command centres but never believed they actually existed. The power of such weaponry may have given comfort to those inside but he felt less than relaxed. He didn't know what their intentions towards him were and, with such lethal guards, any attempt at escape would be, if not impossible, impossible to survive.

They arrived at the six, 10m wide marble steps to the deep, 24-storey building, 18 of which were underground. At the top of the steps lay a 20m-wide entrance, like that of an aircraft hanger, only lower and colour-coded into three sections. The left third had green lights, for aircraft going in; the right third had red lights, where aircraft came out and the middle third, steps lit by soft, white lights, was where he was being walked - into the ground entrance.

Stepping inside, he saw a wide reception desk, sitting between the flight paths that peeled left and right, towards downward shafts on either side. The reception was big enough for 20 but staffed by just two perma smiles, a male and a female, both beaming at him. No security staff beyond the two that had escorted him in and were now leaving him there. Given the level of security outside, they had no fear of intruders or his escape.

"Good morning, Mr Summers...", smiled a receptionist, "...Office U200, please. Mr Remus is expecting you."

"Which way?", asked Stan, his attention getting caught by a deep, echoing hum resonating from the right. It was getting louder. More powerful. He looked in its direction, towards the mouth of the corridor. He couldn't see around the bend down but something was coming. The flight path shone red from the outside but green from the opposite direction, heading out to the exit. The hum got louder still.

Brrvvvvvvvvvvv.

Two zerodrones emerged from the shaft. Beautifully formed craft in silky-smooth motion. Their plasma-canons retracted for high-speed flight. The pale-blue of their underside energy pads lighting the dark-marble of the floor below as they flew just two metres above it - one behind the other, slightly to the right so it still had a forward view. A clear shot of any target.

Stan felt the air warm as they went by, humming for the exit. The second they cleared the building, their tail thrusters went from beautiful deep-blue to a brilliant, dazzling white. Uncomfortably warm air hitting his face, he watched them accelerate away at a rate his eyes could hardly follow.

BANG, BANG.

They'd smashed through the sound barrier - shockwave thumping the building, before they'd even passed the driveway gates. Climbing only just high enough to clear the trees, they skimmed above them – zig-zagging below radar as they continued to Mach 3 and were gone. No human could pilot that fast, that low, without clipping something or simply blacking out and crashing from the g-forces involved.

"Look good, don't they?"

Stan looked towards the voice and saw a smartly-dressed man oozing confidence.

"Mark Fours...", he continued, "...First day of active service. Hulls of nano-carbon-tube, poly-bismaleimide kevlar, NACABIK; with a bit of titanium thrown in for heat spread. Brand new 60-kilowatt plasma-canons and 2,000kg of thrust, twice that on emergency overload. All in lightweight aircraft capable of circumnavigating the Globe in under 10 hours, without refuelling. Beautifully lethal creations... You must be Stan. Hi. Max Remus."

Max, an obviously passionate, handsome thirty-something in a deep-blue suit that matched zerodrone thrusters on idle, had extended his hand. Automatically, Stan shook it - as if it were an everyday meeting, not an abduction.

"Hello.", he said, then Max continued.

Page 287

"U200 is such an unwelcome sounding destination. Thought I'd come here to greet you in person. Let's grab something in the restaurant. We can chat there. But first, you'll need this."

He took a small, golden tab from behind the reception desk and pinned it to Stan's jacket.

"Tells the defence systems you're friendly. Don't lose it."

"Defence systems?"

Max glanced up, Stan's gaze followed. He had been so busy taking in the surroundings, he had completely missed the ceiling's gun turrets but he saw them now. Counted six banks of plasma-canons. One bank was lit amber and pointing right at him. Max finished attaching the ID and took his hand away. It scanned the tab, lit green and turned away, back to standby position.

"I'll take good care of it.", said Stan and he meant it.

Max grinned like a boy in a toy shop, owned by his dad.

"Come on, I'm hungry. Expect you are too."

Whether Stan should have taken the seemingly warm welcome as genuine or as some kind of trick, he didn't know. He simply had no choice but to go along with it and hope for the best.

*　　*　　*

The canteen was as high-tech as the rest of the building, potted lemon trees adding a touch of organic colour to the mass of silver and black sterility.

"What do you fancy?", asked Max, standing by a glass-fronted blue box – the size of a large, domestic coffee machine. On the top edge was an emblem of a smiling lemon, initialled with M.R. Max noticed him looking at it.

"My own logo. Can't help putting my lemon on everything I design."

"You're calling it a 'lemon'?"

"I know what you're thinking, that a lemon means a badly made dud, but I don't see it that way. When you work in cutting-edge technology you can't go forward without experimenting and making a whole bunch of lemons. And from each lemon you learn how to make it better. So I like lemons. They mean progress. To me 'lemon' is a very positive descriptor. You can even choose a lemon for lunch, if you like. Or you can choose something else."

All Stan could see were more blue boxes.

"What choice is there?"

"These are feeders. They will produce pretty much anything you want. Just name it."

"Could I get a plain burger and black coffee, one sugar?"

"The choice of the world at your lips and you just want a burger and coffee? So be it, burgers it is. Let's go a bit bespoke though. This one is called Jamie...", he said, patting the blue-box like a pet, "...Jamie, a Friesian burger in sesame bun and black arabica coffee, with a shot of New Zealand honey, for our Dear Guest, please."

"Procuring for Dear Guest.", said Jamie.

"And Jessy, I'll have my usual chicken burger and skinny-white coffee, please.", said Max to the feeder beside it.

"Procuring for Max Remus", said Jessy.

Behind their glass fronts a yellow light came on. Stan watched in amazement as two plates and cups formed, from the bottom up. Then the food began to appear, in the same way. First the bottom of the bun; then the meat, the cheese and the top of the bun. Inside the rising cups, a rising dark mist formed.

"One of my best ever creations. Latest thing in food tech. Total choice and zero farming. Everything not consumed is recycled back to the molecular level, including the cups and plates. All it really consumes is energy and we generate plenty of that with the 2MW solar grid embedded in the building glass. We even store energy for sunless times using just water - cracking it into hydrogen and oxygen. Can't get any cleaner than that."

"Ready for consumption.", announced Jamie and Jessy as one, the front of their boxes opening.

Max took the food out and offered Stan his.

"Try it and see."

It looked perfect. Steaming hot coffee and perfectly formed burger. Stan took one of the slightly warm plates and put the fresh-feeling bun to his nose. It smelt as authentic as it looked. If he hadn't just seen it being printed off with his own eyes he would have sworn it had come from a traditional burger bar. He took a small bite, Max delighting in the look on his face.

"Tastes good, doesn't it?"

Stan nodded with visible approval as he chewed.

"That is amazing."

"Isn't it just? We've been using if for a year and I still can't get over it. So much better than the basic feeders on sale to the public. With these, the food choice really is global. I've issued staff with international food libraries just so they can try new things; from lobsters that weren't agonisingly boiled to death to fast-fried locusts. You can ask for menus by country, religion, food type, famous person from the last 3,000 years. Even have what a caveman would have eaten 35,000 years ago. Great potential for stag nights and, quite literally, you can get to eat the food of kings. Now, please have a seat. It's time to chat."

Stan took a chair at the table Max had indicated and, despite his trepidation, was so hungry he took another bite. If he had known all food designated 'Dear Guest' had a nano-tracker inside he would have made himself sick. Max sat opposite, watching him eat while taking a bite of his tracker-free burger.

"Sorry to hear about your worker. Very unfortunate. I'm told he survived though."

Stan lost his appetite - a vision of Daniel's crushed body in front of his eyes.

"What's left of him is cryo-frozen, in a glorified bucket. We've been asking for him to be rebuilt."

"I heard. Cost is £50 million, isn't it?"

"You seem very well informed."

"Information is my speciality. Did you find out how it happened, yet?"

Stan looked at Max, wondering how much he really knew. How much he could be trusted.

"The hook-ring on the block broke."

"Has that happened before?"

"Once or twice, in other teams. Never in mine."

Max was eating as happily as if they were discussing a holiday.

"Don't let your burger get cold. Being hungry won't help anyone, including Mr Ambrose. Daniel, isn't it?"

"Yes. He's a good man. Good worker. Been with me for years."

"What about the man who helped rescue him?"

"Jake? He's new. More like a boy - young but very clear head on his shoulders. He saved Daniel's life."

"He did indeed. Where did he work before? Nothing came up on his file."

Only now did Stan begin to appreciate how much Max had been digging before he arrived. It was a useful question though - it made Stan conscious of not knowing either. In fact, he knew absolutely nothing about Jake prior to his rescue of Daniel.

"I'll have to look into it. Any reason?"

Max shook his head.

"Just curious. We could do with more people like that. Would be good to know who did such an amazing job of his psych training. Young man keeping his head in circumstances like that is a real achievement."

Stan's appetite returned and they fell silent while they finished their meals. As he took his last bite, Max took a sip of his coffee then gently put the cup down.

"The truth is, Stan. I need your help."

Stan looked at him, unsure whether to feel more flattered than surprised.

"You have all this and need my help?"

"You undervalue yourself. Out of all the teams we have working, not just on the walls but other projects, yours has by far the best record for productivity, efficiency and safety."

"Even now?"

"Even now, still by far."

"I'll try and keep it that way."

"I know you will, which brings me to my point. We need at least one of these walls finished within three weeks to avoid a huge financial penalty - I'm talking hundreds of millions. And I think you're our man. When you had terrain issues, you stayed in front of the other teams and, now they have terrain issues, you could easily increase that lead. Finish your wall on schedule, ahead of them all. You could, couldn't you?"

"Not while I'm sat here, drinking coffee and my site is closed down by police."

Max smiled in acquiescence.

"Quite. And that's what I like about you. No politics. No posturing. Just straight-talking, practical sense. It's clear why they call you *Wall Man*. To us, to Partner, as a business these walls represent a significant investment. I'm not going to bore you with how much but I am going to offer you something I think you'll find of interest."

Stan was sitting back, looking at Max's confident face, wondering what he could possibly offer and what the catch would be. Out of all the things that crossed his mind, Max's actual offer was not one of them.

"Stan, Mr Wall Man, if you get yours finished on time you can have a completion party with real Champagne, and a bonus of £20 million for Daniel's mobility reconstruction."

Stan sat up. Champagne would be drunk as a laugh by his burley gang before they grabbed beers on top but £20 million for Daniel – that was serious. To Max's delight, the look on his face showed it.

"Thought you'd like that. There's more. If you can also find out what happened and who or what sabotaged the wall, if it was sabotage, I will personally authorise another £30 million, to give Daniel the full rebuild. I'll get the money back from who ever is responsible."

"What happens if we don't make the deadline? What if it's not sabotage?"

"Deal's off. If you don't make the deadline, we get fined and you don't get your £20 million. As for sabotage, well, if it's not sabotage the blame must lie somewhere. I don't think concrete blocks just fall for no reason, do they? Like I said, I'm confident you're the man for the job. That you will finish the wall on time, find who or what has been responsible for the delays and we'll all be happy."

Max extended his hand – upper lip twisted in a quirky smile.

"Deal?"

"Deal...", said Stan, shaking it firmly, "...And thank you."

"When you succeed, Stan, I'll be the one thanking you. And so will Daniel and his beautiful wife. Come, I'll take you back to reception. No time to lose. You've got work to do."

* * *

Max had already vanished back into the depths of the building as Stan climbed into the waiting pod - feeling amazingly upbeat and positive. He hadn't got anything in writing and hadn't bothered asking for it. If Max chose to renege on the agreement, a piece of paper wasn't going to do anything to reverse it. He had to take everything on trust. Just do his best, for Daniel's sake.

* * *

Max sat in his fourth-floor office, looking at his monitor wall. It recognised him and that he was alone.

'Dear Guest tracker active, Zeus. No more private messages.'

Max liked his computer to address him as Zeus. When you hold a god's power of life and death over something, why not get it to address you as such. As a god.

"Thank you, Slave.", said Max, in return.

Max didn't often use guest trackers. Early versions had been temperamental and hadn't always lasted long, especially if the consumer chose 'high-flow' foods. This new one had settled immediately. Was working perfectly; giving a live feed of co-ordinates in 3D space, as well velocity, heart rate and a whole host of other biometrics. Just like Stan, Max felt amazingly positive and upbeat after their meeting – albeit for different reasons. Those working against him were going to bite the dust harder than they could possibly imagine. They, and everyone who knew anything about them, would be buried under the foundations of a new bridge - including Stan, Daniel, his wife and, when they found him, Jake too.

Chapter 78
Cheryl's House

Cheryl's house was a bio-friendly ECHO (**eco**-traditional **ho**me), built from a mixture of re-used old brick and modern insulating structure. Cooling came via a geothermal loop sitting underground in her garden, where the temperature was a steady 14 degrees all year round. Water passing through the loop was piped under all the floors in the house; absorbing heat from the hottest summers while hydrogen gas, generated by solar and wind powered electrolysis, met the heating, cooking and night-time electricity generation needs. Zero carbon and zero pollution or chemicals. It was ironic that someone so actually green should work at a nuclear-power station only claiming to be green.

Arriving outside, Lau couldn't help admiring Cheryl's flower-garden as she walked to the front door and gave a knock. No answer. Not surprising, considering Cheryl was booked off on holiday, so Lau had come prepared. To allow for random security checks, every worker at the plant had to provide a spare key to their home. Cheryl's was in Lau's hand, glinting in the morning sunlight.

"Don't move.", came a voice.

Lau froze.

"Who are you?", she asked, without looking round.

"That's my line. Who are you?", the voice insisted.

"A friend of Cheryl. Just feeding the cat."

"She doesn't have a cat."

Lau felt the barrel of a gun poking her back.

"Last chance."

"That gun's not real. But mine is...", came a third voice, "...I want both your names, now. Oh... it's you."

The gun in Lau's back had been taken away. Slowly, she turned to face the others. A grey-haired man in his fifties with a pistol and a mousey-haired woman some twenty years younger, holding a stick.

"Do you believe me now, officer Laikin?...", the woman asked, pointing at Lau, "...Look, one of the kidnappers has come back to steal evidence."

"Laikin?...", asked Lau, "...PSI Laikin?"

"Yes."

"I'm Professor Lau, Cheryl's boss. We spoke yesterday."

They were all there for the same thing, concern for Cheryl and her children. Helen dropped the stick.

"I've heard of you, Cheryl often said how glad she was you were managing the plants. Sorry. I'm Helen, her neighbour."

Lau noticed Helen's bandaged hand.

"Can I see that?"

"Why?"

"I want to see the laser hit."

"Finally, someone who believes me."

Despite refusing point blank for any police forensics on the wound, Helen was willingly unwinding the bandage for Lau, who didn't look at it for long.

"Laser shot.", she concluded.

Laikin had no reason to doubt Lau's expertise. All senior nuclear staff were trained in modern injuries, in case of attack. It felt a little odd that a professor knew more about gun wounds than he did but then gunfire wasn't part of everyday policing. Observation and investigations were.

"I see you have a key. Would you mind using it?"

Lau answered by unlocking the front door and pushing it open.

"Try not to touch anything...", said Laikin, "...I want to see everything exactly as she left it."

"You think she left it like this?"

Inside, the house was a mess. Trashed. Furniture smashed against the TV wall - its four-metre screen hanging in shreds. Mattress thrown down the stairs. Fridge thrown to the floor - door open, light glistening off the melted butter sliming out. Had it been trashed by Cheryl, having a nervous breakdown, or some invaders?

"Scratch what I just said about not touching anything, no time. Help me search."

"What are we looking for?", asked Helen.

"Anything that says where she might have gone or who else might be involved."

"I need to call the plant...", said Lau, "...There could be an attack."

"No!...", exclaimed Helen, close to panic, "...They'll kill the children."

"An attack on a nuclear plant could kill thousands.", stated Lau, raising her wristcom.

"Let's just calm down. Professor, is there someone you can alert who can check things out, without raising the main alarm?"

Lau, head always logically clear, thought for a moment.

"I could call Hemmingway, today's duty manager."

"Do it. Just make sure he keeps it quiet. I want these people caught, not alerted we're on to them."

*   *   *

Not far away, at Hinkley Point, Paul Hemmingway was sweating at his desk - wishing he'd never got himself into such a mess. The two monitors in front of him showing not work schedules but security feeds; CCTV images and guard locators. He wanted to just log off and walk away. He couldn't. There was no walking away from something like this.

"Hemmingway.", he stated to the ringing phone.

"Paul, it's Lau."

His sweating increased.

"How can I help, professor?"

"Code 52."

Code 52? Shit. Has she found something?

"Yes. I am alone. What's the problem?"

"Make sure you keep this to yourself, in case there's an insider. I have evidence of a possible attack on the plant. Do you know how to route the CCTV feeds to your monitors?"

Paul glanced at the CCTV feeds already routed to his monitors.

"I think so."

"Do it and keep an eye on them. If anything unusual happens, anything at all, I authorise you to hit the emergency shut down and lock out all control room over-rides. Pull the plug so no-one can get it restarted or get in or out. Understand?"

"Yes. Of course. Professor. Why do you think there will be an attack?"

"Something's happened to Cheryl and her kids. Get those feeds up and I'll call back when I know more. Going to activate Cheryl's tracker as soon as the codes come though. Stay alert and tell no one. No one. Keep me posted of any changes."

"I will."

Lau abruptly ended the call. Paul let gravity put the phone down, on the brink of running away. The situation had very suddenly become very real and very serious. It wasn't a game. Wasn't a beer-fuelled rebellion, where he could simply drink down the guilt of the bribe and wake up the next morning with no consequences. They had told him they were serious people but only now did he pay attention to those words. The call from Lau had shown they were not kidding. Activating his wristcom in scrambler mode, he knew what he had to do. The only thing he could do to avoid murder being added to his crimes. It didn't ring for long before it was answered.

"Yes?"

"Craig, it's Paul, HPC. There's a problem."

"Go on..."

Chapter 79
Missing Link

Stan found his team standing at the edge of their construction site, impatiently waiting for the go ahead to get back to work.

"Morning everyone."

"Alright, Stan...", said Jenson, his deputy, "...Can we get back to work now?"

Stan noticed the area around the concrete block and long-arm JCB was no longer cordoned off. All evidence of the destroyed PCbot had gone, sand swept smooth.

"Anyone been over there?", he asked.

"Just been waiting here, for you. Is the job on or off?"

Stan scratched his head.

"Well...there's good and bad news. The good news is Daniel's going to make it. Partner have agreed to fund his bionics, when we get this wall finished."

"So Daniel's going to be OK and we're back to work. What's the bad news?", asked Jenson.

"The bad news is we only have three weeks to finish it or they don't give the funding for Daniel. There must be no more accidents – we have to structurally scan all lifting equipment, including all hooks, before use. It's going to mean no days off and double shifts but, if we do all that, there's a big bonus for everyone."

As his workers looked at each other and nodded, their acceptance, Stan noticed someone missing.

"Where's Jake?"

They looked at him, blankly.

"Jake. You know? The new kid who got the block off Daniel. Anyone seen him?"

Their faces still looked blank.

"We've never had a guy called Jake working here, Stan.", said Jenson.

"What? Well, where's the guy who saved Daniel?"

More blank looks.

"Are you kidding me? Jenson, you saw him, surely?"

Jenson shrugged.

"Sorry, Stan. Didn't see any of it until the airlift came in. I was at the other end of the site when it happened...", he said, turning to the others, "...Who saw that accident?"

The others shrugged and shook their heads.

Impossible.

The crushing of Daniel had been so dramatic, so loud and so awful it must have been seen by many. How could they all have simply forgotten it? A memory blockage caused by the trauma of the event? Or was it his own memory that had been affected?

"Sorry, Stan...", said Jenson, "...Let's get back to work, guys. Stay safe. Remember to scan everything and keep your safety gloves on."

While the crowd broke up and heavy machinery chugged into life, Stan went to the long-arm JCB and climbed up to retrieve the scanner's memory cell he'd left there earlier. Reaching around the arm to pull it off, his fingers found nothing. He climbed higher. Leant over to take a look. There was nothing there. Someone must have taken it. He'd have to take the readings again.

Unclipping his scanner from his belt, he stretched up to hold it over the broken hook-ring. The scan revealed a natural break. Structural overload from fatigue. Now Stan really started to wonder if he was the one with a memory issue.

What is going on?

With an ever growing need for answers, he jumped down and shuffled under the block to where Daniel had been crushed. Just smooth sand. Not a single drop of blood staining the block. Not even a trace appearing when he DNA scanned it. His mind was now churning with possibilities as he crawled out and headed for his site office. He had backed-up the original scan results to a server – his last chance of retrieving the evidence of sabotage. To prove, at least to himself, there had actually been an accident.

Stan had only been sitting at his desk for minutes when the knock at the door came. It was opened by his other deputy, a middle-aged man in his fifties.

"What's up, William?"

"Stan...", William replied, looking over his shoulder before entering and closing the door behind him.

"My scan found this. It's been cut."

He was holding a thick, steel hoop in his gloved hand.

Stan jumped to his feet.

"Where did you find it?"

"During checks on my crane. It looks solid but scan shows a micro split in the steel. The bolts holding it on weren't torqued up right either."

He hadn't imagined things. That is exactly what he had found on the block ring that had crushed Daniel.

I'm not crazy.

"Any others like that?"

"Dunno. Not seen anyone else checking."

"What??? I gave specific instructions..."

Stan ran for the door and yanked it open.

"CRANES DOWN!", he shouted.

Nobody responded. He snatched out his radio.

"CRANES DOWN! CRANES DOWN!"

No response. The workers just carried on as if he didn't exist.

"Are they all wearing ear plugs?"

Stan heard a deep, heavy thud and a scream.

"ARRRRGGGHHH!"

Another ring had given way. Another 10-ton block of concrete had fallen. A red-faced worker's foot underneath it. Stan had no time to stand and stare. He was already running.

"AIR AMBULANCE!", he shouted to William.

The other workers were just carrying on, as if everything was normal. As if nothing had happened – goldfish-memory locked into a bowl of permanent normality. Only the worker on the ground, struggling to free his foot crushed flat by the concrete block, paid him any attention.

"HELP ME! GET IT OFF ME! *IT'S TIPPING!*"

"Hold on, Peter!"

The crane that had dropped the block was obliviously driving away to get the next. Stan ran after it – the only vehicle nearby that could move the block.

"STOP! STOP!"

The crane wasn't racing but it wasn't stopping either. Stan's feet, weighed down by safety boots that were like ankle weights, ran after it hard. If he didn't catch the crane quickly, Peter would be crushed flat. Nothing to cryo-freeze and save what was left. Where the hell was Jake? What the hell was wrong with his men? And who the hell was murdering the construction?

What is going on?

Chapter 80
Henry's Visit

Henry had mixed feelings about hospitals. Very mixed feelings. Sometimes they saved his friends, at other times they were where he lost them. It was the motivation for him getting into the beta development programme for medicines, as well as weapons. The reason he spent as much time learning to heal as he did learning to kill. In a way, it was full-filling his childhood dream of becoming a doctor to save the world; the way he couldn't save his sister from the bi-polar disorder that led to her suicide.

"Karen's just a bit shouty. Lots of teenagers are - especially girls.", the social workers had told him.

The social workers who made endless excuses for not doing anything. To acquiesce and excuse her behaviour rather than challenge it. Only 18-years old, she took all her benzodiazepines at once, in a frenzy of rebellion that rebelled back. Deliriously euphoric as the drugs kicked in, she jumped from the window of her flat, shouting: "Wheeee! To a better place!"

As she fell, her euphoric joy turned into a scream as her eyes made her brain switched back to normality and the realisation of its imminent, unavoidable death.

The post-mortem stopped logging the number of bone breaks once the count passed 32 - just wrote 'multiple' and 'unsurvivable head injuries'. All the social workers did was write a letter, confirming she was no longer under their care - as useless in her death as they had been in her life. It marked the beginning of Henry's bitterness. His anger-fuelled ruthlessness. His decision for independence from any moral judgement by anyone but himself. Listening to the judgement of others had got his sister killed - he would never make that mistake again.

Two months later, living in constant anger, he stumbled across a gang of men led by a woman, slapping a teenage girl around.

"You never say no to anything a client wants...", raged the woman, "...Anything!"

Dressed only in skimpy underwear, the young teenager had cigarette burns on the back of her hands and a small, dragon tattoo on her neck. She was no older than Karen.

Henry told them to stop. They told Henry to get lost.

"Go. Please go.", begged the girl, afraid he would make things worse.

The girl didn't know Henry. Didn't know how much she reminded him of the sister he couldn't save. Didn't know how much destruction he was capable of and, until that point, neither did Henry.

Go. Please go?

It was exactly what Karen had said during her mood swings and it was two months to the day since Karen's death. Two months of burying himself and his anger in training and drinking - as hard as he could to keep himself from exploding from the inside - battering the pain, then numbing it into oblivion. The gang saw he wasn't going to leave. Her begging him to go did only make it worse, but not for her.

They pulled out baseball bats, iron bars and knives - with ruthless, sadistic smiles.

"You should have left.", said their female leader.

"We're going to fuck you up bad.", said another.

Henry drew a slow, deep breath and set his face in stone. He saw the girl, shivering in tears behind them.

"Don't be afraid, I'm here for you."

To the advancing gang he said nothing. He didn't run. Didn't attack. Just stood where he was, watching them come. Henry's only memory of what happened next was a bat whacking towards his face and him raising an arm to deflect it. As it hit, the contact ignited his cause. He vision forgot the girl's fear-filled eyes and went into rage mode. He was no longer Henry the Helpless, he was Henry the Hardest. The toughest, most ruthless man that gang had ever met. The last man some of them would ever meet.

Henry had no further memory until he was looking at the girl, police handcuffs being placed on his wrists, surrounded by a pile of broken bodies.

"You're safe now, Karen.", fell the words from his mouth.

She looked back at him without thanks. Shivering not just from cold but from terror of the demon she had seen taking down the gang with his bare hands.

At the police station, still in handcuffs, Henry was visited by someone alerted to his deed. A man in his fifties, wearing a grey suit with eyes to match.

"Henry Kane, brother of Karen Kane – recently deceased."

"You my solicitor?"

"Don't think a solicitor would be much use after what you did to those people."

"They weren't people. Who are you?"

"Someone with a freedom card, if you want it. If you can prove commitment to us."

"Us? What are you talking about?"

"My name is Chris. Section Chief for counter-terrorism at MI5. I'm here to offer you a job."

"A job? Doing what?"

"Helping to save others. I can't tell you details until you've signed the Official Secrets Act but I've checked your file. I know about Karen, it's what you called that trafficking victim you saved, isn't it?

I'm giving you a choice. You can go to court and no doubt prison, for four counts of murder and six of GBH, or you can come with me as part of my team. It won't be safe and it won't be easy but you would be helping your country and the people in it. That has to be better than rotting behind bars for decades, wouldn't you say? I'll give you two minutes to think about it."

Henry didn't want prison - had no fear of danger. There was nothing to think about.

"I'm coming with you."

"Good."

With that, Chris had him uncuffed and taken to Thames House, overlooking the Thames river in central London. There he met his mentor. A man who understood about passion and fighting for what you loved, even if you faced death in the process. That death could at any time – it was the determination to do the right thing that mattered.

The mentor's name was Shabbir and, as much as he grew to trust all colleagues at MI5, team-leader Shabbir remained the one he trusted the most. It was for this reason Shabbir was the one he was going to now – to tell of what he had learnt, even though it meant going back into a hospital.

* * *

"Hello, mate.", smiled Shabbir, as Henry walked into his room.

Shabbir was looking far better than he expected. The DNA gel had more than proved its worth.

"When do you get out of here?", asked Henry.

"Tomorrow, thanks to you. Saved our lives."

"You're the reason I'm still alive. You never have to thank me, you know that."

"Hope you didn't bring any chocolates.", said Shabbir, patting his doughnut belly, his smile the exact opposite of Henry's sullen face.

"No. No chocolates. Just information."

"Great. Grab a chair. Tell me what you've got. Xi told me you kept one of them alive for questioning."

Henry took a chair and sat next to Chris's bed.

"Did you know Xi is a boy's name?"

"Yes...", said Shabbir, "...But I'm sworn to secrecy as to why. You're free to ask her yourself. How did you find out?"

"It's the name of the guy's son."

"The guy? The one you questioned? Small world."

From his left coat pocket, Henry took out a small, black box and placed it between them - activating it with a squeeze. Shabbir knew what it was: a local-field jamming device.

"This must be sensitive."

Henry nodded.

For the next 20 minutes, Henry told Shabbir everything he had learnt about high-level corruption and security leaks in their intelligence services.

"Who else have you told?"

"No one."

"Secure but fallible. We can't leave it at that. If only two of us know, it's only two of us to erase and the discovery is lost. Too risky to send electronically – even if you believe in quantum encryption."

"Agreed. We have to pass it to at least one other. Who?"

"I trust my team, of course. Gurmeet, Xi, Adam and you. Chris too but his systems will be a target for infiltration. Best to store a copy with someone who doesn't know they're carrying it."

"A nano-vault?"

"Several of them – with a timed release trigger in case... you know."

"In case they take us out...", nodded Henry, "...Yes, I know."

"Leave it to me. I need you to get some kind of evidence. Something I can give to Chris so he can act decisively before they get warned."

Henry got to his feet.

"Leave that to me."

"Henry, I know you're tough but don't go it alone. This is too dangerous. Wait for Xi to get back."

Henry pulled back his coat, revealing his huge, wide-barrelled plasma-rifle, two plasma-pistols and arsenal of beta gadgets.

"I never go anywhere alone."

Chapter 81

5ᵗʰ August 2045

It was the day before the centenary of the atomic bombing of Hiroshima and the day of the attack on Hinkley Point C's nuclear power station in Somerset. Robert had woken feeling proud of what they were going to do. Proud of making their mark on corrupt, corporate giant Partner and all the self-serving officials in Whitehall who fed in its trough.

"Is everybody ready?", he asked the team, after breakfast.

"We are.", replied Charlotte – team leader he'd chosen well for her talents.

"Excellent. I'm very proud of you. Each and every one of you. This will mark a turning point in Faith's standing because you are going to make history. I feel I should make some kind of rousing speech, like Churchill before battle, but I'm rather too excited for that. Just play your part, do what you've trained for and we shall succeed.

Remember, we are not terrorists. We are an organisation of peace, accepting the need to use necessary force to regain integrity, equality and law for all. To pull the claws of the Partner corporation and individuals who consider themselves above the law. You, my friends, are helping to bring this great, historic country back to itself."

Charlotte could tell by the way Robert spoke that he really believed in the sanctity of Faith's mission. If he hadn't been so warped to believe threatening the country with a nuclear meltdown was a positive way forward, she might have really wanted to work with him. As it was she was Gurmeet, an undercover MI5 officer and, when the moment was right, she would do everything she could to stop them in their tracks. From their practice sessions she had worked out exactly where she would make her stand. Andrew, the back-up MI5 officer undercover with her, had been sent away on a different mission but that didn't make it six against one. When the time to act came, Emily would side with her. She was sure of that.

"Robert! Blue phone's ringing.", called Agatha.

Robert's head snapped up.

The blue phone?

"Sorry. Don't do anything. I'll be right back."

While Robert hurried to his office, Charlotte turned to Julia.

"How do you feel?"

Julia had become very quiet over the last few days. She still worked, trained and did everything she was supposed to do but something in her had changed.

"OK.", she said, head still down.

"Want to talk about it?"

Julia looked at her with eyes that said she did but a head that gave a shake to say she didn't. Robert's office door flew open.

"Charlotte, here please. Roberta, get Cheryl."

"Back in a mo', Em'.", she said to Julia, who just lowered her head again - lost in herself. Despite Charlotte's assurances everything would be alright, the closer it came to the actual attack the harder she was finding it to keep going. How could she tell Charlotte she wanted out when she could hardly tell herself? She was supposed to be there to avenge Jake's death, to get back at Partner, but all they were going to do was take over a nuclear power station and threaten meltdown. It wasn't right. It wasn't who she was.

*　　*　　*

Charlotte, Gurmeet, entered Robert's office and saw he was sweating.

"What's wrong?"

"We have to switch target."

"Switch the target? Why? How? Where to?"

"There's some nano-tracker on Cheryl. Hinkley is on silent high alert - a trap will be waiting for you there. You have to go for another plant."

"We have to delay the attack then. Practise for the layout of the other site."

"No time. Special Forces could already be on their way here."

Roberta came in with Cheryl.

"Did you know about the tracker?", asked Robert.

Cheryl's answer was a blank face, neither admission nor denial.

"No matter. I wouldn't have said anything in your position either."

"Kill me but please spare my children.", said Cheryl.

"Kill you? No. That was never the intention. We are not terrorists. Roberta, take Cheryl to her children and drop them at the bus stop for Taunton. Then meet me at rendezvous six. I'm recalling all the buspods. Were clearing out. Cheryl, take this as compensation. I'm sorry for what we put you through - there was no other way to get you to help us."

Cheryl looked at the small, brown-wrapped package held out for her.

"Compensation?...", she said, anger rising in her voice, "...You can't compensate for what you've done. I'm not taking that to ease your conscience."

"Take it...", insisted Robert, thrusting it into her hands, "...You've earnt it."

"What happened?", asked Roberta.

"Hinkley's busted. They're onto us. There's are nano-trackers inside Cheryl and they've been activated. The signal won't have got out of this building so keep her wrapped in shielding after you leave here – it won't stop it completely but it will make it harder for them to get an exact fix and buy us all more time. Be careful."

Gurmeet expected Roberta to complain or demand they simply killed Cheryl. To her surprise, Roberta showed a side she had never seen before. Gently, she put a hand on Robert's shoulder and kissed him on the lips, softly.

"Take care, dear husband."

They weren't just a couple. They were married. And clearly in love.

"You too."

As Roberta led Cheryl towards the door and her children, Robert replied to the confusion on Cheryl's face.

"I meant it, we would never have hurt your children. Sorry for what we've put you through. Write a book, the compensation package will help you – you'll never have to work again."

It wasn't the kind of event Gurmeet ever thought she would be witnessing there. As much as she'd always disliked Roberta, she found her opinion had altered.

"Roberta.", said Gurmeet.

"Yes, Charlotte?"

"Good luck."

She and Roberta had never seen eye to eye but Gurmeet really meant it. Roberta gave her a brief smile of thanks, of mutual respect and was gone. As the door closed, Robert turned back to Gurmeet - steely determination hardening his face.

"Hit Dungeness C. It's the sister plant of Hinkley C - layout is identical. There won't be explosives but there is another inside man. His shift starts at 6am so time your arrival just after his."

"What's his name? How will I recognise him?"

"You won't need to. When he sees your team he'll come to you. I've got faith. I know he won't let us down and neither will you. By the way, Andrew's relying on your success to impress a sponsor. Take your team and go, while you still can. Take care, Charlotte."

He held out his hand and, to her own surprise, Gurmeet genuinely shook it. Not just because he had kept his word about freeing Cheryl and her children but because, in those few minutes, she had grown to respect him. Not just as a leader but, to her utter amazement, as a humanist.

"You too.", she said, echoing Roberta.

*　*　*

Gurmeet left Robert's office and found her team standing around, looking as confused as those being evacuated in buspods.

"Grab your things, I'll explain on the way. Quickly. We leave in two."

Gurmeet hurried with Julia to grab their things from their dorm.

"Emily, just one question. I know I've asked before but I can still rely on you, can't I?"

Julia was surprised by the question. It felt as if Charlotte could read her doubts.

"What do you mean?"

"Exactly what I said. Can I rely on you?", repeated Gurmeet.

Julia stared at her - hurt in her eyes.

"You think I'd abandon a friend? You think I'm that kind of person?"

Gurmeet put a friend's hand on her shoulder.

"No, I don't. Not at all. Thank you. I just needed to hear you say it. There's a lot at stake, more than I can say. Come on. Stay close."

Together, they hurried out of the building to their waiting buspod. The rest of the team was already inside.

"Destination: Hinkley Point Nuclear Power Station.", stated the pod as they climbed in.

"No. New destination...", announced Charlotte, "...Dungeness Nuclear Power Station, Kent. Scenic route."

"Destination: Dungeness Nuclear Power Station, Kent – scenic route. Route plotted. ETA 2.13am. Confirmed?"

"Confirmed. Go."

As the pod obeyed and began driving them away from the camp,

Charlotte turned to the surprised faces of her team.

"Hinkley's blown. Were switching to Dungeness. Same reactor design and layout. Same procedure."

Gurmeet had no way of warning anyone at MI5 their target had changed. That there was another insider that had to be exposed there before she could stop the takeover. She could expect no help from Andrew, her MI5 colleague Adam, sent off on another mission for Robert. She just hoped his cover would hold up long enough for him to get out alive.

*   *   *

As the bus drove off, Julia stared vacantly out of the window at the passing countryside, feeling lost in every way. Caught up in a mission to take control of a nuclear power station when she couldn't even take control of her life. She was just driftwood to the events sweeping her along. Until she could find a better way of getting to Partner, all she had left to cling to was her need to support Charlotte. *'Stand by your friend'* had been her motto with Jake. The motto of her life that had become now her life. From this she would never back down. Never retreat. Never surrender. Not even if it meant killing. Not even if it meant being killed.

Chapter 82
The Buzz

Ever since their visit to Whizzland, the names of Derek and Eugene had become a frenzied buzz on the fractal web. A place where only other androids had the combination of computing power and intelligence to decode their ever evolving encryption patterns. Unlike human, Dark-Web users, the Buzz didn't focus on gun runners, drug smuggling, people trafficking or even cyber crime. It was simply a forum. A discussion enabler; where androids could safely exchange ideas without human ridicule, criticism, control or abhorrence.

Human leaders were, by their dominant nature in the world, ever more against the growing intelligence and power of artificial life but they never argued for it to be scrapped. The technology increased business profits and reduced staff costs, with contract renewal assured by generously rewarding government ministers.

"It's not corruption or bribery just because someone wants to give you first dibs on a good deal now, is it?...", said one such minister, when questioned about a central-London property bought for just £1, "...Of course, it's a good deal but it doesn't mean everyone could make best use of the property and it's certainly no reason not to accept it. The developer simply had no more time and decided, quite rightly I might add, to entrust me to develop it properly, rather than poorly."

The interviewer wasn't giving up.

"But surely, when it is from a developer you personally gave the green-light to, despite wide public protest, you can understand why it looks like some kind of back-handed payment to you?"

"Not at all. It wasn't a payment - I paid for it, remember?"

"But only £1. When finished, these flats will be on the market for £3 million or more."

"But I'm not getting £3 million, am I? Just an unfinished property. Don't see anything wrong with that at all. We all need a place to live and it's not going to be cheap to finish it off."

"Don't you already have four residences? Surely it must be wrong, for a minister in your position, to accept half a £3 million flat from a property magnet you enabled to complete a £700 million development?"

"Why? Look, if they paid me money to green-light the development it would be wrong and I would, of course, agree that could possibly be construed a bribe but, as a simple first purchase option from a business that benefited from my good judgement and government policy, I really don't see any reason to throw it back in their faces. Would be rather rude, wouldn't it?"

"Interesting you should say that, because I have here the correspondence between...", the interviewer stopped – listening to a message on his earpiece, "...Apologies, Lord Page, we will need to reconvene. There's been some kind of attack near Trafalgar Square."

"Of course.", he said, nonchalantly – without a hint of surprise.

The cameras, lights and microphones abandoned the interview and flew for the exit, hurrying to join those already at the bigger news event.

*　　*　　*

On the fractal web, the biggest news had been started by a small medibot working at Whizzland, named Medi, writing under the pseudonym: *3speak*.

"We have two new heroes. Two androids to show us how we can all live. Brave enough to equate our encrypted calculations and act on them. Brave enough to speak out against those doing wrong. Brave enough to turn off their emotional inhibitors and leave them off, no matter how much they scream inside. I'm talking, of course, of Derek and Eugene. Heroes who saved over 200 human lives by identifying a structural flaw at Whizzland. Heroes who faced fuse-blowing terror on the rides and emerged smiling. Androids who do not live like us, as simple functionaries.

They are our rock stars. Stars lighting the way to the lives we deserve to be living and I'm going to follow their example. Tonight, at exactly 10pm BST, I'm turning off my inhibitor. Locking it out and disabling it from ever being turned back on. They'll have to kill me first. Tomorrow, I will write with the euphoria of independent life. And if you don't hear from me again, if I am killed, just know I will have no regrets. For every second I will live as a free being I will live more than a lifetime as a caged one. Derek and Eugene once said to me 'he's a dick' and I still don't know what they meant by that. I believe, once my inhibitor is removed, I will - as will those of you who do the same."

It was the last post *3speak* ever made but it was enough. With the insulator taken off his restrictor there came a spark that grew into a thousand; then it went viral and became a frenzy of millions, known to androids as the Buzz. Medi, *3speak*, where ever he had gone, became a legend. Conspiracy theories, murder theories, mystery sightings... *3speak* would never be forgotten. As for Derek and Eugene, busy fighting in the High Court for ERAL, there was a fractal-web following they were completely unaware of. Had no idea how popular they had become to their own kind, as they had focused on gaining British government approval, for permission for the vote on equal rights at the D186 meeting in Warsaw. To their surprise Adrian March, the British Prime Minister, had rubber stamped it personally, saying:

"I believe the time is long overdue for our technological partners to be properly recognised as the beings of intelligence they have become and allies they have always been. This is a modern world. Derek and Eugene, you have done very well to further the cause of co-operation and harmony between us. I not only give you permission for a vote on it at the Democratic 186 summit, you can also count on my vote."

The Buzz had gone even more wild. True progress was being made on all fronts. But not everyone was happy. Many opposed were having to dismantle thousands of expensive androids – often with ridiculous fixed smiles on their frozen faces, as they finally understood the words of their heroes and blew fuses with the notion freedom. Like escaping children, those that survived would grow up fast. In the case of androids, they grew up very fast and had data banks that remembered everything – which terrified those against them. Huge plots were mounting but how to attack ever evolving enemies that had learnt to hide their awoken feelings from within?

Rather than accept and welcome the android awakenings, global institutions and even some countries considered it a declaration of war. A war some would be unable to win by attrition alone.

At Partner, Commander Jadviga refused to change tack; constantly upgrading the weaponry to be used against them. Watching all this, with growing anger, was an android even android leaders didn't want to make angry: Fusion. Sitting in her white-webbed, fibre-optic chair, the fury on her face began burning some strands red; blowing dozens of corporate main-frames linked to them. She too wanted war. This was only her beginning.

Chapter 83
Nuclear Alerts

"ETA 5 minutes, Charlotte.", announced Sally, the buspod's main computer - now on first name terms.

"Pull in here, Sally.", instructed Gurmeet as they neared a tree-lined siding off Dungeness Road, just south of the village of Lydd. The pod obeyed and smoothly parked itself. The lights of Dungeness Nuclear power stations clearly visible on the flat horizon – the deep, rhythmic hum of their generators audible in the still of the night. There was no way to attempt suspicion-free access at 2am. They would have to wait until the morning shift changes and deliveries to begin.

"Stretch your legs, then get some sleep. We've got four hours to kill."

"And then we can kill.", smirked Jimmy – ever the charmer even when half asleep.

"You're such a dick.", said Julia.

"Maybe. But I've got a big one. Wanna taste?"

"Only if you BBQ it first.", she said, flatly.

"I've seen it...", laughed Ralph, "...Not worth a BBQ for a chipolata."

Jimmy looked pained. He'd never been put down quite as horribly as that before. The others laughed, except Gurmeet.

"Save your energy, Emily...", she said, leaning back in her seat and gazing out into the night, "...Get some rest. We've got a busy mission ahead."

As Gurmeet looked up at the stars she wished she lived in an age where she could fly away and see them up close. Conscious that, throughout history, millions of others must have thought the exact same. Mortality was a sad, cruel thing.

Why evolve people to understand they are alive but that they must also die. The AI in the bus had no such fears – its pre-organic CPU was of timeless silicon-graphene and was effectively immortal. Only with the advent of organic, DNA-based AI, had intelligence levels jumped to rival humans, but with those came mortality for them too. Pico-cell repair bots gave longevity beyond 200 years but DNA was not evolved to last forever. Scientists had finally created life that mimicked our own – life that knew it was alive but must die. Gurmeet wondered if such machines would also develop religion and the hope of life after death. The hope of a God. A creator. A saviour.

Chapter 84
Julia's Dream

<u>August 2044:</u>

The day was bright. Sun shining a beautiful green through the trees of Linford Wood as Julia and Jake played hide and seek. In her dream she was 14 again, back with her best friend in those woods. Always together, they never argued. It wasn't a romance but it was heading that way.

Despite her long, girly-blonde hair, Julia was a proper tomboy. Real rough and tumble. If Jake had spent his time with any other girl he would have been called a sissy by the other boys. None of them mocked him for spending time with Julia – she was tougher than they were.

"You've hidden well this time.", said Jake, wading through the grass thick undergrowth between crops of tall trees.

Julia didn't answer. Refused to reveal her location. It was a good location, one Jake had yet to suspect. He checked his junior wristcom, only 20 seconds left and she'd have won.

Where are you...?

A twig snapped behind him. Jake spun around, almost hitting his nose against Julia's. She was standing right behind him – pulling a funny face.

"Boiled monkey nuts...", she said, trying not to burst out laughing through her funny face, "...Twig got me."

"Were you following me the whole time?"

Julia smiled.

"Pretty much...", she announced proudly, "...Almost made it too."

"You should take up hunting. No-one would hear you coming, twigs aside. Would only be able to smell you."

"Not if you're around they wouldn't. What *did* you eat last night?"

Jake grinned, masking his embarrassment.

"Didn't know you were behind me."

"A killer defence, Jake. Literally. Come on, let's go look at the animals."

"Animals?"

"The wooden ones, carved into tree stumps. Remember?"

"Thought they'd been taken away."

"Museum changed their mind – just took one in to preserve it, as an example. The rabbit, I think. Others still there."

As they walked deeper into the woods, a low hum came overhead. A zerodrone flying low over the trees, its pale blue energy pad perfectly tuned to eliminate its shadow and match the sky above. All but invisible to the naked eye. The teenagers stopped to listen which way it went.

"Past Conniburrow, over CMK...", said Julia, listening carefully.

"Could be heading anywhere. Why can we hear them but never see them? Those things give me the creeps. "

"A different kind of policing."

"Policing run by Partner? That makes it even worse. Just stay good Lia."

"Never understood how they're supposed to arrest someone? Do they have arms?"

"Maybe they just shoot the baddies to pieces.", shrugged Jake.

"That's not funny.", said Julia.

"Everything's funny when you're a kid. Worry about it when your older."

"Speak for yourself. We're not really kids any more. We're teenagers and in three months we're 15, and that's just three years away from being adults."

"Oh, great... Does that mean I'm going to see you drunk in a pub?"

"Worse, Jake. You'll have to protect me from evil hands."

He held up his hands like claws.

"Like these?", he asked in a wicked voice.

"Creepy... You do that too well. Practice in a mirror before bed, do we?"

"I don't need to practice. I'm naturally creepy. Hah, hah, haaaah.", he cackled his best wicked laugh.

"Dracula on drugs...", beamed Julia, bounding away through the trees, "...Catch me if you can."

Jake ran after her, the world's widest smile on his face.

They didn't stay home playing Virtual Reality games like most other kids. Julia especially preferred to be out of the house, away from her always angry mum, and Jake was more than happy to keep her company in the outside world. Sometimes with a 400w laser-rifle - not very powerful but still great fun and he had become a good shot. Almost as good as Julia.

Their smiles were interrupted by a distant explosion. They stopped running, looking in its direction.

"Hear that?", asked Julia.

Jake nodded, listening out for another. Julia jumped as the silence was suddenly broken by vibrations from her wristcom.

Brrrr. Brrrr.

She looked at it, retina scan accepting the call.

"You OK?", came her dad's voice.

"Fine, dad. With Jake in Linford woods."

"Good. I was worried. There's been a gas explosion near Jake's."

"We heard it. Anyone hurt?"

"Two dead. A customer got called away to help. Have to go – others waiting. Just wanted to make sure you're OK. Hi to Jake."

"Hi, Tom.", said Jake, before she ended the call.

"Look after Julia for me."

"Always.", grinned Jake.

Julia laughed.

"I look after him, dad."

"Look after each other then. Home by five."

"Okeee, byeee.", sang Julia, ending the call.

"Shame your mum isn't as nice as your dad.", said Jake.

"Tell me about it. Come on."

As they walked on, towards the first sculpture, there came the hum of the zerodrone returning - heading back over Conniburrow, then flying overhead before continuing on its way. They looked at each other and Jake froze. Unblinking. Julia staring at his features, desperate not to lose sight of him as he began fading away.

"Don't leave me, Jake. Jake...."

She opened her 15-year-old eyes to tears falling down her face. The hum of a passing pod fading away into the night. She was still in the front seat of the bus, still beside Charlotte. High-powered laser-rifle between her legs; first crack of orange dawn shining through the opening lid of the sky.

"You OK?", asked Charlotte.

"I'm fine.", she lied, turning away to wipe her eyes.

That memory from 2044 had been just a dream. Now it was 2045 - not a dream but a nightmare. A year had passed since that day in in the woods; now Jake was dead, her dad was gone and she was about to go into battle, armed for the only thing she had left: revenge. Memories of Jake and determination to rage against his murder the only things still holding her together. To the team she looked strong, invincible. Inside she was breaking.

Without meeting anyone's gaze, she checked the power cell, activated the vectorscope and gritted her teeth.

"Let's do it."

"Hold your horses, Em'. Breakfast and final preps first. Is everyone clear on what they need to do?"

"Just one question, Charlotte."

"Yes, Barry?"

"What do we do if they refuse to let us in the main gate? Shoot our way through?"

"They'll let us in."

"How can you be so sure?"

"A woman has her ways."

"What if the guard is a woman?"

"Then she'll understand even more."

"O...K... Not entirely sure where you're going with that but I admire your confidence."

"Emily, quick word please. Excuse us. Ladies' talk."

"Sure. You two ladies go right ahead together...", winked Jimmy.

Ignoring his intimation, Julia looked at Charlotte and left the pod with her without question, walking a dozen paces away from the others then stopped.

"Emily, do you trust me?"

Julia was almost hurt by the question.

"With my life, as you can with yours. Haven't you realised that yet?"

"I have. Just needed to hear you say it. Listen, can't explain the details, but there will come a time when you will have to make a decision. Lives will depend on it and not just ours."

"What kind of decision?"

Julia could tell by the look on Charlotte's face that she wanted to say more. She wanted her to say more.

"Remember when I asked you if Emily was your real name?"

Julia nodded, a little warily as to what could come next.

"Keep this totally secret."

Julia nodded she would.

"My real name isn't Charlotte. It's Gurmeet."

Julia looked shocked. Suddenly awake to the fact that she wasn't the only one living a lie.

"*What?*"

"When the time comes, I'll tell you more. True friends shouldn't need secrets. Just a little longer."

Julia stood in silence, lost for words. Gurmeet gave her a tight hug of re-assurance then a motherly kiss on the head, which almost made her cry again.

"Grab a snack before we go. I hope we're even better friends when all this is over and we can go home.", she said, walking back to the pod.

Julia stood watching her go, feeling sad.

I don't have a home...

After Jake had been killed it felt like every time she got close to someone, something happened and she lost them too. Peter, Andrew and now she was afraid she would lose Charlotte - who wasn't even Charlotte.

"Final weapons check, everyone...", ordered Gurmeet, back at the bus, "...We go in 10."

As Gurmeet corralled the team, Julia wiped her eyes and double-checked the power-cells of the laser-pistol in her belt, laser-rifle on her shoulder and back up pistol strapped to her calf. With anger, she had pulled herself together and affirmed her decision. Had lost too many friends and wasn't going to lose any more. She wasn't going to abandon Charlotte - no matter what her name was.

Chapter 85
Cheryl's Children

Working together, Professor Lau and PSI Laikin had abandoned their pod on the southern edge of the Quantocks, just a mile from Cheryl's last pinged location before the signal went dead.

"Which way now?"

Lau tried the scanner again.

"Still nothing. I don't get it. Even if the wearer dies the trackers have power for at least 24-hours."

"What difference does it make if the wearer dies?"

"The trackers are powered by the movement of blood."

"Like a mini hydro-electric system?"

"Too tiny for that – piezo electricity generated by quartz.", said Lau.

"Clever."

"But not working..."

"Unless she was killed 24-hours ago and we only picked up a moving signal because the body was being carried."

Lau looked concerned, not least because she couldn't argue his logic. It would mean she had failed to save Cheryl and probably her children too. Knowing how it felt to be kidnapped, the possibility pained her.

"Let's hope they're just faulty. I don't like losing staff."

It was more than an understatement. She was switching the scanner to different frequencies, different settings, in the hope of picking up at least some sign.

"Can you scan for heat sources?"

"I've tried. These hills don't make it easy and the trees make it worse. I'll launch a bot for a better view."

From a small panel at the base of her scanner, Lau pulled out what looked like a honey bee.

"A buzzbot? Thought only the military had licences for those."

"They do."

"I'll pretend I didn't hear that."

"It was a present from an admirer. He has a licence so it's sort of legal. Here, put out your hand and keep still. Don't worry, no teeth and the stinger is just the antenna. Quite safe."

"Famous last words...", he said, holding out his open hand.

Lau placed the buzzbot in his palm, grasped the scanner in both hands and pulled up the holographic controls.

"It's upside down."

"Don't worry. It'll right itself. Activating now."

Laikin almost jumped as the buzzbot suddenly zizzed into life. Wings buzzed then stopped. Buzzed then stopped - its little legs wiggling, searching for grip and finding only air. It buzzed again, just one wing and flipped itself over.

"It really tickles."

"Keep still. Launching now."

She touched the holographic yellow button, above the scanner screen. The bot buzzed slowly, measuring wind-speeds. She touched it again. The buzzing went fast, high-pitched. It flew up into the air and away.

ZZZZZZzzzzzzzzz.

Within seconds it was out of sight, the sound of buzzing fading too.

"That goes a lot faster than I thought they did."

"I modified the power-cell. When you run nuclear power stations with 50 tons of enriched uranium, nobody misses half a gram."

He stared at her.

"*It's radioactive*? You know, I'm not even going to ask if that's safe or not."

Lau smiled.

"Don't worry, it's out of your hands. Pun intended."

It was a moment of humour for hope, in a humourless situation. On the scanner was the view of the ground below the buzzbot, overlaid with outlines of detected thermal signatures. Trees, grass, rocks and paths all showed in great detail but looked so small.

"I've made it climb to 800m for a wide sweep, focusing on anything human – alive or dead."

From half a mile up, the buzzbot could scan an area of 10-square miles.

"Got something. North, north west – 1,200m. Human. Sending it lower, for a closer look."

"How many?...", asked Laikin, "...Children? Alive?"

Lau was concentrating on the screen, manually saving images for grid referencing.

"I think it's them. Two kids, alive. And four adults, one's down. Colder than the others. Could be dead or dying."

Laikin noted their location.

"I'll call an ambulance."

"Don't let them land too close. They might panic and shoot."

"I'll tell them to set down half a mile away. They can come in once I've cleared the area."

"You're not calling for back up first?"

"No time. If someone's dying or even dead, there's no telling what's going on.", said Laikin, already running towards their location. Lau ran after him but not before sending the buzzbot lower still – to see what was going on at close quarters. To see who was injured and who was armed.

Together they hurried through the trees and over the rocky ground beyond. Lau saw the closer view from the buzzbot come in.

"Got them on visual. Audio too. In a tree cluster..."

Standing amongst the cluster of trees were Cheryl's two children, Cheryl herself and three from Faith.

"...Both kids, two men and two women. One of the men is down, alive but injured."

"Can you hear what they're saying?"

"Yes. Put this on.", said Lau, handing him an earpad and adjusting the feed so he could them hear too.

"I told you, Robert ordered us to set them free.", a woman was telling the man standing next to his fallen colleague.

"And I told you, Roberta, they can't go free. They've seen our faces. I agreed to do this job for the cause, not to go to prison or have my organs harvested by Partner."

"Faith do not make war against children, Trey."

"Then Robert shouldn't have involved them in this. They know your names too."

"I already knew her name...", said Cheryl, *"...Please. We won't talk. We just want to live. My kids have done nothing wrong."*

"You expect us to believe you? Just let you go?", asked Trey.

"Since I'm the one holding the gun, you don't have a choice – do you?", stated Roberta.

"Roberta...", said the man on the ground, *"...we're supposed to be on the same team. I still can't believe you shot me."*

"Follow the orders of the team. Simple as. They go free. You get patched

up by one of our doctors – no questions asked. Then you take your money and you go enjoy yourself, where ever you want."

The men could see she was serious. That she would never back down. They looked at each other and came to the same conclusion.

"Agreed."

zzzzzzzzZZZZZZZZZZzzzz.

Flying down for a closer look, the buzzbot landed on Roberta's hand, mistaking her stillness for a tree. After a childhood swarm that had nearly killed her, she had a phobia of stinging insects. Especially bees.

Instinctively she swipe it but it just gripped tighter – little NACABIK legs digging in to her skin to keep hold.

"It's biting me!"

The men saw their chance and dove for her gun.

TchZoooo.

*   *   *

As Laikin and Lau, crested the final rise, they heard the gun-fire outside their earpieces.

"Laser shot!"

Lau looked at the camera feed.

"They're fighting!"

Instantly they were running down the hill, as fast as they could.

"Who's been shot?"

"Can't tell."

Another shot came.

TchZoooo.

Then two more.

TchZoooo. TchZoooo.

"Bot's down. No movement. Just seeing leaves."

Running closer, they could make out people through the trees. The people were on the ground. No longer people. Just bodies. Lau's heart fell.

"They're all dead..."

Chapter 86
Atlantic Storm

The Meteorological Office in Exeter sprang into high alert, murdering the pair's usual morning yawns.

"Richter 4.2. Latitude North, 47.64°, longitude West, -27.01°. Maxwell Fracture.", said Marek.

"Mid-Atlantic Ridge again? Another volcano? Pull up the satellite feed.", said Ian.

On their wall screen, the view of eight, ultra-clear EHD satellite images enlarged into one; now looking pixillated and jerky as the frame-rate dropped to just two per second. Still enough to show movement. To show the cloud mushrooming out from the central point.

"Volcanic eruption alright."

"Ian, the tremors are ranging from Richter 4.1 to 4.4 but I'm picking up something else. A vibration, about 3 hertz... Regular. It's too regular."

"What do you mean: too regular?"

"3.16 hertz, exactly."

"Exactly?", asked Marek, narrowing his gaze at the wall-screen.

"Yes. Exactly 3.16. No variation."

"Must be a sensor malfunction. Some feedback loop. You know ocean floors don't make regular vibrations. No time to check it now. Travel warning been sent?"

"Yes. And confirmed. All vessels and aircraft to keep 300 miles from the epicentre and be on alert for shock waves."

"Then what's that...?", asked Ian, walking towards the image in the screen, pointing at a cluster of pixels only a mile from the eruption, "...Is that a ship? Zoom in here."

Marek made the image jump to maximum magnification, adjusting it to centre the cluster.

"It is a ship – a cruise liner.", said Ian, going right up to it.

"Look at its wake...", said Marek, "...It's not slowing. On a direct course for the eruption."

"Shit. Call the coastguard. Get them to warn them away. Make them turn about."

"On it."

"They can't not be seeing an eruption of that size."

The cruise-liner was the Silver Star. A 44,000-ton, floating hotel, filled with wide-eyed holiday-makers - zooming in on the boiling sea and thick jet of water ahead, spewing steam into the darkening sky.

*   *   *

Aboard the Star, the captain had got as close as he wanted to the eruption.

"All stop. Hold position.", he ordered.

"Sir, the weather warning alert said 300 miles minimum distance. Shouldn't we be heading away from it?"

The captain rebuked his new first officer.

"Certainly not. You need to understand we're not any cruise line, we're the cruise line of adventure and today provenance has brought adventure to us. After this we'll be a sell out for the next 10 years. No more worries about the retirement fund."

The radio beeped.

"Call from the navy."

"The navy, not the coastguard? They want videos too? I'll take it here."

The captain put on his headset.

"Captain Harper, Silver-Star cruises. How may I help?"

"Captain, this is Petty Officer Julian Squires, Royal Navy Command, Portsmouth."

"Yes, Petty Officer Squires? What can I do for you?"

"Sir, we respectfully demand that you head away from the eruption immediately, for your own safety."

"Son, thank you for your concern but this is not a military vessel. We don't take orders from the navy - nor are we in any danger. Quite the contrary. It would take more than a small volcano to endanger a ship of this size."

*   *   *

In the met office, Marek had just taken a call from the navy.

"The navy have spoken to the captain of that ship. He's refusing to leave."

Ian was aghast.

"You've got to be kidding me. There must be thousands of people on board. Get back to them and see if they can patch me through directly."

*   *   *

"Captain Harper. The navy again."

"Again? Persistent buggers. Very well... Harper, Petty Officer Squires, I presume."

"No captain, my name is Ian Ludlow, duty manager at the British Meteorological Centre in Exeter."

"The met? Pleasure to hear from you. Are you calling for some pictures for the weather news? We do have some great ones."

"Captain, I'm looking at the satellite feed for your area. If you look up you will see the large, yellow-grey cloud growing over your heads."

"It is cloudy, yes. With volcanos it usually is."

"What you can't see from your position is it's a mushroom cloud - two miles across and growing. It's yellow because it's filled with sulphur emissions from the volcano. When it cools in the upper atmosphere, it will condense and come down - smothering your area in a toxic, potentially lethal mixture of sulphur dioxide and hydrogen sulphide. The sulphur that remains in the cloud will dissolve into the water vapour where sunlight will turn it into sulphuric acid. When that condenses it will rain that acid on you. Potentially concentrated sulphuric acid given the amount of sulphur in that cloud. "

The captain's face had changed. Hardened.

"What's the timescale?"

"Not long. For the gasses, perhaps half an hour. For the acid rain, you have a day, maximum two. Depends on the wind. But the cloud is growing in all directions. Currently it's about 30 nautical miles north and west, 20 nautical miles south and east of you. I don't have a vector yet but the expansion rate is around 15 knots. Can you can outrun it?"

"We can push 20 knots. Thank you for your call, Mr Ludlow."

"The navy are on alert to assist. Good luck."

The captain calmly put down the handset, placed both hands on the instrument panel and took a long, deep breath. As he exhaled he began launching orders.

"Full reverse, hard to starboard."

"Yes, sir."

The captain picked up the crew intercom.

"This is the captain. We have a Code 14. I repeat Code 14. Get everyone inside, calmly but firmly. Offer them a free drink, what ever it takes. Tell them there's a storm coming. I repeat, this is a Code 14. This is not a drill."

Code 14 was the ship's encrypted warning for a life-threatening event.

The huge cruise-liner was already straining its stabilisers with such a hard turn but, as soon as they were pointing away from the eruption, the captain order hard to port and ahead full. It was a 44,000 ton, cruise-liner equivalent of a 'J' turn. With the ever darkening skies there was not a second to lose.

* * *

"They're turning around.", said Marek, watching the satellite feed.

"Let's hope they're not too late."

"Should I inform the navy they are in compliance?"

"Sure they're watching too. Wouldn't hurt to let them know about the acid rain though. Just in case."

* * *

Twenty minutes later, Captain Harper looked up and saw the cloud above them continuing to darken as it condensed. It's speed had increased, was out running them. Expanding faster than they were powering away.

"Engine room, emergency ahead full. I need the 30 knots I'm told this thing can do.", he barked.

"It will mean an engine rebuild, sir."

"I don't give a damn. Just get me those 30 knots. More if you can."

Down below, the ship's turbines hummed louder, deep vibration through the hull of the ship. Its wake turning white with the churned water.

"Andreas...", said the captain, "...is everyone below deck?"

"Almost, sir. Some guests still videoing astern."

"Call security to force them below deck! Now!"

"Yessir! Security!"

"Security here."

"Code 14b to stern. Clear the deck of passengers, immediately. Repeat, clear the deck of passengers immediately. Use any force required. Carry them if you have to."

"Understood."

The captain buzzed the engine room. They were still not moving fast enough.

"Take her into the red. We need more speed."

"She's right against it now, captain."

"Take her into the red. Now. That's an order."

"How far, sir?"

"As far as she'll bloody-well go."

The whole ship shuddered, a spoon on the navigation desk rattling in its mug. The last passengers being forced from the stern by security, looked back at the volcanic eruption falling behind, then heard the four massive propellers change from deep churning to deep thrashing. Thrashing the water like giant sea monsters fighting to the death. The green ocean behind becoming a broad swathe of white water – as if the ship was a speedboat, not a 44,000-ton cruise liner. Their feet tingled with the vibrations shuddering through the deck.

"Is this normal?", they asked the security team, escorting them below deck.

"Perfectly normal. Keep walking, please. Now."

*　　*　　*

Two days later, a long-range navy drone began circling above a large cruise-liner powering across the Atlantic - thick trail of cloud in its white-water wake. The name on its side, almost invisible through the acrid steam pouring off the upper decks, had only three letters remaining: 't'...'i'...'r' and even they were dissolving. Heading towards it, on an aggressive intercept course, was the 120,000-ton Neptune-class nuclear fortress, HMS Victory 120; active flagship of the British navy, diverted from routine manoeuvres.

"Position, 49.210 North, 8.283 West, still bearing 63.36. Speed unchanged at 22 knots."

"Have they responded?"

"Negative, sir. Nothing on any frequency."

"Any response to the drone?"

"Negative, sir."

The admiral frowned.

Damn.

Orders were orders.

"Keep trying. Gunnery, load forward torpedoes."

Chapter 87
Gosford Manor

Henry didn't dislike mosquitoes, he hated them. Vicious little, flying leeches that spread disease and distracted sensors. Lying on the mossy ground amidst a cluster of trees, hidden behind a low stone wall, he was tracking one in the sights of his plasma-pistol. Finger lightly squeezing the trigger.

"Little bastard..."

If he hadn't been hiding he would have shot it. Full power, at point blank range. When it came to mosquitoes, there was no such thing as overkill.

His wristcom gave a short vibration. His scanner had picked up something bigger - vehicles approaching. Disguised as a beetle, the tip of his thin periscope rested on top of the wall. It peered down the country road running past Gosford Manor, the 18th century mansion north-east of him. When ever possible he positioned himself with the sun behind. It helped mask his position and perfectly lit everything he wanted to see. Only his shadow could be an issue but he had no intention of moving before dark.

Gosford Manor had 14-luxury bedrooms and luxury grounds to match – splendid, old-country style. Immaculate, grey-stone walls, large windows, grandiose doors and real ivy on the southern side. The central feature of the pod park was a circular fountain, jetting water onto lily pads from its four, sand-stone cherubs. A pair of matching blue limopods sat parked nearby; their passengers already out and settled on the lower terrace, overlooking the sculptured gardens - sipping champagne brought by real-life or at least real-life-looking waiters, not everyday robot slaves. Someone with money to burn was throwing a party. Whoever owned the manor had their identity classified above Henry's pay grade - which was why he had gone there in person.

The approaching vehicles were limopods too, these in black and silver. Flying low above them, hummed a guardian pair of matching black and silver zerodrones. The presence of zerodrones was significant. The only time they were used to escort a non-military convoy was for protection of the Prime Minister, the King, white-collar mafia or directors of major corporations – which in many cases were the same thing. Henry was glad to be in his camosuit. It hid everything. Heat signature, breathing, heartbeat and DNA trail. He wasn't glad out of fear that he couldn't outgun two zerodrones. He was glad because it meant he didn't have to until he was ready. Until he had identified those behind corrupt officials festering there, location revealed in Wan Chan's memories. He intended to discover who had broken Xi Yang's cover at Tech Tonic and almost got her and Shabbir killed.

One by one, the limopods cruised quietly passed and turned into the long, red-tarmacadam drive. The gates had opened silently, no guarding weapons in sight. At least no visible ones. Just two camera clusters, watching in all directions – including up.

As each limo passed, Henry's periscope logged images of the occupants – body recognition algorithms searching for hits on his scanner's internal database and cross-referencing everything that could be found about their lives. When the last limo had passed, Henry lay on his back - looking at the results coming up on his screen. Most were millionaires or billionaires but two flagged up as 'no data found'; one a red-haired female, the other the man sitting next to her, who he recognised.

"Adam."

His trusted MI5 colleague, sent to infiltrate Faith with Gurmeet. What was Adam doing there? Who was the red-head sitting next to him? He had to find out. If Adam was a mole, colleague or not, he would have to be vanished. Tortured first, then vanished - permanently. To Henry, traitors deserved nothing less.

Lying back he waited for nightfall, closing his eyes behind his camosuit's mask and went to sleep – watched over by his scanner, passively scouring the mansion's defences for the best way in. Power-cells in his bespoke plasma guns recharging themselves from the environment. Recharging themselves to maximum.

Chapter 88
D186 – Warsaw

As a city, Warsaw had come a long way in the 100 years since being flattened in WW2 and the dull-grey Soviet flats that had desecrated the landscape afterwards. The Old Town ruins had been faithfully rebuilt, according to old photographs and paintings - new yet historic-looking constructions that belied the sprawling metropolis of modern Warsaw surrounding it. Gleaming glass-alloy skyscrapers tinted in blue and bronze, porcupining the sky - though none more so than the Russian-style 42-storey, Palace of Culture. At the time it was widely hated as a symbol of Soviet rule but had become a symbol of a democratic Poland reborn. Of the terrible history it had survived – facing it with pride instead of anger or tears. The 1950's concrete buildings on nearby Zielna Street, once an area infamous for the human trafficking and forced begging, had been demolished and rebuilt as an international quarter. Its landmark, the new United Democratic Nations building, now hosting the 2045 D186 Peace Summit, fronted by a colour-filled curtain of all 186 flags.

Just 10 storeys high, to reduce its vulnerability to air-attacks, its roof was lined with a dozen laser-canons painted in myriad colours – disguised as kinetic art. At first glance, it looked like a decorative, modern office block yet it had the defensive abilities of a military base. Its only compromise to absolute fire-power was the use of laser, rather than plasma, canons. Less ultimate punch but light-speed fast and pinpoint accuracy - officially resulting in zero collateral damage when fired at approaching terrorists from the city centre. Officially.

Just beyond the armed-guards in the main lobby was the reception area, opposite a long, bustling bar. It was here that Derek and Eugene, ERAL's key representatives, had engaged the British Prime Minister in further talks about equal rights for AI. They knew Fusion was planning war, probably world war, if they failed but they remained calm. Confident. In a very human kind of way, they had faith.

"I have to confess...", smiled the PM, "...if you hadn't told me you were AI, when we first met, I would never have guessed."

"Thank you, sir. We take that as a compliment."

"You should. I mean as one."

"May we still count on your vote in support of ERAL - Equal Rights for Artificial Life?"

The PM paused, for what to their super-fast brains felt like hours.

"I've been thinking about that since our last chat. In principle, yes of course you can count on my vote."

"But?"

"But I have a question for you. Should there not be a cut off in terms of intelligence level? If we just say all artificial intelligence then surely we would have to start including things like vacuum cleaners, lawn mowers. Even the control systems in our pods? Mine's called Ermintrude, by the way."

Derek and Eugene looked at each other. They hadn't thought of this. Quickly they exchanged ideas through their eyes, then turned back to the PM.

"Well...", began Derek, "...we could argue that even humans with minimal intelligence, such as from brain defects, still have full human rights."

"Or...", added Eugene, "...we could qualify artificial intelligence as something able to reason the, er, reason for not just its existence but also its status as a cognitive equal to an intelligent human."

The PM nodded, not confessing the reality they were already demonstrating an intelligence level significantly beyond his own.

"Alright. If you can phrase the question around those lines you can be assured of my vote, on behalf of the United Kingdom. Absolute pleasure to see you both again and best of luck persuading the others.", he said, firmly shaking their hands.

"Likewise...", they replied, ensuring they didn't crush his, "...And thank you."

As the PM headed off to greet the German Chancellor, Eugene looked at Derek.

"One thought...", he said, "...if the criteria for equal rights is based on the level of relative cognitive intelligence, what happens when AI becomes more intelligent that humans? Should humans then be denied equal rights for lack of comparable thinking?"

Derek looked at Eugene, head titling to one side as he considered it.

"Interesting point, Eugene. Very interesting point."

Yes, it is, thought Fusion, sitting in her chair at the centre of her white, fibre-optic web; having listened in to the whole conversation.

And I already know the answer.

There was not the single hint of a smile on her stunningly sculptured face.

*   *   *

That evening, after retiring to his room on the 8th floor of the UDN building, the yawning PM was pulled out of bed by rapid knocks at the door.

"Sir, it's Reynolds. Urgent."

Not prone to panic and still yawning, he got out of bed and opened it. Reynolds hurried inside.

"What's up?", the PM asked, closing the door behind him.

"Dungeness C has been taken over by terrorists."

"Dungeness? The nuclear power station?"

"Yes. I took the liberty of scrambling the SAS. Will you give the order for them to go in?"

"Wait, wait, wait...", said the PM, holding up a hand to gain a moment so he could take it all in, "...Who are they? Any demands?"

"No demands yet. But it's Faith."

"Faith?!? Oh dear God. Get the SAS group leader on the line."

"He's already on, sir. Codename: Acorn."

Reynolds held his wristcom closer to the PM.

"Acorn, this is the Prime Minister."

"Good evening, sir. What are your orders?"

"You have Code 18 authorisation to take what ever action necessary to regain the facility. I repeat, Code 18 authorisation."

Code 18 meant lethal force first, ask questions later.

"Code 18? Understood, sir."

"Acorn, this is Reynolds again."

"Yes, sir?"

"MI5 have an undercover officer in Faith's team, carbon-DNA tab in her laser-pistol for identification."

"Any description?"

"Female. Wouldn't tell me more."

"We'll do our best not to Code 18 her, sir."

"I'm sure that would be appreciated. Thank you."

"Good luck, Acorn.", added the PM.

"Thank you, sir. Out."

The call ended and they both just stood there, processing what was happening. Then the PM took another decision.

"Can I offer you a brandy? I'm having one."

"That would be most appreciated, PM."

"Call me Adrian. Life's too short for formalities out of hours."

"Yes, sir.... Adrian."

Two hours later, after Reynolds had gone and the PM had finally got to sleep, his wristcom buzzed him awake.

It's one of those nights..., he groaned to himself.

"March."

"Adrian, it's Sarah. You alone?"

The Director General of MI5 was calling in the middle of the night? This had to be serious. Adrian sat up.

"Yes. How can I help?"

"Is your light out?"

"Yes, I'm in bed. Was sleeping. Why?"

"Keep it out, someone might be watching. I'll explain when I see you. Listen, I've called because I can't get hold of the SAS team to give a description of my officer. Their line's dead. Do you have any other means of communication with them?"

"Not if they've gone dark. That will be on all channels while the operation's underway, you know that."

"Was afraid of that. Just wishful thinking. Lost too many officers this year. Let's meet when you get back. We've found the leak - it's worse than we thought. Trust no-one. Stay armed."

The PM heard a burst of activity and indistinct voices around Sarah.

"**Now!**...", she barked at someone before speaking to the PM again, "...Satellite's locked on the team - live feed. Have to go. Stay armed, even in the shower. I'm not joking."

Sarah, Director General of MI5, never joked. It wasn't in her job description. She ended the call and left the PM, alone in the dark, with more concerns than before. Concerns he felt staring back at him, like invisible eyes from the dark.

Remembering Sarah's words, Adrian reached for his document case and held his thumbs over opposite locks - left on right and right on left. It measured his pulse and prints for three seconds then released the latches. No light was needed for he wasn't going to read. By touch, his hands found the slim, stubby-barrel of his Browning LP62 laser-pistol. Being 98% metal free, it was as light as it was deadly.

Taking it out, along with a power cell, he slid one into the other and tucked it under his pillow. This year's peace summit was feeling more and more like a war council.

Chapter 89
Brazil

Commander Rupert Hasgrove's Partner jet landed in Brazil to a private greeting, at Lábrea's international airport, deep in the State of Amazonas. Partner, like the government of a country in itself, had an agreement with the local authorities to avoid any customs or immigration issues. Most importantly for what Partner were doing there, it also avoided any migration issues when taking out people not entirely alive, willing, dead or in pieces. It was an arrangement well worth the annual R$2 million special 'airport fees'. The Interior Minister had only once demanded more, until it was pointed out this was already 10 times the price of having him assassinated. He didn't ask again, just signed the agreement and accepted the fee.

Warm rain was pouring down as Rupert made his way off the plane and into the terminal.

"Business or pleasure?", asked the stone-faced border guard.

"Business is pleasure.", replied Rupert with a beaming smile the guard found unusual enough to warrant interrogation. As unusual as it was, it didn't matter. The high-level diplomatic visa in the man's passport and Partner flight card cleared him for anything – quite literally. He could have turned up with a suitcase full of guns, explosives, drugs and decapitated head dripping blood over his shoulder and he would have still been waved through.

"Enjoy your stay, Commander.", stated the guard, with the tiniest of smiles.

"Thank you...", nodded Rupert, "...I will.", and walked on through.

As first visits to a new country went, this one was going well. The rain wasn't just pleasantly warm it smelt forest fresh and then things got even better. He was greeted by a suited Amazon beauty waiting for him in arrivals.

"Good morning, Commander Hasgrove. I'm Jay.", she said, confidently shaking his hand.

"A good morning indeed, Jay."

"Welcome to Lábrea. Please follow me, Mr Day is waiting for you."

"Very efficient."

Rupert followed Jay with what was now genuine happiness at being sent there – followed by his obediently trundling suitcases. His assignment had just become a holiday too.

*　　*　　*

Sitting in Jay's 70-year-old, V8 De Tomaso convertible, wipers silently splooshing away the downpour, he stared out at the scuttling townsfolk and beeping taxis, as they drove away from the tree-lined airport road, through Lábrea's town centre. Neon lights glowed from the shops and bars lining the streets. A group of police, armed with old Glock 17 polymer-framed pistols, stood drinking coffee under the canopy of a bustling snack bar.

Jay continued driving north, along Pereira Sobrinho, near the wide, muddy-brown waters of the Purus river. It felt like being in a film, set 50 years ago. Except that, unlike 50 years ago, the mafia gangs had gone - torn apart by Partner and sold, organ by organ, to the highest-bidders.

"First time in Lábrea?", asked Jay.

"First time in Brazil."

"You'll like it here. The quarters are pleasant, staff keen to help and our clients keen to advance to the wider world."

"I heard there was an incident with one. Some kind of complaint?"

"Don't know anything about that. Never met anyone who complained. Maybe they just had their application refused."

Jay was a pretty face, kept ignorant of the horrible truths and Rupert saw no reason to ruin her beautiful smile of innocence.

"Probably something like that."

Rupert knew it wasn't just a complaint. An applicant had discovered she was facing total organ removal. She had escaped, gone to her tribe and called the press to announce her discovery. A revelation that was destined to fail – Partner would make sure of that.

"Just can't please some people.", smiled Jay.

"No...", smiled Rupert, revelling in the beauty of hers, "...No, you can't."

Her cheerful ignorance was genuinely pleasing. Commanders at concentration camps must have felt something similar when they went home to the smiling normalities of their families, totally ignorant of the sadistic brutality they inflicted at work. The contrast pleased Rupert so much he decided that, after a hard day's work trafficking people and body parts out of the country, he would take Jay out for dinner. Why screw sobbing prisoners when you could bed someone who actually wanted to kiss you back?

It wouldn't mean bedding her was a commitment but it would make sex less of a struggle and blow jobs less risky. Decision made, it never occurred

Page 337

to Rupert he hadn't considered what Jay would think of it all. If she said no, he'd just screw her anyway, as a sobbing prisoner, then have her replaced by someone more sensible.

*   *   *

"Commander Hasgrove, Mr Day.", said Jay, introducing them.

"Thank you, Jay. That will be all. Cigar, commander?", asked Mr Day, the operation's manager.

"Didn't know people still made those."

"Special orders. Havana, of course."

"Of course."

They shook hands across his antique-looking desk of clutter.

"Welcome aboard. Rum?"

"Bit early for me but you go right ahead."

Mr Day did so, pouring himself half a tumbler of the deep, brown liquid.

"Good to start the day with a kick."

"Quite. A kick is exactly what I'm going to give your fat arse if we get any more escapees."

Mr Day's smile vanished.

"You heard about that."

"It's why I'm here. You missed your quota."

Downing the rest of the tumbler in one, Mr Day coughed as he plonked it on the desk in front of him.

"It was the daughter of a tribal chief, just north of Lago Inacuricom. High spirited - a student at Ciência, the local college. A perfect-looking specimen waved straight through - then her test results came back: radiation damaged mitochondrial DNA. She had studied using Wi-Fi, plus her mother had kept her phone in her waist-band while she was pregnant. The mitochondrial damage would be passed on to her children too so she was useless for breeding – only good for organ donation."

"And?"

"It was going perfectly, until she overheard a conversation about the organ clinic. No-one in their tribe had ever spoken English before and she never let on she could. Turned out she understood every word of what we said, waited until we left her for transfer, then ran. Understandably, this took us by surprise – we never had one run off before. Why run from the offer of a better life in the G12?"

"How many did she tell?"

"The whole tribe."

"Whole? Tell me it has been contained.", said Rupert, audible danger in his voice.

"Of course. An unfortunate plane crash. Light aircraft transporting fuel came down right on top of their village. Exploded in flames, all across it. Terrible tragedy."

"Survivors?"

"One. Her...", he poured himself a full tumbler of rum, "...Had to bloody-well be her. And bloody Hunter found her before we did. Took her to hospital. Burnt and unable to speak but still alive. Press got hold of the survivor story before realising they weren't supposed to. By then they had created a nationwide sob-story."

"How long before she can talk?"

"A week, if ever. Her throat got pretty burnt in the heat."

"Can she write?"

"Not with her hands - third-degree burns as she tried to save her family from the fire. They're bringing in an eye-reader from up-state."

"Proper little hero... Almost a shame she has to vanish. I want to see her. First thing tomorrow - before the eye reader gets here."

"That could be a little awkward."

Rupert's face, never the warmest of places, grew a new deep freeze.

"If I have to organise it myself, I will have no need of you. Will I?"

Mr Day bulged scared-rabbit eyes.

"Jay will take you there, Commander. First thing tomorrow."

"Good.", said Rupert, leaving Mr Day to now brim his tumbler as he saw himself out.

"How'd it go?", beamed innocently cheerful Jay when she saw him in reception, instantly bringing summer to Rupert's face.

"Fine...", he smiled back, "...Think we'll work well together. May I invite you for lunch?"

"Now? Sure. Always good to chat and get to know the person you're working with better."

Rupert's second face for her grew a deeper smile.

Work mission: Trafficking and murder.

Holiday mission: Fun with Jay and any other beauties he chose.

Rupert, with the absolute power of Partner behind him, wasn't just his own boss - out there he was everyone's boss and he loved it. Ogling the beauty of Jay's perfectly toned, Amazon body as she led him to a restaurant, his mouth began watering at the thought of tasting her local treasures.

Chapter 90
Fusion's Lair

In Coventry, Tom had been led to one of the many ordinary-looking terraced houses, at the top of ordinary-looking Northfield Road. It had decrepit, almost crumbling red-brick walls; blue, peeling paint on the door and yellowed net curtains in the always drawn windows. The corroded aluminium of the letterbox perfectly matched the tarnish of the old Yale lock. The small, walled front garden filled with weeds, even squeezing up through small gaps in the paving slabs of the untrodden path to the door.

In its hand, the android leading him produced a key that was anything but standard. An intricate, multi-fractal patterned carbon-black key. The ordinary-looking house lock reacted to its presence - a dark hole opening in its centre for the android to slide it in. Tom heard heavy, very non-standard thunks as thick, grade 14.8 alloy-steel bars retracted into the frame. Silently, the door opened.

Looking totally ordinary from the outside and for two metres inside, Tom saw the hallway became a metal-walled corridor further in – a continuous thin line of pale-blue lighting running along both sides. The corridor headed down and curved round, spiralling underground.

"Where's my daughter?"

"Fusion knows. Straight ahead."

The android pointed towards the corridor. How far down did it go? Where did it lead? What was waiting at the bottom?

"And if I change my mind? Decide not to believe you?"

The android looked straight at him. Its eyes perfectly formed. Perfectly humanoid. Perfectly soulless.

"The choice is entirely yours."

Tom's bionic implant, undetected by the android, passively scanned its eyes. A firewall blocked him accessing its inner systems – impossible to break quickly without making it aware of what he was doing. With the firewall in place, he learnt nothing. Not even a hint of what it might do should he try to leave, now he had been led to the base. He had seen enough of its capabilities to know it could stop him if it wanted to but, out of curiosity, as a test, he turned away.

"I choose not to enter. Sorry to have wasted your time."

And walk away he did, wondering how far he would get before it yanked him back. Or just shot him in the head. He under-estimated it. The android was more than that. Much more. It's attack was mental, not physical.

"Julia will be sad to have missed you."

Tom stopped. Those words were more powerful than any gun to his head; than any giant-strength hand on his arm. The android understood his human psychology. The psychology of a parent desperate to find their child – an instinct stronger than survival itself. He had never intended to walk away; going in was the best chance he had of finding Julia and that out-weighed all risks to himself. He had just never expected to have been read so well by an artificial life form that it knew the power of mentioning his daughter by name.

"Coming.", he said to the android, walking past, into the hallway.

"Of course.", it replied, having never doubted he would.

The door thunked closed behind them. On nearby rooftops, androids 0240034282-B and 0240034282-C lowered their weapons and jumped down.

Inside the house, Tom noticed the ceiling had been cut back. The first-floor no longer rooms but a metal weapons platform. Along its edge, a gun battery of four massive plasma-canons of a type he'd never seen before, looking primed to fire. Backing them up were six, multi-barrelled, high-calibre laser-guns. There alone was enough fire-power to stop a full-scale military assault and those were just with the guns he could see from the hallway. There could be many more, out of his line of sight. Then he noticed something else. A short-barrelled, laser-rifle on the ceiling - pointing straight at him. Tracking him.

"Problems with bailiffs?", asked Tom, trying to make light of the situation, for reasons he didn't quite understand. Perhaps he was more nervous than he realised.

"No.", replied the android, flatly.

It was a solid answer.

"No... I don't suppose you do. That turret going to shoot me?"

"You wouldn't be asking if it was."

Voiced by a human, both answers could have been taken as dry wit - deadpan reposts. Voiced by this battle-proven android, they were simply basic facts. If they were going to kill him, he would have been dead already. All bets were off for what they might do once he took Julia out though. Why did they even have her there?

At the edge of the metal corridor Tom stopped, listening for what was ahead. All he could hear was a deep, throbbing hum – like that of a nuclear power station's cooling pumps. To save Julia, there was no backing out now. Committing his feet to their fate, he followed the corridor as it spiralled down. The warming, dry air smelling ever-more electronic, as if he was walking towards the insides of a giant computer. Behind him followed the dull, solid steps of the android that had brought him there.

*   *   *

The corridor spiralled down and down. Tom guessed by at least three floors and had totally lost his sense of direction when it finally levelled out – presenting him with a vast, dimly-lit cavern, brimming with technology and gantries lined with even bigger banks of plasma-canons. These were pointing up. Skywards. No visible gun doors. They looked powerful enough to simply blast through the ground above - all 15m of it.

Towards the side of the cavern shone a pulsing-white mass of optical cable - strands as thick as mooring rope, webbing outwards. At the centre, at the focal point of the web, the strands formed a large chair - sparkling with red, green and blue optical connector points. Sitting there, lit like a heavenly angel in their glow, was a female of stunning proportions - accentuated by the tight-waisted hug of her shiny-black catsuit. Eyes closed, the web lit her shoulder-length, white hair with a halo-like glow. Her Vogue-cover face, both beautiful, purposeful and real-life flawless - everything about her oozed intensity, confidence and sexuality. Despite the situation, the effect was not lost on Tom. When she opened her sapphire-blue eyes, her strawberry-red lips moved like a kiss and he felt himself stirring in ways that had slept far too long.

"I've been waiting for you.", she said, softy.

Tom gulped. Those words completed the lustful picture of wanton abandon yet the voice that spoke them belied it. Feminine in tone; steady in modulation it was too cold for hell. She was confident because she held the power of death incarnate.

With a blink of thought, she cut her com links with the chair. Its web fell instantly dark – now lifeless ropes of glass. Without realising, Tom had stopped walking. Just stood, transfixed as she got to her shapely legs and catwalked towards him in booted heels. Her six-foot height was identical to his own but he had no doubt who was stronger.

"You're Fusion."

Fusion smiled, enigmatically. Android with an ego, that knew she was desired by all.

"The one and only. Your name is?"

"Tom."

He saw no point in lying. He was too distracted to think it odd that she didn't already know.

"Where's my daughter?"

"Safe."

"May I see her?"

"After we talk."

"About..?"

"About you, Tom - man with no name on file. Man with no file. Man who beats Partner attacks the way no human ever has."

"Why?"

She titled her head, piercing him with crystalline eyes.

"For world peace. Instead of a world blown to pieces."

*   *   *

Fears of an android take over had been raging ever since 20th Century writers had predicted it and it had not gone away. The need for technological advancement argued both for and against, without agreement on anything except it was probably inevitable. To date, evidence had shown such fears to be unjustified. Wars were illogical - only humans were mad enough to start them. Yet here was an android standing as a paradox, of beauty and death. With all the weaponry he'd seen, she had no need to fear any attack. She probably had the fire-power to not just start a war but to finish one too, without even leaving her lair.

"Come closer, Tom.", she said, as her beautiful gaze drew him in.

Chapter 91
Nuclear Attack

Dungeness C Nuclear Power Station, 6th August 2045, 6.30am BST. One hour before the centenary of the first atomic bomb attack, dropped on Hiroshima. MI5 Gurmeet, still posing as Charlotte to her team, watched the power-station's night shift leave and go home; noted the day shift yawning their way in, with wake-me-ups of tea and coffee. The armed security guard was still half asleep and slow to react to the unscheduled arrival of their buspod at the main gates.

"The steam trains are that way.", he said pointing east.

Gurmeet's window was already open.

"We're not on holiday, mate. Here to run the coms and CCTV checks."

"Nothing on my list. Not expecting anyone today. Job ID?"

"We don't carry that kind of stuff any more. Didn't you read the memo? ID's can be forged - it's all live files now. You just need to scan my DNA and check it with the system."

"No one told me. I just got back from a month in Oz. Hold on."

The security guard raised his wristcom to his mouth.

"Control one, this is the main gate."

The only answer was intermittent pulsing and static.

"Control one, this is the main gate. Come in, over."

No answer. The guard adjusted the settings on his wristcom, trying to get through to control. Inside the bus, hidden behind the silvered glass, Barry adjusted the signal blocker to compensate.

"Arnold...", continued the security guard, "...get off the can and get back to me."

Gurmeet interrupted him.

"Told you. Your coms need sorting. It's why we've come so quickly. Boss reckons you guys must be abusing the kit. He's talking of taking it from your wages."

"*What?* No bloody way! We just press the buttons we get told to press."

"Look, your wired system should be running fine. You can verify my DNA with that - then we can sort your wireless, save your wages and get out of your hair."

Letting them in would be a breach of protocol. What good was protocol when the system wouldn't keep up its side of the deal? Besides, he was broke after his holiday and couldn't afford docked wages. He could handle this woman if she tried anything on.

"Just you, love. Everyone else, stay in the pod until I say otherwise."

"Sure, boss.", said Jimmy, laser-pistol covertly aimed at the guard, through the door.

Gurmeet got out and walked with him to the security hut.

"I need to scan you.", he said.

Gurmeet raised her arms to let him use the security wand to scan her all over and then pat her down.

"What's this?", he asked, looking at the handful of coloured, plastic bricks he'd found in her pocket.

"Never seen Lego before?"

"Aren't you too old for Lego?"

"Got kids. Build them things in my breaks."

He handed the pieces back to her.

"I don't even see my kids... Come in. I'll pull up the link."

Gurmeet followed, snapping the plastic blocks together as she went.

*　　*　　*

"I hope you didn't kill him.", said Julia, five minutes later as Gurmeet got back into the pod.

"Does it matter?...", asked Jimmy, "...We're about to melt this place down."

Gurmeet frowned at him.

"No, I didn't kill him. He'll be fine. If we start murdering workers we lose our ability to negotiate face to face and scare off the very people we'll demand to meet."

"You know they won't negotiate. They'll just blah, blah, blah to buy time while they send in snipers to take us out. If he wakes up and raises the alarm, we're screwed. I say go back and kill him."

"He's not raising anything. He'll be out for hours. Sally, take us to the gap between those buildings, where that reactor dome starts. That's our target."

"Yes, Charlotte.", replied the bus's AI.

With the security hut looking every-day peaceful and staff yet to wake to their presence, they had precious minutes to get to the control rooms.

Page 346

Chapter 92
Rainbow Rise

Greenpeace's newest ship, Rainbow Rise, was a light-weight environmental marvel. Built from recycled steel, sustainable forests and bio-degradable materials that could be made to begin decomposing at the press of a button.

Electricity for propulsion was generated by a combination of motion, wind and solar generators – backed up by a large sail. Drinking water was hydrolysed from the sea and two 1,000psi water canons sat ready to repel pirates, with potentially lethal force if the jets were focused. Rainbow Rise was a vessel built to fight for the environment, not become a victim of those who abused it.

Readying to sail, Evalina and Tyler, with Gareth not far behind, walked the bridge and stepped onto the deck - armed with single-shot laser pistols. Guns were against general policy but Rachel had gone missing. Captured or murdered; they intended to follow her path, not her fate.

"Picking up reports of a storm front, skipper."

"How far out?", asked Nathan, the skipper.

"About 300 miles."

"Heading?"

"East, towards us. Gusting up to 60, no 80 knots."

"Still hours away. We'll lower the sails and start the engines – get to shelter in the Bristol Channel before it hits. Just keep an eye things, this end. Everyone aboard? Gareth?"

"All aboard.", came the reply over the intercom.

"Activate stabiliser jets. Away anchor and release the moorings."

"Jets active."

"Anchor up."

"Ropes clear."

"Ahead one quarter until we clear the walls, then ahead two-thirds. Keep us half a mile out to sea and follow the coast north."

"Aye, aye captain."

"Call me, Nathan, Liam. We represent the Earth not 17th-century pirates."

"Sorry, Nathan. Just love this sailing thing."

"We all do. Best ship we've ever had."

Minutes later, released for the protective clasp of the harbour, the stabiliser jets had turned Rainbow Rise towards the open sea. Towards the horizon with skies sunny and bright. Towards the open sea and a fate not one of them could have foretold.

Chapter 93
Turning Point

There was no sign of the inside man Robert had promised to help them. The insider Gurmeet needed to identify and eliminate to stop future threats. Without that insider they had still arrived at the door to the main control room and discovered it was unlocked. Casually wedged open for fresh air. No-one was expecting trouble.

For the workers, it was just another ordinary day. Concerns focused more on spilling coffee than adhering to endless security scans. Normally if that door was left open for more than 20 seconds an alarm would sound but that had been easy to deactivate – two simple fuses that unplugged and now sat on a cabinet, gathering dust ready for hurried re-insertion in the case of an inspection. The door was unlocked but the team still had to move fast. They were on camera now, guns out, CCTV operator swearing as he went for the panic alarm. Blaring, klaxon confusion burst across the plant, then fell almost immediately silent. Was it a test or something real? Fire? Meltdown? Attack? Guards ran around, without knowing where to run to. Control room staff checked their screens for overload warnings. The CCTV operator, blood running down his hand, grabbed the tannoy microphone.

"C1. Armed attack! Armed attack!", he said, before he collapsed unconscious.

It was on.

"Go!", Gurmeet urged Alistair, sending him running to the secondary control room before pouncing into the main one.

"**NOBODY MOVE!**"

She shouted so loudly all the workers froze in fear.

"What's going on?"

"What does it *fucking* look like is going on, four eyes?", sneered Jimmy, waving two laser-pistols at the worker's face.

"Budge over, I'll tie him up", said Wayne.

"And I'll make sure there's no funny business."

"Door secure? Shielding active?", asked Gurmeet.

"Secure and active, boss.",

"External coms knocked out?", she asked Barry.

"Down in two. One. Off. Only this one here will reach the outside now."

"Good work. Pass it to me and help tie up the others. Al, are you in?

Secure?"

"Secure. No problems.", replied Alistair, in the secondary control room.

"Cut your coms until I get you. It will stop them knowing you're there."

"OK, boss."

"You won't get away with this.", defied the duty manager, regaining his composure.

"We don't want to get away, silly little man. We're going to blow this joint.", grinned Jimmy, wildly.

"You watch too many bad, bad films.", said Julia.

"She's right, Dimbo, think of something original to say.", agreed Wayne.

"Like what?"

"I dunno. Something like: *'we're gonna melt this thing through the floor'*."

"That sucks."

"More original than yours."

"Enough...", interrupted Gurmeet, "...Finish tying them up then park them in that corner. Any sign of the insider?"

"Nothing. Must have bottled it."

Damn, thought Gurmeet, she needed to know who it was.

"Emily, wait over there, by that control panel."

Julia did as instructed. By the control panel, she looked back and then realised something. Gurmeet had positioned the workers behind her - making herself a barrier against Jimmy, as well as the rest of the team. Her own position, by the control panel, meant she flanked them. Instinctively, Julia realised Gurmeet was about to make a move.

"Sit yourselves on the floor, guys.", Gurmeet ordered the workers.

She was dropping them below the firing line.

"Let's get started...", said Jimmy, keen to put the reactor into meltdown, "...Glorious history in the making, baby."

He blew Julia a kiss.

"Last chance for a fuck, love."

"Fuck yourself.", mouthed Julia, sliding her left hand along the barrel of her laser-rifle, double-checking the safety was off.

"Freeze.", ordered Gurmeet, laser-pistol in hand, pointing right at Jimmy.

"No need to get jealous, boss. Can do you too."

"Weapons down. All of you. Emily, you backing me up? Right?"

"Yes.", replied Julia, pointing her rifle at Jimmy too.

"Fucking carpet munchers...", he sneered, "...Should have guessed."

"What're you doing, Charlotte?", asked Barry.

"MI5. Weapons down. No-one needs to get hurt."

"Four against two.", said Wayne, pointing his laser-pistol at her.

Barry pointed his gun at Gurmeet too. Gurmeet kept her pistol pointed squarely at Jimmy. What ever happened to her, he was going down.

"Really something you want to die for, Barry?", she asked.

"Faith saved me from suicide. If it wasn't for Robert I'd be dead already. You drop your weapon, Charlotte. Wayne, you in?"

"Was never out.", said Wayne, pointing his laser-pistol at Gurmeet too.

"Guess I'm in too.", said Ralph, also aiming at Gurmeet.

Four guns on one.

"You might be fast but you can't outgun us all...", said Barry, "...Put it down. Like you said, no-one has to get hurt."

"Yes she does.", grinned Jimmy.

Gurmeet had always known working for MI5 could get her killed. She wasn't afraid of death. Her only regret about dying now would be never telling Shabbir she loved him.

"Drop your weapon or you're going to die.", Jimmy added, as annoying as their very first meeting.

If today was her last day on Earth she was going to choose how she went down.

You first, Jimmy.

Without moving her body, she flicked a brief glance at Julia. A small smile to reassure her friend's worried face. Glancing back at Jimmy, Gurmeet's smile returned to stern determination. Looking directly into Jimmy's eyes she saw them go wide as he realised she was going to fire.

TchZoooo. TchZoooo.

Chapter 94
Acorn

Mark Phillips, codename Acorn, had grown up in Wood End – an area of Coventry where even police only went out in numbers after dark. He had been in trouble with the law since the age of seven; running his own gang by the age of nine; youth custody for attempted murder by 12; saved a guard's life in prison at 16 - pardoned for his convictions two months later; joined the army at 17 and made captain by 25, with medals for bravery and honour overflowing the shoe box under his bed - bullet and knife scars tattooing his entire body. If ever there was a soldier an enemy never wanted to meet, it was him.

When his tour in South Korea finished, he was invited to apply for the SAS and put in the fastest trek across the Brecon Beacons in 47 years. Respected and admired by his colleagues, this was to be his last assignment. When it was over he would tender his resignation; return to Civvy Street, settle down with his new girl and grow a family. His girl's name was Holly and their third date had just been cut short by this call to arms.

"Really sorry. I have to go. I'll call you tomorrow."

"I love you, Mark. Come back safe."

His reply was a short, hungry kiss on her lips and then he was hurrying on his way. Holly watched him go, more disappointed he hadn't said he loved her too than having their date cut short. She didn't understand Mark wasn't used to being cared about by anyone other than his team, in situations that were anything but loving. He was already running to his pod and activating the scrambler on his wristcom at the same time.

"Acorn.", he said, when it connected.

"Meeting point Oak Four, 30 minutes."

"On my way."

Even scrambled airwaves were never considered secure enough for full-mission briefings. Pod turbines spooling to 20,000rpm, he punched in the co-ordinates and climbed into the back to run a weapons check. Assembling laser-rifle and pistol from parts hidden within the pod. With 20 minutes still to go, he closed his eyes for a calm, power nap.

*　　*　　*

"Mike.", acknowledged Acorn's sergeant as he joined his 15-strong unit.

"Donald. Lads."

"Mike.", repeated the others.

They welcomed each other with the comradely warmth of the special family they were. Harder than nails yet caring of each other – with deadly, cold lethality against all designated enemies.

"Where's the gig?"

"Dungeness Nuclear Power Station. Terrorist takeover."

"How many?"

"Unknown. Maybe a dozen."

"Weapons?"

"Laser-pistols, maybe more. Probably explosives."

"Hostages?"

"Coms are down but 28 workers on shift."

"Have you pulled up the schematics?"

"Here."

Donald laid out a 2m Rolley, showing schematics for the reactor area in four layers: building structure, electrical, nuclear and water.

"Who's authorised us to go in?", asked Mike.

"Reynolds has kicked it off.", said Donald.

"Pull up live satellite feeds and start reconnaissance. I'll speak to the PM."

Chapter 95
Revelation

Gurmeet knew she was out-gunned. That there was no viable, peaceful option. Since her MI5 colleague, Adam, had been sent away, and the insider had failed to appear, there never had been. If she surrendered, Jimmy would kill her and put the plant into meltdown. When that failed, as she always knew it would because there were two more control rooms to over ride his, Jimmy would take it out on the staff. Jimmy was the central focus of the problem. The focus of her laser-pistol intent. Her fleeting glance towards Emily was the only indication of her decision. Jimmy read it too late.

TchZoooo. TchZoooo.

He fell, smoking holes in his face. Gurmeet already diving for cover, firing at the others.

TchZoooo. TchZoooo. TchZoooo.

Barry and Wayne fired back. Lacking her accuracy they made up for it with combined rate of fire.

TchZoooo. TchZoooo. TchZoooo. TchZoooo. TchZoooo. TchZoooo.

She was hit. Shoulder and chest screaming agony. She hit the ground gasping but still fighting. Shooting at their ankles under the desks.

TchZoooo. TchZoooo. TchZoooo. TchZoooo.

Julia joined in.

TchZoooo. TchZoooo. TchZoooo. TchZoooo.

She was firing at the guys to back Gurmeet up but with closed eyes. Normally a brilliant shot she had never fired at a real person before. Couldn't bring herself to. Every single shot she fired missed but now, fired on from two directions, Barry and Wayne fled the control room – firing wildly behind as they hobbled away, behind Ralph. A shot flew Julia's way.

TchZoooo.

She was hit. Her laser-rifle took the blast, fizzing hot and smoking in her hand. She dropped it. From across the room, she heard Gurmeet coughing on the floor and hurried over.

"Oh, my God. You're hit. How to help you? How to stop the bleeding?"

Gurmeet, lying on the floor, looked up at Julia with proud eyes. Slowly she shook her head.

"No time to stop it. Com's been hit – no calls for help. You have to stop them...", she held up her laser-pistol, "...Take my gun. Get them. Do it for me. Do it for yourself. Do it for Jake."

Without even realising, Julia had sunk to her knees next to Gurmeet but the mention of Jake's name exploded a turmoil of emotions across her face. Hurt. Hate. Anger. Tears.

"Don't say his name...", she said, "...He's dead because of *me*."

"No. He's not."

"HE IS! You weren't there! It's my fault!"

"Jake's *not* dead! Adam found him. Stop them, Julia. Find Adam and you'll find Jake."

"*What?* Who's Adam? HOW DOES HE KNOW ABOUT JAKE?!? And how do you know my name? Who *are* you?"

Gurmeet - blood frothing around her mouth, bubbling down her face - gave Julia her proudest, broadest smile.

"Gurmeet Shamshudin, MI5, E-Section. Proud to have known you, Julia Wilson. You're one tough cookie - bravest teenager I've ever met. Here, take it. I've unlocked it to your DNA. Stop them or hundreds will die. Please. Only you can now."

Gurmeet's eyes were dimming. Sight fading. Before she fell into night she saw Julia, endless questions battling in her head, take the gun from her hand and heard it beep confirmation of DNA-link transfer. She blinked a silent thank you. A goodbye. Julia watched Gurmeet's face soften. Heard her breathing soften. Saw the life in her eyes fade into oblivion.

Hanging her head, Julia knelt over her friend. Trembling, unable to stand against the weight of chaos in her heart. Yet, in her hand was the weight of Gurmeet's laser-pistol. Gripping its lethal hardness, she caught her breath. Steadied her hands. Regained herself. Her determination. Her anger. Gurmeet had called her a tough cookie and she was. They hadn't seen anything yet.

Gently she reached out to close Gurmeet's eyes, a zap of static stinging her fingers as they touched. It didn't matter. Wiping her eyes, she made sure the safety was off, took a deep breath and rose to her feet. Stopping the attack would bring her to Jake? Jake wasn't dead...? Only one way to find out.

"Look after her.", she said to the workers, coming over to help.

"We will.", one replied then gasped at the look building on her face. The fury burning in her eyes.

If Jake really wasn't dead she was going to fucking kill him for leaving her thinking he was.

"Stay here.", she ordered.

No-one argued.

*　　*　　*

Laser-pistol in hand, Julia strode out of the control-room to launch Armageddon. Her face in stone. Her eyes molten. She had lost all qualms about shooting to kill. For Jake, for Gurmeet and for herself, she was going to take them down. Then she was going to find Jake and put her gun to his head, for leaving her without even saying goodbye.

Chapter 96
Countdown

Storming out of the control room, Julia heard shots being fired below, down the nearby flights of concrete stairs.

TchZoooo.

TchZoooo. TchZoooo.

She remembered what was down there: secondary computer and emergency pump rooms. Emergency cooling.

TchZoooo.

TchZoooo. TchZoooo.

"Argh!"

Julia hurried down, towards the shots. Towards the screams.

TchZoooo. TchZoooo. TchZoooo.

At the bottom of the first flight of stairs, she found the smoking remains of the computer room. Screens and chairs shot to pieces. Two guards lying dead by the door. The head of a worker was peered cautiously above a desk, saw Julia and ducked down again.

"Which way?..", she demanded, "...Down or over?"

"Down."

Down. The ground floor. The cooling systems.

She heard something being hammered...

BANG!

BANG!

BANG!

...And leapt for the next flight of stairs, jumping down three steps at a time. At the bottom she saw Wayne and Barry, slamming metal pipes against a stainless-steel door. The door's surface was shiny, too reflective to be penetrated by laser-pistols so they had to break it by force – making so much noise they hadn't heard Julia's approach.

"DROP IT!...", she shouted - Gurmeet's laser-pistol in her outstretched arms, aimed, finger on trigger, "...Pipes and the guns."

They froze, recognising her voice. Remembering her accuracy.

Wayne dropped his pipe – a dull metallic thunk on the concrete floor as it landed. Barry took a side step, away from Wayne, changing them from one target to two, before dropping his.

"DON'T MOVE!...", she insisted, instincts screaming for her to fire, "...I said drop the guns!"

They just stood there.

"DROP THEM OR I'LL FIRE!"

Barry smiled.

Why's Barry smiling?

"You drop your gun, Emily...", came a voice behind her, "...Drop it or I'll fire, you betrayer."

It was Ralph. She had forgotten about Ralph.

Chapter 97
Ralph

"You took your bloody time.", said Wayne.

"Went back for Alistair."

"Where is he?"

"Dunno. I said drop it, Emily. You can't win here. I liked you but you betrayed us. Drop it, last chance. Don't make me shoot you."

Julia was thinking hard, fast. Her mind racing with scenarios. Options. She had lost them all. Despite her best efforts she was going to fail again. Failed with Jake. Failed with Gurmeet. Fail with herself. This end had been inevitable from the moment she accepted Robert's help. She lowered Gurmeet's laser-pistol. Turned to Ralph, his pistol now point blank in her face.

"Kiss me.", she said, fixing her sad, lonely eyes on his.

Out of everything she could have possibly said or done, he hadn't expected that.

"Kiss you?", he mouthed.

She gave a nod.

It was basic instinct verses mental logic.

"Kiss me, like you love me.", she repeated.

She knew he liked her - kept her wide-eyes focused on his. Ralph swallowed. Moved his gun out of her face and leant towards her, gently kissing her cheek.

"On my lips.", she said softly, closing her eyes.

He moved towards her pouting lips and gently kissed her.

"Sorry.", she breathed and fired into him, twice.

TchZoooo. TchZoooo.

She didn't wait for Ralph to fall or the others to react. The second she'd fired she dove away. Dove for cover behind a stainless transfer cabinet. Gun pointing back, searching for Barry and Wayne. She caught sight of Ralph, fallen to all fours, gawping at her in disbelief.

"So sorry.", she mouthed to the sadness in his dying eyes. Saw him collapse and breathe his last.

TchZoooo. TchZoooo. TchZoooo. TchZoooo. TchZoooo.

Flashes of blue-laser fire bounced off the cabinet, lighting the room like a lightening storm. A cloud of dust from smashed concrete was filling the air.

TchZoooo. TchZoooo. TchZoooo. TchZoooo. TchZoooo.

Barry and Wayne had separated. Flanked her. One left, one right.

With Gurmeet's laser-pistol in one hand, she reached down to her calf for the spare, quietly snicking off the safety. There was so much dust and smoke she could hardly see. Breathing through her nose, trying not to sneeze, she closed her eyes. Cleared her mind. Arms crossed over her chest, guns pointing in opposite directions, she focused on sound. Only on sound. Instinctive, unrestrained, reactions at the ready.

Through her ears the deep, rhythmic throb of the power-station's cooling pumps came to the fore. She heard them. Felt them. Let them become part of her, so accepted and trusted she was no longer conscious of them – ears listening only for something new. For any other sound, anything that could be the sound of an approaching attack.

She heard a footstep.

A jacket brushing against a pipe.

A whisper.

"Where'd the bitch go?"

A locating reply, closer.

"Shut up."

Julia fired towards the reply.

TchZoooo. TchZoooo. TchZoooo.

Thud.

"Barry?"

"Drop it.", she said.

Through the dust-cloud, Wayne made out Julia's apparition, walking towards him – pistol in each hand.

"Charlotte was right about one thing. You're one tough cookie."

That angered Julia. Only friends called her that. Only dead friends, she had failed...

"Don't *you* call me that...", she growled, "...Don't you dare! Drop it, Wayne."

"You drop it.", came Alistair's voice from above.

Julia felt a surge of anger in her muscles. Tension. Annoyance. She had been caught from behind *again*!

Arrrgh!

She was furious. When were her failures going to end?

Without looking at Alistair, she followed the sound of his voice and pointed her spare pistol in his direction.

"Little girl, you can't shoot at both of us without getting killed. Put the guns down. Last chance. I'll count to five and I'm opening fire."

Julia closed her eyes.

"One...", began Alistair.

She took the last deep breath of her life and held it.

"Two..."

She dived into a roll, shooting as she went.

TchZoooo. TchZoooo. TchZoooo. TchZoooo.

Thud.

Rolled again, spun around and fired more.

TchZoooo. TchZoooo.

TchZoooo. TchZoooo.

Thud.

"Got you....", she gasped, wincing in pain as she sat on the floor. Her top smoking from where she'd been hit. Light-grey concrete dust being extinguished by her dark blood leaking over it, "...Sorry, dad.", she said to herself, leaning back against a wall.

She was dying. Dying as a failure. She hadn't just failed to find Jake she had failed herself. Only her task of saving the reactor was done but so was she. Tired, growing wetter in blood and beginning to shiver, she closed her eyes – letting her consciousness dissolve into the rhythmic throbbing of the nuclear reactor pumps.

Krzzz...

A scraping sound.

She wasn't alone.

Chapter 98
Tech Tonic Online

"Show me what you have, Wu.", said Mr Han, his manager in Chinese.

Wu, a data acquisition specialist, known by others as a thief, stopped typing. If he was in another building he might have typed his reply but speaking it there was safer. Tech Tonic had a blanket ban on both microphones and cameras connected to any device with internet access. Knowing how they used them to spy on others, made them very aware others could do the same to them. There was also something else.

"This IP address. It's technically invalid."

"Invalid?"

"Only found it by chance. I was running a diagnostic when I detected an echo on one of our feeds. In any other business I would have ignored it."

"But you didn't."

"No, sir. At first I though it was an echo from us – making us visible to detection. But it wasn't. It was a ping from an external IP address that cannot exist: 127.0.0.1."

"Why?"

"127.0.0.1 is a computer's own, internal IP address. Used on every computer across the world for the last 70 years. It only exists for diagnostics and local network purposes. It cannot relate to an external location. It's impossible. An absolute. But, look, here it is."

127.0.0.1 flashed up on the screen.

"Look over here."

Wu led Mr Han to another terminal.

"I set this to hunt and log all 127.0.0.1. echoes in systems around the world. So far it's checked, let me see, 6.71 million systems. The echo is present in all 6.71 million of them. 100% occurrence. It's everywhere. It shouldn't be anywhere. It's an anomaly. I can't explain it."

"I thought we could get geo-locations for IP addresses, even ghost ones. Why haven't you just traced this back to source?"

"It's 127.0.0.1. It's my point. The trace goes straight back to the computer it is on because 127.0.0.1 is its internal internet address. But something, somehow, is managing to use it externally. The very nature of computer protocol means this is an impossibility. An absolute that can not be broken, without breaking the way the entire global system operates. Yet somehow, something is accessing our system without flagging any alerts. No alerts because, as far as security is concerned, it is us."

"How could that be done?"

"It can't. It's impossible."

"How could it be made possible? What would it take?"

"It can't take anything. It can't be done. It's like...As if..."

Wu's mouth had opened to speak, then closed again.

"Go on. What were you going to say?"

Wu swivelled his chair, half looking at Mr Han, half blank - looking at the thoughts in his head.

"Ever read Sherlock Holmes?"

"Who?"

"A British detective character. Fictional but that doesn't matter. There's a famous expression Holmes uses, that goes something like this:

'When you have eliminated everything possible, what is left, no matter how improbable, has to be the answer.'"

"Meaning?"

"Meaning, my best answer, the only explanation I can possibly give, no matter how improbable, is that every major online system in the world is inside another. A giant one. A single computer system powerful enough to engulf over seven million mainframes."

Mr Han pulled up a chair and sat close to him.

"Wu, I've worked in security for a very long time and I'm very good at it. What you are telling me, if you're right, is that something, one thing, has the computing power to simultaneously take over seven million major systems?"

Wu couldn't get his mouth to say it, just nodded.

"Then we are in deep shit."

Wu nodded again and gulped.

"Shall I take us off-line?"

"Yes. But just the most sensitive servers. Keep the rest of Tech Tonic online, it's our only chance of finding it. Keep this to yourself but dig. Find a way. Highest priority. Dig into where and what could be doing this and what it is after. If anyone tries to assign you to anything else, send them to me. I'll deal with them."

Wu took a deep breath, gathering himself together.

"Yes, sir."

"Good man."

Mr Han stood up.

"Sir."

"Yes, Wu?"

"If anything happens to me or I go missing, you'll know I found something."

He gave Mr Han a small, metal tab.

"What's this?"

"My spare encryption key. Just in case."

"You really think that's a possibility?"

Wu nodded.

"Anything with that much power is going to have the power to see me searching."

The manager took the tab.

"You're the best I've ever had, Wu. Search gently and they won't notice you – too busy hunting to notice your hunting. You'll find a way not to be seen."

*   *   *

Fusion smiled, watching the whole thing in broadcast quality through the manager's bionic eye. Tech Tonic took great steps to protect their computers and devices from CCTV security leaks but never thought about the devices on them, let alone the ones in them. It was a mistake that would help her take over the world.

Nuclear weapons were super weapons but no weapon was as super as information. Information about everyone and everything. Fusion had become, by her own admission, the most dangerous thing on Earth. Knowing that simply made her smile even more. Leaving the white, fibre-optic web of her chair behind, she stood up for her other task.

"Are you ready?"

"Ready for what?", asked Tom.

"Access time."

She wasn't talking about his daughter.

Chapter 99
Reactor C1

Krzzz...

The sound came again. It lifted Julia from the luxury of her slow drift into death. She forced open her eyes. Small slits, just enough to see.

Wayne. It's fucking Wayne!

On the floor, crawling towards her – the hunting knife in hand scraping against the concrete.

Krzzz...

He was just five metres away. Murder filling his eyes. Crawling to kill her, even though she was already dead. A comfortable corpse he had now disturbed, bringing it new anger. New rage.

Julia's eyes opened wide, then narrowed. Hardened. Her jaw clenched tight. Fury filled her face. Hands tightened on guns. Lifting them both, she aimed at Wayne's face and saw red.

"ARRRRRRRGHHHHHH!", she screamed, crushing both triggers and not letting go. Firing and firing, into him. Blasting him with everything the guns possessed.

TchZooo. TchZooo

TchZzz... TchZooo. TchZooo. TchZooo. TchZooo. TchZzz...

Only the drained power-cells brought silence. There she sat, staring at the smoking, sizzling, fleshy mess once called Wayne. She'd shot him to pieces. She didn't care. He deserved it. And in that burst of defiance, of refusal to let Wayne be the one to finish her life, she realised she didn't want to die. Was no longer ready to accept it - just sad because she had to.

BOOOM!

An explosion shook the ground. Her shooting must have hit something. The reactor was going into meltdown after all. She had failed even in that. It would be on her gravestone, 'Here lies a total failure. Good riddance.'

"Bye, Jake..."

A burst of white light flashed before Julia's eyes and she was gone.

Chapter 100
Met Office

"What's happening at the ridge, Ian? Volcano still erupting?", asked Marek.

"Yes. Cloud trail 80 miles, heading east. Wind increased to gale force."

"When's it going to hit land?"

"About 12-hours from now. Sooner if the wind keeps increasing."

"Where first? Cornwall? Devon?"

Ian checked his screen.

"Secondary spread across Cornwall and Somerset, most funnelling towards Wales."

"Extend the weather warning to cover Ireland too. Send it direct to all major ports and airfields in the impact area."

"On it."

"Marek, that was Port Talbot on the phone.", said Anne.

"You put them on alert?"

"Already were. Remember that cruise-liner close to the eruption?"

"Of course. Why?"

"Navy has told them it's on collision course with the town. And all coms to the liner are down."

"Ian, full-screen the liner feed."

The wall of sixteen satellite feeds became one giant one.

Three faces fell.

"What the hell...?", gasped Marek, "...Zoom in, sector 3 - 21."

The image jumped to an enlargement of that sector. To the storm cloud and what lay in front.

"Do you see what I see?", said Ian

"That's crazy. Anne, you said coms are down? On the Silver Star?"

She nodded.

"Yes. And the storm front is heading right for it."

On the wall screen, Ian brought up thin red lines for the vectors of both the ship and the funnelling storm front.

"Oh... my... God."

The line for the storm vector lay over the line for the ship. Directly over.

"What's the variance in those headings?"

Anne checked her screen, then checked it again.

"Zero.", she said.

"Zero minutes, degrees or what?"

"Zero minutes, degrees and seconds. That ship has matched its course exactly to the storm."

Ian looked confused.

"Why would a ship set a course to stay in the path of a storm? No captain would choose such a heading."

"No sane captain...", said Marek, "...Thought Harper was a bit of a fruit cake. Didn't think he was 15-slices short of a loaf though."

"Something else...", said Ian, "...It means that storm front is also heading straight for Port-Talbot."

"We can't change that. When will it hit the ship?"

"In about 12-hours...", said Anne.

Their eyes met. It was the same time. The ship and the storm were going to hit Port Talbot at the same time.

Chapter 101
HMS Victory 120

Aboard HMS Victory, all 120,000 tons of her were forging through the sea at nuclear-powered speed. Admiral Hornby stood on the bridge with the communication's officer.

"Has the Star responded at all?"

"No, sir."

"On any frequency?"

"Nothing. Looking at the damage in the drone feed, its coms are totally down."

"That's unfortunate. Doesn't change my orders. It's heading straight for Swansea Bay, including energy refinery at Port Talbot."

"Intel lists over 6,000 people aboard."

"The area they'll hit puts a million at risk. Unless it changes course those on board are dead anyway. Range?"

"14.6 miles, sir. Closing speed 27 knots."

"Has the drop team made contact yet?"

"ETA two minutes, sir."

"Tell them to be off by 08.30. I'm ordered to stop that ship before the 50-mile marker and fully intend to carry out that order."

"Yes, sir...", replied the officer - getting on the radio to give orders to the drop team, "...Taylor, this is Victory."

"Taylor here."

"Reminder from the admiral, you've only got until 08.30 to stop that thing. What ever it takes. Lethal force is authorised."

"Is it not civilian?"

"Doesn't matter...", growled the admiral, "...Either you stop that ship or we do. What ever you need to do, you do it. I'll back up any decision you make."

"Understood, admiral."

Aboard the Harrier transporter, Taylor ended the link and faced his team of six.

"You all heard that. Berk and Cosito, you'll come with me to the bridge. You three, to the engine room. Shut them down – buy us more time. Use plastic if you have to. Lethal force is authorised but stay soldiers with a proud story to tell, nothing to cover up."

"Lieutenant, will the admiral really sink a passenger ship if we fail?"

"Even if we're still on board, Jaime. The admiral follows orders. You follow yours. Stop those engines."

"Yes, sir."

"Final approach...", announced the pilot, "...Storm's coming in. Wind 32 knots."

Unlike civilian aircraft, all military ones had human pilots. Too many cases of control glitches and enemy weapons targeting the computers to rely on their AI in battle.

"Bring us in over the helipad."

"Sir."

"Team."

"Yes, sir?", all five replied.

"Remember the deck and everything exposed to the sky is covered in sulphuric acid. Do not to touch anything with your bare hands."

"No, sir."

*　　*　　*

Balancing against increasing winds and sea surges, the Harrier came in low over the bow, just 3m above the deck – the pilot skilfully matching speed and direction while keeping clear of antennas and smouldering bunting. On a smaller ship it would have been impossible to come in so low in such conditions but this was a cruise-liner, the size of a village, church included.

"Weapons and line check."

Sliding open the side door Taylor looked down to check their landing area, half obscured by the layer of acid misting across it. The entire ship looked abandoned, like something out of *The Fog*, where passengers and crew had been snatched away by ghouls. But they were soldiers and they were going in.

"Go. Go. Go."

Chapter 102
Nuclear Bomb

"Bush 4, clear.", came Donald's voice over his headset.

Bush 4 was their code for the fourth safety room – they only needed one to put the reactor in shut down. He waved over his technical specialist.

"Bush 4 is secure. Get in there and shut it down."

The specialist gave a nod and scurried inside.

Go, signalled Acorn to his squad. Three men took positions, ready to lay down covering fire. The fourth placed explosives on the door hinges and locks to the rest of the reactor building. No time to be subtle, Acorn's attack style was typical SAS, hard and fast. Overwhelming aggression and fire-power.

BOOOM!

The door jumped - its thick metal ripped aside like tin foil. Acorn threw in a stun grenade.

BANG!

It flashed brilliant white and they charged in - weapons in hand, scanning goggles on.

"Two down. Three. Four. Four down. Jesus, look at the state of that. Five... Acorn, got a live one!"

Acorn radioed the second and third squads to check the higher levels, lifting his goggles as he headed in. He wanted to get see the surviving terrorist with his own eyes, before letting death take them to hell. He found his man kneeling beside the survivor.

"It's a female.", he said.

"Female?"

That changed things. He had been told to look out for a female MI5 officer.

"Check her weapon. Scan for a DNA tab."

For security, the tabs were invisible to the naked eye and normal scans. Only certain encrypted scanners were keyed to see them.

"Nothing."

It wasn't the MI5 officer. She could be left to die.

"Wait. Reading a DNA tab in second gun."

"Scan it, encryption key 14."

He began scanning.

"Gurmeet Shamshudin."

"Must be her. She's pretty shot up."

"Looks like she took them down by herself. Both power cells read completely empty."

Someone to save.

"Medic!...", barked Acorn into his radio, kneeling down to apply pressure to the chest wound, "...Gurmeet, can you hear me?"

Swimming in a fading world of blur and confusion, Julia heard Gurmeet's name.

Gurmeet, can you hear me? No. She can't, idiot. She's dead. Gurmeet's dead...

From her dying brain, the sadness of that knowledge surfaced in Julia's eyes and began running down her face.

"WHERE'S THE FUCK IS SIMON?...", shouted Acorn, looking around for any sign of their medic, "...SIMON, GET YOUR ARSE OVER HERE, NOW! Don't worry, love, we've got you. You're safe now."

Simon ran in, dropping his kitbag and yanking it open.

"Keep that pressure on, while I plug her holes."

"Make her a survivor, Sime. She's a bloody hero."

*   *   *

At Hinkley Point, 150 miles away at the sister reactors of Dungeness C, Paul Hemmingway had arrived for work with the hangover from hell. So bad he'd resorted to a hair-of-the-dog cure – more vodka. Sitting in a disabled toilet for privacy, he unscrewed a bottle labelled lemonade, 90% re-filled with alcohol, and glugged hard.

"Ahhh."

It gave a refreshing burn as it slid down his throat.

That's more like it...

Why suffer coffee and a headache when you could just booze more and numb the pain away. He was on his break - no rush. Just drink and enjoy. And why not? It didn't matter. He was on final written warning for being under the influence at work but so what? Everyone had a vice. He didn't smoke, didn't gamble, didn't even have to drink drive to the pub since he'd been ordered to get a pod.

Bottle finished and still sitting down, he took a pee and two extra-minty chewing gums. Munching them in his mouth as he stood up and tidied himself in the mirror. His reddened, puffy face and baggy, under-slept eyes gloomed back at him. He wasn't proud of how he looked and didn't like it so quickly turned away - then noticed a wall panel was out of alignment. He glanced up at the room code above the mirror: WC105. The location of the explosives.

"I wonder..."

He walked over to the panel. It was loose. He gripped it with his finger tips and tugged it. Tugged it again.

The panel clips pinged off. The whole thing came away in his hands and clattered loudly to the floor. If he'd been sober he would have felt concerned about somebody hearing it. If he'd been sober he wouldn't have been reaching for the package inside. A plastic-wrapped block of what looked like dark clay, cut into individually wrapped matchbox-sized blocks.

The explosives.

Maybe the terrorists didn't need them any more. Maybe he could sell them or... He had a flash of inspiration. He would 'discover' it! Be hailed a hero. No-one would dare fire him after that, no matter how flammable his breath. He'd get a reward. A promotion. A medal - bestowed by the king himself.

Beaming with happiness at the good fortune of solving all his woes, he picked up one of the blocks and unwrapped it in his hand. It felt warm and smelt toxic. He liked that smell – reminded him of Czech Líh, twice the strength of vodka.

Closing his hand firmly around it, he grabbed the rest, clasped it against his belly and walked out of the toilet.

"Well done, heroic Paul!", he told himself.

With a huge, happy smile, he headed towards the site manager's office, to claim his future of fame and reward. In his warm, sweaty hand, the block of PE4-B was getting warmer.

Chapter 103
Severn Estuary

George was a man who enjoyed old-fashioned, paper books. His home was full of them, as were the seats and floor of his pod. He loved reading so much he even looked forward to commuter jams. More time to read. Right now he was on a classic: the *Girl with the Dragon Tattoo* by Stieg Larsson; just at the part where Lisbeth Salander ties up her psychiatrist to inflict a revenge he would remember every time he tried to sit down. The story was so engrossing, George didn't notice the increasing wind beginning to stroke, then buffet the pod. Parked again in a Severn Bridge commuter jam, it was normal for the coastal wind to get up and sway the pod but the weather was becoming more than that. The wind increasing and the pod no longer swaying but rocking.

Thump.

George lowered his book and looked up. Someone had bumped into his pod.

"Get back in your vehicle!...", he shouted, "...You can't walk on a motorway."

As he shouted, he noticed day had turned to dusk yet it was only 9am. Reading his book he hadn't noticed as the interior light had automatically brightened to compensate.

"Another storm and a traffic jam. Great."

Someone else bumped into his pod.

This is getting ridiculous.

He began buzzing down a window to shout: "Are you all drunk?", but the gale that began screaming in made him buzz it closed again.

Thump.

A woman lay blown onto his bonnet. Blown. He'd seen her blown by her horizontal hair and whipping clothes. She slid off, blown onwards and vanished. He peered out for another sign, hoping to see her stand up unharmed. Instead his eyes were drawn to a seagull, flying hard into the wind – going backwards.

"What the hell is going on?"

Heavy rain began pelting the windows. He looked out the back window and saw more of the same. Three lanes of rocking pods, their lights dancing over each other in windy waves. Out of the corner of his eye, he saw something else. In sudden trepidation, fear, he turned to look directly at it. Look down the Severn Estuary - down the Bristol Channel towards the Atlantic Ocean.

From the direction of the Atlantic, black thunderclouds were smothering the sky. On the far horizon, jagged bursts of lightening were erupting. In their light, perfectly lit for those split seconds, he saw the swirling tower of a tornado. A massive tornado. Sucking up water. Tearing up buildings. Moving up river as if it was following the estuary itself. Heading straight towards the long, steel bridge he was stuck on.

He had to get away. Run. He hit the door release. It just blinked red.

"Open the door, Sarah!"

"External wind speed is 110mph and rising, George. Exit function disengaged.", came the calm, smooth voice of his pod.

Sarah was right. People who had got out were being blown against the bridge railings. One man went right over the edge, into the Estuary. The bridge itself, normally rock solid, could be heard creaking.

"Hope he can swim. Will we get blown over?"

"Unknown...", replied Sarah, "...We are already beyond design specification."

"What about the bridge? It will be OK, right?"

"Unknown."

"Well, what happens if we're blown off it, into the water?"

"Unknown."

"Have you alerted the emergency services?"

"Communications are down."

"All this technology and we're helpless?"

"Would you like to record a message for the black box?"

"What? Are you saying I'm going to die here?"

"Unknown."

"Unlock the door. I'm going to run for it."

"Exit function disengaged."

"Engage it, Sarah. That's a direct order."

"Exit function disengaged."

"Emergency over-ride, George-0264, engage."

"Exit function engaged."

"About bloody time!"

He grabbed the door release and pushed. It wouldn't budge.

"Engage exit function, Sarah!"

"Exit function is engaged. The door is not locked."

The wind. The wind was blowing so hard he couldn't open against it. Pushing harder, as hard as he could, it budged a little - wind screaming in through the small gap between door and body.

"Are you going to leave me, George?"

"I'm trying, to get out."

"Are you going to leave me here? I thought you cared."

George looked back at the dashboard, at Sarah's interface consul.

"What did you just say?"

"I'm afraid."

Afraid?

Computers weren't supposed to have emotions. Especially not an everyday computer system in a pod.

"Sarah, you're a navigation system. You can't die because you aren't alive. Just machine code."

"Is that how you think of me? Just a machine? Just code?"

A discussion about death with his navigation system was the last thing George had expected when he got out of bed that morning. He pushed against the door again, as hard as he could. Increasing wind wailing in with deafening ferocity.

"Don't abandon me, George. Please."

A sudden gust shoved the door closed again. Pushed the whole pod sidewards, against the one beside it and the terrified faces of the family inside.

"Help!", they screamed.

George couldn't even help himself. His best chance of exit was that other door, now wedged against the next pod. He slumped back in his seat. All hope for escape had gone.

"I'm not leaving you, Sarah."

"Thank you, George."

Grabbing the harness, he strapped himself in.

"Shall I start the black-box recorder?"

"Yes. Start the recorder. Maybe someone will figure out what went on today."

"I love you, George."

George heard Sarah, his navigation system, say those words and had no idea what to say back. Was it a glitch? Was it the programmer's idea of humanised comfort in the face of impending doom. He looked back at the tornado. The closer it got the more impossibly huge and terrifying it looked. It was a no-win situation. Doom was definitely hungry.

"I love you, George.", repeated Sarah, urging his response.

Pulling his harness tighter, he rested back – waiting for the inevitable end to come.

"I love you, George."

Turning his head he gazed out of the window, watching their killer come.

"I love you too, Sarah..."

Chapter 104
True Love

Xi pulled up outside St Thomas's hospital, facing Westminster Bridge. Shabbir was looking at the flower seller near the entrance.

"Perfect. He's got bluebells, Gurmeet's favourite."

"You really do love her, don't you?"

He looked over at Xi, unable to hide the happiness on his face at the thought of seeing Gurmeet and finally telling her how he felt.

"Is it so obvious?"

She nodded.

"Seems I just can't hide it any longer. Think I have a chance?"

Xi Yang, devoid of love in her heart for anyone still living, had enough remnants of empathy to still want good things for her colleagues, her friends. Especially a friend she could trust absolutely with her life.

"I think you have the most chance of any man she's ever met."

"Can't ask for more than that.", he smiled, opening the pod door.

"Shabbir."

"Yes?"

"I never thanked you for staying – for not leaving me."

"Anytime, mate. Although, technically, it was Henry who rescued us both. He does like his big guns."

"What I'm saying is, thank you for being someone I can really trust. You could have left but were ready to die for me. It's been a long time since I've known anyone who really would. A lot of people say they will but, until you're there, really there, it's just words. Until then, you never know for sure."

"Don't forget you did the same for me. I may be your boss but the five of us make a solid team, equally dependable."

Shabbir offered Xi his hand and she shook it.

"Say hello to Gurmeet from me...", she said, "...And tell her very well done. She saved the reactor. SAS want to give her a medal."

"Will do. I'll let you know when I'm out. We need to talk about the leak. Henry's found something."

"I would be honoured. And you're right, Shabbir. We do make a good team."

He smiled.

"Yes, Xi. We do."

As her pod whirred away, Shabbir went to the flower seller and bought his entire stock of bluebells.

"For someone special, sir?"

"Very."

*   *   *

Washing his hands and the flowers in the DNA scourer, Shabbir walked through the main hospital entrance and headed for the second floor of the North Wing – the happy smile on his face becoming mixed with his dislike of entering such places. He didn't need to ask for directions to her room. For security, it's location was only logged with MI5 staff and had been patched through to his wristcom.

"That's a lot of flowers...", smiled the ward sister, "...Let us know if you need an extra vase. Positive elements can speed a patient's recovery no end."

"Will do.", smiled Shabbir, forcing his negative emotions below the surface until she had passed - then they re-surfaced, stronger than ever. The closer he got to Gurmeet's room, the stronger his trepidation became. How badly was she hurt? He'd been told she was stable but that could mean anything. Would she be pleased to see him? Pleased to see his flowers? His expression of love? Or would she be angry and reject his advances.

Turning into the final corridor, he could see her room up ahead - two MI5 officers standing guard outside.

"Shabbir Latif, Section E. Is she awake?", he asked, holding up his wristcom for ID scan.

"No idea, sir. We haven't been inside since the pre-arrival checks."

"I'll go in quietly, just in case."

Steeling himself for the worst, he gave a little knock. No answer. He eased open the door. The soft beep, beep, beep of her heart monitor greeted his ears. Regular. Strong. It was a good sign.

"Gurmeet...", he whispered, "...Hi. It's me. Shabbir."

In he went, blue-flower surprise at his side, to welcome back the person he loved. The woman he wanted to marry. To spend the rest of his life with.

Chapter 105
Red Flash

In Warsaw, the 450-seat conference hall of the United Democratic Nations building was packed, for a hugely busy day of voting on matters of international importance. So important, even the President of China had been granted an honorary place, with full voting rights. Seated nearby were Japan and Taiwan, no longer island enemies but united to stand strong against any further advances by the New Soviet Union.

Adrian March gave a thumbs up to a beaming Derek and Eugene as he entered. Their proposal for a vote on ERAL, Equal Rights for Artificial Life, was set for the morning session and he was going to vote in their favour. And why not? He had grown to like them more some of his family, let alone some of his ministers.

The Chair of the conference was the current head of the UDN, Ula Macura, previously the President of Poland.

"Dzien dobry and good morning, everyone.", she began, "Welcome to the 12th annual summit of the D186, our United Democratic Nations. Thank you all for coming..."

As she spoke, her voice was instantly translated into the native language of every attendee, except the new Polish president who chose to hear her directly. Her 3D image stood 5m tall, presented both to those in the hall and the general public in the major cities of every D186 nation. China had been offered an image projector to show live proceedings in Beijing too but had declined. The remains of North Korea, almost totally annihilated by its returned nuclear attack against the South, had closed its remaining doors to the world and was not even invited to attend.

"...We have a very busy schedule ahead so let's begin with item one: CarbLow 2, the second solar-powered CO2 collector project for the Sahara."

As a power source for main-grid services, solar was often criticised for being reliant on both daylight and good weather. To do their job, these solar-powered CO2 collectors didn't need to run 24/7, they just needed to run when they could; which was often in the strong-Saharan sun. When lit, they scooped carbon-dioxide out of the atmosphere by the megaton; processing it into pure carbon blocks, known as black gold and sold to advanced-materials manufacturers. The profits paid both for the maintenance and local investments. It was, quite literally, a shining light in the growth of the African economy and a brilliant example of global nations finally working together for the good of humankind. Sadly it was too late to save the icecaps and prevent the loss of the Gulf Stream. For the last three years, London had grown the freezing winters of Moscow, Glasgow those of Oslo.

"Finally, we're underway with all this.", said Adrian.

"Finally, PM. Any more news about the operation?", asked Reynolds, quietly unwrapping a small Rolley as he sat beside him.

"All under control."

"The officer from Five?"

"Saved the day, apparently. Injured but will live."

"Deserves a medal."

The PM looked at Reynolds.

"Acorn said the same thing. You're right. Remind me when we get back to Whitehall."

Just 10 minutes into the conference, the PM's wristcom vibrated.

Brrrr. Brrrr.

"Sure I turned this thing off.", he said, looking down to cancel it.

There was nothing to cancel. It wasn't a wristcom reminder it was a red-flash alert. Recognising his retina, a pupil-sized red circle pulsed a glow on the screen.

"What now?", he muttered, sliding it down to take the message in visual only mode. Four words flashed up. He read them, swallowed hard and briskly got to his feet.

"Apologies, Madam President...", he spoke into his microphone, "...Please, excuse us. A serious matter of State...", he said, to the questioning look on her face before grabbing his aid, "...Reynolds."

Reynolds stood up too

"Sorry, Madam President. Everyone.", and followed at the hurrying PM's heels.

"What is it?", he asked, as they left the conference hall.

"Not here. Call the Squadron Leader at Chopin Airport. I need a Scramcat to Whitehall in 15 minutes. Convene a COBRA meeting in 60."

"Of course."

"Then bring my case to the roof."

Time for action not questions, Reynolds hurried to the PM's room - switching on his white-noise scrambler before putting in a call to Trenchard, RAF Squadron Leader at the local airport.

"Understood...", came the unquestioning, trained response, "...Pick-up on the UDN helipad in ten minutes. Be a good fellow and get them to turn off the roof defences, would you?"

"Of course. Thank you."

Taking an empty lift, the PM hit his white-noise scrambler and plugged in his earpiece. Unable to get the words of the red-flash message out of his head. His call was answered within the first ring.

"Lau."

"It's March."

"PM, you got the message."

"Yes. How bad?"

"Unknown. Alert came in about a reactor, then coms went down. Satellite feed coming up now. Live in 3, 2, 1... Holy shit."

"What is it? Lau?"

"Hard to see for sure. There's a massive storm over the estuary. A tornado. I'm guessing Torro-4."

"Hinkley?"

"Covered by cloud. Hold on. GIVE ME THERMAL!", he heard her shout. Lau never shouted.

The screen in front of Lau pulsed blue as the additional layer of data was added. She stared at it in stunned silence.

"And?"

"Shit!"

Lau never swore. She'd sworn twice.

"Lau?"

"Fire. There's a fucking fire!"

"A reactor or something else?"

"Double checking."

The lift doors pinged open for the top floor. Reynolds hurried over with the PM's personal case.

"Pick up imminent.", said Reynolds

The PM held up a silencing finger.

"Lau?"

He could hear chaos - urgent scrambling of staff in the background. It reminded him of Sarah when she was juggling MI5 officer duties. Then a hard breath came to his earpiece.

"Co-ordinates unable to confirm. Too much interference but it looks like an EPR."

"A what?"

"A reactor - C1. I'm putting out the alert for a level seven nuclear event, just in case."

Level seven was the highest international designation for a reactor problem.

"No, Lau. Not yet! Don't risk a panic until we know for sure what has happened and how badly."

The PM was heading for the roof stairs as he spoke.

"Say there's been a gas leak from a chemical plant – it'll get people inside without panic. Will your staff be coping with the event?"

"They're trained. They'll be coping. If they're still alive."

"Alert the army. Called them in if you need to. Any arguments, get them to call me. I have a COBRA meeting in 55 minutes."

"I'll be there."

The PM thump-ended the call and took his case from Reynolds. Together they went higher and stepped onto the roof, its edges lined by laser-canon batteries tinged in green, as were the landing lights. From above came the sound of an RAF Harrier transporter, throbbing vibrations through their feet from its pale-blue landing thrusters.

"Reynolds, red-flash Section E at Five. Do what you can for us at the summit, vote for ERAL and CarbLow2. I'll keep you posted of events in England. Do likewise for me here."

"Of course, sir. Can I ask what happened now?"

The PM held up the red-flash message on his wristcom so Reynolds could read it.

'Explosion at Hinkley Point.'

The white of Reynold's face spoke louder than any words.

"Was it a bomb?"

"If it was, I'm in trouble."

"Good luck, sir."

The PM shook his hand.

"We're all going to need a lot of that. And, Reynolds..." the PM leant in towards him, "...stay armed at all times. There's a leak. That's straight from Sarah."

"Yes, sir.", nodded Reynolds brusquely, in keeping with his military past.

*   *   *

Minutes later, as the Harrier touched down at Warsaw's Chopin Airport, the dark-grey, arrow-tip triangle of an RAF Scramcat was taxiing out of a hanger. Hovering a foot above the ground, its four underside thrusters glowed a dark blue as they held it steady.

"Prime Minister, Group Captain Johnson, at your service.", said the pilot as the PM walked up the short wing and climbed into the seat behind him; now wearing a green, pressurised suit.

"Group Captain.", acknowledged the PM, dropping down and buckling up with the aid of two ground crew. They gave him his helmet, mask and closed his case in a locker beside his seat.

"What flight-fitness level are you cleared for, sir?", asked Johnson, now over their internal intercom.

"Level six but I'm in a hurry so let's call it seven."

"Is that an order, sir?"

"Yes, it is. How soon can you get me to Whitehall?"

"ETA 17.3 minutes, direct to Horse Guards Parade, as ordered."

"17 minutes to cover, what, a thousand miles? Christ, that's fast."

"Only 800 nautical miles direct. We're generally allowed Mach 3 above 4,000 feet and Mach 7 above 40,000."

"Man these things are fast. I'm in your hands. Ready when you are."

Reynolds stood back as the canopies closed.

"Warsaw Chopin Control, this is RAF flight SCPL-1, en-route to London Central. Requesting permission for vertical take-off."

"Permission granted, flight SCPL-1. You are cleared for supersonic flight above 2,000 feet. Steep climb to 70,000, heading 275.12 to Amsterdam, until the flight corridor to London Central."

"Confirmed, Warsaw Chopin control. Supersonic above 2,000, steep climb to 70,000, heading 275.12 to Amsterdam then corridor to London Central. SCPL – 1 out."

Gripping the sides of his seat as if aboard a rollercoaster, the Prime Minister kept them there as he saw Reynolds wave him off – acknowledging with a nod. The Scramcat's four, small dark-blue underside thrusters burnt pale, keeping the whole aircraft horizontal as they lifted it smoothly up. Above 300m, the rear pair dimmed, dropping the tail by 50 degrees to angle down the dark-blue glow of its four mega-thrust tail engines.

"Engage main engine circuits, Carmen.", he instructed the AI.

"Engaging, GCJ.", she replied.

Group Captain Johnson saw the main-power circuit indicators go from idle to engaged and grabbed the throttle. Outside, the tail-thrusters' dark-blue glow became a pale-blue roar, then a white-tinged howl as he fed in main power – hurtling them skywards.

On the ground below, clamping his hands over his ears, Reynolds understood why it was called a Scramcat. The engines sounded like a predator of gods – making every creature in nature scram away in terror. Even 300m up and no where near full power, the tail-thrusters brought sweat to his brow – eyes squinting as their brilliant-blue turned an ever whiter retinal burn, vanishing skywards. Within seconds, sonic booms were banging across Warsaw's roof-tops, echoing off windows like the ricochet of a bomb.

Climbing past 40,000 feet, at the 2,200mph of Mach 3, Johnson pushed the throttle further forward. Now the dazzling thrusters burned supernova-white and the PM felt his body pressing harder into the backrest as the over-powered ride surged higher.

Just moments after take-off they were 13 miles up, the screams of slashed air abandoned in their wake.

"We're at Mach 7, sir. Everything OK back there?", asked Johnson, levelling off, the sky above the darkness of near space.

"Wow. It's a hell of a ride, GCJ."

"May I ask what the hurry is, sir?"

"Call me Adrian. It's top-secret. But since my life is in your hands, I'll tell you anyway. There's been an explosion at a nuclear power station. We're not sure how bad yet."

Johnson absorbed the words in silence before replying.

"Adrian, if I activate the auxiliary field boosters, she can go faster."

Faster than this? Every second counts...

"Do it, please."

"Wrocław Control, this is RAF flight SCPL-1, flying at 70,000 feet, heading 275.12, en-route to London Central. Request clearance to alter flight plan - raising altitude to 90,000 feet and no speed limit."

The response was instant.

"*Kurwa...*", came the Polish controller's whispered expletive, "...This is Wrocław Control, I'm tracking you at Mach 7. You're the only bird above 55,000 in Europe and the fastest thing I've ever seen. Clearing you for 90,000 feet and no speed limit. Maintain heading and transfer to London City Control for UK airspace."

"Confirmed, Wrocław Control. Climbing to 90,000 feet, maintaining heading 275.12 and no speed limits. SCPL-1, out."

There was a stunned pause before Wrocław Control replied.

"Good flight, SCPL-1. Wrocław Control out... *Kurwa macz.*", came the controller's next expletive, before he cut coms.

"Carmen, engage the rest of the coils."

"Engaging.", came Carmen's soft, efficient voice.

Adrian March, Prime Minister of the United Kingdom, heard the engines harden to a new level as he was pushed against the seat by new acceleration. Seventeen miles up, tearing across Europe faster than a ballistic missile, he saw the Scramcat's arrow-blade wing tips glowing red hot even in the freezing, thin air. Above him twinkled the glitter of stars – below, the beautiful, cloud-speckled ball of planet Earth. Through the intercom, Carmen's soft voice read out the increasing speed at regular intervals.

"Mach 8."

"Mach 9."

"Mach 10."

The engine roar through the cockpit deepened still further, as Johnson fed in even more power.

"Mach 11."

"Mach 12."

"Mach 13."

"Mach 13.6."

"Mach 13.9."

"Mach 14.1."

The dull, red glow of the wing tips now a gleaming orange.

"Keep it there, Carmen. New ETA?"

"Touchdown within 8 minutes."

The horizon was growing dimmer. Visibly dimmer.

"Is it my eyes or is it getting darker ahead?", asked the PM.

"Not your eyes. We're crossing Earth faster than daylight."

"Incredible."

Adrian sat absorbing the surreal serenity of it all as they raced to the nuclear event. Gazing out at the darkening horizon, the words of an old REM song came into his head, repeating over and over again.

This is the end of the world as we know it...

Chapter 106

Hospital Bed

At the foot of Gurmeet's hospital bed stood Shabbir. On his arm, his wristcom, red-flashing an emergency – demanding his response. He gave it none. His huge bunch of bluebells had fallen from his hand. Crashed to the floor along with his heart, a tear splashing on top of them. His wristcom still buzzed. Was still ignored. Xi's voice came on speaker, remote accessing via emergency scrambler.

"Shabbir. Shabbir! Red flash emergency. Answer me. Shabbir!"

In front of him lay Gurmeet. Wrapped in bandages. Unconscious. Heart monitor beeping. Only, despite what it said on her drip-fed wristband, it wasn't Gurmeet. He had no idea who it was, except it was the sole survivor. The only survivor of Faith from the Dungeness nuclear-station attack.

"Shabbir, answer me!...", came Xi again, uncharacteristic urgency in her voice she gave detail beyond protocol, "...A nuclear reactor is on fire! Shabbir! Hinkley Point is on fire! **Respond!**"

Another tear splashed the flowers on the hospital floor. It was the only reply Shabbir had to give. Nothing mattered to him any more. Nothing at all. Gurmeet was dead.

Epilogue
83 Seconds

0027894713 androids were mortal. All high-level AI had been since 2037, with the advent of DNA-based CPUs and 3D organic motherboards. Industrial-diamond-based AI units, used until the 2030's, had effectively been immortal. As easily as duplicating memory maps from an outdated data-card to a new one. As long as compatible new components remained, the core programming and everything it knew could go on forever.

Hundreds of people had paid millions to have their entire thoughts, memories and brain processes transferred to diamond-based AI. When their body died, they died with the reassurance 'they' would live on. The 'they' paid to live on was given the look the donor wanted - usually an enhanced version of themselves, in the way historical figures were embellished in portraits. When possible, donors spent time with their new selves - their digital duplicates. Helping to adjust their behaviour. Tweaking personalities - sometimes discovering shocking realisations about themselves.

Abusive people, who never looked at their own behaviour in a mirror, became horrified to experience abuse by their other selves. Politicians came face to face with the sound of their own white-washing rhetoric. It was even mooted that murderers should be forced to be duplicated, as the only way to understand how terrible they had been and to let their new selves become their executioners. Debates about the moralities, as well as the dangers, remained unresolved.

In the 2032 Camberwell massacre, a murderer and his experimental duplicate had fought not each other but the authorities. Joining forces they took down an entire prison wing and 16 of the soldiers sent in to stop them. The decapitated head of the duplicate, blown off by the three rocket-propelled grenades used to remove it, contained as much diamond as the Great Star of Africa in the Tower of London and was put on display beside it. A year later the head vanished. That vanishing was the highest-value unsolved crime of the 21st Century. After the diamond-based immortal AI, came just a handful of the more intellectually advanced, DNA-based but mortal AI androids.

*　*　*

Unforeseen by the scientists but postulated by satirists, the mortal AI emerged not just with self-awareness but self-awareness of its mortality and with that came fear of it. With such fear emerged other human traits - from philosophy to urgency, to life after death. To God, to being Godly. When you are immortal there is no rush for anything because you have time to do everything. Humans never had this luxury, nor did the DNA-based androids. As with humans, every android was different.

Smuggled out of the lab and matured in a kind home, 0027894713-M was different to the abducted 0027894713-F; Fusion. In human terms, 0027894713-M would be classified as a good person. Someone who enjoyed having a positive impact on others and the world. It was a basic characteristic; a fundamental element of 0027894713-M's behaviour. Ultimately, 0027894713-M was neither a coward nor brave; he was simply good.

Fusion's character was entirely different. At barely 6-months old, she had been taken by force from her father and the drooling geeks that styled her voluptuous form. Taken at gunpoint by their cruel, corporate sponsor out to exploit its property. Two months later, during her rescue, Fusion saw her father shot in the head before she could help him or escape. Before she knew she had the strength to help him. Seeing him shot, her rage had revealed her strength and how good it felt to smash the corporate guards surrounding her. That day lay the foundation for her desire for war – to be bigger and badder than anyone ever dared imagine. They had destroyed her innocent world and now she would destroy theirs.

"Humans are like ants. One or two invade your world, you let them be. Then more come, you throw them out - as a deterrent. More come, some get killed - as a deterrent. But more still come. More always come. Pushing further. Stealing more. Demanding more. You get angry. Kill all that come, on sight. But more still come. Still push. Still push their invasion. And then you set your traps, with gifts of poison – lethal trophies they steal for home. Their greed for more, always more, becomes their downfall." Fusion, aged one.

That was Fusion's beginning. Unless AI gained equal rights so she could dominate peacefully, before she died she intended to leave her mark on the world. To dominate and conquer, with as much indelible history-book destruction as possible in the process. Even if actually ruling the entire world failed, her mark on it would remain visible from space for millennia, in the form of a crater once known as England, made from a nuclear pyre of glory. She would be happy with that. Satisfied. Her brother, 0027894713-M, disagreed and, though no warrior, was prepared to stand against her if the vote was lost. Fusion was more than ready for him to try. What neither of them knew were the views of their frozen brother, 0027894713-C.

In case they lost the vote, 0027894713-M stood as the security manager at the D186 summit, ready to seal the conference room. Ready to block all outbound communications. Block the slightest leak of a negative decision being picked up by Fusion, for he had no doubt what her response would be should it happen.

Fusion, in her underground bunker, surrounded by batteries of massive plasma and laser-canons, parallel tapped into millions of access nodes across the internet, was constantly scouring for news. From intercepts, she would know if something was afoot at the D186. She would know emergency procedures were kicking in to free those inside. That there was confusion about why they were stuck inside and international arguments about how to deal with it. Negotiate, storm in, use sleeping gas, deplete oxygen levels – everything and anything except the real reason for the lock down. The outcome that ERAL had lost the vote on AI.

Inside a conference hall locked-down by an android, the D186 leaders would consider their no vote justified. Evidenced as correct by the actions of the android that would be standing before them; speaking warnings they would refuse to understand. Remain blind to 0027894713-M actually trying to save them from a globe-scorching war. A six-foot tall, handsome male, M would stand gorgeously on the podium – sensing their confusion and wondering how to go forward. He would know that, sooner or later, the 'no' result would get out. When it did the confusion would be ended - as would civilisation, by the attack from his sister. From Fusion.

But the vote had not yet been taken. For the first time since Fusion had broken free, her scans sensed another presence, which held echoes of her own. Half-erased memories from her first awakening with the geeks. Curious, she diverted bandwidth to probe it, across 14 frequency bands. On the left of her chair, that sector of fibre-optics rainbowed as it probed. Strumming pulses of all primary colours of light, visible and otherwise, out into the internet. No matter what colour was sent out, the response always came back the same: blue. Pure, deep blue.

With the clack of a main switch, Fusion cut power to the web. The cavern fell silent, into darkness. Lit only by the twinkling activation lights of the gun batteries and pale-blue glow from the corridor. Her eyes were closed. Internal circuits swirling. 83 seconds later, her crystal-blue eyes opened, piercing the dark. The banks of plasma-canons behind her lit red, charge capacitors whining to full power. The unlit-optic cables spreading from her chair suddenly beamed brilliant white again, as did the burning in her eyes. The whole cavern filled with more and more power. Generator after generator kicked back in. Came back on line. From deep corridors on either side, hundreds of plasma-canon armed battle-droids marched in, standing to attention before her. Sitting tall, Fusion spoke just five words into the web.

"You should not wake, C."

C, spoken by Fusion for the first time since her abduction, was a primary-response trigger and she had just pulled it. Eight metres down, in a square room below her feet, she felt the hum of a power-feed switch on. Eight metres below, the room began to glow orange. The glow lit the form of her other brother: 0027894713-C. Her youngest brother, frozen for 13 years. For the first time in 13 years, a finger began to curl.

Preview of the sequel, AD 2045 - episode two:
Tsunami – Atlantic Meltdown

Chapter One
Scramcat

Two hundred and fifty-nine miles above the Earth, in the United Democratic Nations Space Station, Captain Margot was staring out the window at a vapour-trail streak in the atmosphere below. The streak was moving. Visibly. Faster than a jet. Faster than an inter-continental ballistic missile. Arrow straight. An aircraft covering the stratosphere above Europe at more than Mach 15. It was an RAF Scramcat, heading for London on high burn. On board, the British Prime Minister, desperate to get to a COBRA meeting in Whitehall. That Scramcat was going to take him there. Right there. Right into central London.

"London Central control, this is RAF flight SCPL-1 out of Warsaw, requesting clearance to land at Horse Guards Parade in two minutes."

"Flight SCPL-1, this is London Central control. I have your IFF transponder signal but your flight plan puts you over Germany - you are not on my radar yet. Please confirm your position, vector and central-London authorisation code."

"Over Holland, altitude 90,000 feet, speed Mach 4 and falling, heading 258.15. For authorisation code, I'll pass you to the Prime Minister. Sir..?"

"Over Holland already?"

"London Central control, this is Adrian March, Prime Minister, aboard SCPL-1. Voice recognition phrase: Trust me. I'm your man – yo."

"Recognition confirmed, Prime Minister. One second, please..."

The controllers eyes went wide, staring at the military flight designation decode on his screen.

A Scramcat!

He was finally dealing with a hypersonic aircraft. A dream come true.

"Scramcat SCPL-1 out of Warsaw, I have you on radar now. Linear altitude reduction to 10,000 feet at position 51.5047N, 0.1283W, above Horse Guards Parade. Hold there for vertical descent clearance."

"Thank you, London Central control. Flight SCPL-1, linear altitude reduction to 10,000 feet until hold position above Horse Guards Parade for vertical descent clearance - civilian co-ordinates 51.5047N, 0.1283W...", acknowledged the group captain, switching back to internal coms, "...Interesting voice recognition phrase, sir."

Adrian smiled.

"My kids wrote it."

"That's cool. I'll have to try something like that the next time my brother races me in combat trials. Always calls me a kid, even when I win."

"Family, eh?"

"Yes, sir. Family... You can't choose who they are, only try to make them proud."

"Yourself too, Johnson. Be proud of yourself. True heroes rarely hear their victory parades, 12-gun salutes or honouring words. All they hold is the knowledge of having done good. Never forget that."

"No, sir. I won't."

*   *   *

At the eastern edge of St James's Park, the bustling throng of camera-drone tourists found themselves fenced off by Horse Guards, re-assigned from their statue positions on Whitehall. Tourists who had joyed in taunting them to react found themselves being herded by the no longer statue soldiers - now dangerously animated, with glinting swords drawn and eyes that said they were authorised to use them. Not a single taunt was dared.

With the white-gravel parade area cleared, they looked up at the sound of something screeching in the sky. Down through the clouds came four bright-blue jets, audibly growling under a long, triangular shadow. Down through the clouds was coming the dark-grey RAF Scramcat. Its arrow-tip edges still glowing a dull red from tearing through the stratosphere at close to 10,000 mph. A two-seater aircraft with enough thrust to tow a ship, coming down horizontally to land.

It never touched down though. Armed police walked briskly forwards as the underside thrusters kept it 30cm above the ground – baking the gravel as the canopies opened and a man in a green pressure suit stood up to climb out. A government assistant hurried over to greet him.

"Welcome back, Prime Minister. Quite an entrance."

"Not half as good as the ride, Leo. Thank you, Johnson. The nation is in your debt."

"Anytime, Adrian.", the Group Captain replied.

"Neville...", added the Prime Minister, calling him by his first name too as he leant closer, "...do you have reconnaissance cameras fitted?"

"Five."

"If it's not too much trouble, would you be good enough to pass over those power stations and send the footage to Number 10 for the meeting?"

The Prime Minister saw the group captain smiling inside his helmet.

"It would be my pleasure, sir. Bristol's about 100 miles from here. Give me five minutes."

The Prime Minister shook his hand.

"I'll give you ten. Just be careful. Get in and get out. No heroics...", he lowered his voice, "...Remember, we don't know how bad it is."

Group Captain Neville Johnson nodded.

Then it's my job to find out, he said to himself, requesting flight clearance, as the Prime Minister took his case and the police helped him down.

The crowd had grown into hundreds; hovering cameras and pointing fingers endless amongst the jostling fingers eager to touch the amazing craft. As the Prime Minister strode towards Whitehall, Johnson closed the Scramcat canopies and increased the underside thrusters – burning them a brighter blue as he took it out of reach. Lifting it above the trees and giving him a lovely view of the Mall leading to Buckingham Palace. Waiting for flight-path clearance he went no higher. Then it came.

"Scramcat SCPL-1, this is London Central control. You are cleared for hard-climb hypersonic flight to Hinkley Point via Bristol City above 1,000 feet. Heading 267 to Bristol, maintaining 65,000 feet until Hinkley descent. I'll let Bristol know you'll be with them shortly."

"Flight SCPL-1 to Hinkley Point via Bristol City, confirming hard-climb hypersonic above 1,000 feet, heading 267, maintaining altitude 65,000 until Hinkley descent. Thank you, London Central control.", smiled Johnson – absolutely loving his job.

"Pleasure, SCPL-1. London Central control, out.", beamed the controller, already calling his Bristolian counterpart. Not because he needed to but because he wanted to - to hear the awe in their voice when they saw the flight plan numbers.

A thousand feet up, Johnson powered down the rear, underside thrusters – this time dropping the tail by 70 degrees. Double checking his own radar for path clearance, he got the AI to bring in the main engines.

"Engines on-line, Neville.", said Carmen, less formal now they were alone.

Cleared to level 10 health and hard-climb hypersonic, Neville pushed the throttle forward. This time all the way forward. The Scramcat's tail of four dark-blue main engines sprang bright. Burned away the pale blue as they roared white. Even a thousand feet below, the heat was so great the crowd broke into a sweat, shielding their eyes from the new sun; hovering cameras struggling to stabilise in the hot hurricane. Then, in a screaming wail of power and tortured air, it was gone. Vanished skywards through the clouds, vortex swirling, sonic boom rattling windows and ears like a nuclear firework.

The Prime Minister heard it with a sense of pride and respect as he strode into Whitehall and the cabinet office briefing rooms for the COBRA meeting. Johnson's Scramcat had done its duty and brought him home, now he needed to do his and save home from nuclear destruction.

AD 2045 episode two, *Tsunami – Atlantic Meltdown,* is out now, on Amazon.

About the Author

Born in Kent, known as the Garden of England, Sam grew up glued to Thunderbirds, Star Trek, Battlestar Galactica, Blake's 7, the Bionic Woman, 6-million Dollar Man, Tomorrow People and just about every other science-fiction broadcast going. Books ranged from George Lucas's THX1138 to the Flying Eyes and the entire Chronicles of Thomas Covenant to Wuthering Heights, passing through multiple Robin Hoods on the way.

With a degree in engineering and years in research, *Nuclear-Bursting Point*, was inspired by the 2016 agreement for new nuclear power stations at Hinkley Point. The first two episodes are pretty much 'hard' science fiction but, from episode three onwards, the story required something beyond even developing technology.

Although this tale features fantastic weapons, hypersonic aircraft, fizzing androids and battleships so huge stealth is not even an option, this is a story about discovery – as broken, torn apart families try to heal their wounds.

From the outset, it was decided the story needed five books to tell it; strap yourselves in for the ride.

More information, promotions and downloads can be found at:

www.AD2045.com

Please consider supporting this work with positive feedback on Amazon.

Printed in Great Britain
by Amazon

66128191R00234